VIPER'S CREED

THE CAT'S EYE CHRONICLES

BOOK 2

T. L. SHREFFLER

www.catseyechronicles.com

The Cat's Eye Chronicles

Sora's Quest (Book #1)
Viper's Creed (Book #2)
Volcrian's Hunt (Book #3)

PROLOGUE

Crash awoke from the dream with a start.

It dissipated as soon as he opened his eyes. Stars glinted above him, pinpricks on the pitch-black horizon, the ground cold and moist. From the stillness in the air, he knew that it was early, early morning.

He stood, looking across the flat plain, a dark ocean of wavering grass. The residue of the dream lingered, its cold hand on his back, as if warning him of something....

What? he thought, studying the broad expanse of the lower plains. *What am I overlooking?* He felt keenly disturbed, as though a predator stood just beyond the fringe of grass, watching him, filled with murderous intent. But was the threat far away or nearby? It was like watching a heavy storm cloud approaching. *How long before it reaches us?*

A large flock of crows suddenly appeared in the sky, flapping loudly against the dead night air. They cawed and squawked to one another, rushing by overhead. Dozens, perhaps hundreds. The mass of birds was so thick, it blacked out the stars.

Crash stared. Crows flying at night?

Then he noticed a certain skittering in the underbrush. Rabbits, mice and ground squirrels dashed through the dry grass, all following the same direction as the crows. The more he watched, the more he saw. Sparrows, black birds, swallows...all darting across the plains, fleeing west.

What is this? he wondered. A fire? An earthquake yet to strike? Yet there was no firelight on the plains, no telltale smell of smoke. The ground remained cold and solid.

Crash pondered the animals thoughtfully. *Why are they running?* Deep in the pit of his stomach, he felt like he already knew the answer.

A bush rustled, and he turned around to find his companion, Burn, returning from his watch. Small leaves, curled and dry from the summer climate, crunched beneath his boots. It was difficult to move soundlessly. They were camped next to a thicket of spindly trees tall enough to offer shelter from the elements. Burn had spent the last several hours in the branches, taking a better look at their surroundings.

"So they woke you?" Burn asked softly, glancing at the sky where the crows were still flying by. "I wonder where they're going."

Crash nodded. So he wasn't just imagining it. "They're fleeing from something."

Burn paused next to the assassin and gazed at the horizon. He turned his face into the wind, his flared nostrils sniffing the air, his long, pointed ears twitching; Wolfies' senses were naturally heightened and sharp. Finally, he pointed toward the northeast. "There," he murmured. "Far away, at the base of the mountains." He looked troubled. "It smells like...blood."

Crash's eyes hardened. Volcrian. Had to be. The bloodmage was approaching—though Crash doubted he was close because if he was, they would know it by now.

"He wants my head," Crash replied. "We should go our separate ways. He would most likely let you go. This isn't your fight."

The Wolfy's eyes turned hard. "It *is* my fight," he murmured. "Or have you forgotten what he did...?"

Silence. No, Crash hadn't forgotten. He only wished that Burn could forget—Burn was one of those rare, upright, honorable men who deserved a good life. But if they continued traveling together, they would both end up dead.

Now Crash could feel the bloodmage's presence descending onto the plains, a malevolent force, unstoppable. He seemed larger than before, easily detectable, powerful.

"We should leave the mainland," he finally said.

"Aye," Burn grunted softly in agreement. "Might be our only option. We can travel south to Delbar, take a ship overseas...we have some backtracking to do." They were currently traveling north, and had planned to traverse the mountains to the distant ice fields. If Volcrian was close, however, they would need a faster route of escape. Overseas would do.

Crash's eyes turned to the south, tracing the constellations in the sky. To reach the port city of Delbar, they would have to pass through the region where they had left Sora more than six months ago.

Should I warn her? he wondered. Hopefully, Volcrian would leave her alone now that she wasn't traveling with them anymore. If they showed up at her house, they would risk drawing the bloodmage there, too. *No,* he decided. Better to stay away.

"We leave at dawn," Crash said determinedly, and turned back to the copse of trees, ready to keep watch. The crows continued to fly overhead, growing in number.

CHAPTER 1

The poles definitely did not look inviting.

About a full hand's width in diameter, they were wooden, moss-covered and lined the meadow like solemn sentinels. They started low to the ground, progressing around the field in a half-circle, growing taller and taller until they reached the height of a man. Sora had never seen anything like it.

"What are these?" she asked, and gave her mother a skeptical look.

"These, my dear," Lorianne said, "will make you a true fighter!"

Lori had awakened Sora at the crack of dawn. The two women had dressed and eaten a hasty breakfast. Then her mother had led her out into the fields, gray mist hovering above the frosty grass, and into the forest beyond. They entered the overgrown clearing soon after.

"I constructed this place especially for combat training," her mother said, "though it hasn't been used in a while."

Sora was confused. The poles looked degenerate and rotted; with a bit of effort, she dug her fingers into the soft wood. A firm shove might have sent one toppling to the ground. She couldn't imagine what they were used for. Was she supposed to practice sparring? She raised an eyebrow. They didn't strike her as very challenging opponents.

"I don't get it," she said plainly. "And why wouldn't you let me bring my staff? What's the point?" Her staff was her best weapon, the only thing that felt natural in her hands.

Her mother grinned, a mischievous glint in her eye, and said, "Climb one."

"What?"

"That one, right there." Her mother pointed to a short, stout pole nearby. It was only about a foot off the ground, Sora stepped on top of it easily. Then she stood there, balancing on one leg like an awkward stork. She felt a little foolish.

"Okay, now what?" she asked, trying not to get annoyed.

"Now jump to the next one."

Sora looked around, trying to see where the next pole might be, only to find it almost a yard away and a good foot higher than the first. After a bit of eyeballing, she swung her arms and jumped, landing clumsily on the other foot, wavering to keep her balance.

"And now the next one," her mother said immediately.

The next one? Sora looked for her next landing place, only to find it another yard away and a whole foot higher. At this point, she shook her head. "You're crazy!" she exclaimed. "I can't jump over there and land. I'll break my ankle! No one can do that!"

Her mother's mischievous grin widened. "No one?" she asked in amusement.

Lori walked boldly past her. She leapt lightly onto the third pole, as though it were a normal doorstep, and proceeded to dash across the clearing from one to the other. Sora's mouth dropped. Her mother was magnificent! Fluid! Graceful! She danced across the pillars, climbing to the highest and then bouncing down to the lowest. When she finished, she came vaulting back in Sora's direction, and landed at her daughter's side with an elegant twirl.

She had crossed the entire clearing and back in under five minutes.

Sora was eighteen, but had only known her real mother for about a year now. The woman was full of surprises. She still couldn't believe her eyes.

"This is called 'step training;' it's to gain balance and confidence," her mother said knowledgeably. "This is an old, old technique. It's also the way your assassin friend trained."

Her assassin friend.

The reminder of Crash was unexpected, and Sora quickly turned away. Well, he hadn't truly been a friend, but definitely someone who had changed her life. The mention of Crash left her flustered and tense, not a welcome feeling, though she didn't mention it. He had left a year ago, traveling away with their mutual companion, Burn. An entire year...but she still thought of them every day. *Every. Single. Damned. Day.*

"Now *you* do it," her mother said, ignoring Sora's reaction, or perhaps oblivious to it.

Sora turned back, clenching her teeth, forcefully shaking the memories away. She certainly wasn't going to give up if her mother could do something like that, *and if this is what Crash can do, then I'm going to do it too!*

She and the assassin had started off on pretty bad terms—he had kidnapped her from a disastrous birthday ceremony, killing her supposed father, and had whisked her away into the night—but things had changed. They had grown close, somehow. "Close" seemed almost too much. Perhaps familiar? Was there another word for it? Crash was not the kind of man who inspired warmth, and yet...she missed him strangely, in rare moments of the day, when she was knee-deep in housework or out riding through the forest. She yearned to see him again, though she wasn't sure why. A cloud would shift overhead or a crow fly past, and she would turn to look, imagining it was him.

Or Burn, she reminded herself. *I miss Burn too.*

Blushing, she slowly turned on her pole so she was facing the next one, and carefully aimed. *There's no way I'm going to make that without a little momentum.* Swinging her arms at her side, Sora summoned her courage and launched herself across the open space, flying toward the next pillar. *Oh, gods!*

Amazingly, she landed on her target—for about two seconds. Then she overbalanced and tumbled head over heels with a yelp. She fell four feet to the ground, landing with a clumsy thud in the dirt.

"You've got to be kidding me!" she exclaimed. She picked herself up, brushing dust and grass from her clothes. "That's the hardest thing I've ever done in my life!"

Her mother winked at her. "And with enough training, it'll soon be the easiest. You'll be able to jump across rooftops, climb fences, vault through trees...! I'm going to take you out here every morning for at least two hours until you can climb like a squirrel. Feel free to practice whenever you want, though."

"Sure, whenever I want," Sora muttered. She couldn't help but feel a little disappointed. She wanted to fight again, feel the surge of adrenaline in her muscles, the excitement of combat. She missed using her staff and daggers. She cleaned her weapons daily to keep them from collecting dust, but other than that, her staff might as well have become a broom handle. She spent most of her time doing chores now. Not the life she had imagined so long ago, when she had plotted to run away.

"Don't look so glum!" her mother chided. "These small exercises will make all the difference. But we don't have time to practice now. We have an appointment in town."

"In town?" Sora asked. "An appointment? Another one?"

"A sick farmer this time," her mother said slowly. "Seems like the infection spread from the animals...to the man."

"Huh," Sora frowned. Unusual.

Her mother was a Healer, one of the few in the region, and some farmers traveled for weeks to see her. She always had a steady flow of work, and since moving in, Sora had learned quite a few things about the healing trade. She had become an assistant in some ways, a personal maid in others. But that was country life, wasn't it? One person wore a lot of hats.

Sora was used to an army of maids doing her laundry and turning out her sheets, or cooking her meals, or cleaning her dishes. Her adoptive father had been a rich Lord, well known on the High Plains, but there had been no warmth in that house; instead, only a distinct feeling of imprisonment. A year ago, she had willingly given it up—though sometimes she wondered why. Housecleaning was hard work!

Lorianne turned abruptly and started back across the fields, pulling up a few plants as she went, or snatching leaves from certain vines. Collecting remedies.

Sora followed with a sigh. Another day of dealing with the sick. It had been exciting at first, learning how to mix potions and sew up wounds, but after a long winter of colds and a warm spring of hay fevers, she was absolutely, without a doubt, tired of it.

* * *

The small farmhouse was about four miles away. Sora recognized it. They had visited only three weeks ago to deal with sick chickens, and had found over a dozen hens with gummy eyes and blackened beaks, their feathers falling out in odd clumps.

When Sora saw the farmer, she thought he looked much the same.

He laid on the bed restlessly, tossing and turning with a fever. After wrapping a cloth over her mouth and pulling on her leather gloves, she mixed a concoction of yellowroot and mint at her mother's direction, which would help lower his fever.

Lorianne collected samples of mucus from the back of his throat. "Strange," she murmured, holding a vial up to the light of the window. "It's clear. No color."

"What does that mean?" Sora asked.

Her mother glanced at her and spoke softly. "It means that he's healthy. His body isn't fighting an infection."

The farmer's wife stood in the background, silently wringing her hands. She had the tough, weathered look of a woman who could work the fields. Her hair was tied up in a kerchief, her arms tight and sinewy.

Lorianne passed the farm wife a rag to hold up to her mouth. "This disease looks contagious," she said gravely. "Be careful not to breathe in his air. Have you shared any meals with him? Laid in his bed? It's probably unsafe for you to be here. Can you step out of the room?"

The woman paled and nodded, and quickly left, closing the door tightly behind her. Sora glimpsed a small boy standing in the hallway, staring at them with wide eyes.

"Mom," she said, turning back to Lorianne. "You said there's no infection. So how can it be contagious?"

"It's not," she said, lowering the rag from her own mouth. "Something else is happening here." She looked at Sora sharply. "This isn't a normal sickness, and I have my suspicions....We need to use your Cat's Eye."

"My...my Cat's Eye?" Sora paused. She touched the stone under her shirt. It hung from her neck on a silver chain. "But why...?"

"Because I think this is a curse."

"A curse?"

"Yes. Here, touch his body. See if you sense anything."

Sora hadn't used her Cat's-Eye necklace since arriving at her mother's house. She had always thought it was an old family heirloom, but a year ago, discovered it was far more than that—an ancient weapon from the War of the Races.

Truth be told, she didn't know a lot about magic, and neither did most people; it was all but myth now. But she had learned a lot since discovering the Cat's Eye. She raised her eyebrows slightly, wondering what her mother was getting at. She knew magic existed —had seen enough on her adventures to be sure of it—but a curse?

When Crash kidnapped her so long ago, he and his companions had taken her through the Catlin swamp, which was under a spell to keep out trespassers. Her necklace made it possible for them to cross the swamp and escape from Volcrian, the Wolfy mage who had hunted them. The Cat's Eye was not just a simple pendant—it was an old, old artifact, back from the time of the races, when the world had been at war. The necklaces protected the bearers from magic; ate it up like parasites, feeding off the supernatural energy.

"I'll try," she said, and with only slight hesitation, reached out to touch the man's wrist.

Shhhhnnnnt!

Sora's hand snapped back. The immediate energy shocked her fingers and she heard the dim whisper of bells in the back of her mind, like a distant passing wagon. She shook her head slowly, trying to clear it. It had been so long since she had experienced magic, since she had felt the Cat's Eye awaken and move....

"Sora!" her mother exclaimed.

She looked up. Her eyes widened. The body of the farmer had gone rigid. As she watched, the man's eyes rolled back into his head, his mouth opened, and he suddenly sat bolt upright. His blind face turned toward Lorianne.

Then something dark gushed from the man's mouth. It looked like a dense river of black, slimy worms. The worms spewed outward, flinging through the air, projecting straight at her.

Her mother gasped, stumbling backwards. The worms landed all over her arms and chest, squirming left and right, climbing up her skin. They were looking for an opening, a path into the body.

Sora reacted instantly. She reached up, touching her Cat's Eye, summoning its presence in the back of her mind. Her ears began to ring in response, the urgent jangle of bells. The necklace rushed to life.

Then she lunged at her mother and wrapped her tightly against her body. *Please,* she thought fiercely, *protect us!* With a vicious crackle, the energy of the necklace enveloped both of them. The worms screamed—screamed! Small, buzzing cries, like mewling kittens. With another fizzle, they dispersed, vanishing into small puffs of smoke. Their energy was absorbed into the necklace.

Silence. The two women sank to the ground.

"What...what was that?" her mother asked, panting, obviously shaken.

They both turned to stare at the bed, where the old farmer was lying down, snoozing peacefully.

"I-I don't know," Sora frowned. "But...the worms weren't real, they were magic. The Cat's Eye dealt with them. Could they...could they be part of the curse?"

Her mother nodded, slowly recovering. She finally dropped Sora's hands and climbed to her feet. Her eyes never left the bed. "Maybe...I've never seen anything like it." She prodded Sora's shoulder. "You should touch him again, to see if the curse is gone."

Sora glanced up at her mother. Gross! "Really?" she asked, wrinkling her nose. "Why don't *you* touch him? That was disgusting!"

"I'm the one who got covered in worms!"

"Yeah, well, I don't want to be next...." Sora sighed. She knew she had to do it since her mother didn't have a Cat's Eye. So she stood up and crossed the room carefully, wiping her sweaty hands on her pants, wary of the sleeping farmer. Finally, she reached out a shaky finger and touched the man's wrist. It felt warm, dry...normal. She closed her eyes and sank deep into her mind, where the bond with the necklace resided. Mentally, she nudged it. *What is happening here...?*

Wwwhuumph! Instantly, darkness flooded her vision. Sora felt a jolt, but this time she resisted the urge to remove her hand. She let the Cat's Eye take her where it wanted to go.

It was as though she had been sucked into the man's body. She could suddenly feel his laboring breath, the stab of pain with each inhale, the heaviness of the quilt and an overwhelming nausea. *Hot, so hot....*Her eyes filled with images: a swarming darkness, like legions of insects, and a nasty, crawling sensation in her gut. Then the sound of a voice, low and lethal, murmuring against her ears. *Hushhh.*

And then—something burst in her chest like a red hot boil. She took a sharp breath. *Hatred.* So much hate....

Fear stabbed her. The impressions were intense, close to overwhelming. She summoned the Cat's Eye and the light sound of bells met her ears—like a clinking in the wind.

When she opened her eyes, she saw a green light surrounding her hand. Like cool water, the power of the Cat's Eye flowed from her fingers, stretching across the man's fevered skin. Then she felt the necklace draw the heat into itself...slowly suck inward...until it pulled the fever inside, like water into a duct.

With a small burst of light and a final tinkle of bells, the Cat's Eye went silent.

Sora looked up at her mother. She felt winded...but strangely exhilarated. When was the last time she had dealt with magic? A year ago, to be sure, before Crash and Burn had left. She could feel the necklace more firmly now in her mind. She had almost forgotten the sensation, as though another person sat just behind her eyes. She hadn't realized it had grown so quiet. The lack of magic over the past year had made it dormant, sleepy.

"Well?" her mother asked.

"His fever broke," Sora said. She knew this for a fact, though she had removed her hand from the farmer's skin. "It was...strange. As though he had been possessed by hatred. I don't understand it."

Her mother nodded slowly, her brow furrowed. "I've been watching for something like this," she said quietly.

Sora looked at her, surprised. "What do you mean?"

"Now is not a good time to discuss it," she said, glancing at the door, and Sora was certain that the farmer's wife stood just beyond, listening with an acute ear. "But I have noticed many animals acting strangely. Those chickens from three weeks ago were not just sick. They were attacking each other. Last week I saw the same thing with a herd of cattle. Only last night I saw four hawks collide in a battle over our house. There is something dangerous afoot here. I need to return to my library."

Sora nodded, thinking of her mother's library back at the cabin, filled with thousands of books. She had only read a handful of them in the past year. The woman had spent her entire life collecting them; everything from children's stories to tales of the Wanderer, historical accounts of the War of the Races, alleged spellbooks, maps and geography.

"Let's go," her mother said, packing up her supplies.

Sora nodded numbly, her hand traveling to the necklace under her shirt. The small, circular stone felt warm to the touch, as though she had dropped it in fire.

* * *

By the time they got back to their house, Sora felt like she had dropped her head in fire, too. The sun was high in the sky and harsh to her eyes; even blinking was a pain.

She staggered off her horse and walked to the house, eager to get away from the sun. Once inside, however, the headache only grew until her temples throbbed. She paused next to the doorway, one hand on her head.

"Are you all right?" Lorianne asked, worried.

"Fine," Sora said. "A headache...I think I need to take a nap." Perhaps using the necklace had affected her more than she had thought.

Her mother frowned and nodded. Then Sora dragged herself upstairs to her bedroom. It seemed like each footstep was twice as heavy as the last. For a moment, she thought she would collapse straight onto the floor, but she didn't want her mother fussing over her, so she forced herself up the narrow wooden stairs, down the long hallway and into her bedroom. She barely managed to close the door behind her, then slumped into a large, overstuffed armchair, too tired to make it to the bed.

What's wrong with me? she wondered, pushing her head back against the soft chair and tightly shutting her eyes. Had she somehow caught the farmer's sickness? It couldn't be possible. Her Cat's Eye protected her from magic. It had been a curse, after all; not a disease. Certainly not contagious.

But she continued to feel more and more sick until she finally gave up, allowing her thoughts to fade into swimmy darkness. Maybe she needed a nap. That was it. Just a nap and she would be fine....

CHAPTER 2

She was standing in the field, looking down at Dorian's cold, lifeless body. His eyes were glassy, empty, gazing up at her. She had buried her good friend a year ago, but she could still conjure up every curve of his face, the slope of his nose, his pointed chin and silver hair.

A peculiar shudder ran through her. She forced herself to look away, biting her lip until the pain made her concentrate on her surroundings.

The field was dead. The earth torn up, like great hands had dragged across it. A dense haze covered the dream, as though the very ground was rotten beneath her. The air stunk with the residue of diseased bodies. Chickens pecked across the surface of the earth, clucking and bickering with each other, their eyes like gummy red beads, their beaks black with infection.

She focused past that. In the distance she could see a figure moving, his form vague against the background of the swamp. She frowned, and as in the nature of dreams, lifted from the ground to glide smoothly over the fields, drifting steadily toward the strange figure.

She had to hover quite close to get a good look at the traveler, floating just above his head, and then she grew confused. Was it Dorian again, this time creeping through the trees? No, she had just left his dead body. Then who...?

A gust of wind swirled around the figure's cloak, and a face turned in her direction. Sora's eyes widened in fascination. His features were delicate, with the effeminate touch of a Wolfy mage. No, it wasn't Dorian, though the man was of the same race. His eyes were smaller, narrowed with malice and alight with cunning. His lips weren't lush like Dorian's, but thin and pale, set in a narrow line. His nose, though pointed, was obviously masculine, and his overall frame was broader and taller—still rather lean compared to most men. Sora felt an odd knotting in her gut at the sight of him, and some inherent dislike bloomed in her chest.

Everywhere he stepped, the grass turned brown, and his shadow spread around him like a pool of darkness.

He raised a delicate nose to the air and sniffed, his long ears twitching, then his head snapped around and his eyes looked right at her.

"Who watches?" he called. He stared at her—pierced her.

Then she was off flying again; the field disappeared in seconds. Acres of farmland swept by below her, the crops bent and withered, dying...then a small forest, then more dead fields until finally she crested a hill. Then she found herself overlooking a port city. She could hear the sound of people coughing, the moans of women and the cries of children. It seemed like a dark cloud hung over everything, as though the world had been thrown into a permanent dusk.

Sora got a good view of the houses and shops before she was soaring again, down through the streets, twisting and turning past flower stalls and brick walls, dirty cobblestones, the sun glinting off windows...then she arrived at the docks.

Crowds, bartering, the dull impression of voices....

A young man with aqua-colored eyes and red hair stepped off the plank of a giant merchant ship. A crow perched on his shoulder ruffled its feathers and squawked, perhaps annoyed by her presence. She didn't recognize the traveler's face, but he looked vaguely familiar.

Then she was whisked away again, this time over the ocean, across waves and waves, endless waves. In seconds she had covered countless miles, heading swiftly toward a series of green islands.

She moved in closer to the main island. A circle of gigantic stones rested amidst a field of green grass overlooking the ocean. Sora dove down to its center, then was pulled up a rock path to a strange marble pedestal atop a hill, mere yards away from a steep drop, straight into the crashing surf. The pedestal was shaped like a claw, as though meant to hold something small and round, like a rock or a small pebble, a marble, or maybe even...a Cat's Eye.

The vision changed, sending her into a whirl of chaos, the scenery spinning around her, flashes of woodland and ocean and rock. The Wolfy mage stood close by, staring at her, grinning. As she watched, he slowly raised his fingers to his mouth; they were covered in blood, and he licked each one clean, as though devouring a great delicacy. A dense, impenetrable darkness seemed to be spreading from him, oozing out of his pores, dampening his clothes and overshadowing his face, until all she could see were his eyes....

There was an abrupt shout; she tore her gaze from the evil face. Next to her stood another figure, someone living and breathing whom she knew very well.

"Trapped again?" the assassin whispered. He reached out to touch her hand. Her heart twisted at the sight of his dark hair, his green eyes....For a moment, she felt relief.

"You came back for me," she murmured.

"No," he said. But it wasn't his voice. No, someone else, a darker voice, impossibly deep and crusted, like rusted metal....It sent needles of fear through her heart.

"You're not Crash," she whispered, stepping back, her pulse thudding in her ears."Get away from me! Who are you?"

"You mean...what am I?" the voice taunted.

Abruptly her vision narrowed. She felt as though she were looking through a tunnel, the world focused solely on his face; then Crash's face smeared, and in its place was a pair of glowing red eyes. Fire leapt in their depths—fire and darkness. The creature smiled.

She screamed.

She turned and ran, wind whipping around her, completely blind. A dull murmur reached the edges of her hearing, nagging, but she continued to run through the black space, glints of light all around her, stars or fireflies or something similar. A shushing sound grew in her ears...voices...rushes and whispers: "Who hast the nerve to light thy fire, to steal thy blade and risk thine ire...."

The chanting continued, and Sora covered her ears, wondering how to escape from this nightmare. Somehow the voices beat through her defenses, speaking as one, constant and insistent. "Emotions powered in the fight—around thy neck, burning bright—when thou dost run, do not fall— hence the destruction of us all."

And finally—finally—the voices stopped, only to be replaced

by a much more familiar sound, like the brush of wind chimes, but louder, ever more urgent. The clink of bells made her think of a galloping horseman, faster and faster, thundering in her direction. It could only be one thing....

* * *

"Sora! Sora! Wake up!"

Sora sat up with a start, bursting from the dream like a wild horse, grabbing her mother with hands of steel. Her body was shaking, trembling, and she clung to the woman like a rope in a dark ocean. She still felt trapped by the intense dream, as though it would rise up at any second and consume her again.

They stayed like that for a long moment, both women breathing, holding each other, until peace seeped back into the room. Sora finally let herself sag backwards onto the sweat-soaked chair. Her lungs shuddered in her chest.

The two looked at each other. Sora realized her headache had gone; tears were streaming down her cheeks. Tears? Numbly, she wiped at them. She couldn't get the image of Dorian's dead body out of her mind, or Crash's evil, maniacal eyes. She could remember the dream clearly, vividly, like a poem or a song. It took her mother's voice to bring her back to her surroundings.

"And so it begins," the woman whispered.

"W-what?" Sora replied.

"Dane had these symptoms. Nightmares. Visions from the necklace."

Sora nodded, still shaken. Her true father, Dane, had worn the necklace before her; in fact, he had died wearing it, which meant that his spirit could be trapped inside, still bonded to the Cat's Eye. But nightmares? No, this had been real, tangible; she had tasted the air and had heard Crash's voice as though spoken into her ear. It was a vision. She had never had one before, but she knew what it was instinctively. Something had transferred from that farmer; some residue of the curse. Her Cat's Eye had awakened—and was trying to tell her something.

"I saw sick people," Sora murmured. "The earth was barren. Dead crops. Disease. It spread over the land like a dark shadow...." She looked at her mother warily, waiting for an explanation.

Lorianne sighed. "The Cat's Eye isn't a dead rock. It's part of you now, just like your pulse or your breath. It knows your heart and mind," she said slowly. "I think it's trying to warn us. The farmer's curse...is part of something much larger. Something that has to do with this...."

Sora hadn't realized until now that her mother was holding a package. She watched as Lorianne unwrapped it. Her skin prickled.

She already knew what was inside.

A thick, dark sword hilt, wrapped in leather, no blade.

Sora recognized what had been a true sword not so long ago—a rapier, to be exact—wielded by one of Volcrian's minions, a wraith made of powerful blood magic. The specter burst upon them shortly after they escaped from the swamp, catching them all by surprise. The sword had killed Dorian, and then the wraith had plunged it straight through her ribs.

She almost died in the fields next to him. Sometimes she wished she had. It was strange, the guilt of a survivor. She spent more time than she wanted to admit visiting his grave, thinking about his death, wondering if she could have prevented it—and knowing she could have.

Crash and Burn had left her the sword hilt as a strange memento. Neither had explained why.

"So?" Sora asked. "What about it?"

Lorianne held the hilt tightly, as though it could still hurt her daughter. She spoke quietly. "A bit strange, don't you think, that a creature made of blood and magic would wield such a weapon...?"

Sora shrugged. In all honesty, she hadn't thought much of it.

"Do you know much about Wolfy magic?"

Sora shrugged again. "Only that they use blood to work their spells. They're supposedly the strongest of the races, though I don't know if that's true...."

"It is," her mother said shortly. "Blood magic is a tricky thing. It's not like elemental magic or nature magic. It crosses boundaries. The wraith that Volcrian summoned was powerful. It was a human spirit tied to a magical form, turned into something evil and soulless. The wraiths are not part of this world. They come from another place, the underworld, far beneath the earth. Where the Dark God sleeps."

Sora nodded. She had heard the lore of the races before. There was a god for each of the elements: Wind, Water, Earth, Fire, Light and Dark. But only the Wind Goddess was worshipped now. The races were all but extinct; some humans believed that they had never existed in the first place. They were slowly being forgotten, and their gods with them.

"Each of the gods and goddesses has a sacred weapon," her mother explained. "In this case, the Dark God has three: a rapier, a spear and a crossbow. I was reading this," she said, placing a book in Sora's lap. It was a sizable tome, difficult to lift, the pages worn and dusty. "The spell that Volcrian used to summon his wraiths is forbidden. If the Wolfy race were still powerful, he would be imprisoned by now. It is strictly forbidden by the Wolfies, and all of the races, to raise the dead, because when things return from the underworld, sometimes they bring stuff back with them...like these weapons. The sacred weapons of the Dark God, released once again into the world of Wind and Light."

"All right," Sora said, nodding slowly. She didn't know much about the old ways, the laws of the Wolfies or other races, but she could remember most of the lore of the Elements. "So the Dark God had sacred weapons. Why does that matter?"

"If these weapons fell into the wrong hands, well...."

"What?"

"They have the potential to awaken the Dark God fully. To cause pain and suffering unlike any seen in thousands of years. This sickness that is spreading, it is not just a disease. It is a curse. Residue from the Dark God that is now seeping into the land. We need to destroy these weapons—and Volcrian—before it is too late."

Sora sat back, her mouth hanging open. She looked down at the rapier hilt, then back at her mother. She didn't know what to say. Finally, she cracked a smile. "Really, Mum?" she said cheekily. "Are you sure your eyes aren't tired? Maybe you need a nap, too."

"Don't laugh!" her mother replied, but she was grinning. "Sounds dire, doesn't it? These things were common once, back in the time of the races, when magic was an everyday occurrence. People knew these things and they respected the old laws. But with the races gone and magic all but a myth, it's a very dangerous time for Volcrian to invoke this spell. There are few who know how to stop him."

Sora nodded. She could see that. Most people either scoffed at magic or whispered about it worriedly, as though it were bad luck. Her eyes fell to the rapier hilt again and she studied the old leather wrappings. She had often wondered about the rapier in the last year. The handle looked ancient, worn, like a relic from a forgotten time.

But a sacred weapon? Something of legend? Truly?

"The Cat's Eye," she said, putting a hand to the necklace again. "The vision. That's what it was telling me."

"What did you see?" her mother asked.

At first, Sora didn't want to relate what she had seen—in truth, she couldn't make her voice work—but she knew she had to confess, especially if the curse was real.

But when she thought back to the dream, all she could focus on was the sight of Dorian's body. *Dear gods, Dorian....* The loss of her friend was still a fresh wound. It had been a shattering experience, seeing him fall in battle, his blood spraying the fields. The sight of his body occasionally rose up in dreams, usually in the background, in a closet or a corner, or behind some cracked door....She would catch his shadow under a tree, his voice from beyond a river. But never had she been this close, standing right next to him, as though he had just fallen at her feet. Never had it felt so...*personal.*

Suddenly, she found it impossible to keep the words inside. Half-choked, she began her narration, describing Dorian's dead body in the fields, the stranger near the woods, the acres upon acres of rotted farmland, the diseased city, the distant islands and Crash's terrifying transformation. And the words, over and over, circling in her head. *"Who hast the nerve...."*

Lorianne bowed her head in thought. Sora finished, describing the sound of the Cat's Eye, its thundering, urgent presence in her head, like the clambering of horses' hooves. She waited for a response, thinking back on the dream. Part of her was hopeful—maybe it meant nothing—maybe her mother had read too many horror books. But Lori's silence stretched on, and Sora's hands became clammy.

A minute more passed; finally her mother spoke. "This is very serious."

Sora swallowed hard. "Do you think the Cat's Eye is warning me about Volcrian?"

"More than that," Lorianne said. "I think the Cat's Eye was trying to tell you how to stop him."

Her mother opened the book and began flipping through pages of text. Sora hadn't read this specific volume before, though she recognized it from one of the shelves about magic. "The Cat's Eye hasn't had magic in some time," her mother said thoughtfully. "It must have come into contact with Volcrian's residue when it absorbed the curse. It knows him, certainly...and knows that he follows you."

"That's all just in theory," Sora said.

"Well, your vision was certainly specific. This isn't the first time the necklace has tasted his magic." Lorianne paused, her finger landing at the top of a column of text. "Here it is," she continued. "There are only certain places that the weapons can be destroyed and returned to the underworld. This might be one of them. The Lost Isles."

"The Lost Isles?" Sora asked, with an arch of her eyebrow.

"Yes, the island you described in your dream. The Harpies still live there, I believe, and they are the race of Light, natural guardians against the Dark God. They have a sacred stone structure there that could be useful."

Sora turned to look out the window, taking in a slow breath of air. "I don't understand. What about the rest of it? Why Dorian? Why dream about his body?"

"Because your friends are in danger," her mother replied. "Isn't it obvious? Volcrian is on the hunt to kill them, and his hatred is bringing something terrible into the world. The Cat's Eye is trying to warn you. You said you lost him, right? That he couldn't follow you through the swamp?" Her mother bit her lip.

Sora nodded.

"What if he's picked up the trail again?" Lorianne stared at her intensely, her hands tight on the armrests.

Sora paled. *Volcrian?* "Then...then he is coming here...." It was the only logical place he would go. She had never met him face to face, but it was a name she had learned to fear. She felt as though he might appear next to her if she spoke it aloud. He was on a hunt for vengeance, bent on killing Crash and anyone else who got in his way.

He was the reason they had risked life and limb to pass through the swamp; the reason Crash and Burn had left her here at her mother's cabin. They wanted her safe, out of the way—or at least, that's what they had said. Sora knew the truth: she would have just slowed them down, another burden. She had caused Dorian's death and she might cause theirs as well. What good was a rich, spoiled noblewoman, anyway?

But I'm not like that anymore, she thought, her hand clenching in her lap. Was she?

"On his way here?" she repeated quietly, thinking.

Her mother nodded. "To be honest, I've suspected it for some time since they left. It would have taken Volcrian many months to cross through the mountains, because he couldn't enter the swamp. But now seems to be the right time for him to arrive. He is hunting Crash. He will follow him wherever he goes, including to this doorstep. I think this curse precedes him. He is much closer than we realize. In the vision, you saw him at the border of the swamp, correct?"

Sora nodded.

"Then he must be on his way." Lorianne gave her a pointed look.

Sora stared at her mother, horrified. In the dim light of her bedroom, she could barely make out the woman's troubled face, so much like her own. She frowned slightly. "Great, just great," she muttered. "Well, what am I supposed to do? Go off and find these lost Isles? Seems a bit much."

Her mother gripped the pages of the book, folding the corners in her hands; she seemed frustrated and didn't readily have an answer. This was a side to Lorianne that Sora hadn't seen yet. "I don't know," she said tensely. "But you need answers, and fast. This plague is unnatural and evil, and we might be the only people who know about it. You must find Crash and warn him. You must also travel to the city of Barcella, to the Temple of the Goddess. It is almost a hundred miles to the west, toward the coast. Speak to the High Priestess. Visions are not so uncommon in their order. She can advise you."

Sora nodded slowly. The Temple of the Goddess...she had never visited one before. There had been a shrine on her father's land, fairly close to their house, where they had gone to pray and light incense on certain days of the year. But that was the extent of her knowledge of the Goddess and Her disciples. "So...so what? Is that what I'm supposed to do?" she asked incredulously.

"Well, you must do something!" Lori demanded. "You're the one with the necklace. The dream could mean many things, but you will need to consult someone more experienced than I—and you need to find your friends. The Cat's Eye is concerned with more than just a plague. The Cat's Eye is always, first and foremost, in tune with your heart. You must find your friends and warn them. Then you must find some solid answers about how to cure this plague."

Answers. Cure the plague. Despite all her longings, the thought of hunting down Crash and begging him for help made her gut twist with anxiety. He had left her behind for good reason and she doubted he wanted to see her again. He was not the kind to stick out his neck for others. "I'm sure they're just fine without me...."

"Obviously not, if you are receiving visions. Volcrian is on his way, I'm certain of it. Your friends probably don't even know he has found their trail."

Sora nodded. That much, she could understand. She remembered her last encounter with Volcrian's magic. The wraith, a ghost-like apparition smothered in black rags. Its magic had been powerful, terrifying, its very presence like a demon from the underworld. It had killed Dorian effortlessly...and had almost killed her, as well. She still carried the scar on her ribs where its blade had pierced her through. The blade had been destroyed by the Cat's Eye shortly afterward, but the hilt remained.

She hadn't been able to save Dorian...but perhaps she could save Crash and Burn.

"Okay," Sora said. "Okay, I'll do it."

At this, a tension settled on the room. *I'm going to do this. I'm going to find Crash...although how, I have no idea!* And what would she say when she found him? Would he believe her? Or would he dismiss her as crazy? No matter what scenario she envisioned, she felt pathetic. Weapons of the Dark God? A plague? Why would he buy into that? Crash was an assassin with a shady, secretive past. She knew hardly anything about him—only that he wasn't a hero.

Come now, her inner voice chided, *no use getting a stomachache over it!* Trying to warn them of Volcrian's pursuit was noble enough. It was something she *could* do. And the plague was real, she could vouch for that. Her Cat's Eye was proof. Crash would listen to the necklace; he was the one who had first told her about it, after all.

When her mind turned to the thought of traveling again, she felt a sudden thrill of excitement. Sora flexed her hands, full of anticipation. Her year in the cabin had been far too long. Her bones itched for more adventure, a horse beneath her and a new breeze on her face. She wanted to wander like a vagabond, no ties and no true destination—following the wind.

They've been gone for a year, she thought. *How am I going to find them? I don't even know where they were headed.* Yet it was a fleeting worry, easily answered. The solution came to her as she looked at her mother. She hadn't found this woman by chance alone. No, the Cat's Eye had led her straight through the dangers of the swamp to her mother's doorstep. It had focused on the hidden yearnings in her heart and made them a reality. She knew the necklace could lead her to someone else important, someone buried deep inside of her—like her lost friends. Perhaps she only had to ask. When she touched the stone subconsciously and heard a soft chiming in response, she knew that would work.

So this is it. In a single day, everything had changed. It struck her again that she would truly be leaving soon. To find Crash and Burn? *Admit it, Sora, you've been longing for this all along!*

"Mom," she said quietly. "I—well—I guess I have to go."

Lorianne nodded slowly. Sora's eyes narrowed in the dark; were those tears on her face? She didn't truly want to know. *If she's crying, then I might not be able to leave.*

"I'm sorry," she murmured, for lack of anything better to say.

Her mother sniffled loudly, confirming Sora's suspicions, then said in a shaky voice, "It's safer for you to go. If Volcrian found you here...."

They sat in silence for another moment. Sora was worried. What if Volcrian arrived and attacked her mother? The mage was evil, insane, destroying anyone who helped Crash or Burn. She wanted to tell Lorianne to leave, or to come with her, but she knew her mother was stubborn. *I just wish...*she thought, watching as her mother thumbed the pages of the book. *I just wish I could tell her these things.* But they were still new to one another. Awkward strangers, despite the powerful bond of blood.

Sora pulled her mother into a startlingly tight embrace. There was nothing to say, no way to explain how she felt. She thought she might understand what was in her mother's heart, but they had been apart for so many years. *We've spent no time together, really.*

Her mother left her on the doorstep of a rich Lord, allowing her to grow up in another household, in a different way of life. She couldn't hang around with Lorianne for the next sixteen years, trying to make up for lost time. She had to move forward.

"When shall I leave?" she asked. "This is all moving so quickly; it seems like just yesterday...." *Just yesterday I awoke to find myself wounded, and in this strange bed.*

"As soon as you can," her mother said steadily. "There's no time to lose!" Her tone was unexpected. She pulled back from the embrace and looked Sora in the eye. "It's dangerous to ignore the warnings of a Cat's Eye. We can't afford to wait. It's almost dawn anyhow—did you know that you were asleep all night? Here, I'll make you a good breakfast and have Cameron pack your saddlebags."

Cameron was her mother's stablehand and general hired help. A simpleton. He had received a bad head wound from a horse several years ago, robbing him of his ability to do complex reasoning. Her mother had kept him on as an assistant.

Despite her words, Lorianne seemed reluctant to stand up. She held Sora's hands for a long moment, then finally sighed. "You need to get dressed and I need to start cooking." Slowly, she got up on her feet.

Sora sat for a moment in silence. She knew her words were true, that the vision had been urgent. But she still felt bereft, as though she had swallowed a pocket of air. *Leaving home already?* She yearned for adventure, yes, but she didn't truly want to leave her mother quite yet....

No use trying to puzzle through it. She dressed quickly and made her way downstairs in her new black riding pants and boots. When she reached the bottom, her mother was standing there with her weapons in hand: a staff and a pair of daggers.

"Oh," Sora said, taken aback. Her mother wordlessly pressed

the weapons into her hands. She could feel the familiar weight of the staff. It was made out of dense blue wood—witch wood, the salesman had called it, so many months ago. It, too, was said to have magical properties, though she hadn't been able to find anything about it in her mother's library. She ran her hand over the staff's length, feeling its firm weight. Her fingers went to the top end, where the initials K.W. were carved, the mark of some previous owner. It was impossible to tell how old the weapon was; the wood was nigh indestructible, and wouldn't even chip under a sword blow.

Sora took the daggers; she slipped one into her boot and one up her sleeve. Then Lorianne handed her one last artifact. The rapier hilt, once again wrapped in cloth. Sora held it carefully, staring at it, suddenly aware of its importance.

"A sacred weapon," she murmured. Somehow, she had expected it to be more impressive. She waited for it to do something extraordinary—but of course, that didn't happen.

"Make sure no one sees that you have the rapier," her mother said. "In the time of the races, there were many sects trying to get these weapons, secret societies, cults and other hidden orders. Those groups might still be around today."

"This decision to leave really is quite sudden, isn't it?" Sora asked quietly.

"I suppose," her mother answered brusquely. "But I want you gone from here as soon as possible. If Volcrian were to find you...." She abruptly turned back to the kitchen and made herself busy, taking down a pan and lighting the stove.

Sora didn't want to speak of it, either. She was suddenly, painfully aware that she might not come back from this journey alive. The possibility crawled around in the back of her mind, poking her like a big, black beetle.

But she couldn't think of failure, not now. Who was to say that anything bad would happen? She tried to be positive. With any luck, she would find Crash and Burn safe and well, living somewhere far from Volcrian's reach. *Knowing those two, though, I doubt it.*

Sora continued packing her bags as her mother cooked. Lorianne had a way of humming to herself, no matter what she was doing. The sound pervaded the room, tickling at Sora's ears, drawing a small smile to her face. *I'm going to miss this.* Sometimes, she imagined that her mother's voice made the food taste better.

She lingered in the doorway of the kitchen, watching her mother, awkwardly running her fingers over the door frame. She wanted to speak...to offer some sort of comfort...but Lorianne seemed somehow unreachable at that moment. More like a distant friend than the woman who had birthed her.

Thunk. An onion appeared on the sideboard, near Sora's hands. Lorianne put a knife next to it. "Want to help?" she said. She caught her daughter's eye and smiled.

Sora smiled in return. Then she cut the onion, without crying.

They ate breakfast together—eggs, onions and toast—and wrapped some leftovers for Sora to take on the road. They walked outside together. Cameron was already waiting there with her horse. It was a dappled mare with short, stout legs and a fluid trot. She had ridden the steed several times before; it was one of her favorites.

Cameron tinkered with the saddlebags, securing ropes,

adjusting the stirrups and saddle blanket. He was short and stooped, with a bald, blunt head and big ears.

"Well...I suppose you're going to be gone for a while," Lorianne said from her position in the doorway. "Write to me in a few months, will you? Let me know you're safe."

Sora nodded. They both stood awkwardly for a moment, looking at each other helplessly. Finally, Sora put her arms around her mother. "I love you," she whispered. She had never said those words before—she never thought it would be so hard....

Lorianne looked as if she would cry again. "I'll be waiting for your return."

The two held onto each other, then broke apart. Her mother seemed to be drinking in every part of Sora, her eyes roving over her face, jumping from feature to feature.

Finally Sora nodded, turned, and walked briskly to the horse.

The beast stamped his foot impatiently as she checked the stirrups and mounted. Cameron stood to one side, giving them plenty of room. She waved to him and, with one final look at her mother, turned her horse toward the dirt road.

* * *

The path was long and winding, wide enough for a wagon to fit on, the sides crowded with bushes and ferns. Tall fir trees lined the road, their branches heavy with needles and pine cones, the air rich with their scent. Sora's eyes traveled to the end of the distant road and she imagined what lay beyond the dense woods. Through the trees, past the nearby town, and then...nothing but horizon. Miles and miles of open plains. The sun was just peeking over the hills, a new day. It seemed full of promise.

She nudged the mare forward and they started off down the trail. Excitement filled her, growing with each clip-clop of the horse's hooves. Her heart sang with the knowledge that she could go wherever she chose, wherever the Cat's Eye led her. Her adventure was beginning again—this time she wouldn't stop until it was truly over.

Soon Sora was out of view of her mother's house. The sun warmed her face, and she was accompanied by the sonorous calls of birds.

CHAPTER 3

During the late summer, the sun would suck the moisture from the grass, burning it to a flimsy yellow. Her mother told Sora that brushfires were common in these parts. Even a simple magnifying glass could light the plains on fire.

For now, though, summer was still a few months away and the fields were a springy green cushion. Sora took a brief rest in the fields while her horse rummaged for fresh grass. It was about mid-afternoon...she had to find her direction.

She lay down on her back, obscured by the tall strands, breathing in the moist air; she felt sheltered from the larger world, momentarily invisible. She reached up to touch her necklace, running her fingers across its warm, smooth surface. It had always felt more like skin covered by a thin film rather than a rock.

Her mind wandered to her friends: the dark assassin who had kidnapped her so long ago, and Burn, the Wolfy mercenary, a giant warrior and one of the last of a dying race. She could clearly remember their faces, their specific traits and features.

She meditated on their images for a while, attempting to communicate with the Cat's Eye, to describe what she needed. Something stirred deep in her mind, like the beginnings of a dream. A dull noise reached her ears—the jingling of sleighbells. That was the same sound the necklace always made, the gem's subtle way of communicating with her. She didn't know if all bearers heard the same sound, but her Cat's Eye always used bells.

Sora received a clear impression that the necklace had already decided the course of her journey. She had never used the necklace like this before, and was a little disconcerted at having to read its nudges and impressions. She sank into a deeper meditation, her breathing slowing, her limbs growing heavy. Over time, the world slipped away. She was floating in a black space, with no sensation of the wind or grass beneath her, as though she had entered a dark tunnel.

Then, vaguely, she felt like she was standing on rocks or sand—and a long, deep corridor stretched before her. *Where do we go from here?* she asked silently. The words echoed in the deep emptiness, as if she was talking in a void. Had she been heard?

After countless minutes, perhaps even an hour, she felt the necklace nudge back at her, like a hand resting on her shoulder. She was startled back to consciousness.

She climbed to her feet without a second thought, as though directed by a clear voice and turned southwest, across the plains. *That way.*

Her horse grazed a few dozen yards to her left; he saw her and trotted over, bumping her with his nose, eager for attention, even slobbering on her shirt. She gave the mare a handful of oats so it wouldn't set its attentions on her hair, grinning wryly at its antics. All of her mother's horses had distinct personalities and were excellently trained. Sometimes, they seemed close to human. She wondered if Healers had a certain affinity with animals.

Sora mounted, then looked around. *West.* She could feel the Cat's Eye urging her in that direction, like a finger poking into the back of her head. Who knew how long she would have to travel to find her friends—it could be another six months. *No, it would be sooner than that.* She wasn't sure where that thought came from, but it crossed her mind with the slight chiming of a bell.

She shook her head, her thoughts swimming with this strange, new communication from the necklace. For so long, it had been silent...but now, it was wide awake.

After only a bit of hesitation, she started off across the fields.

* * *

Days passed—she had been traveling a week or more. Sora grew accustomed to sleeping under the stars, although she had to admit that the trek was a bit lonely. Sometimes she talked to her horse out of sheer boredom. At night, she was never certain if she should light a fire, since the plains were large and flat and any sort of light was easily visible. She saw ground squirrels, rabbits, foxes and owls; luckily, nothing bigger than a deer. She didn't waste time trying to hunt; that was one skill she had never learned. She ate from her rations instead, something that she was very good at.

Finally a shape appeared, an oblong shadow on the horizon with thin clouds rising above it. As she neared, she recognized a trail of smoke off in the distance. A town—had to be.

She was miles away from home and had never traveled this far across the grasslands before. At least the town in the distance gave her a tangible direction. A small smile spread across her face. Maybe she could find an inn and stay the night. The thought of sleeping on the cold ground again was not very appealing. It had been frosty the last few nights, and she had been forced to cover herself with her saddle blanket. *Ugh, the smell....*Now she stank like horse sweat. Even worse, she was almost out of rations. She would need to refill her bags at a few trade stores.

She continued forward, pushing her horse at a slow canter. The afternoon stretched on. Toward sunset, the town became fully visible on the grassy plain, a circular colony with tall wooden walls and wide, flat rooftops.

She reached the front gates a few minutes later. Her horse slowed to a walk, and she approached the entrance curiously, uncertain of what she might find. Tassels and bells hung from the wooden archway, clinking dully in the light breeze, small emblems of the Goddess. She had seen similar charms on barn doors and storefronts. One guard stood on either side of the tall gates, dressed in heavy steel armor. They nodded as she passed.

Sora stopped when she was just inside the gate, glancing back at the guards, who had already returned to scanning the fields: two grimy, pimply young men. From their expensive-looking armor, she guessed they were King's soldiers, probably recruited from local farms. She decided to try her luck—*what could it hurt?*

"Excuse me," she asked politely, "I was wondering if you've seen a man pass through here recently. Maybe you'd remember? He's about so tall, black hair, green eyes, wears dark colors....?"

The guards turned to look at her in surprise. One of them, a sunburned redhead with giant splotches of freckles across his nose, scratched under his helmet. "You talkin' about the Ravens?" he asked. "Aye, we caught a few. I think there was one that kind of matched that description...."

Sora's eyes widened, curious. "Ravens?" she echoed. "Like...birds?"

The other guard choked out a derisive laugh. He had straw-colored hair and a stern, serious face, too gaunt to be handsome.

"No, miss. As in outlaws and thieves. The Ravens are a notorious group of bandits in these parts."

"More like pigeons, really!" The freckled one added with a wide grin. "Or crows. They hop around in people's trash and take whatever's shiny."

"Quiet, Don," the blond guard said coldly. "The Ravens are lawless, bloodthirsty criminals, no doubt about it."

Sora mulled the words over in her head. *Lawless, bloodthirsty criminals.* Her companions weren't the most respectable types...but the thought of them hiding out in the tall grass and then attacking caravans made her want to laugh. And they certainly wouldn't have been caught by a pair of acne-covered farm boys....

"We arrested the pair just last night," the blond guard continued. "Fools tried to steal from the town treasury. Now they're locked up in the cells. Just who is this person you're looking for, anyway?"

Their eyes narrowed suspiciously, but Sora didn't answer immediately. Instead, she looked down the well-worn streets, at the hard-packed dirt and empty vendor stalls. She experienced a moment of horror as a brood of hens hobbled into view, their beaks black and splotchy, feathers missing from their wings. No one else was in sight. The town was eerily quiet.

Then she frowned. "Oh, an old friend, I don't know if he's a bandit, though. He's been...ch...missing for quite a few months. Think I could take a look?"

The freckled soldier raised an eyebrow. "A look at the prisoners?"

"Yes," she nodded. From their wary expressions, she realized how strange she must sound; they must not get a lot of travelers asking to visit their jail cells. She widened her eyes, trying to look innocent and naive. "He's been missing for so long, and I've been so worried!"

"Right..." the redhead said slowly. The two soldiers shared another glance, then looked back at her. "Could we see your wrists first, miss?"

"My wrists?"

"Aye," the blond guard spoke up. "Let's see 'em."

Sora frowned, but complied. She dropped the reins and rolled up her long sleeves, showing the guards her bare, white wrists. The guards looked at them carefully, and one even stepped up to the horse, taking her small hand in his and turning it over, inspecting it closely, as though she had a knife up her sleeve. Which she did, but she was far better at hiding that.

"She's clean," the blond guard said. The freckled one looked relieved.

Now it was Sora's turn to stare incredulously. "Clean? Is that what this is all about? Well, honestly, I haven't bathed in several days. Road dust has a way of clinging...."

"No, we meant your wrists," the redhead soldier interrupted her. "You don't carry the mark of the bandits. They always brand their members...scar them with fire...you know, to identify them." He looked a little pale at the thought.

Sora felt her lips twist into a grimace. "Brand them?" she echoed. "Like cattle?"

"Aye...or slaves."

She wasn't sure what to think of that.

The blond guard motioned for her to follow, and turned toward the guardhouse. "If you'll come with me, miss, I'll show you the prisoners."

She dismounted her horse and tied it to a nearby post, then followed the blond guard toward a large brick building next to the front gates. The redhead stayed behind to keep watch. He turned his back to them, staring out across the plains.

"I take it you're not from around here?" the blond asked, looking at her curiously. Now that they were alone, he seemed more relaxed.

"Just passing through," Sora said, somewhat guarded. It occurred to her that Volcrian might travel this way as well in the next few weeks. She might have already made a mistake by speaking to the guards. They would certainly remember her if anyone described her appearance.

"Ah," the soldier said. "Well, better that way, I suppose. You should be careful on the road. We've been fighting off the Ravens for years now. They'll go after anyone—caravans, travelers, children. I've even seen them make off with stray chickens."

"They sound more like jackals than ravens," Sora commented.

"Aye, they're bandits, through and through. We killed the old leader almost eight years ago, shot through with an arrow. For a while, things died down, but in the last few years, they're more active than ever! They've been attacking towns, raiding our warehouses, stealing livestock and robbing inns." The soldier leaned close, as though sharing a secret. "We suspect they have a new leader, but no one's got close enough to see him."

Sora nodded, listening with half an ear. She didn't really care about bandits, not if it didn't involve her friends. She had heard rumors of such things back home, when speaking to the farmers who passed through her mother's village. They had talked about terrible, depraved outlaws who watched the roads, but she hadn't realized the problem was nearby—or that the bandits were even real. She wondered if the Ravens would eventually make their way further north to her mother's area. She couldn't help but feel a little concerned. Her mother lived out in the woods by herself, after all.

"Here we are," the guard muttered. He withdrew a keyring and unlocked the heavy iron door, nodding to Sora to pass through.

She stepped into the cool, shadowy interior. The floor was tiled and swept clean. It appeared to be a common room; there were a few wooden tables and a barrel of water—or, she suspected, ale—in the corner. The narrow windows along the far wall let in faded light, casting the room in a pinkish glow. Tall and long, the windows were barely wide enough for her to fit an arm through. Also on the far side of the room were stairs leading to a lower floor, probably to the jail cells. A rack of weapons and heavy iron shields rested against one of the walls; no other soldiers were in sight.

"The patrol should be back any minute now," the guard mentioned, following her gaze to the rack of weapons. "They usually return at sunset. I'll let you have a glance at the prisoners, but you should probably go before the Cap'n gets back. He might not like it."

Sora nodded. Wouldn't want to upset the Cap'n, whoever that was. Then her stomach growled. She considered turning around and leaving to seek an inn for the night, but she had already come this far. She might as well see who they had downstairs. One thing was for certain, though....She doubted such a place could hold her companions for long.

They traveled down the narrow flight of stairs. Sora found herself in a broad room with jail cells lining each wall. The place was more or less clean, but weighed down by the heavy smell of urine and human waste. She gagged on the stuffy air, feeling its thick texture in her mouth. There was no ventilation. How long had it had taken that stench to build up?

"Here's the two we captured," he said, pointing down the row of dark cells.

He took a step forward, but suddenly a strange noise reached them through the walls. Sora was surprised that any sound could penetrate that dense building. It was hollow, like a horn or a bugle.

The guard next to her stiffened, then gave her an apologetic glance. "That would be the Cap'n back from patrol," he said. "I've got to meet them at the gate. I'll be right back. Don't go anywhere!" He turned and ran up the staircase, his boots slapping on stone.

Sora watched him go, then turned back to the dark, dank cells. She would just take a glance and be done with it. She thought of calling out Crash's name, but something about the gloom stopped her. Although she doubted that her companions were anywhere close by, she still started down the length of the room, flinching at each shadow. *Ugh,* she thought, spotting a small movement in the corner. *Rats!*

The first prisoner she came across was not very impressive. She thought at first that he might be dead, he was so thin and ragged, until she saw the hollow rise and fall of his chest. She took a step closer to the bars and raised an eyebrow. Blinked. She was so tense that she had fully imagined her assassin friend lying there on the ground, dressed in rags, as bony as a buzzard. But a second look revealed a haggard stranger with dishwater-brown hair and a grizzled face. Not her assassin friend, by far.

Then something moved in the next cell over. There was a

muffled groan. Sora frowned; it was a girl's voice, unexpected. She walked to the next cell and stared at a small heap inside it, curled in a ball on the ground.

The girl unwrapped herself, slowly sitting up, stretching her pale, skinny arms. She looked up with wide gray eyes, and Sora was struck by their color—lavender, in the shadows.

The prisoner didn't say a word, only stared with those large, soft eyes. She was so thin and small, at first Sora thought she was a mere child, but small mounds of breasts were protruding from her chest. Still, she couldn't have been more than fourteen. Her hair was thin, blond, platinum in the murky light, falling in wispy tufts to her shoulders. She was dressed in swaths of rags, in an assortment of different colors and fabrics. They looked like things she had pulled off of laundry lines or found discarded along the roadside. Her face was dirty and gaunt, with hollow cheeks and an alarmingly dark bruise on her jaw. Sora had the sudden urge to reach out and touch her, to assure herself that she wasn't a ghost.

"What...what are you doing in here?" Sora asked, shocked.

The girl's soft, vulnerable expression suddenly changed, and Sora was met with the face of a street child, hardened and suspicious. "What does it look like?" she asked sarcastically. "They arrested me."

"For what?"

"None of your business!" she spat venomously.

How does a child like this wind up in jail? Sora wondered, ignoring the girl's attitude. Incredibly young and small, she looked as harmless as a fly. The girl tried to rise to her feet, but the effort took her longer than it should have; she was terribly thin and weak. Sora wondered when she had last eaten.

"How long have you been here?" she asked.

"I don't know, a few days," the girl said. "They threw me in here with this other guy. They'll hang me for sure before the week is out." Her eyes flashed defiantly. "That's what they do to us, you know. Hang us."

Sora frowned. She wasn't necessarily against hanging criminals, but this girl was far too young to be executed. She could remember when she was that age, she hadn't known not to steal honey scones from the manor's kitchens. What could this child possibly have done to warrant hanging?

"Why?" Sora asked again.

The girl sat up straighter, looking her in the face, her eyes narrow...then suddenly she sagged, as though the wind had been taken out of her. "Stealing," she finally said, looking to the ground. She appeared even younger now, like a small mouse. "That's all."

Sora's heart went out to the street urchin. Where were her parents?

A sudden door slam broke the silence. Sora jumped slightly and turned toward the staircase. She could hear footsteps approaching, the soldier returning to check on her. She bit her lip, conflicted, then glanced at the girl. No one so young deserved to be hanged.

The guard appeared at the bottom of the steps, another man by his side, this one older and grayer, with a grizzled chin and pronounced nose. The older man stared at her with cold gray eyes.

"I see we have a visitor," he said, his gaze lingering on her wrists. Sora knew what he was looking for, and turned her wrists out. She figured this was the Cap'n. He had a tall, confident stance, like a man used to giving orders.

He nodded sharply to her, then glanced at the girl in the cell. "Do you know this one?" he asked.

On sudden inspiration, Sora nodded, surprising even herself. "My sister," she said, raising her chin slightly. She tried to hide the tremor that went through her. She had a gut-sinking feeling that she was about to get into trouble....

The Cap'n looked even colder than before. "Sister?" he grunted. "So you're related to one of these thieves?"

"Sh-She deserves a second chance," Sora said. "Look at her, she's just a child! She doesn't know any better."

The Cap'n snorted. "Miss, I have seen twelve-year-olds slit a man's throat! She certainly knows better than to get mixed up with outlaws. It's unfortunate that you two are related. We have strict laws about these things." The Cap'n turned abruptly, nodding to the guard next to him. "Jesse, lock her up."

"Wh-What?" Sora exclaimed, her eyes going wide. "But I didn't do anything!"

The words landed on deaf ears. She could tell that some unspoken rule had been broken. Apparently this town wasn't very forgiving of criminals—or their supposed families.

The guard had a regretful look on his young face, but she watched him draw a short knife from his belt. There was a rope in his other hand. "Best to come peaceably," he said, brow furrowed. He took a careful step toward her. "We probably won't hang both of you."

Probably? Sora watched the man approach, shocked, then her reflexes kicked in. With a flick of her wrist, she slipped the knife from her sleeve and lunged forward. The guard's surprised yelp was his only reaction. She plunged the knife into his shoulder, then smacked his head back against the wall. His helmet fell off, clanging across the ground. The guard collapsed, blood running from his head wound.

Sora withdrew her knife and leapt after the Cap'n, who was slightly more prepared. He attempted to grab her wrist, but she kicked him squarely in the knee. It was a fierce kick, much stronger than she had intended, and a high-pitched screech ripped from his throat. Then he fell to the ground, his leg hooked at an unnatural angle. She brought the hard butt of her knife down on his head, cracking it back against the floor, and with a hollow gasp, the Cap'n went limp.

Sora grimaced at his unconscious body, slightly surprised at her own reflexes. She had been practicing with her mother for a full year, but she hadn't thought she'd improved so much. She wiped her knife clean on the tail end of the man's cloak, averting her eyes from his crooked limb, then turned back to the cells.

When she straightened up, she found both prisoners staring at her, their fists tight on the bars. The buzzard man's mouth gaped open. His skull stood out repulsively beneath his tightly stretched skin. The young girl's eyes were as wide as soup bowls.

"You...you...." the young girl said.

Sora didn't waste any time. She couldn't turn back now, and she hadn't laid out the soldiers permanently. They would be awake soon, perhaps within the minute. She yanked the keys from the Cap'n's belt and dashed toward the girl's cell. The ring had about a dozen or so keys jingling from it, and she flipped through them, trying to control her fingers, which were trembling from adrenaline. She tried the next key, and the next. Luckily, by the fourth key, she grabbed the right one. The lock turned with a rusty *crriiick.* She yanked the cell door open and held out a hand to the girl.

The girl stared at her. Her wide, lavender eyes were absolutely luminous. "Wh-what are you doing?" she finally exclaimed. Suspicion came over her face like a dark cloud. "You claim to be my sister? I've never seen you before in my life!"

Sora's mouth dropped. "Of course I'm not your sister!" she exclaimed. "Can't you see—I'm trying to get you out of here!"

"Why? Why should I trust you?"

"You can ask me later, but we don't have a lot of time." Sora looked at the girl in exasperation. "Do you want to live or not?"

The tension ran out of her shoulders at this, and the girl nodded wordlessly. She dodged out of the cell, avoiding Sora's hand, obviously still wary.

"Hey!" the buzzard man shouted. "What about me?"

Personally, Sora didn't like the looks of the man. She could see the branding marks all up and down his arm, scars in the shape of flying birds. A Raven, indeed. He looked like he had been one for countless years.

The girl shook her head, echoing her thoughts. "No way," she said. "He'll go straight to the others and rat us out!"

"I wouldn't!" the man said. It sounded genuine enough, but Sora wasn't convinced.

"Yes, you would!" the girl shouted, fear creeping into her voice. "I saw what you did to the last two! Bastard!"

There was no time for an argument. Sora grabbed the girl's arm and pulled her toward the stairs, away from the man in the cell. The man started banging his hands against the bars, making as much noise as possible. "Help!" he screamed, once he saw that they were leaving him behind. "Help! Guards! There's a breakout!"

Sora threw the keys behind her on last-second inspiration. They skidded across the ground toward the man's cell, but she didn't stop to see if he could reach them. The banging stopped, so he was at least distracted. *Well, that shut him up,* she thought, dragging the young girl up the stairs behind her. It would buy them a little bit more time. Hopefully the keys hadn't slid too close. She didn't necessarily want to break him out of jail...but that wasn't her problem anymore.

They reached the top of the stairs and dashed through the singular room. Two soldiers stood in the corner, both drinking tankards of ale, half-undressed, their cuirasses and shirts off. They looked up, mouths open in mid-conversation. Sora ran straight for the door.

Luckily, the soldiers took a long moment to recover. She rammed open the door and sprinted into sunlight, the girl stumbling behind her. She glanced around, looking for her horse...her horse, anywhere, her horse...*there!*

Her mare was tethered to the same post, next to a line of other steeds that belonged to the guards; one could tell from their decorative saddles. The street urchin dropped Sora's hand and sprinted to the nearest horse, untying its reins.

"What are you doing?" Sora demanded, even as she swung up into her own saddle.

"I'm not going to ride with you!" the girl said. "They'll catch us in no time!"

She had a point. Sora nodded and turned her horse toward the gates. Just then, the door to the guardhouse burst open and two shirtless men ran outside, swords in hand, yelling at the top of their lungs, "Escape! Help! Raise the alarm!"

But they were too late.

The girl freed her horse, a tall, gray steed that was a few years past its prime, and dragged it around to the front gates. She was a blunt and heavy-handed rider. Sora suspected she was self-taught, but now was no time for a lesson.

With a firm kick of her legs, Sora's mare leapt into an immediate gallop. They took off into the fields, running at top speed, her steed huffing and snorting. Full night was almost upon them, with only the barest rim of light on the horizon. She could see stars winking down at her, as though cheering her on, congratulating her on her good luck. She let out a slow breath, easing into the horse's pace. Good fortune, indeed. They would lose the guards easily under cover of darkness, and by morning, they would be far, far away.

* * *

"Are you all right?" Sora looked at the girl curiously.

They had ridden all night. Eventually, they found a river and followed it upstream, hoping it would wash away their trail. Sora was confident that plan had worked. There were no signs of pursuit.

Now, if only they could find a good campsite, sheltered from the wide, flat plains. Sora was becoming tired—a solid twenty-four hours without sleep. She glanced over her shoulder when the girl didn't answer. "Did you hear me?" Sora asked.

The girl followed awkwardly, jostling with each step of the horse, too small for her saddle. She looked exactly as she had in the jail cell: skinny, pale and wan.

"I'm fine, thanks," the girl grunted. "Whatever you want, you're not gettin' anything. I didn't ask for your help."

It seemed to come out of nowhere. Sora paused, unprepared for the attitude. "Uh...what do you mean?" she asked. "And what could I possibly want from a street child?"

A harsh laugh ripped from the girl's throat, strangely uncharacteristic of a child. "Are you kidding me? You just saved my life. No one would do that for a stranger without asking for something!" She leaned her head to one side, her face tight with suspicion. The predawn light had a way of making her skin whiter, like ice.

Sora frowned. Maybe her act of heroism hadn't been such a good idea. "I don't want anything," she said, insulted. *No wonder no one helps each other. Just look at the thanks they get!* "I just thought you were too young to waste away in a jail cell. But if you were happier there, I can always take you back."

Now it was the girl's turn to look surprised. Her eyes widened, a pathetic look that was fast becoming familiar. Her horse came to an awkward halt, and Sora stopped, too.

"Why did you help me?" the girl asked. "How do I know I can trust you?"

Sora wanted to sigh. She was annoyed and not in the mood to prove herself to anyone. "I just wanted to help. I don't know. Maybe I should've left you there. Seems like you're not very happy about escaping."

The girl pouted, sticking out her small lips. "But I'm a Raven. Look, you can see my mark." She stretched out her left wrist, showing a cruel, raw burn. It was still fresh and scabby. Sora winced and glanced away, resisting the urge to touch her own wrist. "You're not supposed to help bandits," the girl said. "The soldiers will hang you now. You might as well have a brand like mine."

Sora had to resist the urge to laugh. Big words coming from a thirteen-year-old! "You're really cute," she said, trying to hide her smile. "I don't care if you're a Raven or not. You're too young to be hanged for your crimes. Don't you have a family to return to? Somewhere to go?"

The girl shook her head slowly.

Ah, well, that explained a few things.

"I'm an orphan," she said. "My grandmother passed two years ago. I don't have anyone—*especially* not a sister."

Sora frowned, once again insulted. Who did this brat think she was? "Fine," she snapped, and turned her horse around. She was no good with kids, anyway. "Go back to the Ravens and continue your life. I won't say anything."

"Wait!" the girl called.

Sora glanced over her shoulder. "What?" she asked, letting her irritation show. She wasn't about to escort this girl to a bandit camp. That would be like stepping on a wasps' nest.

"I–I didn't mean to be rude," the girl started hesitantly. Sora kept listening, but didn't stop her horse. "I...well...living on the streets doesn't make you very trusting. I'm just trying to protect myself."

It sounded sad and lonely coming from someone so young. Sora grimaced, wishing she wasn't quite so soft. *Ugh, here we go again, getting all wrapped up in other people's problems.* She finally stopped her horse and turned back, a half-felt glare in her eye. "You're being a brat," she said sharply.

The girl's eyes were like two shiny puddles of water. "Not a lot of people are nice to orphans," she burst out. "I didn't expect you to help me out of that, I...I really am grateful!"

Sora nodded. "So...you really tried to steal from the town treasury?"

"Well, yeah," the girl shrugged.

"So you're a thief?" *Like Dorian?*

She shrugged at this, too. "Sometimes, I guess. I joined the Ravens a few months ago. You do what you can to survive."

"Uh-huh," Sora said skeptically. She didn't think poverty was necessarily an excuse to become an outlaw. Bandits did more than just steal. But the girl probably didn't know any of that.

Sora thought of her old companions, of the times she had spent around their campfire. Assassins, thieves and mercenaries. At least they had carried some sort of inner integrity, walking the line between lawful and lawless. Then she thought of the other prisoner, the buzzard, that sorry scrap of human debris. A shudder ran through her.

"You know," the girl said, all attitude gone. "That was really brave, what you did...."

Sora resisted the urge to snort. *That was nothing.*

The girl grinned, brushing a pale strand from her eyes. "What do you think of traveling as a pair? I've been wanting to get away from here, and you...well, you seem like a good person."

Sora was surprised by the change of attitude. *So she's finally caught on.* But could they really travel as a pair? Honestly, she'd been hoping to return the girl to her parents. "I'm looking for some friends of mine," she finally said, reaching up to touch her Cat's Eye, hidden under her shirt. "I don't think...."

"Then I'll help you," the girl said firmly.

Sora blinked. *How much help can a thirteen-year-old possibly be?* One more mouth to feed, and she was already low on provisions....

Then again, it was a long, lonely ride. Her horse wasn't the most interesting person to talk to, and she couldn't just abandon a child.

Sora wondered how far they were from the town, and how desperate the guards were to find them. It was impossible to tell. Finally, she let out a long groan. "All right. I suppose so," she agreed. The girl was bound to bring trouble—but she could handle it.

A smile broke across the girl's face. In that moment, she transformed from a ragged street child into a young woman: pronounced cheekbones, wide lips, a slight dimple in her chin. Her unusual coloring only added to the effect.

Sora stared. *I've seen that coloring before,* she thought, frowning. *I've seen it...but where?*

She turned away and pushed her steed into a trot, perhaps a bit harder than she meant to. The moment was broken, and she was eager to leave it behind. Why was she suddenly so unnerved?

The girl followed. "They call me Laina, by the way," she called, her voice soft on the wind.

Sora sighed, already questioning her decision. "I'm Sora."

And the two continued across the fields.

Where have I seen it before....

CHAPTER 4

The days passed more quickly with Laina there, despite Sora's initial reluctance. Aside from the occasional bout of attitude, she proved to be useful at setting snares. They managed to catch quite a few rabbits. It was a relief, because Sora didn't know much about hunting or tracking animals, and truly, she wasn't eager to learn. She had to grit her teeth every time they found a rabbit in a snare, and forced herself to push a knife through its throat. It was ironic, to be sure. She could lay out a full-grown man—kill a Catlin by shoving a spear through its gut—but snaring rabbits gave her the willies. *Ridiculous,* she thought, more than once. *What would Crash think of all this?* Doubtlessly the assassin would sneer in disgust, then force her to kill more woodland creatures until it didn't bother her.

She shivered with that thought, but it slowly turned to longing. *Where are they?*

The Cat's Eye answered, *Soon.*

Despite her skill at setting traps, Laina proved to be clumsy and useless at pretty much everything else. She tripped over bags, led her horse into brambles, spoke far too loudly and would even choke on her food. Sora tried to impress upon her the importance of silence—*besides sparing my sanity, our voices carry much too far over the fields*—but Laina either ignored her or genuinely forgot. She had a bossy, prying sort of curiosity, and often asked about their quest: who Sora's friends were, why she was trying to find them, and where exactly they were going. (*Isn't it strangely dry for spring? Shouldn't there be more rainfall? I bet it's going to be a hot summer. I hope we find them soon because I burn really easily. Have you noticed there's a flu going around? Best to stay out of cities, I think. Say, we should go to the ocean!*).

Sora wasn't ready to share all of the details yet. She was still hoping to run across a caravan or maybe a small village and convince the teenage thief to go her own way. *I can't babysit forever,* she thought, watching as Laina attempted to ride her big, unwieldy horse.

Besides that, Sora still held a sliver of doubt about her Cat's Eye. She had never used it like this before, as a sort of supernatural compass. Although she had a firm sense that it was leading her somewhere, but she wasn't exactly sure where that might be. She often found herself wondering what Crash and Burn would think of Laina. She doubted their meeting would go over well. *Maybe I should learn to set snares. I could set one for Laina and catch her in it...and leave her behind....*Sora laughed to herself.

Sometimes, after her companion fell asleep, she would take out her rapier hilt and marvel at it. A sacred weapon of the Dark God, straight out of legend, now resting in her hands. Her mind would wander back to that day Crash and Burn had left, to their mud fight in the rain, how she had laughed until her body ached. She could remember Crash's sudden easiness, his hands running up the sides of her ribs and hitting all of her ticklish spots, as though they had known each other for years....

Then, the inevitable pang of loss. She missed them sorely. Every night before she fell asleep, she would imagine a scene when she finally caught up with them. *Will they be glad to see me?* she wondered, fearing the worst. *Will they welcome me back?* She had been a burden before, but now things were different. She could hold her own. Or at least, she thought she could.

It was on one such night, perhaps after a week of travel, that Sora fell asleep next to the fire...then awoke some hours later, inexplicably alert. Had it been a dream, or had she really heard something...?

She wasn't usually a paranoid sleeper. It was the wilderness, after all, and animals made noises...but after opening her eyes, she noticed a strange silence. No hooting owls, no scampering mice. No crickets.

She lay silent for a long moment, her staff in hand, her eyes traveling across the tall grass. *What is it—a wolf? A wildcat?* She hoped so; animals were easy to deal with. A wind brushed through the grass, passing over them like a wave, and then the fields grew still again. Their fire had burned down to a mere handful of embers, and her eyes were well-adjusted to the shadows. She had to suppress the urge to call out. Her heart was pounding, her ears straining so hard she thought they might twitch against her head.

Then she saw them. Vague outlines hunkered down in the grass. They were creeping slowly around the fringes of their camp, toward Laina's sleeping form.

It happened within seconds. A twig snapped. Then a body partially emerged from the grass, leaning toward Laina, and Sora saw the glint of a knife. She didn't hesitate. Leaping out of her bedroll, she swung her staff in an upward arc and smashed it squarely into the stranger's face, or where she assumed his face was, hidden by shrubbery. He fell back with a muffled cry.

Someone else leapt out of the grass—two someones—but Sora

was prepared. Whirling her staff, she turned and rammed it into a shadowy ribcage, sending her attacker staggering back into the bushes. There was a yelp—a woman's voice.

The second man swung at her with a knife, but she leapt back a short distance, dodging the blow. She brought her staff down over his head, putting her full force behind it. *Crack!* She dropped him into the ashes of the fire. He let out a mumbled groan, then lay still. She was sure the coals were still burning, but the man made no move to stand up, or even to roll to one side. She frowned. *I must be stronger than I think.*

Twirling her weapon with ease, she turned full circle, her eyes scanning the grass. There was a thrashing sound and the scrabble of feet. She saw the dim shape of a woman running off into the fields, awkwardly bent because of her damaged ribs. She considered giving chase, but hesitated, her eyes returning to Laina. She didn't want to leave the girl alone. *Is it just me, or were they targeting her?*

It seemed that way, thinking back on it. The attackers had circled around her side of the camp, going straight for the sleeping girl.

When she looked back up, the shadowy woman was gone. Sora wondered who she was. Hopefully just a thief looking for easy coin. She waited for a long moment, staff in hand, prepared for another attack. A hushed wind blew across the fields, ruffling the tall, dry husks. Nothing.

She finally went to check the bodies. The first man was sprawled backwards in the bushes. She gasped softly when she saw his face. The staff had connected perfectly with his nose, leaving a bloody, pulpy mess behind. She gagged. He certainly wouldn't be getting up again. She could tell that he wasn't breathing.

Then she turned back to the body in the fire. His clothes were beginning to catch flame, and she quickly rolled him over, patting the embers on his shirt. The last thing they needed was a bushfire.

Her eyes widened when she finally got a look at his face. Instant recognition. *Dear Goddess, he looks like a skeleton!* It was the buzzard man from the jail cells, the one she had left behind. *He must have gotten hold of that key,* she thought, quickly searching the body for weapons. She found two knives, a compass and a water flask. Beyond that, there was nothing, no food and no money. Her eyes fell to the brand on his wrist, and she was struck by another idea. The Ravens. Had they followed all the way from town? How desperate were they for a bit of coin?

Her eyes returned to Laina. The girl was still asleep. She was like a corpse, dead to the world. Sora smirked. A herd of horses could have stampeded past and she wouldn't have stirred.

She set down her staff and grabbed hold of the bandit's body, dragging it around the fire into the grass. It was hard work. The man was skinny, no doubt about that, but he was well over a foot taller than she and probably close to 180 pounds. Sora, who barely capped five feet, couldn't believe her own strength. She thought of the long hours of practice she had put in over the past twelve months, the poles her mother had made her jump, the rope climbing and the bucket lifting. *Apparently all that training paid off.*

When the camp was clear of bodies, she moved next to Laina and reached down to touch the girl's shoulder.

Laina shot bolt upright, twisting wildly, her scrawny fist swinging through the air. Sora caught her wrist with ease and tried not to laugh. "It's just me!" she said, grinning in irony. *She slept through that whole fight, but lay one finger on her....*

Laina stared at her, blinking owlishly, her mouth slightly open. She didn't bother apologizing. "Oh. I was having the strangest dream...."

"Right, and I just hid two bodies in the grass. We need to move camp."

"Huh?" Laina grunted.

Sora pulled the girl to her feet and led her to the unconscious—or perhaps, dead—bandits. Laina paled visibly at the sight of the crushed face, then turning her eyes to the other body, grimaced. "Oh, *him.*"

"I was going to ask you..." Sora started slowly. "Do you know why they followed us? It seems like they've gone out of their way. They were very focused on you." She thought back to the knife in the grass, the way it had hovered over Laina's sleeping body.

Laina nodded, obviously shaken. "Let's get out of here," she said.

"Right, but..."

"I told you back in the jail cell!" Laina exclaimed, her eyes bright in the darkness. "They're going to come after me now. Once a Raven, always a Raven. If you abandon them, they kill you. It's just how it works." She turned away fiercely, her movements short and tense.

"But...but you escaped from jail. You're starting a new life, remember? And you're so young!"

"Age doesn't mean anything!" Laina exclaimed. She was already heading toward her horse, taking clumsy strides through the grass. "When you become a Raven, you enter their family. It's a gang, get it? And if you leave, they kill you. It's part of the deal. You're either all in or *all out.*"

Sora nodded slowly at this. She understood what Laina was saying...it just seemed so barbaric. *But not as barbaric as the Catlins,* she thought. And truthfully, not as barbaric as the guards back in the jail cell, who would gladly execute a young girl. She sighed to herself. Barely a year away from her manor, and she was still being surprised by people. Would it ever end? She thought of Crash, of the way he had first treated her, like a spoiled, naïve little girl. Perhaps it was still true. Maybe she just hadn't suffered enough to understand how the world worked. *Well, that is rapidly changing,* she thought with a grimace.

Laina was gathering her belongings, packing her saddlebags and readying her horse. Her haste was disturbing. Sora realized they must be in a worse situation than she had originally thought. *You're either all in or all out.* The Ravens had followed them far into the fields—a lot farther than the soldiers had. *I shouldn't have let that last bandit escape,* she thought, her gut sinking. Now they would return in force.

What have I gotten myself into? Sora started to roll up her own sleeping blankets, biting her lip in worry. How long until the Ravens found them again?

She and Laina mounted their horses a few minutes later. Laina looked at her, silently asking for a direction. Sora touched the necklace under her shirt. She couldn't allow herself to be distracted. *Crash and Burn.* She had to remember that she was on a mission.

It took a long moment for the Cat's Eye to stir, then tendrils of consciousness looped through her, expanding slowly from the base of her skull, like smoke. She felt a twitch in her hand, a silent compulsion. With a slight nod, she turned her horse.

They continued southwest, toward a wide river and lonely stretch of trees.

* * *

Days passed. The grasslands were beginning to change. There were patches of trees now and a few ranches spread out. Every now and then, they saw campfires at night, or heard the distant sound of horses; Sora always had the sense that they were being tracked.

It was evening when they saw the riders. They were unmistakable against the sunset. In a place as barren as the fields, Sora didn't need to look twice. These weren't just innocent farmhands coming home, tired from a long day's work. The horses traveled on a strict course—directly toward *them*.

She turned to Laina. The girl had already seen the silhouettes on the horizon and was staring with wide eyes.

"They've seen us," Sora said.

Laina nodded. "It's them," she replied. "I know it is, look how fast they're riding. We need to get out of here!" The panic was obvious in her voice.

Sora nodded in silent agreement. The riders were close enough to have hailed them if they were friendly. She didn't like their silent approach, the way they shot forward, as though bent on running them down.

"Follow me!" Sora said, though she had no idea where she was going. There were at least four riders on their trail, probably more, too many for her to handle on her own. She turned her steed toward the west, where they had been following the border of a forest. It was a tall, open wilderness, mostly pine and oak trees, but they still had a chance of finding cover. They could evade their hunters, especially with night so close at hand.

She kicked her horse; the brown steed leapt beneath her, sensing her urgency. It took off through the grass, easily jumping over rocks and stones. Laina's horse wasn't quite so agile, and Laina herself not such a skilled rider. The gangly gray steed had longer legs, but still managed to slow them down, stumbling over hidden rocks and holes. Sora looked over at her smaller companion several times, expecting the girl to fall from the saddle. Laina bounced and jiggled on top of the giant horse like a doll strapped to a buggy.

They reached the trees after only a few minutes, but a deep ditch separated the fields from the woodland. Sora navigated her steed down carefully, pushing her way through spindly bushes and clumps of vines. Laina pulled up short. Her horse pawed the earth, snorting, reluctant to proceed.

Sora reached the bottom of the ditch and clomped through a thin stream of water, then started up the other side. "Come on!" she yelled, turning to look over her shoulder. "Just push your way through!"

"I'll fall off!" Laina exclaimed.

"Then fall!" Sora yelled back.

She paused, watching as Laina danced nervously at the top of the slope, then finally her horse started forward. Sora's eyes scanned the top of the ditch. The riders had been no more than a mile or two behind them; she expected them to reappear at any second. Their time was limited. Why couldn't the girl hurry up?

Finally, Laina made it to the bottom of the ditch, her clothes covered in leaves and thistles. Impatient, Sora reached over and grabbed her horse by the reins, then dragged it forward, pushing them both up the opposite hill. She directed her own horse with her legs and used her upper body to steer Laina's. It seemed to take an eternity before they entered the fringe of trees.

When she looked back, the horizon was a deep red. The sunset cast brilliant flames across the sky, and the riders were practically on their heels, close enough to be clearly visible. There were six of them, and she could have almost made out their faces, if not for their hoods and cloaks. They reminded her of Crash on the night he had kidnapped her—lethal. Definitely Ravens.

"Follow me, and don't slow down!" Sora hissed, and she turned her little mare into the trees. There was no easy way to pass through, so she made her own trail, diving into the brush. As far as she could tell, Laina followed. They rode somewhere between a trot and a canter, taking the route of least resistance, the shadows deepening on every side. She hoped that the coming night would dissuade the riders—that the bandits would give up and wait until morning. But they were so close now, she doubted they would stop.

"This was a bad idea; they'll catch us for sure!" Laina gasped from somewhere behind her. "I can't even see where we're going!"

Sora ignored the girl's complaints, an irritated frown crossing her face. *If it wasn't for me, you'd be dead already.*

"You know, I don't think we should have left the fields," Laina called. "The horses could hurt themselves in the woods, and we don't stand a chance on foot! Are you listening, Sora? More Ravens could be hiding out here waiting for us! This might all be part of their plan!" Her voice cut off. Sora couldn't help but sigh in relief. She glanced back to see that Laina had ridden smack into a low-hanging tree branch and was rubbing her forehead.

"Keep quiet," Sora said, "or they'll hear you for sure!" She actually didn't know if this was true, but at least it would shut the girl up until she could think of a better plan.

They moved deeper into the woods, Laina now silent and sulky behind her. Every now and then, the girl would grunt or mutter, complaining about her horse and the thick bushes, but Sora ignored her. She was too busy looking forward, trying to listen for any trace of pursuit. *Maybe rushing into a dark forest was a bit hasty,* she thought, catching a spiderweb in the face. She brushed it off, trying not to scream, running her hand desperately through her hair. *But where else can we go?* She didn't hear anything behind them, but then again, the forest was alive with sound: nighttime bird calls, crickets, squirrels in the trees, deer in the brush. The two horses made a lot of noise, too. How was she supposed to tell if they were being followed?

Half an hour passed and Sora began to relax. Surely the bandits would have caught up with them by now...maybe they had given up. The brush was nigh impassible, after all. *We'll just have to keep moving.* She blinked, already feeling weariness settle on her shoulders. Darkness had fallen, and, besides the occasional glimpse of the moon, everything was black.

They passed a rather thick clump of poplar trees, and Sora's horse suddenly tossed its head, raising its nose to sniff the air. It continued to turn its head, looking around the trees. An uneasy feeling entered Sora's stomach, and tiny hairs stood up on the back of her neck. She could feel her steed growing tense beneath her, the muscles bunching in its shoulders and haunches. Not good signs. She thought of Laina's words, that perhaps more Ravens had circled around them and were already waiting in the forest. She had the sudden, terrible sensation of being watched, though she couldn't tell if it was just anxiety. They could be surrounded right now; she had no way of knowing.

The two travelers entered a small clearing. They came upon it without warning, the brush opening on all sides, revealing a hard stretch of dirt and wet leaves. The half-moon shone down upon them, casting a silver glow, and Sora's horse came to a sudden halt. It put one hoof forward. Paused. Backed up a step. Laina's horse stopped behind them, still obscured by the trees.

Sora's first thought was of Laina's safety. The girl was incapable of fighting and hadn't even attempted to play with the blades she'd been given. Knives were useless if you couldn't use them. *She might be annoying, but I don't want her killed,* Sora thought, glancing around.

Her sense of alarm was growing. She could tell they were definitely being watched. Abruptly, Sora turned to look back at her traveling companion. "Laina, get off your horse and go hide!"

At that moment, an unseen object whistled past her—*thuuunk!* A dagger! It landed hilt-deep in the tree next to her head. It would have hit her, but her steed abruptly whinnied, rearing and dancing to one side. That sent Sora tumbling sideways out of the saddle, unprepared for the sudden movement. She landed with a small "oof" of surprise, her staff jammed against her back, one foot caught in a stirrup.

She kicked her foot free just as her horse took off into the trees, whinnying madly, pushing its way through a thin patch of bramble. She leapt to her feet; no time to worry about the beast. Then she dodged to one side, led by pure instinct. Another dagger whistled past her. A dark blur followed the dagger, and Sora brought out her own knives, ready for the next attack.

So there were bandits in the woods. She should have known! No wonder they had given up the chase so easily.

By the strength and speed, she judged her foe to be a man. His knives whistled close to her and she leapt away just in time to save her neck. Then the Cat's Eye began to jingle, a dull chiming in her ears, and its unnamed presence awoke in her mind. She felt its power melt through her, sinking into the nooks of her shoulders, the joints of her hands. She felt as though her eyes had suddenly opened.

It happened far more naturally than ever before. The Cat's Eye joined with her mind, and everything became clearer: the trees, the ground, the moon above. Her mother told her that each bearer left an imprint on the stone; the knowledge of past warriors lived inside it. With moves she never thought she could have mastered in her short lifetime, she dodged and ducked, easily evading the man's attacks.

Feinting to one side, Sora felt her back touch a tree. *Uh-oh, wasn't this my first lesson in fighting? Never get yourself cornered!* She ducked beneath the next swing and came up on the man's other side, then brought up her daggers. Blocked. The man was a much better fighter than any of the bandits she had faced so far. He was fast, almost too fast, even with the help from her necklace. One thing was for sure: hand-to-hand combat was getting her nowhere.

Sora broke away from her opponent and leapt across the clearing, putting several feet of space between them. Then she faced him, crouching slightly, observing. To her surprise, he followed her lead, breaking off from the fight and standing back to watch her.

Who is he? she wondered, but when she tried to see his face, she found that it was too dark to make out clearly. He wore a hood pulled low over his head, his clothing as black and muddled as the foliage. *It doesn't matter, a foe is a foe,* she told herself, and concentrated on his wickedly pointed knife.

It was time to act. She sprang forward, dagger outstretched, hoping to catch him off-guard. The man turned just in time to deflect her blow, but she nicked him; she felt her blade snag on his clothing and the slight pull of flesh. Sora couldn't see where she had hit him, but there was blood on her knife.

They were in close combat again. He tried to grab her, his hands going to her wrists. She barely evaded him and landed a kick to his ribs, trying to force him back, but he wouldn't give her any space. It didn't seem to matter where she struck; he had a way of blocking her, of trapping her hands. And then, suddenly, he lashed out—*wham!*—and struck her squarely in the chest. Sora staggered backwards, winded from the blow, only to smash into the trunk of a tree. He was on her in a second, no space between them, no chance to even breathe. He grabbed her roughly and rammed her back against the tree again, hard, his knife against her throat.

Anger burned inside her; all she could think of was Laina lying helplessly in the woods. The Raven pressed the knife against her throat to kill her, and she brought her knee up hard into the man's unprotected groin. With a grunt, he keeled over, and Sora brought her elbow down on the back of his head.

The blow should have dropped him, yet he shook it off. Surprised by this, for a moment she didn't know how to react. Then he suddenly reached out and fastened his hand around her knee and with powerful fingers, squeezed the joint.

She cried out. It felt as though her knee were breaking! Her knife fell from her hand. The man released her, though she didn't know why—perhaps her scream had startled him—but she didn't give him a second chance. Without hesitation, she reached for her staff, which was strapped to her back. She pulled it out, holding it in front of her, shifting from her sore leg.

The man picked up a long branch from the ground, holding it in an identical fighting stance. Sora's mouth dropped open—absurd! None of the Ravens so far had been trained fighters; just petty thieves with old, rusty knives. She couldn't remember the last time she had fought an opponent, staff-on-staff.

She lunged forward, enjoying the feeling of the familiar weapon in her hands. The man moved to meet her, fearless and confident. He ducked her swing, then brought the makeshift staff up into her ribs. *Uff!* Sora hadn't expected the blow; that had slipped straight through her defenses. She staggered back, the wind knocked out of her.

The man took another swing, the staff whirling in his skilled grasp, but she ducked to one side just as it sailed over her head. She leapt away, trying to put some space between them, but pain stabbed into her foot, cutting through her boot and into her heel. With a grunt, Sora hobbled backwards, off-balance. The moon glinted and she saw her dagger on the ground, stained dark with blood. She cursed herself for her own carelessness, realizing she must have stepped on it by mistake.

In that second of hesitation, the man was on her and had her down on the ground, sprawled in the wet leaves. He held her pinned down by sheer weight, then put his staff to her throat and pressed it down to cut off her air supply. Feeling her control slipping away, Sora was filled with a sudden, intense fear. Terrible things could happen to a girl in the wilderness. Her mother had warned her. Men were capable of evil, despicable acts....

She reached out to one side, grasping for anything that might aid her in her struggle. Finally, her hand connected with the bloody dagger on the ground. Perfect!

Desperate, she grabbed the knife and lashed out wildly. She didn't know if she had cut him, but he sat back fast. Sora took her chance and launched herself to one side, rolling in a circle. Suddenly he was below her and she sat astride him.

He was prepared for the move. When she looked down at him, he had a long dagger in his hands, a new weapon he had pulled out of his cloak. Moving on instinct, she grabbed his hand and tried to take the knife away. It was a pure match of strength. Sora tried to keep her balance as he twisted beneath her; she cursed her light weight. *If only I were a little heavier!*

The man flipped the two of them over again easily. Now she was on the bottom, her legs astride him, his hips pressed against hers in an unexpectedly intimate way. She wasn't prepared for it. Suddenly she couldn't concentrate—she felt his hips, his torso, his thighs pressed against her, hot and powerful. She had never been under a man before; somehow, she hadn't envisioned this exact scenario. His body was large, heavy, muscular. She let out a harsh breath. Her control broke. She had been wrestling with the knife, but suddenly her arms caved and her body quivered with adrenaline and nerves, no longer able to resist his strength.

The man pressed the knife against her throat again. They held that position, each panting and heaving for breath, their bodies locked together. Sora didn't dare move. She tried not to think of the position they were in, of all the stories her mother had told her cautioning her to be careful. She let her chest rise and fall, the air choking in her lungs, fear and strange anticipation surging through her belly. He was a worthy fighter, for sure. It made her blood race.

Finally, she gasped, "W-who are you?"

There was another long, silent moment.

In a violent movement, the man dropped the knife and yanked back her hood. A rare beam of moonlight cut through the trees, illuminating her face. He stared at her, blocked by shadow, unreadable. He gazed for a long time—longer than she thought reasonable. Sweat dripped down both sides of her face and she felt cool air on her skin. There were leaves in her hair.

Fear coiled inside her again. She was acutely exposed in this position, defenseless. He could do anything he wanted to her.

Then he pulled down his own hood.

It took her a long moment to make out his face, which was turned away from the moonlight. But slowly, the angles and planes became visible. And finally, the color of his eyes. Green, like the deep meadows of the forest. All the air left her for a second time. She had seen green eyes like that before. Could it...could it *really* be....?

"C-Crash?" she whispered. No, impossible! She blinked, expecting it to be an illusion, like the man she had seen in the jail cell. But those glowing, vibrant eyes caught the moonlight and, for a moment, seemed as bright as fire.

He stared at her as though she were a ghost. She tried to shift from under him, but was suddenly uncertain. Why wasn't he letting her go? The memory of her vision came roaring to life again, his maniacal laughter, the evil that had oozed from his body. His eyes flickered over her, a shadow crossing his face, something dark and heated and feral....

Then he quickly sat back, lifting his weight off her. He allowed her to slip from beneath him, then rolled onto his feet, standing up and sheathing his knife. He held out a hand to help her up.

Sora was shocked, to say the least. He still hadn't said anything. She should have expected this. *He's never been the chatty type.*

When she took his hand, she was surprised to find herself shaking. Or maybe it was him? He pulled her to her feet. She let out a slow breath, amazed at the battle they had just fought. *Dear Goddess, what if I had killed him?* She almost laughed at the thought. *As though I could.*

Suddenly, there came a rustling from the bushes and a hulking figure appeared. She recognized the golden, wolf-like glow of his eyes, which burned through the night like a wild animal. "Burn!" she exclaimed, unable to keep the relief from her voice. It was certain now. She wasn't dreaming. She had finally found them!

She would have run to the giant mercenary—her heart felt like it might burst from her chest—but he was holding tight to the struggling, hissing form of Laina. From what she could tell, the girl was fighting for her life, with no results. The Wolfy looked down at his captive in amusement, then back to her. A wide smile was on his broad face.

"Well, isn't this a pleasant surprise!" he exclaimed. His booming voice shook the night, breaking the moonlight's spell; she doubted that he was capable of whispering. "We thought you were a pair of those bandits. They attacked us a few nights back and took our horses and supplies."

Sora's mouth dropped. "You thought we were bandits?" she asked in disbelief. "But we thought *you* were bandits!"

The Wolfy laughed again.

"This is all very funny," Laina said, her hair in disarray and her tone nasty. "But it would be much more fun if you would let me go!"

"Oh, sorry," Burn grinned again, a sheepish twinkle in his eyes. Laina broke away from his muscular arms and jumped to Sora's side, still carrying the panicked, slightly-winded look of an escaped rabbit. She stared at Sora and the two men.

"Okay," she finally said, sizing them all up. "I take it these are the two you're looking for?" She put her hands on her hips, her eyes darting back and forth. She looked absolutely silly.

Sora sighed. "Yeah, these are the two," she confirmed. "Laina, the Wolfy over there is Burn, and this is Crash." She motioned to the man next to her.

Laina's eyes landed on Crash and she paused, a frown tugging at her lips. Sora frowned too, then turned to look at him, wondering what was going on.

Crash was glaring. Hard. In fact, he looked so scary that she wanted to run screaming back into the woods—if only for a moment. She had seen that look before, long ago. *It's not a good sign.*

"So, Laina, why don't you come with me and tell me all about yourself," Burn tactfully broke the silence. "Our camp is a ways over there through the trees. We were just about to set a fire." He glanced at Sora meaningfully. "We'll leave these two to talk."

Laina and Crash stared viciously at each other for a moment longer, then she slowly nodded. With apparently no qualms at all, Laina turned and linked her arm with Burn's arm, and the two walked off into the woods.

Sora shook her head at the sight. She could remember her first meeting with Burn; he had a way of dissolving tension. Then she turned to look at her assassin friend. Blinked. Crash was now staring at her, a strange expression on his face.

"What?" she asked, her eyes straying to the cut on his cheek. It was shallow, but visible. She fought the urge to grin. So she had landed a blow after all....

"Been practicing?" he asked, a thin trace of amusement in his voice.

Now she couldn't keep from smiling. Coming from Crash, that was a huge compliment. "No," she said, trying to be humble. "It's mostly the Cat's Eye...which is actually why I'm here right now, but, uh, I'll get to that in a moment." Her voice faltered. Now what? "Just why are you guys so close, anyway? It's been a year!"

He shrugged, his eyes scanning the clearing. "That long?" he asked, as though he hadn't thought of her at all, which was probably true. "We're on our way to the port of Delbar. For a while we were doubling back north, but we decided it would be better to leave the continent. Catch a ship overseas." He paused. "This is certainly unexpected."

Oh. Sora nodded, her stomach sinking slightly. A part of her had hoped they had been coming back to visit her.

Then the assassin strode past her to pick up one of the knives he had dropped. She picked up her own knife and sheathed it smoothly, suddenly awkward. She had been so set on finding him for such a long time....Now that he was here, she wasn't sure what to say.

"So why are you here?" Crash finally asked, wiping off his blade and tucking it under his cloak. "I thought I told you to stay put. You were supposed to forget about us."

A lot easier said than done. Sora realized that the man she had glimpsed on their last day together was not about to resurrect himself. No more mud fights or tickle wars. She prepared herself to deal with the cold, familiar Crash. Business first.

"I had a vision," she said. He looked at her steadily, making her flush in embarrassment. Somehow, she thought that would mean something. "Well, a dream, maybe, but it was from the Cat's Eye. It meant something, Crash. I've been learning about these things. I...." She wondered how she was supposed to communicate with him, explain the sickness that was spreading across the land, the sight of Volcrian, of Dorian's body in the grass, of the islands and his own terrible transformation....

He continued to stare at her, then said tonelessly, "Sit down."

"What?"

"Sit down. Your foot is wounded. Then tell me about this dream."

She frowned and moved to one of the trees. She sat down at its base, purposefully selecting a beam of moonlight so they could see each other. Much to her surprise, Crash knelt down before her and gently tugged off her boot. Then he pulled off his gloves, inspecting the cut foot, his fingers deft and hard with callouses. She tried to ignore his firm, warm hands, the touch of skin against skin. It was surprisingly difficult and distracting.

With a deep breath, she started her narrative.

She did her best to describe the illness that she and her mother had discovered; how it had infected the livestock, then the farmers, and had only been cured by the Cat's Eye. Then she began to describe the dream. It was still branded in her memory, as though it had happened just a few minutes ago, so intense that she could still smell the ocean air, hear the call of seagulls and the rush of waves. Strange, because she had never seen the ocean before.

As she talked, he wiped off the wound and bandaged it with strips of cloth. The only sign that he was listening were the glances he gave her whenever she paused. Once finished, he sat back and gazed at her intently. His full attention was unnerving, but she continued, once again horribly self-conscious. She couldn't tell what he was thinking; couldn't read his face. She went on to describe the book her mother had found, the forbidden Wolfy magic, and finally, the discovery of the Dark God's weapons. Crash lowered his eyes then, staring intently at the ground.

Finally, she ended her story with how she had met Laina. His eyes avoided hers, his face drawn. He looked down at the crushed leaves beneath their feet.

"Do you have the rapier hilt?" he asked slowly.

She nodded. "Do you want to see it?"

"No, it's fine," he murmured. Another pause. "And the other weapons...they have manifested as well?"

He spoke about them as though he knew about the Dark God and the curse. As though he had known about it for a long time. She frowned—but how could he know?

"My mother seems to think so," Sora replied. "Though honestly, I haven't seen them....I'm assuming that Volcrian summoned more than one wraith."

Crash nodded. "Well, if the sickness is any indication, then she's probably right. Your mother is a wise woman."

More silence.

Sora cleared her throat. "She...she said that we need to travel to Barcella, to speak to the High Priestess of the Goddess. She'll be able to interpret my vision."

Crash nodded again.

It wasn't the reaction she had been expecting. She hesitated. Then, "I wish I could say that it was just a dream...but I remember it perfectly, Crash. It still wakes me up at night. The Cat's Eye...."

He looked at her sharply. "I'm not questioning you," he said. "I don't know a lot about the artifact, but I trust you wouldn't run out here on a whim. You realize that destroying the weapons might require you to release the necklace?" His gaze settled on her throat, where the stone lay hidden under her shirt.

No, she hadn't. And to be honest, Sora had avoided thinking about that for a long time. When she first put on the Cat's-Eye necklace, it made a psychic bond with her mind...if she removed it, the bond would break, her *mind* would break...and she would die. The backlash of a broken bond would destroy her from the inside out.

She nodded, unable to speak.

"And you're willing to do this?" he asked softly.

She didn't know what to say.

His words sat heavily between them. She wondered, briefly, if he would stop her. If he would refuse her help, force her to turn around and go back to her mother. She could suddenly, easily imagine it. Part of her was relieved by the idea. It would be better than breaking contact with the necklace, slipping into a coma and slowly dying. But so far, that wasn't part of the plan. It would also mean standing by while a plague overtook the world. She couldn't imagine doing that, either.

And she would never see her companions again. They would have to run from Volcrian indefinitely, leave the continent, head to some other faraway land, some place with different languages, customs and clothing. Perhaps far to the west, where there was nothing but rocks and sand.

She breathed deeply, but it was Crash who spoke.

"If your mother said there is a plague, then I believe it," he said quietly. "Did you think I wouldn't?"

Sora felt a knot forming in her throat. Why was she suddenly so emotional? "The thought had crossed my mind," she said.

Crash let out a long, slow breath. Then he nodded. "I wasn't sure what the rapier hilt was when I first saw it, but I had my suspicions. And I've seen this sickness that your mother talks about. Burn and I just passed an entire field of cattle, all dead. If you're willing to do this, then so be it. We will travel to Barcella...." His face grew hard. "But we must hurry. I am certain that Volcrian is on his way."

Sora swallowed. Really? He would travel with her? She hadn't realized she had been holding her breath, waiting for his rejection....

Crash released her foot. "Barcella is about two days' travel to the south," he said. Then suddenly he was standing, pulling away from her, turning back to the trees where Burn and Laina had disappeared.

Sora looked after him, studying his tall, dark frame as he walked away. Then Laina's laughter drifted through the woods, shaking her from her thoughts. She rose to her feet, brushing herself off. "Do you have anything to eat?" she asked, following the assassin into the trees.

"Squirrels and berries," he said, and she caught a hint of humor in his voice. "Just like old times."

CHAPTER 5

Volcrian knocked on the door and waited impatiently.

He had tied his horse to a tree at the edge of the property. It was a good animal, obedient and docile, no hidden agenda. So far, it had lasted the entire trip around the swamp, crossing treacherous mountain slopes and broad valleys, and still it showed no sign of tiring. Quite a fine beast, worthy of its previous owner, the late Lord Garret.

Volcrian had killed the man, drained him of blood, and taken his steed. He was sure the act was justified, though he couldn't waste time trying to remember why.

The town he had come across was small and isolated. Its east side fringed the Catlin swamp, its northern end cut by a long, rocky trail—which, if one followed far enough, would lead straight to the mouth of a mountain pass. It was the direction Volcrian had traveled from. For a year now, he had ridden through the highlands, spending nights in river basins or on dry, flat, deserted hills.

They weren't proper mountains like the ones he had seen in the far, far north, thousands of miles away, above the City of Crowns. There, the great peaks and slopes of The Scepter climbed over twenty thousand feet into the sky. No, these were highland mountains, made of rocky gray stone, windswept and rolling. But still, it had been an impossibly frustrating detour. The swamp was vast. Traveling around it had taken more than twice as long as cutting straight through.

A frown touched Volcrian's lips. The swamp's curse was ancient and powerful, as old as the Catlin colony that lay hidden within it. Compasses failed. The sun disappeared for months at a time. Travelers became disoriented and lost.

His prey had used the Cat's-Eye necklace to travel through Fennbog swamp, which was otherwise impassible to humans and Wolfies alike. All because of that stupid girl. She was an inconvenience...but easy enough to track, if one asked the right questions.

The town had been full of chatty farmers and midwives. He had been surprised by just how easy it was to find the girl's trail. No one remembered the Viper or his Wolfy companion, which was not unusual, since the assassin avoided being seen. But the blond girl with the pretty stone necklace, oh yes, that sounded just like the Healer's daughter...*awkward little thing, arrived about a year ago, none of us even knew the Healer had a child. Nice enough, though!*

Yes, nice enough to leave a clear, blazing path, straight to the Healer's house.

Volcrian shifted impatiently and knocked again, slightly irritated that the woman would take so long to answer her door. Didn't she know it was urgent? Finally, his long ears picked up movement from inside the house. A small smile settled over his lips. *At last.*

A chill wind blew, unlikely for this time of year. The last rays of the setting sun illuminated the doorway as it opened. His cloak drifted around him gently in the breeze. Surprised, Volcrian looked down at the figure who stood there.

"May I help you?" the woman asked, with a slightly puzzled smile.

He was stunned, to say the least; that was an emotion Volcrian did not enjoy. At first he had thought it was the girl herself, but no, this woman was far older. An easy mistake to make, perhaps. He had only ever seen the girl in glimpses, fragments of vision perceived through his monsters and wraiths. This woman was mature and wore a low scoop-neck shirt, with no necklace in sight.

His eyes narrowed momentarily, taking in her classically beautiful features and short stature. She had the toughened appearance of having lived a well-traveled life. His keen nose picked up the scent of herbs from inside the house: salves, potions and powders. He could even see a stain on the floor, sunken into the wood, a remnant of blood from years past. The aura of a Healer was unmistakable.

"Ah, Ma'am, I was wondering if you might assist me. I am searching for a lost companion," Volcrian murmured politely, with a thin smile. He waited for an invitation to enter the house, but the woman didn't move. Instead, a bright smile fixed itself on her face.

Why is she looking at me like that? Volcrian shifted slightly, uncomfortable under that gaze.

"And just who are you looking for?" she asked warmly.

Volcrian hadn't been expecting this open, disarming smile. Most people were suspicious of him based on his appearance alone. His silver hair and long, pointed ears were a sure indication of his race; he was far from human. He listened now, using his heightened senses. His ears picked up the steady beat of her heart, the calm cadence of her breathing. She was perfectly at ease.

"An old friend, actually," he said. "A girl who wears a Cat's Eye.

Word has it that your daughter meets that description."

The smile stayed in place, the telltale heartbeat didn't flutter, there were no signs that his words meant anything. "My daughter left here quite some time ago; I don't know where she is." Honesty. Truth. He could smell it.

Volcrian nodded slowly. "Then perhaps you have seen a man with dark hair and green eyes, and a Wolfy mercenary, nigh unmistakable."

The woman continued to stare at him steadily. "I have many patients," she finally said. "They come from all over the lowlands, even the coast. Do you know the vow that a Healer takes?"

Volcrian shook his head slowly. Healing was an art that he had never bothered to study. It wasn't magic, though strange energies were known to manifest in healing at times. Humans were incapable of *true* magic. *Like rats or pigs.*

"We take a vow at the beginning of our apprenticeship to help all people, all creeds, *all races*," the woman said. "It is the backbone of our order. Can you fault us for that? A true Healer cannot choose sides, nor can she choose her patients. I do not remember the people you speak of. But they might have passed through."

Volcrian was troubled by this. She was hiding something, she had to be—but she was cleverly avoiding lies. She must know about his race, his heightened hearing and impeccable nose. It had once been said that a Wolfy could detect a lie a hundred yards away.

But that didn't make his task any easier. For the past several years, he had hunted the assassin, killing all who helped him even in the slightest way. He had planned to do the same to her, if she admitted her guilt. Such was his duty to his dead brother.

But the woman spoke sense. Healers served all peoples, even

the Wolfies, even the guilty. Perhaps, most especially, the guilty. And he certainly wasn't innocent. This woman stared at him with clear, perfect eyes. He could see the purity of her trade inside her...and she could certainly see something in him. He knew she did. Healers could see suffering; they could sense it as surely as they could cure it.

"I have traveled far," he murmured.

"So I guessed," she replied. Her eyes sharpened, falling to his crippled hand, which he kept curled close to his body. "I see you have a damaged limb. That's a bad omen." Her eyes traveled back to his. "Do you know what you are doing?"

Volcrian had heard as much before. A knife of hatred pierced through him. It had been the assassin who had crippled his hand, who had brought him this bad luck. "I am doing all that I can to set things right," he murmured.

"You're doing too much, perhaps." Suddenly, it was as though the woman was speaking directly to his thoughts, to his mind. "You are a Wolfy mage, and your blood magic knows no boundaries. You must realize what you are doing. You cannot control what you have set in motion." She gave him a piercing stare. "I saw the hilt of the blade that almost killed my daughter, and I know where it comes from. You have released something dark into the world, something bred on vengeance and hate. The gods were laid to rest a long time ago, and for good reason."

Volcrian opened his mouth, but was at a loss. What was she talking about? The gods? And how did she know of the rapier? She must have helped the girl and the assassin, she as much as admitted it....He tried to take a step forward, to lift his arms and put his hands on her throat, but he felt stiff, heavy, like sunken wood. "What do you mean?" he demanded.

"There were laws in the old world. Rules among the Races. You have summoned your wraiths, and with them comes a dark magic that not even you are aware of. You're lucky that your race is all but extinct. If the old ways were still followed, you would be killed for your transgressions. What you do puts us all in danger."

A chill went up his spine. The woman's words rang true in his mind, clanging together, making his ears hurt. He felt sick, suddenly nauseous; pierced by a poisoned arrow. He wanted to turn around and leave as quickly as possible.

Ever since pursuing the blood arts, he had felt changed, tainted, as though he was no longer quite truly himself. And the wraiths...they did his bidding, yes, but he didn't know where their weapons came from, or by what means they existed in the world. He had created them, following the spell as one would a recipe—but he didn't understand *why* it worked, *why* it was possible to bring the dead back to life. Too much knowledge had been lost.

"What...what do you know about it?" he asked, his voice hoarse.

"Only what I can see." She nodded to him. "And a Healer can see much. Your skin is pale. Your hand pains you. You have dark veins on your arms. You are releasing a curse into this world, a disease that was buried centuries ago. You must stop this quest for vengeance."

Volcrian's eyes flashed. "No. Never."

"Yes. Now," she hissed, with even more vigor.

They stared at each other, the Healer and the mage, the tension building. Volcrian knew what he must do—grab the sword at his waist, pull out the blade, shove it through her small, thin ribs.

Spill her blood, serve his brother, ease his hatred....He must...but he tried to move his arm, and it felt clumsy, weak. *True Healers serve all creeds.* It was an ancient order, back from before the War, passed down for thousands of generations. Her art had changed her; it protected her, just as she protected the sick and the dying. They carried the favor of the Goddess. Killing a Healer was said to be the worst luck of all.

He didn't know what to say or do. But one thing was certain—he couldn't stay here.

"I thought a Healer was supposed to tend to all of her guests," he sneered.

"Not even I can cure your hatred," she replied, her voice smooth as a river. "It has already destroyed you."

Volcrian couldn't take it anymore. With a growl of frustration, he whirled away from the doorstep, stalking back across the front yard. He couldn't reach his horse fast enough, and he swung up into the saddle, dragging its head forcefully toward the road.

"I should kill you for helping them," he shouted over his shoulder, his voice thick with rage. Then he laughed; a raw, terrible sound. "But I'll kill your daughter instead."

Then he wheeled his horse toward the road and took off at full gallop, the wind pushing against him, his teeth bared in a terrifying grin.

* * *

Lorianne caught herself against the door frame. His words punched her in the gut, knocked the wind out of her. She slowly collapsed to her knees, sinking to the floor, waiting for the wave of dizziness to leave her. *I will kill your daughter.* His voice spun around in her head. *Your daughter.*

His presence had been like a cold, burning stake driven through her lungs, spreading ice through her veins. She felt sick. Paralyzed. Frozen.

She had thought Sora would be safe. The mage was after the assassin, not her own flesh and blood...but he had barely asked about the two men. No, he had come calling for the girl with the Cat's Eye. The girl who, under any other circumstances, would be upstairs in her bedroom, or out in a forest somewhere, riding her horse and exploring the woods. Lorianne paled at the thought. What if she hadn't sent Sora away? What if she had kept her locked up in her room, barricaded from the world, as she had so desperately wanted to do?

I'm no good at this, she thought. She had never been a mother; parenting did not come naturally. How was she supposed to raise a child who was already grown? Was she a friend, a confidante—or a guardian, a provider? She had abandoned her daughter at a Lord's house, telling herself that she would be raised by a rich family, that Sora had no need of her. She had missed the girl's entire life; everything that made her who she was. Her own heart, cut out and returned to her, transformed into an awkward stranger. And now she couldn't even protect her.

Giving up her daughter had been like cutting off a leg. For countless years, she had remained numb, stifled. She had absorbed herself in Healing, telling herself that it was her purpose, that it all made sense and that it was for the best.

But no. Nothing made sense until Sora had turned up on her doorstep, inches from death, bleeding all over the floor.

With a surge of strength, Lorianne got back on her feet. She had abandoned her daughter to protect her—but she would not turn away again. Volcrian was a dangerous man. His magic was tainting him, eroding his mind as surely as it poisoned the world. She had never felt power like that before. It was beyond human, beyond Wolfy—beyond any of the races.

Blood was a dangerous thing. It opened doors.

And Lori would have to find a way to close the doors. What about recovering the other sacred weapons? Curing the plague? She had a feeling that the Cat's Eye was important, but she didn't know enough about the necklaces. The stones had been discovered during the War, then destroyed shortly thereafter, far too dangerous to continue using.

She needed answers, and there was only one man who could help her.

"Ferran, you bastard," she muttered, grabbing a cloak in one hand and a quiver of arrows in the other. "You'd better be ready for this."

* * *

They spent the night in the forest.

Laina and Burn were talking on the other side of the fire. Sora was glad the girl had found a friend; her curiosity had a new target. She was asking the mercenary an endless stream of questions: about his race, his sword, his hair color and even his pointed teeth.

Sora settled next to Crash, who had his arms crossed and his back against a tree. Burn and Laina's conversation slowly took over the camp.

"So you enjoy stories?" the giant asked the orphan.

"I love them! I can't read all that good, though...but I've just about memorized all of Kaelyn the Wanderer's tales."

Burn laughed. "Kaelyn the Wanderer! You know of her, do you?"

"Of course! Who doesn't?" Laina exclaimed.

Sora had to agree with her. Kaelyn was a personal hero of hers as well, and the reason why she had wanted to go adventuring in the first place. The great warrioress had lived before the War of the Races. The Goddess had called upon her to stop the War and unite the races in peace. It hadn't worked, but her acts of heroism had grown into legend. Her name had been a bright torch for humans, especially later, when their kind had been enslaved for more than a hundred years.

"I know that she played on a magic flute that controlled the Four Winds," Laina said proudly.

"But do you know the names of the Four Winds?" Burn asked.

Laina frowned. Sora watched her think. "North, South, East, and West?"

Burn smiled ruefully as an ember popped in the fire. He prodded the wood with a long stick. "Close," he said, "but they have other names in the Old Tongue: *Aiet, Tuath, Iar* and *Deas*. They were the Four Winds of the Goddess. Legend has it that they would appear as men and women to deliver messages from the gods. On the old maps, you will see them written at the very edges of the known world. Travelers used to think that, if you walked far enough in one direction, eventually you would fall off the world and all you'd have is the Wind."

Laina laughed at this. "That's absurd!" she said. She gave him a wry, pointed look.

Burn grinned in response. "Well, that's what they thought. The Winds sat on four thrones, all at different ends of the earth. I'm not sure which name goes with which Wind. The Old Tongue is all but forgotten now."

Sora was listening with half an ear. She had read most of the tales of Kaelyn the Wanderer, and although she didn't remember any mention of the Old Tongue, she knew most of the legends by heart. Her eyes traveled up to the night sky, where the stars twinkled and gleamed through the tree branches. At this time of year, the Wanderer's constellation would be low on the horizon, barely visible. She sighed quietly, wishing she could find the stars now; the cool blue light had a way of offering comfort.

Laina was asking something else. Burn chuckled. "Oh, I don't know how to speak the language, only a few words that my parents taught me. They say that Kaelyn means First One in the Old Tongue."

"Well, of course, because she was the first female warrior!" Laina said.

"Perhaps. She was certainly the only one ever written about." Then the Wolfy looked over at Sora, a slight grin on his face. "Your name means something, too."

"Really?" she asked with interest. She saw Crash's eyes open for a moment, and knew that he was also listening. "What?"

"Sky."

"My name means Sky?" Sora was surprised and somewhat amused. In a way, it was appropriate. Her eyes returned to the stars, searching in vain for the constellation.

"What does my name mean?" Laina asked eagerly. She sat

forward, bouncing slightly in place.

Burn looked down at her woodenly. "It means 'pig snout,'" he said.

Laina's mouth dropped open.

They stared at each other, and then Burn let out a loud, booming laugh. "Just kidding! I'm not sure. It might not mean anything."

Laina didn't seem to know how to respond. At first, she scrunched up her face, a pout on her lips. Then she forced out a small laugh, though it still seemed that she didn't get the humor. Then she pointed to the book that was in Burn's hands, something that Sora hadn't noticed until now. "Well, why don't you read a passage, then? My grandmother always used to read books to me. Sometimes she would sing stories as well. When she sang...it was as though the story came to life in the air."

Sora saw Crash glare in her direction. She couldn't blame him; she doubted he was a fan of stories and grandmothers and children.

Burn nodded, opening to the first page in the book. "This one is called *The Wanderer*," he said, fingering the tattered pages. "I've carried it for quite some time. It was Dorian's favorite, too."

Sora wished, quite fervently for a moment, that the thief was with them beside the fire. She could even imagine what he would say, a little smirk lingering around his lips, his eyes bright with cunning. "*A favorite? Nonsense. My favorite story is the one I'm living.*"

Somehow, the group around the fire was incomplete without him. Laina could never be a replacement for Dorian.

"Go ahead," Sora said suddenly, wanting to distract herself from the memories. "Read a page."

Burn nodded. In his deep, earthy voice, he began:

In this world, there was a time before humans existed, before the five races came to the earth. This was a time when the land was stripped down to its bare elements: Wind, Fire, Water, Earth, Shadow and Light.

Each of the elements were like gods, but far greater than gods. They created the world, and therefore created Life. But the elements were not perfect. They argued among each other, unable to agree upon anything. They shunned the outcast element, Shadow. This constant arguing led to chaos and disarray.

Wind, who was known for its wisdom, came up with a way to create beings, creatures that could inhabit the world. Wind hoped that by joining with all of the elements, it would give birth to different creatures and create harmony and love between them.

Wind approached Light with this idea, and they created the first race, the Harpies, magical beings with violet eyes and moonbeam hair. The Harpies were so pure that they were thought to be the children of stars, and their voices were perfectly in tune with nature.

Then came the Dracians, creatures of Wind and Fire, a species with giant leathery wings and scales. The Dracians were hot-headed and jubilant, with a love of games and mischief.

Next Wind joined with Earth to create the Catlins, a fierce and wild race that took to the forests. There, they cultivated the land and grew giant colonies out of the trees.

Last, Wind joined with Water, but while they were joining, some of Water froze and became ice. These ice shards turned into the Wolfies, creatures of the arctic, with pointed ears and sharp teeth. Pure Water created humans, a simple race with a love of stories and a Healing touch.

Shadow was left out of the joinings. This element was an outcast, hated and feared for its consuming darkness. None of them knew how powerful Shadow was, nor how trustworthy. Therefore Shadow was kept far away from anything that the other elements did. Not even Wind, with all of its wisdom, thought to approach the darkness.

Wind, who was always cunning with words, convinced the elements that it was time to leave the physical world, to allow the races to grow and flourish on their own. But each of the elements were reluctant to leave their children. In their stead, they created the gods and goddesses to govern over them.

Light created a god, one that would watch over the Harpies and all celestial objects. It was given a sword of fire as a sacred weapon, so that it may defend these realms if necessary.

Water created a goddess that would govern all bodies of water; she was gifted with a violin, to play her music and control the waves of the ocean.

Fire created a god to watch over the Dracians and all else passionate in nature; this god was given a sacred harp that would cause flames to burst up from the lands.

A goddess was made by the Earth, and she played upon a lute in the deep forests, watching over the animals and the mountains.

Lastly, Wind also made a goddess, and gave that goddess a flute. She would be the guardian of wisdom, knowledge and fate.

When Shadow heard of their activity, it grew angry and jealous—unspeakably so. It could not create its own race, so it, too, created a god, one that would govern evil and darkness.

Hatred entered the world, and all of the foul things that came with it: greed, sickness, madness. This god was given three weapons, because Shadow wanted it to be the most powerful: a crossbow, a spear, and a rapier to pierce the heart....

The elements were furious at this transgression, and they knew it was time to leave the physical realm. They disappeared into the night sky, taking Shadow with them, leaving this world to its fate.

And the Dark God, deemed the most dangerous, was confined deep under the earth in an eternal slumber. But even sleeping, His evil penetrated the world and cruel, power-hungry men were born. Those with evil intent had a natural way of seeking out the God. Over and over, His powers were summoned. And over and over, warriors of the Wind Goddess, deemed Wanderers, were called upon to put him back to sleep.

And if one could collect the three sacred weapons of darkness, then they would have control over the Dark God's wrath, and plagues would sweep the land....

"Okay, stop!" Laina cried, putting a hand on Burn's arm. "That's a frightening story. What does it have to do with Kaelyn?"

"She was one of the Wanderers," Sora said. "The first Wanderer. She was summoned by the Goddess to find the sacred flute and prevent the War of the Races...."

Laina was shaking her head. "Well, they're all just legends," she said. "I guess it's dumb for me to be afraid. The book isn't even accurate! My grandmother told me that Shadow *did* create a race. It was pure evil. They would kidnap children and sacrifice them to the Dark God...."

"That's not true," Sora said, waving her hand dismissively. "I've read this legend a hundred times. There's no race of darkness, and you're lucky there isn't, because you'd probably be their first victim."

Laina glared at her, a stormy expression crossing her face. "My grandmother wouldn't lie!" she growled. "I heard it from her own lips, and she took the story with her to the grave!"

Laina was obviously upset, her small chest heaving. Sora backed off; she didn't want to argue, especially about something so personal. She looked at Crash instead, hoping to change the topic.

The assassin was staring at Laina in annoyance. The girl shied away from his gaze and turned back to Burn, continuing the conversation, ignoring them both.

Sora reached over and touched his shoulder. "If you stare much harder, you'll set her on fire," she said with quiet humor.

"That girl will be trouble," he said testily.

She frowned. "She has a name, you know."

"And I'll be happy to forget it."

Sora let out a small laugh, remembering how long it had taken him to actually use her own name. Except back then, she had feared him. Now...now things were different. Or at least, she thought they might be. She felt closer to him, though his silence was still intimidating.

Things are different now, I don't have to be afraid of him, she thought, trying to convince herself. "You really are conceited, you know that?" she finally said, bracing herself for his reaction.

Crash glanced at her, but didn't respond. She might have seen a smile play around his lips, but it was a mere flicker. She had to wonder at that.

"Well, I'm getting some sleep," Burn said, closing the book and putting it away. This was followed by a loud yawn. Then he gave Crash a tired look. "Will you take first watch?"

"Of course," he replied.

"Then I'll see you three tomorrow." The Wolfy moved over to his bedroll, and after a moment, Laina followed suit. Her bedroll was set up next to his, as close as she could get without seeming invasive. Sora wondered if she felt safer that way.

She sat with Crash by the fire, watching her friends settle down for the night. She wondered if she should say something, but the assassin seemed quiet, withdrawn. Then she too decided it was time for bed.

* * *

Crash gazed into the fire. He watched its exotic dance, felt its warmth, and shared that warmth somewhere deep in his blood.

His eyes wandered to his companions. He didn't like the new girl, Laina, not at all. She was a nuisance and a manipulative one at that. Her very presence grated on his nerves in a way that Sora would never understand. What had she been thinking, allying herself with this street rat? The child was rude and unskilled, with nothing to offer but a snotty nose—and he wasn't a fan of baggage.

His gaze traveled to Sora, who twitched restlessly in her sleep. He knew she wasn't fully unconscious; he could tell by her breathing, by her shifting eyelids. He watched as she neared the fringes of a dream. Somehow, her presence made him relax. He wasn't sure if he liked it or not. Relaxing could be dangerous.

It had only been a year, yet she seemed different, older

somehow. Even her face had changed: tanner, gaunter from living on the road. But it was obvious that her heart was soft, wide open and still young. She was a fool to come after him. He had done nothing but put her life at risk. Why would she pursue him now...*and why do I feel so compelled to let her?*

He watched the fire play over her hair, over the lean angles of her face. Somewhere deep inside of him, he wanted to speak, to confess himself....It was a strange urge, and confusing to him. Why tell her all of his secrets? She couldn't understand who he was. Not even Burn knew his full past, his years spent in the Hive, a childhood of intense discipline, schooled by generations of assassins. His very nature made him separate from the world, scorned by it.

And yet, looking at her face across the fire, he wanted to try....

Who are you kidding? some inner voice mocked. *She will never accept what you are. How could she?* She was still young and fresh out of childhood. She still believed in things like justice, truth and fate. He didn't know how to tell her otherwise. Justice was a human concept. Nature had no order. The Wind hadn't brought peace to the elements, hadn't brought love to the races. All things were still chaos. Just because she wanted to save him didn't mean it was possible.

But with her...with her, he felt different. Like he could be someone else.

You're not Crash, the voice whispered. *You're Viper. Or have you forgotten?* The assassin, the killer who had won his Name at fourteen, a protegé. A boy of Laina's age, already with blood on his hands. Such were the ways of his people. He had been the best...or perhaps, the worst. It was a rueful thought.

And even if he told her his real Name, if he confessed it, she wouldn't know what that meant. What was the Viper? *The one who hides in the grass.* An elite assassin. Death for hire.

Crash looked down at his hands, at the blade that he had sharpened. Its hilt was worn by generations, passed from one Viper to the next and to the next. In some ways, he felt that he had failed. Those who carried this blade were not supposed to live this long, to think like this.

But that's why he had left.

His eyes returned to Sora. He had to protect her. He owed her that much. If she was willing to risk so much for him, for the world, then maybe he could risk the same for her. And it went deeper than that. Viper was a creature, a shadow, a ruthless mask. Crash was a man.

As long as she didn't know his true title, as long as she didn't know his true self, he was changed. Free of the endless faces of his victims. Free of the knife, of the Hive, of his own dexterous skill.

And free to protect her, from his enemies and from himself.

CHAPTER 6

The city of Barcella was only a day's ride away, which was surprising. Counting back, Sora realized it had been more than a month since she had left home, and the days were growing much hotter.

They packed up camp early and set out just as the sun breached the wide plains, which Burn referred to as the lowlands. "Not many farms out this way," he explained, nodding to the dry, rocky ground. "Bad soil, hardly anything grows but weeds and scrub grass." He led them out of the thin patch of trees, doubled up with Laina on the large gray steed. "A few days past Barcella, there is a ridge of hills called the Thumbs. Then, past the rolling hills, there is the coast, the ocean and the city of Delbar." He finished with a broad sweeping gesture.

"How do you know so much about the area?" Sora asked.

Burn grinned. "I've been traveling quite a few years longer than you have," he said. "And who in the lowlands hasn't visited Barcella, and prayed at the Temple of the Goddess? It's a well-worn road."

Sora knew this was true; she had heard travelers speak of that Temple in her mother's town. Barcella contained one of the four great Temples that graced the lands. It was known as the Western Light, the supposed Throne of the West Wind.

Burn and Laina rode in front while she and Crash rode behind, two to each horse. Sora's dappled mare didn't appreciate the extra weight and swished its tail with each step, ears flicking in annoyance. Sora couldn't help but agree with the beast. She didn't like sharing a saddle, especially with the dark assassin, who had always been keen on personal space. Now her breasts were pressed against his back, her thighs against his legs. She had to hold onto his hips. The rocking of the horse was...distracting....

The bandits from the night before had disappeared. Sora counted herself lucky; the Ravens might have become discouraged when they entered the forest, or perhaps ran off after seeing Crash and Burn. Those two warriors were definitely intimidating, well-traveled—and armed to the teeth. Whatever the reason, the lowlands were empty, an endless sea of yellow and white grass before them, a hazy horizon.

It was mid-afternoon when Sora began to hear a strange noise. At first she thought it was her Cat's Eye, since it reminded her of sleighbells. But the necklace always resounded right inside her ear, partly within her own head; this sound rose and faded with the wind.

Toward late afternoon, the city made its first appearance. The sight began as a small speck that grew rapidly as they neared, with spiraling towers stretching up toward the sky. The closer Sora got, the more ornate the walls: limestone painted with curving, swirling shapes, as though gusts of wind had solidified into rock. A gentle chiming was in her ears. The closer they came to the city, the louder the sound became.

The wind blew again and she saw glints of metal flash in the sunlight. Perhaps thousands of small metallic shapes were hanging from the large wall—wind chimes? She squinted. The wind blew again. Yes, wind chimes—dangling from every available surface.

Charms and baubles swirled and danced in the light. With each gust of wind, glorious sound cascaded through the air, shockingly akin to music, a wondrous cacophony that made her jaw drop, her mouth gape in amazement. Must have carried for miles across the plains. Perhaps even more surprising, it was pleasant to the ears; not a chaotic splash of noise, but a soothing rush, ebbing and flowing like a river.

She stared in fascination. Then her eyes traveled to a large building that towered above the walls of the city, jutting up like a giant, spiraling seashell. It was dome-like, with towers and scaffolds, the roof tiled with a swirling mosaic of brightly colored stones; lime greens, deep purples and brilliant reds. She recognized the golden emblem perched on top, spinning on a weather vane. This was the Throne of the West Wind.

"They founded the city here because of the intense winds," Burn explained, following her eyes. "Something to do with the land formations. The winds here never stop, and at certain times of the year, can be deadly. They say entire houses have been uprooted from the ground."

Sora nodded, too stunned to say anything, imagining an entire house being lifted into the air. She had noticed that the breeze faded at times but never disappeared; dust and pollen blew into her eyes.

The city grew larger and larger. She couldn't believe the size of the walls, built of a dull gray stone that was obviously native, an extension of the surrounding bedrock. She could also see where an older section of wall abutted the hills east of the city. "It looks like the walls were rebuilt at one time," she said, pointing out the brighter, newer stone to Crash.

Crash nodded, though he seemed distracted by his thoughts. "This city was a fortress once, back in the time of the War. It's been destroyed and rebuilt several times. These walls are hundreds of years old."

"Aye," Burn called, overhearing their conversation despite the racket made by the bells. "The sewers run through the buried streets of the old city."

"Creepy," Laina added.

Sora looked back at the walls with renewed interest, swept up in her imagination. She pictured a fortress smashed by magic, leaping flames, shining weapons, siege engines and war.

It took them a surprising amount of time to reach the front gates. A long line of travelers waited outside, people of varying heights and dress, some talking amongst each other, some standing quietly, others tending their horses or wagons.

"Do we have to wait in line?" Sora asked as they neared the gates.

Burn nodded. "Most come here on a pilgrimage of some kind or another," he said. "The soldiers check everyone who enters the gates."

Sora nodded, her eyes returning to the giant Temple. As they rode toward the end of the line, her stomach growled. She sighed in resignation. *Looks like we won't be eating any time soon.*

* * *

Three hours later, they finally entered the city, the sound of countless bells ringing in their ears. Surprisingly, once inside the wall, the sound was not so intense. It was muffled by wood and stone, drowned out by the rumble of evening foot traffic. Barcella was by no means a small city; twenty-thousand citizens lived within the whitewashed structures and slate-tile roofs. Most buildings were two or three stories high, crammed close together, and connected by wooden balconies. Streamers, flags and banners hung along the main boulevard, advertising shops and restaurants.

Sora never would have guessed that Barcella was built on top of another city. Everything looked sleek, clean and new. The well-maintained streets were laid with brick. Colorful flowers graced pots along the main thoroughfare, and vines spilled over the windowsills. The windows were mostly made of stained glass. Bells and charms swayed gently in doorways and over balconies. Horse-drawn buggies were parked along the main street, their drivers casually waiting for the next passengers.

"This looks like a rich city," Sora observed, gazing first left and then right. She wished her head would rotate in a full circle; there was too much to look at.

"A lot of rich families donate to the Temple," Burn said knowingly, "which pays for the street maintenance."

"And for the guards who enforce that maintenance," Crash muttered darkly.

"How do you mean?" Sora asked. She leaned forward, catching his eye as he turned around.

"There's a hefty fine if you don't keep up your property," Crash explained. "And for littering, too. So don't throw anything on the ground."

Sora nodded, glad he had said something about littering. She had been seconds away from tossing an apple core over her shoulder. Instead, she glanced around, making sure no one was watching... then shoved the core into a nearby bush. *I'm not putting that sticky thing back in my saddlebag.*

"If we go to the Temple, they will certainly give us a warm meal and a bed for the night," Burn said. They stopped their horses at an intersection and looked around, trying to decide the best route forward. "They are good to travelers here. Then Sora can arrange a meeting with the High Priestess."

"Will she even want to see me?" Sora asked, glancing at the large Temple in the distance.

Burn chuckled at this. He seemed amused by every question she asked. "She won't have a choice if you request an audience. The Priestess is here to serve us, not the other way around."

As he spoke, a line of small cloaked figures marched past, hoods pulled low over their heads, eyes directed at the ground. They each held a thick rope with a large ornamental bell at the end.

Sora stared at them skeptically. "Don't tell me those children are part of the clergy...."

"Acolytes of the Goddess," Burn explained. They watched as the line moved by at a slow, meditative pace. Sora wanted to laugh. Based on the size of the acolytes, they had to be even younger than Laina.

"They are chosen at age five," Crash explained quietly, as though reading her thoughts. His voice was low and soft. "Farmers and nobles alike bring their children from hundreds of miles around to be accepted into the Order. It's a lifetime commitment." His tone turned dry. "And a convenient way to get rid of an extra daughter."

"Or son," Laina said.

Sora gave a start; she hadn't realized the young girl could hear them. Laina was staring at Crash with narrow lavender eyes, but she turned away before he could return her look.

"Where do we go?" Sora asked. "Should we follow them to the Temple?"

"That would make the most sense," Burn replied.

"Then what are we waiting for? I'm starving," Laina said. "Let's go!"

Burn nodded and started forward, guiding his large gray house through the crowded streets. With a slight nudge of his leg, Crash led their horse after the line of acolytes and down the crowded city street toward the distant towers of the Goddess.

The acolytes walked at an irritatingly slow pace, and Sora entertained herself by looking around the city. Men and women rode past in little buggies, each pulled by a single horse. Shopkeepers polished windows and laid out wares. Some nodded respectfully to the line of acolytes, or said small prayers in their wake, but most ignored them as if they saw this sight every day.

Up ahead, she could see men in leather armor strutting back and forth, armed with cudgels and polearms.

"City guards?" she asked, lifting an eyebrow.

"Not quite. Street patrol," Crash replied dryly. "Poorly trained fools in service to the Temple. Good thing they didn't see you throw that apple."

He was teasing her—had to be. She highly doubted he cared about littering. Sora rolled her eyes. "That's ridiculous, fining someone for throwing an apple core....It's fertilizing the ground!" Why would rich people make such a law? *Seems like more of an inconvenience.*

Laina stuck her tongue out as they passed. The patrol looked up and glared at them, his eyes cold and hard.

Crash stared back as their horse strolled leisurely by. Eventually, the man looked away.

Sora grinned at this. *Not so tough now, are ya?* She stuck her tongue out at the patrol too, then leaned forward and wrapped her arms around Crash's waist.

* * *

A commotion became apparent as they approached the Temple. They were a block away from the large chiseled doors, riding in the shadow of the tower, and the streets were packed with people. Suddenly it was impossible to continue on horseback.

A few members of the street patrol milled around, hanging at the back of the crowd, not doing much. Sora and her companions dismounted and continued on foot, pushing their way to the Temple.

When they reached the gates, the crowd opened up to reveal an old farmer and his wife kneeling on the ground. Their faces were tan and leathery from the sun.

A woman stood before them dressed in long, purple robes, the white cowl around her head hiding her hair. From the emblem on her right shoulder, Sora guessed it was one of the minor priestesses, though she wasn't sure of the rank.

The farmer's wife was sobbing, and Sora saw a small child no more than a year old wrapped close to her breast.

The noise from the crowd was considerable, but Sora could overhear the farm wife speak.

"Save her!" the woman cried. "Please, save my daughter! I can't lose another child...."

"Pray over her, at least!" the farmer yelled roughly. "My entire herd has died this past month, possessed by some strange spirit. They attacked and killed each other! There is a curse on my land and we have need of the Goddess' touch!"

The priestess looked on helplessly. Her lips were tight, her eyes large and watery. "I-I'm sorry," she said, spreading her hands. Her voice was soft and high-pitched, like a cooing dove. "I've done all I can. We have no magic; we can only hope that the grace of the West Wind works through us...."

"Then what's the point of prayer?" the man yelled. "If the Goddess can't save my herd and can't save my child, then who needs a Temple? We should just tear it down!"

The rest of the crowd surged forward, taking up the cry. "Tear it down!" they screamed.

Sora gasped as she was shoved forward. The weight of the crowd rushed up and struck her like an ocean wave. Crash grabbed her arm to steady her.

"I've lost two sons this year to a strange sickness!" a woman called.

"My crops won't grow! The fruit is rotten!" another yelled.

"Aye! And the fish are dying in the rivers!"

"The chickens are losing feathers! Their beaks turn black!"

The priestess was backed up against the gates now, a panicked look on her face. There were no other priestesses in sight, and the crowd looked extremely angry, with red faces and glaring eyes. A few people carried swords or walking staves, and shook them at her threateningly.

"I-I'm sorry," the young priestess repeated. "Truly...we haven't heard of all this before. We must go to the High Priestess and consult her wisdom. Please, have patience!"

"Patience didn't save my son!" a short, gnarled woman screamed from the crowd. Then she launched forward, whirling a large broom handle over her head.

The woman lunged at the priestess, and Sora lunged too, swinging her staff outward. She caught the broomstick in its upward swing and swept it from the woman's grasp, sending it spinning over the crowd.

The woman turned to stare at her.

In fact, the entire crowd turned.

Sora stood out clearly in front of the Temple, her heart racing, looking around. Everyone seemed focused on her. In truth, she was a little surprised. She hadn't thought before acting; it had been pure instinct. *Now what?* she wondered. Her eyes traveled helplessly over the stunned crowd, then she signaled Crash and Burn.

At her cue, her companions stepped forward. All four turned to face the crowd. Burn unsheathed his massive greatsword and several people stepped back. It was a bulky blade, wider than an open hand and taller than most men.

"Might as well wave," Crash muttered next to her. "When Volcrian travels this way, we'll have a hundred people to identify us."

"Oh, hush," Burn grunted. "What was she supposed to do? Let the priestess be killed?"

Crash's silence was unnerving.

Sora tried to shrug it off. If the crowd got angry again, she would be stampeded into the ground.

"Wait!" she cried, throwing up her arms and addressing the onlookers. She thought back to her mother's house, to the farmer with the flaky skin and clear bile. "W-wait just a second! I can help!"

The crowd broke into murmurs, whispering amongst each other.

"How?" a young man yelled.

"I...I've seen this sickness before!"

Burn glanced at her, surprised, but she ignored him. Instead she turned to the farmer and his wife, who were still stooped on the ground, hunched over their baby girl.

"Hand her to me," Sora said, and held out her arms.

The farmer looked highly suspicious, but the mother did as commanded, obviously desperate. She handed the baby over to Sora, who held her, running a hand over her small, chubby face. She recognized the dry rash on the skin, the fever, the shallow, painful breaths.

Briefly, she called upon the Cat's Eye. She closed her eyes, reaching into her mind, asking....

The Cat's Eye's presence surged inside of her, like a gasp of air, as though it had been waiting. *Now.* She jolted, surprised, and heard the dim chiming of a bell.

She touched the baby's nose confidently. With a flash of green light, the Cat's Eye sucked the curse out of the baby, drawing the magic into itself. It was a small pool of magic. There were no worms like before, but a bitter taste came to her mouth, as if she was drinking lemon juice.

Sora staggered, momentarily dizzy, slightly winded by the exchange.

The crowd gasped. The murmur grew to a rumble. Everyone craned their necks to see.

Then the baby started crying.

The little girl looked healthy. No rash, no fever. The farmer's wife scooped her from Sora's arms. It was a hearty wail for such a small baby, not at all the cry of a sick child. The father and mother stared, their mouths hanging open. Then, slowly, they both started crying, tears streaming down their faces.

Finally, Sora turned to the crowd. She paused, her eyes growing wide. The people looked furious.

"Liar!" a man screamed. "She hurt the baby! She's no Healer! She's evil!"

"No!" the farmer's wife yelled. She stepped in front of Sora smoothly, holding up the child as evidence. "My daughter is crying! Her lungs are cured! She can breathe!"

Another murmur passed through the onlookers.

"Cured?"

"A miracle...."

"Who is she? What did she do?"

"Did you see that light?"

"The Goddess! It is a sign from the Goddess!"

Sora turned quickly to the priestess, who stared at her with an unreadable expression. "Please," she said. "My companions and I must speak to the High Priestess. It's urgent. And it has to do with this sickness...."

The crowd continued to murmur behind them. A few people were already trying to get her attention, shouting out, begging for cures. Sora tried to shut her ears to the noise, tried not to feel the heavy press of bodies behind her. Her heart ached for the people.

She wished she could help every single one...but there was no time.

After a long moment, the young woman nodded. She unlocked the front gates. "The High Priestess only holds audiences in the morning," she said. "But I think she will make an exception."

Sora turned to her companions. Laina's eyes were wide and confused. Burn kept his sword drawn. Every now and then, he pushed back the crowd with his blade, a reproachful look on his face. Crash watched her silently, expressionlessly, as he always did.

She waved to them. "Come on!" she said. Then she started forward. The four entered the gates, the farmers pushing at their backs, trying to touch Sora. As they entered the Temple grounds, several city guards arrived on the scene, brandishing swords in an attempt to disperse the crowd. Sora watched the gates shut behind them, the mob swirling outside like a dammed river.

Beyond the Temple walls, the four found themselves in a surprisingly serene garden, with citrus trees growing on either side. A stone path led through emerald green grass up to a broad, decorative set of doors. The Temple was constructed of a strange material whose shimmering colors were like that of an opal, or mother-of-pearl. It was truly a majestic building. Sora's eyes followed the spiraling towers up their full length, high into the sky. The monstrous central tower was connected to two smaller ones by arching bridges. She looked away before she got dizzy.

"Please wait here while I alert the High Priestess to your presence," the young priestess said, then lifted her robes a bit and shuffled off.

As soon as she was gone, Laina turned to look at Sora. "What was that you did for the baby?" she demanded, her face scrunched. "That didn't look like a Healer's touch. That was magic!"

Sora stared at the young girl, wondering what to say. She felt tongue-tied and a little embarrassed at making such a spectacle.

Thankfully, Burn spoke for her. "A Cat's-Eye necklace," he said briefly. "Sora is one of the few to possess one. I'll explain the whole thing once we see the High Priestess."

Laina's eyes narrowed stubbornly. Sora recognized the look; it meant she was about to ask a million more questions. But at that moment, the young priestess reappeared. She looked flustered, her brown eyes wide in amazement.

"She is expecting you," she said, breathless.

"What?" Sora asked, unsure if she had heard correctly.

"Yes, she says you are late. She wants to speak to you immediately...and alone." The woman's eyes traveled over her companions.

Sora didn't know what to think about that. She frowned, suddenly suspicious. "But how....?"

"I will come too," Crash said flatly.

The priestess opened her mouth to protest, but the assassin stepped up to Sora's side. He didn't have to speak; his presence was enough. As soon as his shadow fell across her, the priestess shuddered, a doubtful look crossing her face. "I suppose...if you would prefer...."

"We prefer," Sora interjected.

The young priestess nodded, turned, and paused. She glanced over her shoulder at Laina and Burn. "If you have need of shelter, the dorms are across that way, and the kitchens too. Ask for Marian. She'll take care of you."

Then the priestess led them into the Temple.

CHAPTER 7

They entered an expansive domed room with wide stone floors and large marble pillars. The walls were the same curious material as the outside, smooth and shimmery. Across the room, a large statue of the Goddess stood, reaching up toward the ceiling, a stone flute held to Her lips. It was a familiar statue; similar figures stood in all of the minor temples and shrines that Sora had ever seen. She could remember one in her garden long ago, back at her stepfather's manor.

The walls were painted to mimic the wind, a myriad of swirling colors, but in the deep shade, they were barely visible. The wall sconces were not lit.

"In summer, we only light the building in the mornings," the priestess explained. "When the Temple is closed, we douse the fires to keep it cool."

They headed toward a staircase on the right, which led upward into the tower. As they climbed the spiral stairs, Sora exchanged a glance with Crash. She was reminded of the Catlin swamp where giant hollow trees spiked into the sky, filled by similar spiral staircases they had climbed for hours just to reach the top. *It all seems so long ago.* She wondered if he was thinking the same thing, but when she met his eyes, she couldn't be sure. His gaze was eerie in the calm shadows.

They reached the top of the tower's staircase and entered a circular chamber, directly on top of the Temple's main room. It was broad and empty. The floor was a swirling mosaic of tiny tiles, each the size of Sora's thumbnail, a rainbow of purples, greens and reds, as though someone had spilled candy across the ground. There were no windows. The only light came from a series of sconces on the far wall, which shimmered with pearlescent light.

In the center of the room an old woman sat on a large, dark-blue pillow. Her silver hair, intricately braided down her back, was woven with small gold bells and purple ribbon. A veil made of soft gold cloth covered the lower half of her face. Sora looked above the veil at the woman's eyes. Old eyes. Wise eyes. Was that a hint of recognition?

The young priestess bowed slightly and opened her mouth to speak, but the old woman cut her off. "Thank you, Clara."

The girl's eyes widened and she bowed again quickly, then turned and hurried away back toward the staircase. Sora watched her go, wondering at the brief dismissal.

"So you have arrived," the High Priestess said, remaining seated on the large cushion. Then her light blue eyes gazed at Crash, and she said, "Why are you here, Dark One? I did not summon you."

Crash remained slightly behind Sora, lingering at the doorway. "I wonder why," he said stoically.

Why indeed? Sora echoed. Her curiosity was piqued. *Dark One.* She could remember her mother calling Crash by a similar name.

The High Priestess and Crash shared a long, tense look that stretched on into silence. Then she frowned and turned back to Sora, as though Crash didn't exist. When she spoke, her words resounded off the chamber walls, amplified by the domed roof. "It has been some time that I have dreamt of a girl with a Cat's Eye," she said. "It is a rare stone that you bear."

Sora nodded. Dreams? She waited for an explanation, but the Priestess didn't speak again. Finally, she said, "You've dreamt of me?"

The Priestess nodded. "I have, child. Many who enter the Order are graced by visions from the Goddess. It is not magic...but Her will."

Sora nodded, still uncertain. She snuck a glance at Crash. Again, unreadable.

"I...I've had a vision, too," she said slowly. "From the Cat's Eye."

The woman nodded, her bells jingling slightly in her hair.

Sora continued, "There is a plague coming, a supernatural one. The Dark God's weapons have entered the world." It felt strange to say that; she wondered if the Priestess would understand.

But the Priestess' reply was unexpected. She spoke in a dry tone. "Do you know much about our Order, child?"

"I...uh, not really...."

"I am the High Priestess of the West. It is the duty of a High Priestess to commune with the Wind...to receive, in essence, visions. Every night I dream...and most nights, the Wind tells me things. I have heard of your Cat's-Eye necklace...and I have heard of the dark hilt that you carry in your bag."

Sora blinked, surprised. She shifted the satchel on her shoulder. To be honest, she had almost forgotten about the hilt. It seemed almost silly—just an old chunk of metal wrapped up in rags.

"Yes," the Priestess continued. "I know of this plague. Those who are sensitive to the balance in the world know that there is a rising darkness, something tainted in the land."

"My mother said it is the essence of the Dark God," Sora offered.

"And so it is," the Priestess replied. A look of speculation came over her face. "Not many know of such things. Your mother must be knowledgeable, indeed, to have come to that conclusion." The old woman stood up. To do so, she had to use two canes, one in each hand. Sora hadn't noticed the canes lying next to the pillow.

When she stood upright, the Priestess was much shorter than Sora, which was a surprise. Her amplified voice made her seem like a giant, as though Sora was speaking to the real Goddess and not just an old woman.

The Priestess stood in the center of the chamber. "The sacred weapons have entered the world, and there is much to fear, young traveler. The Wolfy who summoned them may not understand what he has done, but there are people who have waited years for this opportunity...generations, even." Her eyes turned to Crash, his presence icy in the shadows. "You would be familiar with this, Dark One. They are your creed, are they not?"

Sora turned to stare at Crash, surprised. What were they talking about?

The assassin was as blank as a stone wall, and stared back at the Priestess coldly. "No," he said flatly. "Not my creed. But...I have heard rumors," he finally replied. "They call themselves the Shade. A cult, if you will, existing in secret since before the War of the Races. They wish to harness the power of the Dark God."

Sora frowned. "Really?" she asked, unable to keep the skepticism out of her voice. "Why didn't you tell me this?"

Crash shrugged. "It is only a rumor."

The High Priestess spoke. "No, it is a reality," she said. "Our Order has existed since before the War. So has the Shade, and so have many other things that have been forgotten by the human world, such as your Cat's Eye." And then the Priestess said something almost identical to her mother. "It is a dangerous time that we live in. Very few know how to stop this curse."

"But...do you?" Sora asked, turning away from Crash.

The Priestess nodded. It looked painful from her standing position, old and stooped. "Yes," she murmured. "There has been a shift in the balance of things. This plague...it is unnatural. Magical, perhaps. And your Cat's Eye has proven useful against it. I have had visions of this. Your Cat's Eye will be instrumental in returning the dark weapons to their rightful place, back to the underworld. But first, you must destroy the one who has summoned them. It is the only way," she said solemnly.

"Volcrian...." Sora murmured. She said the name softly, but it echoed around the room, as though the walls were laughing at her.

"He is slowly becoming a vessel for the Dark God's power, possessed by hatred and bloodlust. You must kill him," the High Priestess said. "But that task grows harder each day. He is becoming something more than a simple mortal. You must lure him to the Lost Isles. Use the sacred, sacrificial stones of the Harpies to drain him of his life. Then, you must gather the weapons and destroy them."

Sora was silent. She turned to look at Crash again. She didn't know why; he didn't offer any comfort, any sense of strength. But she needed time to gather her thoughts. *This is crazy.* It was too much. She could remember seeing the Lost Isles in her dreams, the sacred circle of stones. Her Cat's Eye had showed them to her....But it still seemed like an indomitable task.

"How?" Sora asked. "How are we supposed to do this? We don't even have the other two weapons...."

"Then you must find them...or, actually, they will find you!" The High Priestess let out a strange, croaking laugh. "They are with the wraiths, of course, and I daresay they are hunting you. Not very smart creatures, but deadly. They will stumble across you eventually; you have only to wait and be seen. As for how to destroy the weapons...there is a sacred ground, not on the isle of the Harpies, but elsewhere. A Temple of the Dark God, long forgotten. You must find it. Perhaps the Harpies can help...but I have seen...I have seen someone else. Unexpected allies."

The Priestess' voice was dropping. Sora got the impression that their visit was draining the old woman of her strength. "You can sit down..." she started to say.

But the High Priestess shook her head. "There is not much else to tell you, child. I am glad that you arrived here safely. The sorcerer follows you, dogs your steps. Use your Cat's Eye to kill the mage. Travel to the Lost Isles, to the sacred stones where the necklace will suck the life from him. Then destroy the weapons. This is what you must do."

"And the Shade?" Sora asked.

The Priestess nodded slowly, meditatively. "Hmmm. Yes, they seek the weapons. They are drawn to them. But I think...perhaps...you have a protector." Her eyes traveled to Crash again.

Sora turned to look at the assassin. He didn't meet her eyes, but kept them trained on the Priestess. *A protector? Damned unlikely*....She had spent the last year training with her mother; she could protect herself.

But she wondered what Crash knew, what he was keeping from her. Perhaps nothing at all, and yet...he had known about the Shade, and he wouldn't meet her eyes now. He had told her nothing up to this point. She wondered how he knew about the Shade; whether he had dealt with them before. *Dark One.* Could she trust him?

She had traveled for weeks, expecting him to help her...but on second thought, she hardly knew him.

"If that is all," the Priestess said, "I must be excused. I rarely take audiences this late in the day, and, as mundane as it might sound, it is my suppertime. We have food and shelter for travelers. You may stay as long as you wish...but remember, time is of the essence." She ended her words with a brief, careful nod. Sora got the vague impression that she was smiling, though it was impossible to tell behind her blue veil. Then the Priestess turned and walked slowly toward the opposite side of the room, where a separate door stood behind a low curtain.

Sensing they had been dismissed, Sora turned and headed back the way they had come, toward the spiral staircase. She passed Crash swiftly, barely sparing him a glance. She wasn't sure what she had expected from the meeting...but this wasn't it.

She dashed down the stairs, suddenly distraught. Journey to the Lost Isles? Destroy Volcrian? Use the Cat's Eye...perhaps at the cost of her own life?

It suddenly seemed a little much.

"Sora," Crash said from behind her, but she only walked faster. She wanted to get out of the Temple, out into clear air where her thoughts were less muddled. Her head swam from all of the information, and she touched her Cat's Eye, trying to steady herself.

"Sora!" he called more firmly.

No, she didn't care. She went down the stairs, out the door and into the courtyard in under a minute. She didn't know where she was going, just that she needed to think, to gather herself. Anxiety twisted in her gut. *What have I gotten myself into?* The presence of the hilt seemed twice as heavy in her bag, weighing against her arm.

"*Sora!*" A hand grabbed her shoulder. She turned, using one of her mother's tricks to slip from Crash's grasp. But he countered it and grabbed her again, this time in an unbreakable hold. "Stop. Be calm."

"Calm?" she demanded. They had paused under a low tree, heavy with lemons. "*Calm?* Are you deaf? Did you hear any of that?" Her hands were shaking. *Dammit.* She dropped the satchel to the ground. "What am I even doing here? Better yet, what are *you* doing here? You know more than I do, but you didn't say a thing! Are you here to help me or to spy on me? What is the Shade?"

Crash rolled his eyes. "It's just a story. Where I grew up, they were more of a legend, something our Grandmasters spoke of. You shouldn't believe everything that old witch tells you. She's a Priestess, not a Goddess. Her visions are just as accurate—and just as interpretable—as your own!"

Sora shook her head. "I don't know what I'm doing."

"Maybe. But we still have to do it."

She glared at him. He was evading her question, as usual.

"Why are you here, Crash?"

He didn't answer immediately. He looked down at her instead, silent, thoughtful. She became trapped by his gaze; his roguish, handsome face. It had always reminded her of a wolf or a jackal, something predatory.

"Because...." he said slowly. "This is my fault."

She waited for more, but he didn't say anything else. *His fault?* She finally frowned. "It's Volcrian's fault," she grunted. "But all right, I can see your point." Maybe the man had a conscience after all.

Then, surprisingly, Crash threw back his head and laughed. It was a short, biting sound, not entirely humorous. "I've been running for some time," he said quietly. "For a long time, actually, though not always from Volcrian. I need to face what I've done."

She didn't know what to say about that. *What I've done.* And what was that, exactly? It seemed he was talking about more than just Volcrian's brother. She let out a long, slow breath, her thoughts racing. What about before that? What kind of life had he lived? And where was he going now?

That's it. He's just...going, with no real direction, and somehow she had gotten swept up in his wake. Did she regret it?

"Hey!" a voice called suddenly. "What'cha guys doing?"

Sora turned to see Laina and Burn walking towards them. The two were loaded down with trays of food. Laina had a huge grin on her small, mousy face; she was even chewing a piece of cheese. "The spread is delicious!" she shouted. "And fresh! They killed the chickens just this afternoon!"

Sora sighed. After meeting with the Priestess, the last thing on her mind was food, but she knew she had to eat. And eating was better than thinking about their conversation, the road ahead and the massive burden dumped on her shoulders. All because of a Cat's-Eye necklace. *Talk about being in the wrong place at the wrong time.* She wanted to journey, to explore...but to save the kingdom?

And no one even knew the plague was real....

She shared one last glance with Crash, then picked up her satchel and started toward her companions.

Chapter 8

After filling in Burn and Laina on what they had learned from the Priestess, they all decided to head to the port city of Delbar, where hopefully they could book passage to the Lost Isles.

"But isn't that a legend?" Laina had asked, bouncing up and down on her cot in the dormitory. "I mean...what ship actually travels that far?"

"The one we pay for," Crash grunted.

They awoke early the next morning. Sora was eager to get on the road. They restocked their horses with provisions and snuck out of the city on back streets, avoiding the main thoroughfare, where some farmers were still keeping an eye out for the girl with the "healing touch." Then they continued through the lowlands, traveling between the subtle hills, doubled up on the beasts. The grass was bent and windswept, and slowly the sound of bells faded behind them. The tower of the Goddess disappeared, along with all hint of civilization. No roads. No houses. Only the hot, open landscape.

Burn walked next to Laina's horse after a few hours, giving the beast a rest. Sora once again found herself in the saddle with Crash. *I wish I could have a horse of my own,* she thought, eyeing Laina's steed enviously. *And why does he always get to ride in the front?*

Burn and Laina chatted away happily. The girl's shrill laugh could be heard every couple of minutes, along with Burn's deep chuckle. Sora wondered how he could stand her.

"He used to have kids," Crash murmured, as though reading her thoughts.

Sora blinked, surprised by this. Burn had never mentioned anything about children on their previous travels, and she hadn't thought to ask.

"Used to? What...?" The statement slowly sank in. "What happened?"

"Killed," Crash said. "By Volcrian."

Sora went pale. Her stomach turned over. She didn't want to know any of the details—she would ask Burn himself when they got a moment alone. *Perhaps that's why he travels with Crash,* she thought, wondering about their strange alliance. One would think that the Wolfies would support each other, with so few left in the world. Burn and Volcrian were the last ones now, supposedly. She had heard it from his own mouth. Dorian would have made three, but he was gone....She got the sudden, distinct feeling that dirt was sticking between her fingers, and she wiped her hands on her pants.

A bead of sweat dripped from her forehead and trickled down her nose, where it hung for a moment before continuing its downward journey under her shirt. She stretched her cramped back and glanced over her shoulder at Laina and Burn, just as the giant mercenary pointed to the grass.

"There, did you see that movement? That's a field mouse scampering about. We've eaten one or two of those little buggers before. Isn't that right, Crash? They tend to be bony though juicy, if you can find a fat one."

"How can you see so well?" Laina exclaimed. "That's amazing!"

"It's not truly the eyes. I usually hear them long before I can see anything," Burn explained.

Sora sighed, tired of their chatter. She looked behind them at the long trail they had left through the high grass. A breeze blew across, causing the grass to shine and bend in a wavelike pattern.

She frowned, sensing a twinge from her Cat's Eye, and sat up a little straighter. Looking around, she saw nothing but grass, although she had felt a brush of warning, heard a vague chiming. Perhaps it was just the clink of the saddles. She shifted again. Was it her Cat's Eye, or Laina's laughter ringing in her ears? She ran her hand through her hair. Maybe it was just a headache.

No, more than that. Something wasn't quite right about the rolling plains, and she was growing alarmed. Crash seemed to sense it, too. He stiffened in front of her, and she noticed his hand hovering close to his sword. Even the horse was slowing down, its steps becoming more hesitant. Over the assassin's shoulder, she could see the steed's ears flicker.

"What is it?" she murmured into Crash's ear.

"Quiet," he breathed back, turning his head slightly toward her. She pulled back right before they bumped cheeks, strangely flustered. *He's still treating me like a beginner. Didn't I just beat him to the ground a few days ago?*

The horse abruptly shifted beneath them, letting out a short whinny of alarm as it half-reared, lunging forward.

Then the ground moved.

Sora grabbed the saddle with a yelp. She tried to stay on, really she did—but it was impossible. A second later, the earth gave out under them.

She tipped out of the saddle. The horse managed to propel itself forward, dashing away from the hole, but Sora wasn't as lucky. She fell into the caving dirt. Rocks and grass gave way beneath her, and she heard the snap of branches.

It was a trap, it had to be, a pitfall cunningly disguised in the grass. She threw her arms over her head, pelted by a shower of rocks. She landed hard, the wind knocked out of her. She could hear Laina's voice—and then lots of people shouting.

When she finally regained her breath, Sora wiped dirt from her face and looked up at the cloudless blue sky. She could hear the cries of battle and the clanging of swords. What was going on? She had to marvel at the skilled person who had set the trap. She was surrounded by snapped branches that had been woven into a strong mat covered in dirt and rocks.

She used the wall of the hole to help herself stand up, wincing from her bruised rump. Then she looked for a way out. She was desperate to see what was happening, but the hole was perhaps ten feet deep. It sounded like an outright war up there. She could hear Burn's battle cry, an unmistakable howl, followed shortly by a very human scream.

Her thoughts first went to Crash, but he would probably be the last person to scream. Then she thought of Laina. Her heart leapt to her throat and she tried to scramble up one of the walls, but the dirt gave way under her hands. Who was attacking?

And then she realized—the Ravens!

Had to be. She wanted to kick herself. Since meeting with the Priestess, she had completely forgotten about them. They were the masters of this territory; she couldn't imagine who else would be able to disguise such a trap. Volcrian had more direct means.

"Laina! Hang on!" she yelled. Another scream, definitely the voice of a young girl, ripped through the air.

There was another roar in response. That was Burn. She could never mistake his voice; he sounded absolutely furious. She had to find a way out! Placing her back against the side of the pit, Sora looked at its depth and width. Altogether, she guessed she had about a dozen feet to maneuver in, and a good distance to jump.

She unslung her staff from her back. Although she hadn't tried anything like this before, there was no time to waste. Steeling her nerves, she launched into a run, sprinting at top speed. As the distance closed, she brought her staff down into the corner of the wall and catapulted herself into the air.

Because she was so light, Sora wound up vaulting much higher than she had anticipated. She overshot the ground and flew through the air, lifting her staff over her head to keep balance. Then she got a quick look at her surroundings. The Ravens were everywhere, dirty mercenaries dressed in bits and pieces of mismatched armor, darting around like flies.

She landed near Burn, who swung his sword back and forth, but the giant blade was too big for close combat; it was like trying to kill gnats with a hammer. Crash was somewhere to her right, having abandoned the horse, his dagger flashing and zipping through the air. He had already laid out two bandits, but there were countless more, buzzing around on every side.

But where was Laina? Sora brought her staff around, smashing it into the head of one of the Ravens. Then she turned, looking for the girl, her eyes scanning the tall grass. There were too many foes...and Laina had disappeared.

"Sora!" she suddenly heard, a bare snatch of a cry on the wind. "Someone help!"

With a few swift jabs, she broke loose from the mob of outlaws and charged through the long grass, certain she had heard Laina's voice. Now she could see a trail through the grass where a body had been dragged. Burn's roar split her ears and she hurried, knowing that the fight would soon be over and the Ravens would regroup somewhere else.

Her clothes gave her no camouflage against the tall yellow weeds, but no one followed her. Soon the sounds of battle were remote. She could see signs that Laina had been pulled through the area, threads of her clothing and footprints in the loose dirt, and so she continued on course, following the crushed grass. Sweat dripped down her face and stung her eyes, an irritating distraction. *It's horribly hot for spring,* she thought, wishing a cloud would pass overhead. The glaring light made it hard to see.

Abruptly she straightened up; her keen ears had heard a sound on the breeze. Her eyes combed the fields around her, listening intently. There was no sign of movement, but a sudden shiver ran down her spine.

Purely out of instinct, she threw herself to one side. A long, thin blade whipped past her, almost invisible against the grass.

She brought her staff down, but the sword was no longer there. Then she spun around, her heart in her throat—and gasped. A man stood at her back, as though he had risen from the very earth. For just a second, she thought it was Crash. Her eyes flickered over him in shock. His hair was the same perfect black, though longer and shaggier. One eye was closed by a permanent scar, a gruesome deformity that twisted down the left side of his face, while the other eye glinted with a malicious green light.

"Playing hero?" he hissed, and the sword moved like lightning. She brought up her staff, deflecting the blow. It was a clumsy block;

she was completely unprepared.

He laughed at her, and in sudden anger, Sora kicked out her leg, attempting to trip him. Her foot passed through empty air as the man leapt up and *over* her, spinning expertly, landing perfectly on her other side.

Her mouth dropped open. *Gods, he's like a cat!* She had never seen a move like that before.

"And just what is a pretty morsel like you doing out here?" he asked, serpent-like. "Are you frightened? Yes, I think so."

"Don't flatter yourself," Sora growled. Then she touched the necklace under her shirt and gave herself over to the Cat's Eye, summoning its power with a tendril of thought.

The necklace roared to life. She felt its energy run through her limbs, making her loose and confident. The spirits of past warriors still existed within the necklace, snatches of skill and technique. As her muscles tightened with several lifetimes' worth of experience, she attacked him, twirling her staff with ease.

The man dodged her first thrust and brought his sword down to cleave off her hand—but she pulled back, lashing out, missing his throat by a quarter of an inch. She kept at him, attacking with a volley of blows and jabs; she struck his chest, his knee, his arms. Finally, with a firm whack to his hand, she forced him to drop his sword to the ground.

"Not what I was expecting, I'll admit," he said, rubbing the injured limb. His eyes slid over her in an oily way that made her gut churn. His gaze was unnerving, sickly, like poison. "You wouldn't make a bad outlaw, you know. Would you consider joining us?"

Sora glared at him, disgusted. "Let Laina go," she said.

The man raised an eyebrow. "Sorry, my dear," he murmured.

"But she has a price to pay."

Sora lunged at him, infuriated. "Bastard!" she yelled. "She's just a child!"

The Raven was ready for her. He ducked under her staff, smooth as water, and grabbed her arms. Then, before she could react, he spun her around and bodily shoved her into the grass, falling with her, pinning her to the ground face-first. Sora let out a shriek of outrage, but it was useless—he was strong, far more powerful than she, and heavy against her back. He slammed her face into the dirt with one hand. She could imagine the grin on his twisted, scarred face.

"Beautiful girls are hard to come by," the man mused. "Maybe I'll take you with me."

Panic bloomed, tightening around her lungs, her heart skittering. It was hard to breathe with a mouth full of dirt, and her nose was smashed by the pressure on her head. Sora bucked and writhed, trying to break free, but the Raven's grip was rock-hard. "Mmm," he murmured hoarsely. "Keep moving."

Wham! Suddenly, some unseen force struck the bandit, knocking him sideways. He leapt off her, a curse on his lips.

Instantly freed, Sora rolled over and leapt to her feet, reaching for her staff, prepared for another attack.

Her eyes searched the grass.

She spun around, dragging in breath after desperate breath, expecting an attack from any side...but nothing happened. She kept turning, looking, waiting for the blow of a fist or the swing of a sword....

But the man was gone.

What happened...?

There was a large rock in the grass that hadn't been there before. Sora could imagine that someone had thrown it, but when she looked around at the fields again, she was alone. Except....

"I figured you could handle yourself," Crash's voice reached her.

She whirled again, her heart in her throat. The assassin was kneeling in the grass nearby. How had she missed him? It was as though he had been invisible just a few seconds before. She could have sworn that her eyes had passed over that very spot.

He was inspecting something in the dirt—the sword dropped by the bandit. He picked up the thin blade, rolling it over in his hands, then threw it to one side. "Worthless," he grunted.

Sora finally regained her breath. She frowned, staring at the sword in the grass. It was rusty and looked like it hadn't been sharpened in a while.

"Who was that?" she finally asked. The question tumbled out of her mouth before she could think about it. Then she murmured, "He...he looked like you."

Crash sat back, his face impassive. "Did he?"

"Yeah." She recognized that tone. Guarded. She grinned instead, trying to make light of the question. "Any lost relatives hanging around here? A brother, perhaps?"

Crash shrugged. "Family's complicated," he said. "You could say mine are mostly cousins."

"So, a cousin of yours, then?"

"No," he said flatly, and left it at that.

Sora was too tired to pursue the topic. Sweat poured down her face. She felt as though the sun was blistering her forehead. With a heavy sigh, she sank down in the grass next to him, wishing she could just lie flat in the dirt and take a nap.

Surprisingly, Crash shifted closer to her. "Are you injured?" he asked.

"No," she said, slightly irritated.

"I didn't think so."

"Good."

There was an awkward silence. Sora wondered why he was there. He had admitted letting her handle the fight on her own. Who knew how long he had watched before he had intervened...but now he worried that she was injured? She wanted to smack him in frustration. He had no faith in her abilities. How many times would she have to prove herself?

The grass hissed and shushed. She tensed. A moment later, Burn appeared nearby, his massive sword slung over one shoulder. "Well?" he demanded, panting. "They disappeared, ran off into the brush before I could stop them. Did we get her?"

Sora blinked and looked at Crash. "No...?"

He shook his head wordlessly.

"Dammit," Burn muttered. "Damn it all!"

Sora echoed the sentiment. "I agree," she growled. "We need to rescue her...."

"Why?" Unsurprisingly, it was Crash who spoke. "She's a nuisance anyway. Just let her go back to her kind."

"You're kidding, right?" Sora spit out the words. "It's not that simple!" *He must not know,* she thought, trying to calm herself. *He can't be so heartless.* "They see her as a traitor. They're going to kill her."

"Worse than that," Burn said. "She had your satchel with her."

"What?"

"Your bag."

"*What?*" Sora's eyes widened. "With the hilt?"

Burn nodded silently.

Sora sat in stunned silence. She could remember tying the bag onto her horse that morning. How had Laina gotten her hands on it? Was that on purpose? Were the Ravens somehow after the hilt, too? No, that didn't add up; it had to be a coincidence. She shared a strained look with Burn, momentarily overwhelmed. "Then that does it. We have to go after her!"

Crash didn't say anything. Sora had the horrible feeling that he had known the Ravens' plot; he didn't seem surprised by the news at all. She wanted to scream at him in frustration. She could remember moments from their last adventure when they had traveled through the swamp. Secrets he had kept. Manipulation. He was terrible at times, needlessly cold—inhumanly so.

"I'm the one who got her in this mess," Sora said. "She's counting on me...."

"How?" Crash asked abruptly. "How is this your fault? She's the one who joined them. And what if she's lying about the whole thing? Do you know for a fact that they will kill her? She took the hilt with her, after all. She knows now what it is. You don't know if she's telling the truth."

Sora shot him a fierce glare. Of course the assassin would say that. "Shocking, coming from a murderer," she grunted.

Crash looked at her steadily, his face like stone. Harder than stone.

Sora stared back. She didn't turn away, but something about his gaze made her shiver, made her grow cold under the sun. She wanted to cave, certainly. His presence had always made her want to relent, to give in and follow his command.

Then again, he was usually the one to pull them out of trouble. She knew she could trust his judgment, that she was being stubborn and foolhardy. He didn't have any reason to help Laina, no reason at all, and from what she could tell, they didn't like each other. Could she blame him?

He had treated her much the same when they had met, more than a year ago...even though he had been the one to kidnap her, to seduce her into the unknown....

"Well, we need to get the hilt back, either way. I say we follow them," Burn interjected, breaking the tense silence. "Have a look at their camp, see what they're up to. If Laina's lying, then we'll grab the hilt and continue on our way. But if not...." His eyes hardened. "I won't let a child be killed."

Crash looked at the Wolfy. Sora had the feeling that he wasn't used to being ganged up against. "We're wasting time," he said harshly. "Volcrian is right behind us. If he catches us with Laina, then she'll be dead anyway. We need to get the hilt, but rescuing her will take too long. We need to get to Delbar and get off the mainland."

Burn stared back at him evenly. "We save the girl first," he said. "She's just a child. We're not leaving anyone behind."

It seemed that Crash didn't know what to say to that. Sora could hear the gravity in Burn's tone. It was the voice of age, of experience, of someone who didn't argue. She wanted to taunt the assassin, point a finger in his face, stick out her tongue...but she abstained. Maybe he would finally grow a heart. Maybe he would understand.

But when he turned back to her, his expression was

unmistakable.

He'll never change.

"Fine," Crash grunted, as though it had been his decision all along. "We follow." Then he picked up the bandit's sword and snapped it over his knee.

CHAPTER 9

The Ravens' camp was spread out before them.

It was close to twilight, the sun a fragile arc on the horizon. They had followed the trail left in the grass to a long-dried river basin, where the plains dipped down into a rocky strip of earth. Bonfires and broad tents were scattered everywhere. The outlaws strode back and forth, pausing to chat with friends, passing around wine skins and chewing on legs of meat. To the left was a series of large wagons, probably from merchants they had killed. *This is a successful band of thieves,* she thought, surveying the items spread throughout the camp. Chests, crates, barrels, piles of cheap jewelry and furs, abandoned furniture—a loom? *What could they possibly need a loom for, of all things?*

There were many more bandits than Sora had expected. She tried to count them from where she crouched on the ridge above the camp, obscured by a large bush, but gave up after reaching one-hundred. A few mismatched flags waved above their tents. They looked like town flags or folded bedsheets, sewn over with the rough symbol of a flying bird. *Appropriate for a bunch of jailbirds,* Sora thought, and snickered to herself. Their clothes were so shoddy, she could practically feel the uneven stitches with her fingers. They obviously didn't know much about sewing—*or how to use a loom.*

Besides that, the camp seemed fairly organized, at least for a group of homeless criminals. For some reason she had pictured muddy, starving hooligans fighting over bowls of slop and sleeping in their own filth. Instead, the horses were corralled on the far side, the cooking area was separate from the sleeping tents. There were spurts of laughter and the occasional strum of a guitar.

Then the wind shifted, and she caught the foul scent of the latrines. She rescinded any credit she had given them, as small as it might have been. *Ugh, gross!* She resisted the urge to gag. Burn had been rubbing his nose earlier—with his heightened sense of smell, it was a wonder he could stand it. She returned her attention to the camp below, nonchalantly pulling her shirt over her nose.

A large group milled about the center of the camp, calling animatedly to each other. Sora could catch snatches of conversation. *"Make it slow this time...think she'll scream...hope she lasts long, the last one died in an hour."*

Were they going to torture Laina before killing her? That's what it sounded like. She shuddered.

The Ravens were an even mix of men and women, though strangely enough, most of the women were far older than she. Perhaps widows or divorceés forced into poverty, nowhere else to go. Some even had children. She wondered why anyone would turn to such a life. Surely there were better alternatives...?

It was plain to see where Laina was kept. For one thing, there was a large cage off in the distance where a ragged girl lay, curled into a ball. A large crowd surrounded her, almost as large as the group in the center of the camp. As Sora watched, she saw several bandits throw rocks at the cage, yelling and taunting, but a few guards pushed them back. Their hatred seemed genuine. They were building a large pile of wood and debris in the center of the camp. Were they going to burn her at the stake?

Sora banished any doubt of the girl's honesty; Laina was definitely a victim. Her eyes scanned the camp, wondering where her satchel might be, but it was impossible to spot.

Crash and Burn had decided on a rough plan before approaching the camp. "Simple is best," Burn had said knowingly. Sora didn't know if she agreed with that, but at least it was easy to remember. The two men would create a distraction, then search for her lost bag. When Laina was left alone, Sora would make her move and break the girl out.

She shifted so her knees were touching Crash, then asked quietly, "What's the signal?"

"I doubt you'll need one," he said. His eyes didn't leave the scene before them. "When everyone leaves the cage, then go to her. You might have to take out a few guards, but I don't think that'll be a problem."

He cast her a glance and Sora felt strangely happy. Perhaps he recognized her skill after all. "Remember," he continued, "in and out. Nothing fancy, and don't stick around waiting for us. As soon as you get her, take the horses and leave. You remember our rendezvous point?"

"Yeah...." she gripped her staff in sweaty hands. They had decided on a copse of trees several miles away, in the opposite direction that the bandits would expect them to travel. "You'll be okay?"

Amusement flashed across his eyes and he arched an elegant black brow. The rest of his face was hidden behind a black veil, the mark of his trade. She hadn't seen him wear it since he had kidnapped her from her manor, almost a year ago. "You have to ask?"

Now it was her turn to snort. "Of course, I forgot. You're invincible. And immortal, I might add. Did I mention infallible?" She grinned in turn. "It's not like I've ever saved you from drowning...."

"Did you?" he said dryly. "I seem to remember that. You should get going. Burn will be in position by now."

Sora looked around and saw that, indeed, Burn had disappeared. *Darn, I forgot to wish him luck.* She stood, still hunched below the rim of grass, and turned to go. "Watch out for that guy with the scar," she said over her shoulder, a last-minute thought. "He knows what he's doing."

"Hmm," Crash murmured.

Sora started along the top of the ridge. *Blend!* she thought to herself, trying to stay low and inconspicuous. If she stood up too straight, her presence would be as obvious as a lighthouse.

"Be careful," the assassin's voice trailed after her.

She turned back, unsure if she had heard correctly—*am I imagining things?* It seemed almost sentimental coming from someone like him.

But he was gone, nothing but weeds and rocks in his place.

"I will," she muttered, if only to the wind. Then she scuttled on her way, crawling around the outskirts of the large encampment, making sure to avoid the firelight. The sun was setting; it was perhaps a half-hour before full darkness. Shadows were everywhere, the landscape smeared with gray, so she blended in perfectly. She reached the side of the camp closest to Laina's cage and hunched low in the bushes, only a few dozen yards away. At this distance, she could clearly see her friend's tiny form, the men who paced around her prison, old knives shoved into belts, and the firelight that glinted off the eyes of the crowd.

It seemed like no more than a minute later, there was a shout from across the camp. Heads turned. Murmurs of confusion. She squinted, trying to see what was happening on the opposite end of the river basin.

Then a shuddering, echoing roar split the air; it could have been a bear or a lion, though Sora knew it was Burn's battle cry. There was a chorus of terrified whinnies followed by more and more shouts, the thunder of horses' hooves and a cloud of thick dust. She grinned, licking her lips in anticipation. The horses had broken loose from the corral—or had been set loose by her companions—and were stampeding through the camp, panicked eyes rolling, smashing into boxes and tearing through tents.

Chaos exploded. Screams shattered the lazy twilight. She could already see fires spreading, taking easily to the dry grass and wood, trailed by the maddened horses. The Ravens scattered, screeching to one another, leaving Laina's cage and running to put out the fires. There were perhaps fifty horses in all and the mess was catastrophic.

Only one guard remained at the cage. He fidgeted uncertainly, watching the camp disintegrate into panic, turning a blade nervously in his hands. Sora waited impatiently, hoping he would leave, but she couldn't waste too much time. She had to move while the chaos was at its peak. Finally, she decided it was time to act. Lifting her staff in one hand, she slunk down the hill, dashing swiftly from bush to scrubby bush.

She snuck up behind the man, quiet as a ghost, and delivered a firm *whack!* to the back of his head. He dropped like a stone.

She paused, braced for a fight, then stared at the body in

disgust. *Pitiful!* she thought. Hadn't they expected some sort of attack? One would think so, but perhaps they weren't that organized.

She turned to look at Laina and found the girl sitting up, staring at the stampeding horses and spreading fires. Her eyes were wide. "You guys don't mess around," she said, amazed. Then she blinked. "For a while I thought you weren't coming."

"We had to convince Crash that you were worth saving," Sora said, intending it to sound lighthearted, but the girl went pale. She regretted the comment, but there was no way to take it back. "Come on, let's get out of here."

"You can open it, right?" she asked, indicating the door of the cage. Sora leaned down to inspect it. The bars had been tied shut with metal wire. It didn't look very strong. She rolled her eyes.

"Oh, please," she grunted, and took out her knife. With a firm, hard shove, she pushed the blade under the wiring and heaved upwards, slicing through it with minimal difficulty. Within seconds, the wire was cleaved in half and she yanked the door open. It shrieked on its hinges, a horrible scraping noise.

Laina sprang to her feet and out the opening, quick as a rabbit. Sora followed suit. *They'll notice what's going on any minute now.* "We need to go!" She took the lead, charging up the hill, throwing caution to the wind and making a mad dash to their tethered horses.

Abruptly a shout reached her ears. "Look!" she heard from somewhere behind her. "Lookie there! She's gettin' away!"

Uh-oh, not good! Sora grabbed the girl by her skinny arm and hauled her up the hill faster.

Surprisingly, Laina pulled back.

"Are you stupid?" Sora snapped. "Go!"

"But Burn!" she exclaimed. "We can't leave him behind!"

Sora was momentarily shocked, but continued to drag the girl along. "He's fighting for you. Don't let his efforts go to waste!" she said. She didn't know if the girl would understand...but she was suddenly reminded of her younger self, as though from another life, saying much the same thing.

They reached the top of the hill and plunged into the tall grass. In this area, the fields were wild and golden, the grass arching almost above her head, a thick mass up to her shoulders. Some of the weeds had broad tufts on the ends, like fluffy white cattails, taller than a man. Spider webs glistened in the near-darkness.

The horses were tethered only a few dozen yards away, but it was slow going through the shadows. The light was merely a gray afterglow in the sky. Sora had to trust her instincts and sense of direction. She listened for the vague shifting and shuffling of the beasts, which were still out of sight.

Laina was even slower, the tangle of plants far above her head. There was no other option but for Sora to drop back next to her.

"Are you okay?" she asked. "Did they hurt you?"

"No, I'm fine..." Laina panted. "Just...so tired...."

"The horses should be close," Sora said, hoping to encourage her. But when she looked back up, she realized that she had no idea which direction they were heading. The thick shrubbery offered no help. She kept listening for sounds from the beasts, but the clashes of battle were getting louder and the wind was blowing in the opposite direction. There was no time. She picked a route at random and took the lead again.

Behind them, the crash of bodies could be heard.

Crash fought through the disorganized crowd of bandits, looking for one in particular.

They swarmed in every which direction, chasing fires and dashing after horses. A few leapt in front of him, brandishing swords, but he slipped through them like a wraith, cutting down those who got too close. He was silent, fluid, as calm as a winter lake...except for one thought, which kept circling in his mind like a lone hawk. *Where is he?*

Burn fought next to him, cleaving left and right, taking down several bandits with each swipe. Eventually they stopped rushing in and kept their distance, watching warily, uncertain.

"We have to get out of here before we get too deep into the camp," Burn called to him. "Do you see Sora's bag anywhere?"

"No, but I know where it is," Crash replied confidently.

Suddenly the assassin spotted him. His prey had harnessed one of the horses and was struggling toward the opposite side of the encampment, two other riders with him. It looked like he was trying to escape.

A rare grin passed over Crash's veiled face. Too easy. He could have thrown a knife to end the ordeal; his aim was perfect at this distance, and his hand itched to do it. He had already picked out the man's exposed neck, or perhaps his chest, unprotected by a thin linen shirt. But no, not this time. Crash wanted more than that. He needed to see those sickly green eyes; needed to know for sure....

"Go," he called to Burn, and waved his hand, motioning to the edge of the camp. "Get out of here. Go meet Sora."

"You sure?" Burn yelled. Then a bandit jumped at him from behind a pile of wood, thinking to take the Wolfy off-guard. He caught the man in mid-air and tossed him to the side.

"I'm sure," Crash said, a glint in his eye. "See you in an hour."

"Right." Burn turned and started back toward the open plains. There was a horse milling around next to a spilled basket of hay. Crash saw him reach for the reins of the large beast.

Then the assassin went after a horse of his own and managed to grab one within a minute, unharnessed and wild from the fire. He caught the beast as it passed, jumping onto it bareback, firmly gripping the mane. After a short struggle of wills, he won control, then charged effortlessly through the masses. He was faster now that he had a target, directing the beast with his legs. It was the way he had originally learned to ride, back in his youth, when he had spent hours and hours on the beach, dashing through sand, rushing the surf and practicing with his bow.

He galloped to the other side of the camp, following his prey's trail. No one tried to stop him. On horseback, the Ravens barely glanced at him, too busy putting out fires.

His prey's trail led up the opposite riverbank and into the fields. Crash thundered after him, up the rocky ridge, into the wilderness, pushing the beast as fast as it could go. They danced over rocks and plunged through the tall grass. The light was dead in the sky, full nightfall upon them, the stars gleaming up above. If anything, Crash could see just as well in the darkness, his eyes bright and his senses attuned.

Within minutes, he caught up with them. Three figures struggled ahead of him, caught in a thick patch of bramble, the grass so high that the horses were practically drowning.

He drew his dagger and, with skilled aim, sent it flying through the neck of the nearest rider.

The first bandit fell from his horse, crumpling silently, so sudden that the beast didn't even respond. The other rider noticed and turned, eyes searching the darkness warily, but Crash leapt from his steed and entered the tall grass, becoming invisible. He drew another knife from his cloak, this one smaller, thinner, and with a flick of his wrist, sent the blade spinning into the second man's throat. The second rider fell just as silently as the first, almost gracefully, like a swan into black water.

The last one was their leader. Crash could sense his presence in the darkness; it was firm, confident.

The man leapt from his horse, landing smoothly on the ground. He peered into the shadows. Though Crash hadn't moved, the man's eyes went directly to him, staring at the thick patch of brush where he crouched. He knew this was the same one who had attacked Sora, and who doubtlessly had her bag....They faced each other, a mere yard apart, and Crash stared at that scarred face.

He could remember the scar...recognized it. He could even remember the knife that had dealt it—a fine blade that his teacher had given him, so many years ago, long since lost in a river. They had been boys then, fighting for a title, a Name, too young to know anything else. Now they were older...but he doubted the man had forgotten

His opponent stooped to the ground briefly, tugging the blade from the throat of the first rider. In that moment, the clouds shifted overhead and a full moon appeared, silver light cascading down upon them. The blade gleamed. The Raven's eyes flickered over it. Then he grinned.

"I remember this dagger," the man murmured. "Viper." His voice slid through the air like thick oil. "Fate is strange, indeed."

"As I recall, they exiled you," Crash replied, summoning the memories as though from a dream. How long had it been? Ten years, at least.

"I wanted that Name: the Viper," the man laughed softly. "Wanted it badly. But you earned it...." He tossed the blade back to him. It landed at Crash's feet. "Yes, they exiled me after I lost that match."

Crash picked up the dagger, gazing at it, lingering. They had grown up in the Hive, a nest of assassins trained in the killing arts. It was their heritage, their tradition. Born nameless, they had to earn their titles through combat. And if one competed for a Name and lost, he was exiled.

"What do they call you now?" Crash asked.

The man shrugged. "I'm the Raven leader," he said. "I have made a life here, you could say." Then he grinned. "But what is the Viper doing so far from home? On a mission? Or...have you abandoned the Hive?"

Crash didn't reply. The truth was much more complicated than that, and he wouldn't waste his time explaining it to a dead man.

"You have something that belongs to me," Crash said instead.

"Do I?" the man replied. A sickly grin twisted his face, the scar contorting into a snarl. "To you...or to the Dark God?"

Crash's heart gave a vague thump, though he didn't show it. So the bastard knew—of course he knew.

He didn't have to ask the next question; the Raven leader continued talking. "The girl brought it to us, tried to barter for her life. It didn't work. But, ironically, I *do* know someone who would be eager to take it off your hands...."

"Who?"

"A mutual acquaintance."

Crash's hand tightened on the dagger. His mind raced momentarily, summoning up images from the Hive, the colony, supposed Brothers and Sisters of the assassin trade. He pictured each and every one of them, but he didn't know who belonged to the Shade, and there were many different Hives.

"I'm done with this game," Crash said, and he took a step forward, leaving the safety of the tall grass and entering the bright moonlight.

"Wait!" the bandit said, and danced backwards. He pointed to his horse, where Crash could see Sora's bag hanging from the saddle. "A trade. I can barter for you. I am meeting with them in Delbar. We'll split the money."

Crash continued to walk forward. "I have no need of money."

"Forgiveness, then...acceptance back into the Hive, where we belong...we don't need to be alone."

"I left the Hive."

The man stumbled backward, overwhelmed by Crash's presence. Then a strange, frantic light lit his eyes, like a cornered animal. With a flick of his wrist, a knife appeared in his hand and he lunged forward, swiping wildly, attempting to cut anywhere he could reach.

Crash caught the blade with his own. He deflected the blow and grabbed the man's wrist, twisting it up and over his head, smoothly snapping his arm as he brought it down behind him.

The man screamed.

"Where are you meeting them?" Crash asked calmly.

The man was gasping, whimpering. "At the port...the docks...." he choked out, barely able to speak. Crash shoved him backwards and the man collapsed to the ground, his broken arm limp and useless next to him. "Please..." he begged. "Please, I just wanted my life back."

"We aren't alive, or have you forgotten?" Crash murmured, slowly walking forward, following the man across the ground. "Death is our creed, our way. You're a pathetic specimen of our kind."

The man's mouth opened. Then closed.

Crash knew what he needed to do. It wasn't for glory, for justice—nor, even, for Sora. This man was dangerous. If Volcrian found him, he would doubtlessly ally himself with the mage. It was too much of a trail, of a witness. And he knew too much about Crash's past. What if Volcrian turned his sights on the Hive? He had left it years ago, but he didn't want it destroyed.

His heart began to pound, blood rushing through his veins, his hand tight on the blade.

"So...so what then, Death has come for me personally?" the man finally said. There was irony in his tone, despite the fact that his teeth were gritting with pain.

Crash let a small smile twitch his lips. Then he lunged forward with his dagger. He had expected more of a fight, but the man crumpled beneath him without a struggle. He held the blade to his throat, pressing him back against the firm earth.

"I want this," the man murmured. He let out a hoarse laugh, spittle touching his lips.

"Do you?"

"Yes....Can't you see it? There is no happiness in the world for our kind," he said. "We have trained beyond it. Removed ourselves from it. In its place sits a demon who only wants to destroy, to damage, to crush. We don't belong here, Viper. I'm tired of this loneliness. An entire band of outlaws, and no one will ever know what I am. We've both forsaken our home. Do you ever regret it?"

Crash shuddered unexpectedly; it moved through him like a brief wind. There was truth in the Raven's words. A terrible, dark truth. It was second nature now, the thin barrier dividing him from the rest of humanity. For all of the fire in his blood, he still felt cold, somehow absent from the world.

"We have always been this way," he murmured. "Living in shadow since the Elements combined...."

"And you think it's natural?" the bandit challenged.

Viper couldn't take it anymore. These questions had plagued him for too long and asking a million times wouldn't bring an answer. Man or shadow, he would rid the world of one more menace. *I am the menace,* his thoughts murmured, but he brushed them aside. Doubt was an illusion. All things were meant to be destroyed. There would be no guilt in this act.

"Do you think they won't come for you?" the bandit asked suddenly. "You hold the dagger, the Name. They'll find you, Viper. They'll take back what is theirs. Aren't you tired of looking over your shoulder? You've had a few good years, I'm sure. But they are on their way. They will come to reclaim you."

Crash shook his head. He had worried about this long before he had met Volcrian, especially during that first year on the road. Always on the lookout for others of his kind, never sure if he would wake up alive.

But now, he had the firm sense of being forgotten. Unknown.

The man's eyes glinted, as though reading his thoughts. "You think they've given up?" he asked. "Or do you think you've changed? What, are you human now?" He grinned. "Are you trying to be? I bet you are, little snake."

Crash stared at him. *What am I?* Was he the Viper, the one who hid in the grass, still and silent until an innocent passerby stepped too close? Cold-blooded, fanged, his words as sharp as his own knife? He had earned that Name, once upon a time. There had been Vipers before him and there would be more to follow. It was a station and a title; the only one he had ever known.

Except for Crash, the silly nickname Dorian had given him that night by the fire, when Sora had sat scared and shivering on the ground. It was her name for him now, *Crash Crash Crash.* She had saved his life too, once upon a time. She had seen something worth saving. He closed his eyes momentarily. She, of all people, deserved to know who and what he was. *But she will never trust me again.*

It was foolish for him to regret that. Sentimental. *Enough of this.* Questions did not bring answers.

"I am the fire," Crash whispered. *"I am the darkness."* It was a mantra, a prayer, the beginnings of a ritual, a ceremonial killing. He could see recognition on the bandit's face, the spasm of fear.

Crash never broke eye contact. *"I am not Death,"* he finished the verse. *"I am its vessel."*

The Raven opened his mouth to speak. Then Crash shoved the knife through his throat.

* * *

Laina tripped twice and Sora mentally cursed the girl's

clumsiness. It was hard going through the long grass and the bandits were getting far too close. She gritted her teeth as she stubbed her toe on a root, then Laina swore loudly as she crashed through a massive spider web. This noise was followed by several audible shouts of, "They're over there!" and "Get them!"

Sora pulled the young thief around a large thistle bush, panting, desperate...then, abruptly, the horses came into view. *Oh, thank the Goddess!* she thought. She had been randomly stumbling through the dark for some time now, trying not to panic.

Suddenly, the girl screamed.

"Laina!" Sora exclaimed. The girl collapsed behind her and Sora grabbed her arm, her weight dragging her down. She lifted Laina under her shoulders and carried her the final few yards to the horses. Laina was unresponsive. Sora awkwardly tried to push her up into the saddle, but the horse kept dancing away.

Sora paused to focus on Laina—maybe the problem was more than just nerves. The girl was shaking and whimpering, and it didn't take long to see why. A thin shaft of wood protruded from her shoulder. Sora's eyes widened at the sight of the arrow. The girl was damned lucky that it had missed her chest, the obvious target.

Gods. Now what should I do?

"Laina, come on..." Sora said desperately. The sounds from the bandits were frighteningly close; they were seconds away from discovery. "Work with me here, focus! You have to get on the horse. Then we'll be gone like the wind."

The thief seemed about to pass out. "Sora," she choked.

Sora could tell she was trying hard to bear the pain. At any other time she would have been sympathetic, but now she was only annoyed.

"Just get on the damned horse!" she exclaimed.

It seemed to snap Laina out of her stupor. She straightened up suddenly and grabbed the reins with her good arm. "Okay," she blurted. With stiff movements, she swung up into the saddle.

Sora dashed to her own steed. A few seconds later, they plunged through the tall grass, making their way to a sparser stretch of grassland, guided solely by the stars above. Finally, they disentangled themselves from the coarse bushes. With a fierce kick, she sent her horse into a full gallop, dragging Laina's steed along with her. The girl was curled against the horse's neck, stiff with pain. A few arrows chased after them, but they were sorry shots, and the bandits had no horses of their own at hand. Still, she didn't let herself breathe until they had covered at least a mile.

It's all my fault, Sora thought guiltily, looking at Laina's small form. *I should have never brought her in the first place. It's too dangerous.*

"Laina?" she called above the wind and thundering hooves. "Laina? Can you hear me?"

"Uhn," was her only response.

"Hang on just a little longer." Her stomach did a flip as the girl swayed dangerously. What if she fell off and broke her neck? "Do you hear me? Just a little longer!"

"Okay..." the thief's voice gusted away. Her eyes were half-closed. Sora wanted to say something reassuring, but the words wouldn't come. Instead, she focused on directing the horses.

The meeting place, a small patch of trees, loomed up before them perhaps a half-hour later. Her eyes searched the woods and saw no one, but she knew her friends had to be there somewhere. She and Laina had taken longer than planned.

Approaching the trees, Sora slowed the two horses down to a walk. The beasts were both frothing at the mouth and covered with a sheen of sweat, and she felt exactly the same way.

A shadow darted out of the thin copse of trees. Sora looked up, alarmed, until she recognized Burn, who headed swiftly towards her.

The giant arrived just in time to catch Laina as she fell out of the saddle. Sora once again felt guilty. She looked down at the orphan, then at Burn's shadowed face. "Thank you for getting her this far," he said solemnly. "I'll take her from here."

Sora was too tired to say anything, and nodded in response. Now that the adrenaline had left her, she was as limp as a rag doll. Her eyes followed the two back to the fringes of the trees until they disappeared. Once she was sure no one was watching, she let the weariness wash over her. She slumped forward in the saddle, resting her sweaty head against the horse's soft mane. She breathed in the mare's musty scent, absorbing the warm smell. It reminded her of her mother's stables, the scratching of chickens and the thin beams of sunlight. She closed her eyes, momentarily wishing to be there. The beast whuffed quietly in response.

She reached up a heavy hand and gripped her Cat's Eye. The small stone offered great comfort, and she held it for a moment. Her mind drifted back to her mother's house, and she envisioned the garden outside, the warm kitchen and the feeling of a soft feather bed.

Suddenly a hand touched her knee. She didn't even have the energy to flinch.

"Sora?" a voice asked quietly.

Her eyes opened to slits and she looked down. Crash stood

next to her horse with the reins in one hand.

"Did you get the bag?" she asked softly, her voice barely audible.

He nodded, and she breathed a sigh of relief. Before he could ask, she said, "I'm fine, just tired. Laina's with Burn. She took an arrow in the shoulder, but I think she'll be all right." She opened her eyes and looked down at him. She had the strange urge to touch his face, so close to her hand.

"Can you walk?" His gaze was intent.

She yawned again. "I'd better ride. I'll fall over if I don't."

"I believe so."

He didn't smile, but she caught his humor. Sora grinned. " Oh, come now, I'm not that pathetic."

"I'm only agreeing with you."

Another slight jab, but she was too tired to roll her eyes. She closed them instead, pressing her face once again into the horse's neck.

The assassin led her into the woods. By the time they reached their camp, he was not only taking care of two tired horses, but a sleeping Sora as well.

Chapter 10

Lorianne reined in her horse and stared at the old pub. The sky was gray and overcast, the ocean like lead. The small town of Pismo sprawled awkwardly around her, a handful of salt-worn shanties held together by rusty nails. A myriad of fishing boats were tied to a thin, spindly dock, which spread out into the ocean like a glistening wooden web.

Not exactly where she had imagined Ferran to be.

She glanced down at the letter, gripped tightly in her hand. He had written to her last year, ironically; a strange little note, brought by caravan. *"Heard you've settled in the lowlands,"* it read. *"Might visit some day. Be well."* She hadn't heard from him in almost a decade before that. Not since Dane's death.

The thought of her old lover brought on a small twinge of regret, but that was all. Sora's father and her first love. It amazed her how much time had passed. For years she had cried and screamed, howling for his return, an endless Winter that had never quite thawed. But Winter did thaw... and time had carried him away, useless flotsam, an abandoned raft drifting far out to sea....

Her hands tightened on the letter. No, she hadn't seen Ferran in a long while.

She could hear music from within the tavern. She dismounted and led her horse to the rear, where she tied it to a wooden post. She glanced around, looking for a stable boy, but there was none. With a small shrug, Lorianne entered through the back door.

The sounds of a fight were clearly audible, even before she reached the main room. There was the general scuffling and cussing, a glass tipping over. She paused at the end of the hallway, looking into the tavern proper, an eyebrow slightly arched.

The room was small and dingy, with a low slanted ceiling that caved downward in the middle. On the far side, about five men were deeply engrossed in a card game. Closer to her, however, were three men scuffling on the floor, groaning and fumbling drunkenly.

A waitress danced back and forth around the edges of the fight, a tray of beers in one hand. The look on the young woman's face was almost comical. Lori covered her mouth, stifling a smile.

Then the bartender threw a chair across the room, and it crashed into the brawling men. The waitress shrieked and the other patrons looked up from their card game.

"Break it up!" the bartender yelled, coming out from behind the counter. "Break it up! Do ya have to do this *every* weekend?"

"He started it!" one man said, a short, stout fellow with close-cut blond hair. He wiped blood from his lips and stood up. He was shirtless, his chest and torso chiseled with muscle. Lori recognized the sunburns and weathered face of a sailor.

"Aye," his companion said. "We won the game, fair 'n' square. He bet us two hundred gold—where's our money, eh?"

Finally, her gaze landed on the man crumpled on the floor, his brown hair falling into his face. He wore a loose tunic, recently ripped down the front from the fight. A bright, colorful tattoo of a phoenix splayed across his chest, its wings spread in a myriad of greens and reds. Lori grinned slightly, pleased by her own intuition. She had suspected he would be at the tavern....*And, of course, I'd find him in the middle of a bar fight.*

Ferran spit blood out through his teeth in a long, thin stream. Then he grinned. "Ain't got no money. Spent my last coin on that drink." Then he reached out a hand, and the waitress handed him his beer.

Lori rolled her eyes. The two sailors looked furious, but the bartender was shaking his head, as though he had seen this a thousand times. "Sit down, sit down," he said, pulling out chairs. "I'll git you a round on the house. Just no more fightin'!"

The sailors glanced at the bartender, then sat down at a different table, casting angry looks in Ferran's direction.

Ferran didn't move from the floor, but sat against the wall, drinking his beer. Lori watched him. He was older now, she could tell. A few more lines around the eyes, and his hair slightly longer than she remembered, unkempt. But his fit, athletic body was the same—and his tattoo was just as bright as the day he had gotten it. She could remember that, too. He must have had it touched up somewhere along the road.

She waited for him to notice her. It didn't take long. He took a deep swig of beer and glanced around the room. His eyes landed on her. Passed. Returned.

Stared.

He blinked twice, then stood up slowly, an odd look on his face. He glanced down at his drink suspiciously, as though someone had drugged it.

"Lori?" he finally said.

"Aye," she replied softly.

The waitress and the bartender looked up at her, but she ignored them. Instead, she watched as Ferran poured the drink out on the floor, letting the amber liquid seep through the floorboards.

"Damned visions ain't supposed to talk," he grunted. Then he turned, slammed the cup down on a table, and left through the front door.

Lori's eyes widened in surprise and she followed him briskly. The bartender watched her go.

"Ferran!" she yelled, exiting the building, looking left and right. It was about mid-afternoon but the streets were empty, the small fishing village all but deserted. It was easy to spot him, though, heading toward the spindly docks. "Ferran, wait!"

"You're not real!" he yelled back, and kept walking.

Damn, he's more drunk than I thought! She dashed after him. From his lopsided, wandering gait, she knew he wouldn't go far. "Slow down, will you?"

"You can't tell me what to do!" he yelled over his shoulder. "You're just a figment of my imagination!"

"By the Goddess, Ferran! I'm right here!"

He reached the water's edge and paused, obviously unsure of where to go next. He swayed slightly in the wind. She finally caught up to his side and stood behind him, frowning, unsure of what to expect.

Finally, slowly, he turned around.

He didn't say anything, just stared at her from head to toe, starting at her face, then roving down her body, lingering on her hips, her boots, then back to her eyes. He was flushed from drink, but his gaze was a sharp, cool gray, just like she remembered it.

Then he slurred, "Did you shrink?"

"What?"

"You're smaller than you were." Then his eyes narrowed again. His hand reached out to touch her hair. It was fluffed and windswept from her long ride, and she hadn't had a chance to comb it. Lori felt a twinge of self-consciousness. *Really?*

"Huh," he said, then laid a heavy hand on her shoulder, patting her arm. "You feel solid."

"Ferran, *it's me*," she said sternly, and looked him straight in the eye.

Finally he focused on her, his eyes widening, as though coming out of a dream. He stared at her, new realization dawning on his face. "By the gods, Lori," he said, then looked around at the ocean, the decrepit houses, the little pebbled streets. "What are you doing here?"

"Looking for you!" she exclaimed. She threw off his hand, wrinkling her nose slightly at the boozy smell of him. "But I didn't think I'd find you like this! What the hell were you doing in there? Gambling? Drinking?"

He shrugged, his eyes going glassy again. "Eh, well, fishing season's over...."

"It's spring, you fool. The fish are just hatching! I can't believe this. I came here to ask you for help—but looks like I won't be getting any!" Lori turned around, suddenly angry, and started back up the street. "What a waste of time!"

"Now wait, just hold on a minute," Ferran said, and strode after her, easily matching her stride. "What do you mean, you need help? Of course I'll help—I owe you as much! What are you hurtin' for? Money? Well, ain't got a lot of that, but I'm good around a house, I can build things, you know, hammer 'n' nails 'n' such...." He finished with a bit of uncertainty.

She kept walking, absolutely furious.

Finally Ferran stopped, pausing next to a low, rickety fence.

"Y'can't just appear out of nowhere and then leave!" he yelled after her. "Come on! Have a drink with me, at least!"

"No time!" she yelled back, turning slightly toward him. They stood on a slope, and she looked down at him, her eyes glancing over his tall form, well over six feet. He had always been the lanky type, skinny as hell, taut with muscle, not even an inch of fat. He had bulked up now, his jaw wider, his shoulders heavier. His thirties had done him good.

She shook her head, trying not to get distracted. "I don't have time, Ferran," she repeated. "And I have quite a story to tell. If you're willing to sober up and listen, then perhaps I'll stay."

Ferran nodded, his face solemn, eyebrows low. "You should at least eat," he said. "I've got food at home. Let me cook you dinner."

Lori raised an eyebrow again. He had a point; she couldn't leave until the next morning, her horse needed a rest. *And I do as well.*

She nodded. Perhaps he could still help her. He was a drunk, depreciated mess, but who else could she turn to? Who else might know about the Dark God?

"Right," he said, and waved to her. "I got me a little skiff down at the docks. This way. So...what brings you to Pismo?"

* * *

After a few more days of traveling, the fields appeared to be coming to an end. If the hilly terrain wasn't indication enough, the smell of salt on the breeze was unmistakable. It was a smell that Sora had read about many times in books, but had never experienced herself: a strange mix of fish and freshness. The sun was directly above them, but the heat of the fields had died off, gusted away by a consistent wind.

For the past several days, they had been on the lookout for trouble, especially since the Ravens had tracked them before. But so far, they had evaded any search parties. They had reached their destination without incident.

Sora rode with Crash behind her in the saddle. She had insisted on getting the first sight of the ocean. She didn't need his tall frame blocking her view. Burn rode in the lead, Laina's reins tied to the back of his saddle. Her steed plodded along behind him. She needed the help. Her wounded arm was strapped to her chest with strips of cloth, held stiff so that she wouldn't move her shoulder. The wound had been stitched, and Sora had been the one to do it; more techniques she had learned from her mother. She had a nagging suspicion that Crash could have sewn up the wound as well, but he hadn't offered.

Laina was uncharacteristically quiet, bearing the pain. The arrow had pierced deep into the muscle and would take several weeks to heal.

Crash shifted behind her, his chest against her back. She glanced over her shoulder to see him dig a hand into their saddlebag. After a moment of rummaging, he tugged loose an apple, then rubbed it on his pants. For anyone else, it would have been normal...but it was easy to forget that the assassin was just another human being who needed to eat and sleep, and might even have a fondness for fruit.

The hill they were on was a lot taller than it seemed, though the slope wasn't very steep. Sora noticed, with growing excitement, that they were almost to the top. She could hear the call of birds, cries like she had never heard before; a hollow *caw* that was much too high to be a crow.

Suddenly, a large white bird flew into view, quickly followed by a dozen more.

A few more paces and their horses finally reached the top of the incline; Sora gazed in amazement.

Below a series of jagged cliffs was a city so vast she couldn't see its limits. Endless miles of tiled roofs were painted every color imaginable, like a field of gemstones. There were stout chimneys, flying banners, skylights and weather vanes. Beyond the city was a long strip of ocean, blue and sparkling in the afternoon light, that stretched on forever, disappearing into a silver haze across the horizon.

Her eyes traveled inland. Giant ships bobbed gently next to a long, wide dock. Tiny specks of movement indicated the presence of sailors and merchants, horse carts, donkeys, oxen and other livestock. Her eyes widened as she took in all the vessels; everything from titanic seafaring ships to tiny dinghies and fishing boats. The dock was close to a dense web of streets, paved in bricks and stone.

"Sora," came Crash's voice in her ear, his breath warm across her cheek. "Close your mouth, you look like a fish."

Her mouth shut with a snap, but she continued to watch the scene with fascination. She could tell Crash was smiling when he gently reached around her and tugged the reins from her hands.

"The ground evens out this way," he said, and led them to the south, where the hill started to descend. Burn followed wordlessly, with Laina's horse in tow.

***

The port city of Delbar was huge, enough to make Sora feel very small and insignificant. It was even bigger than the city of the Goddess, nowhere near as orderly and perhaps twice as crowded. People with carts and wheelbarrows passed on every side. Peasants and nobles alike strutted along, some in a frantic hurry, while others stopped right in front of her. She would carefully guide her horse past them, avoiding their toes. The quality of the air in Delbar was also notably different, with none of the dust or heavy perfumes of Barcella; a sea breeze made everything seem fresh and clean.

She passed by a large group of women screeching outside of a bakery, waving tickets in the air; children ran around with dogs and played with ropes and sticks. It was enough to make her head spin; the noise was far worse than the endless bells of the Goddess.

Then she became distracted by the vendor carts, by the sight of brilliantly colored silks, velvet shoes, robes and hats...and the next thing she knew, she couldn't tear her eyes away. There were rich reds and purples, sky blues, deep golds. *Business, Sora, we're here on business,* she told herself firmly, forcing her hands to stay at her sides. She longed to touch the soft fabric, to feel its coolness on her skin. She hadn't experienced the luxurious sensation of silk since her manor days.

After what felt like hours of walking their horses, they spilled off the main road and onto the docks. Sora got her first close look at the ships; they bobbed and rocked on the water like giant cradles, a myriad of colors with different shapes of sails. Some were tall and narrow; others were broad and square. The hulls were covered in seaweed, barnacles and the occasional mussel or spiraling seashell.

A two-masted ship with three decks and several sails, each the width of a rooftop, had just docked in front of her. As she watched, sailors and dock workers began securing ropes to the mooring. A dock boom rested to one side, a lever-and-pulley contraption to unload crates from the ship's hold. *This must be a merchant vessel,* she thought, interested.

"See that short man with the ledger?" Burn asked, following her gaze.

Sora gave a start. She had been so focused on the ship, she hadn't noticed Burn join her. He walked his horse next to hers, one hand on the reins.

"Yes," she said, noticing a man with spectacles and a big velvet hat, holding a ledger in one hand and a large quill in the other.

"That's the dockmaster. He collects a fee from every boat in the port. If you can't pay up, they take your cargo."

Sora's eyes widened. A large man in a long blue coat approached the dockmaster. "That's the Captain," she guessed.

"Looks like it," Burn agreed. "They're probably bartering over prices right now."

Sora nodded, absorbing the scene. "How much does it usually cost to dock a boat that size?"

"Oh," Burn said nonchalantly, rubbing at his chin. "Maybe five-hundred gold."

You could buy a house for that amount! She thought, glancing around at all the ships moored to the docks. There were hundreds of them. This city is making a fortune! Everywhere, people walked back and forth, carrying luggage, ropes, nets of fish, shopping bags, tackle boxes. She shook her head slowly. *This place is a madhouse!*

Crash took control of their horse, his arms still around Sora and his hands on the reins. The horse walked down the thick wooden planks of the dock, Burn falling in step behind them. Then they stopped. She looked around, wondering why; Crash prompted her out of the saddle. She dismounted and he followed, landing silently. She shifted uncomfortably from foot to foot, stretching her legs. She had been in the saddle far too many days.

They stood in front of a two-story building that looked like an old country house, complete with balconies and smooth white columns. The windows were made to refract light into an array of colors that spilled onto the street. Sora gazed at the tiny rainbow-colored puddles, impressed. Sailors and other characters walked past her, casting sideways glances, probably wondering what had caught her attention; then they continued about their business.

"What's this?" she asked, looking the building up and down.

"A hotel," Crash said.

"What? Really?" She raised an eyebrow. "It must be incredibly expensive."

Crash shrugged, his eyes sliding away from hers. "I happen to know the owner," he said casually. "It's one of the safest establishments in the city. They have hidden watchmen posted in the lounge and upstairs rooms to make sure there's no trouble." He nodded to the broad double doors, painted a pristine white. "This is where we're staying."

Sora nearly choked. In her past life back at the manor, she might have expected such treatment. But now she was so used to sleeping in the dirt, the thought of stepping foot through those doors seemed wild and unimaginable.

"Truly?" she muttered, looking over the facade of the building.

She was nervous. Perhaps there was a back door they could go through? She hadn't seen her reflection in two days, and if Crash and Burn's appearance was any indication, she was a disheveled mess.

With that thought in mind, she walked over to the edge of the water, hoping she might catch sight of her reflection. There was a low railing along the side of the docks, and she leaned against it, staring down. It was a good ten or fifteen feet to the water. At this distance, the water was a dark bluish-green, and she could see seaweed and other debris floating beneath the surface. She wondered how deep it was. She had read tales of giant sea monsters with tentacles as big as trees, tempests that could swallow islands, and whirlpools that sucked entire ships into the deep.

For now, however, the ocean waves lapped shallowly against the docks, almost apologetically. *Nothing to see here,* it seemed to say. *Move along.*

"Did you drop something?" came a voice from behind her. It spoke in a strange accent that she had never heard before. When she turned around, a man with dark red hair and bright blue eyes was standing there. His face was shaped nicely, with a proud chin and a sharp jaw framed by a closely tailored goatee. A large black bird on his shoulder fixed her with a beady eye. Something about him was familiar, and Sora stared, trying to place him. He grinned and the moment of recognition was gone.

"Well, whatever ye lost ain't comin' back. Sometimes larger things will float in with the tide. 'Twasn't a child, was it?" The man chuckled. "Naw, a joke, 'tis all. And ye best be careful of any hats— the wind will take 'em right off your head! I've already lost seven hats this year."

At first, Sora could only stare at him, speechless. Then she glanced around. Where exactly had he come from? "I-I didn't drop anything," she finally said, and cleared her throat of its stutter. "I was just looking at the water. You see, this is my first time to the sea...."

"Fascinating, ain't it?" he said merrily. The black bird shuffled on his shoulder; Sora thought it might be a crow, though it looked larger. The man leaned next to her, looking down at the waves. "Never gets tiring. I remember the first time I saw the Vast. I must've been just a wee babe," he said. "Never ceases to amaze, though."

"The...the Vast?" Sora asked.

"The ocean, dear. Ah, here we go!" The man stretched out an arm and on cue, the bird swooped down at the water, flapping its big wings, and returned with a sopping wet lump of material. The man then wrung it out. Sora identified it as a wide-brimmed brown hat. She stared in amazement.

"Don't know what poor fellow lost this one, but it looks like a good fit," he said, putting the wet hat on his head. "What d'you think? Am I quite dashing?"

Sora tried not to laugh. Was he trying to be funny? "Yes...quite dashing," she grinned.

The man beamed back at her.

Then a black-gloved hand landed on her shoulder, and Sora let out a yelp of surprise. A voice from behind said, "Talking to strangers again?"

Sora turned around. Crash was standing behind her with a decidedly impatient air. "Burn and Laina just departed. The girl wanted to see more of the city." He didn't sound very happy about it. "I think we should take care of the rooms before they get back."

Sora nodded, forcefully ignoring his attitude. "I suppose," she agreed, then turned back to her new companion. "Uh, this man was just, eh, telling me about the Vast."

"Is that so?" Crash didn't sound at all enthusiastic. He looked the red-haired stranger up and down, from his tall brown boots to his sopping wet hat. He was a good head shorter than the assassin.

The man nodded at the hotel. "Nice place," he said, his eyes traveling over them again. "Expensive."

Crash's face darkened. "Come on, Sora." He grabbed her upper arm and wrenched her toward the hotel. "Let's not wait around."

She tried to pull back, embarrassed. "Hey, let go!" she exclaimed.

His hold loosened, but it was no less firm.

She walked away with the assassin, irritated, as the man watched. She felt embarrassed more than anything. When they had crossed to the other side of the street, she looked at Crash, her eyes narrowed. "That was very rude," she hissed. "We were just chatting."

"He could be a thief. You don't know city types. You're from out of town, and it shows."

Sora's mouth opened, surprised. "And what is that supposed to mean?"

Crash gave her a pointed look, but didn't reply.

I'm not some innocent country bumpkin! she thought, but it was only a short burst of anger. She reminded herself that she really shouldn't be surprised by this. Crash had a tendency to think the worst of everyone. He was suspicious to the point of paranoia...*but he's usually right, isn't he?*

She shook the thought away. Then he pushed her through the hotel doors.

The room they entered was bright and cheerful, although close to deserted. The only occupant was a lady with vivid red hair standing behind a large desk.

Sunlight streamed through the windows, spilling shards of light on the ground. The floor was not covered in straw like the inns she had seen before; rich blue carpet cushioned her feet. She slightly lifted her boots, wincing at the muddy footmarks they left on the lovely rug. There was an archway to one side, where the carpet turned into a swirling display of pastel tiles; she could see tables and lanterns set up throughout the opposite room. It was a restaurant. But the tables were not made of standard wood; they were of round, sturdy, smooth marble, like giant birdbaths.

A beautiful tile mosaic of an underwater city filled the entire wall in front of them. Behind the woman at the desk, a staircase led up to the second floor. And from the way the stairs were positioned, it looked like one could walk straight into the mosaic city, up through the tiled front gates.

As they stood there, a pair of richly dressed patrons in heavy satin robes and scarves walked down the staircase. The woman wore a long, deep purple gown with gold brocade. The man was in a burgundy suit, with a tall feathered hat stylishly slanted across his forehead. Their collars were decorated with the pins and insignia of the First Tier. They glided down the stairs together and passed the front desk, nodding to the desk clerk, who looked up.

"Have our carriage drawn to the entrance," the man said curtly as they swept out the front door. Sora caught the slightest glance of distaste from the noblewoman before they disappeared.

She immediately felt self-conscious. She could remember those looks from the nobles who would visit her manor, usually cast in the direction of a stable hand or a smudge-faced kitchen boy. Her cheeks flushed.

A bit of motion caught her eye and Sora looked up again. The red-haired woman had come out from behind her desk and was now approaching them. She was tall, lithe, and her blue eyes were trained on Crash.

"And how can I forget that face?" she said, a strange smirk around her lips. Then she gave Sora a brief nod, dismissing her as easily as a dust mote. "How long has it been? Three years? Four?"

Crash shrugged. "I'm here to call in that favor," he said quietly.

The desk clerk looked uncomfortable for a moment. She glanced around, as though suspecting that the walls had ears. "Now isn't the best time. Business has plummeted due to crime on the docks. It's been a slow season."

"Then you have a spare room," he said bluntly.

She frowned, a stern look coming over her face. Sora decided that she liked this woman who didn't seem at all intimidated by Crash. "We're also in need of your spare coin."

The assassin shifted, standing up a little taller. The woman took a slight step backward, perhaps unconsciously. Sora changed her mind. No one was immune to Crash's presence. She could feel unnerving energy radiating off him.

A few lanterns flickered in the restaurant. She wondered if that was a coincidence.

"We'll only be a few nights, until we can secure passage overseas," Crash murmured.

"Hm." Another long pause.

Finally, Crash said, "I spared your life once. Should I take it back?"

The woman's eyes darted between them. Her face paled. Sora had a hundred questions wanting to be asked, but she bit her tongue.

Finally, the desk clerk sighed. "I have a small room on the third floor that's reserved for royal messengers, but it's vacant for now. You can use it."

Sora saw the glimmer of a smile pass over Crash's face. "We are grateful."

"I'm sure," the woman said wryly. Then she reached to her belt and undid a large keyring. She picked out a long brass key and transferred it to Crash's hand. "I keep a master key to all of the rooms," she said. She glanced over them again. "And please, do clean up a bit. We have an image to uphold." Then, without any further words, she turned on her heel and walked away, exiting into the restaurant.

Sora waited until she was out of sight, then looked at Crash. "What was that all about?" she asked.

"A botched job, long time ago. I spared her life," the assassin replied. "I don't think she likes to be reminded of it." Then he started for the stairs.

Sora stared after him and suppressed a shudder. For some reason, his words felt like a slap in the face. Spared her life? Why? Had there been something between them? Or had he been hired to kill her? It left a sickening feeling in her stomach, sudden uncertainty. *Just who is this man traveling with me?* she thought, her eyes following him. A murderer, for certain. She had always known that about him. Why was she so surprised?

Her hand traveled to her Cat's Eye, hesitantly touching the stone through her shirt. She and Crash had become friends, yes...she had trusted him with her life on countless occasions. But what kind of friendship was this? Really, they barely knew each other.

They climbed two sets of stairs to the third floor. The hallways were decadent, with soft, shell-colored wallpaper and little basins for washing one's hands. Crash led her to the right wing of the third story, the farthest room that faced towards the ocean. All of the doors were white and rounded at the top with ornate trim. She waited as he unlocked their room.

He led her inside, and Sora's eyes widened.

She felt, perhaps, like she was falling in love.

Three large windows overlooked the docks and ocean, and a polished wooden floor shone beneath her muddy boots. There was a large marble table and three easy chairs; through the foyer were two hallways leading to two separate rooms, both of which had a view of the ocean.

One hallway led into an aqua-color carpeted bedroom with two large beds and a white marble bath large enough to fit three people, complete with running water; that was something Sora had never seen before. A white desk and chair stood near an open window, with gauzy white drapes billowing lazily in the wind; two white chests were at the foot of the giant beds. A mosaic of a beautiful mermaid adorned the wall opposite the windows.

The other room, far more masculine in decoration, had a midnight-blue carpet and two large beds. A black wardrobe and a dark cherry desk were next to the window. The tub was the same size as in the other bedroom, blue marble instead of white, also with running water, both hot and cold. There was a large painting of the surf breaking on the bow of a ship.

Sora and Crash admired both of the rooms. She walked to the window and looked down at the busy street. Then she walked back into the foyer and sat in one of the big easy chairs. She noticed a basket on the small table, filled with a bottle of wine and a pile of fruit. She wasn't a fan of wine, but she loved peaches, and grabbed one off the top.

After a minute, Crash sat down too. She smiled at him. "I feel like a queen," she said jokingly.

He raised an eyebrow, then took an apple for himself from the basket. "Really? I thought you'd be used to this."

"Well...my manor was just as nicely decorated," she admitted, remembering her large green-tiled bathroom and the decadent silks and scarves draped around her bedroom. "But I never really got the chance to travel."

"And is it worth it, giving up all that for a bit of travel?" he asked.

Sora was surprised by the question. In all honesty, she hadn't thought too much about her manor since leaving it, especially after discovering that the noble Lord had not been her real father. She shrugged, suddenly awkward. "I like my independence," she said. "I think it's better."

She let her eyes travel to a nearby window. From where she was sitting, she could just see the masts of the ships. More worries assaulted her mind. "How much money do we have for a ship?" she wondered aloud.

"Not enough for four people...even if we can find one heading for the Isles, which I highly doubt."

Sora frowned and looked at him. "Why do you doubt it? Aren't there any ships that head that way?"

Crash shook his head slowly. "The Isles are a tricky place. Sailors believe they're cursed. Then again, sailors believe a lot of things are cursed. I hear there are a lot of unusual storms out that way."

"So what should we do?" she asked.

"We need to find a captain and a crew foolhardy enough—or desperate enough—to take us there. And that's going to cost quite a bit more coin than just a ticket overseas."

Sora sighed in distress, her good mood gone. How were they supposed to make all of that money within a few days? They couldn't stay at this hotel forever, and Volcrian was surely on their trail. She still saw his image in dreams occasionally, his shadow looming out of alleyways or just beyond their campfire, his hands grabbing her from behind in an ice-cold grip. She couldn't tell such fears to Crash or Burn—they sounded silly even in her own head, but they were very real. She really hadn't slept peacefully since leaving her mother's house.

Thinking of sleep, she found herself sinking back into the easy chair, lured by its soft feather cushions. *No,* she told herself, trying to keep her dry, uncomfortable eyes open. *We have planning to do. We need to figure out our next step.* But her body suddenly felt so heavy...and the breeze from the open window was so sweet on her skin...the freshness of the air, the lulling rhythm of the waves. She closed her eyes, if just for a moment....

CHAPTER 11

Crash watched as Sora fell asleep. Her tiredness overcame her suddenly. He was surprised that it hadn't struck sooner—they had been traveling at a relentless pace since recovering the hilt.

She was beautiful when she slept, her face soft and open. He had the unexpected urge to touch her smooth skin, but he didn't let himself think of that. Instead, he changed his clothes, added a few daggers to his belt, and grabbed her satchel out of her room.

When he had recovered the bag from the bandits, he had found a letter inside it, along with the hilt. By the crispness of the paper, he knew the letter was recent, perhaps only a month old. It was a request for information. Three drawings of the sacred weapons, instructions on what to do if they were found...and a reward. It was sheer coincidence that the sword hilt had landed in the bandit's hands...but not so coincidental that the Shade were looking for it.

Speak to the owner of the Fine Pointe Tavern. He will give you further directions, the note read.

Crash could vaguely remember the Fine Pointe. Despite its highbrow name, it was a dirty little pub on the waterfront at the south end of town, or the "sunken end," as the citygoers called it. He had lived in Delbar for several months, back when he first left the Hive. It was a good place to get lost, filled to the brim with criminals, lowlifes, and unknown faces from exotic lands. He had once entertained the thought of catching a ship overseas, perhaps to the distant kingdoms in the West, where they said the deserts stretched on endlessly and the jungles were deep and fierce.

But he had gone to Crowns instead, the King's city, where he had been contracted to kill Volcrian's brother, ultimately sealing his fate.

Crash slid out of the hotel room and down the hall, taking a separate staircase meant for hotel workers only. It led him down three flights, past the kitchen and out into the stable yard. None of the workers glanced in his direction. Dressed in smart blue uniforms, they ran back and forth, carrying buckets and tack or hay for the horses.

He stepped out onto the street and headed toward the "sunken end" of town. True to its name, the city of Delbar was built on a slight incline, with the streets wending at a vague, downward slant. Because of this, the debris and refuse would wash down to the "sunken end" with each rain. That included human scum, as well.

He walked until the ships by the dock became low and grungy, some withered by age or abandoned in disrepair. The further he went, the shabbier the houses became, until he passed hollow buildings with roofs built from reed mats. The people changed too. The bright colors became washed out, the clothes were rattier, older. Barefoot children ran along the street, carrying sticks and rope, shouting and playing. Eventually he found his way to a small tavern, propped up between a shipping yard and an abandoned warehouse.

He entered the dark building. The tables were mostly empty, the chairs propped up on top of them, as it was still early in the day. A few waitresses sat in the back of the room, passing a bottle of wine around and chatting quietly, perhaps sharing the latest gossip before work. He headed directly to the bar, where the tavern owner sat with a tankard of ale, his stock inventory spread out before him.

"We're not open," he grunted as Crash stepped up to the bar. "Come back at sunset."

"I'm not here for a drink," Crash said. The man glanced up. He was definitely human, bordering on fat, with frizzy gray hair and a large handlebar mustache gracing his upper lip.

He gave Crash a narrow look. "Then you seem to be confused," the man said. "This is a bar, pup. Now go back to your boat and wait for sundown. I don't like pushy people."

Crash threw the letter on the table. "I've come about this."

The man continued to frown. He picked up the letter and unrolled it, carefully bending back the paper so it would stay open. Scanned the text. Then he glanced back at Crash, apparently less impressed than before.

"You ain't jokin'?" the tavern owner asked seriously.

Crash shook his head.

The man rolled his eyes. "Damn superstitious nonsense," he blurted out. "Well then, let me see it."

Crash hesitated, not expecting the request.

"The weapon, kid. Let's see what you got."

He didn't like it. Though he doubted the tavern master truly knew what the hilt was, he didn't want to risk putting it out in the open. The Shade could be watching at this very moment, perhaps disguised as one of the waitresses. Crash glanced at the back corner discreetly, surveying the four women; they wore low-cut, sloppy dresses, their hair piled on top of their heads. It was impossible to tell which one might be a spy—all of them looked suspicious.

He didn't know much about the Shade; only children's stories, leading back to the War of the Races. Supposedly, assassins of the Hive might also be part of the ancient Order, though they would never admit to it. There were many different colonies of assassins and the Shade stretched through all of them, a secret society of fanatic believers, servants to the Dark God. Some said that the Order had even pervaded the human world, infiltrating those with money and power.

He knew one thing, however—if the Shade was made up of assassins, they were all highly trained.

He set the bag on the table slowly, thoughtfully. Knowledge of the hilt would put Sora and the others in danger, but he didn't seem to have much choice. He would have to be careful on his way back, take plenty of detours, make sure he wasn't being followed.

He opened the bag and quickly brought out the hilt, allowing the tavern master to look at it, though he didn't set it on the table. Then he shoved it back in the bag before anyone could catch a glimpse. He could already feel eyes on the back of his neck.

"Hmph," the man said. "Not exactly a sword. But all right. Here," and he handed Crash a small, folded slip of paper, closed with a wax seal. "I'll let 'em know you're in town. They'll meet you at the bell tower in two days. Here are some further instructions."

Then the man turned back to his books and continued his accounts, ignoring Crash as though he didn't exist.

Crash turned and glanced around the room again, but none of the waitresses' eyes met his. He left the pub quickly, dodging out into the streets, submerging himself into the deepest traffic possible. No one followed him, but he kept an eye over his shoulder, looking for anyone who might lurk in the overhang of a building, or perhaps trail at a distance. He saw no one.

But he could feel it in his gut. Someone—or something—was watching him.

* * *

Far away—fields and fields away, as a matter of fact—a silver-haired figure arrived at a large town. The outer walls were strung with hundreds of bells, which shimmered and clanged with each gust of wind. He wanted to stuff cotton in his ears. The sound was disgusting. It jarred his teeth. Made his fangs hurt.

Volcrian dismounted at the city gates and entered the town slowly, hood lowered, shuffling close to the ground. To a stranger, he would have appeared ridiculous—but he was scenting the area, picking up hints and traces of another visitor, a female, the same scent he had followed through the fields....

"Hey!" a voice hailed him. "You there! Halt! We inspect all visitors who pass through these gates."

Volcrian turned, still bowed low to the ground, and opened his arms graciously to the approaching guard. "Sir," he said, a slight smile on his lips. "I am but a humble servant of the Goddess, here to worship at the Temple."

The guard, a dark-haired young fellow better suited for farm work, looked him over. He couldn't have been more than eighteen. "I'll be the judge of that," he said, with an unexpectedly hard tone.

Volcrian grinned again, then stood up straight. He was a few inches shorter than the lad. "You still offer refuge to travelers, do you not? I request a night in the Temple and provisions. I am a starving wanderer and I need rest."

The boy looked him over again. His appearance, at least, would echo his words. He knew his cheeks had grown more gaunt from the road, and his eyes were dark and sunken from nights of restless sleep. He had been having strange dreams of late...odd, worrisome dreams of being smothered in the earth, his arms locked to his sides, twisting and turning, full of rage....*Etienne,* he had thought. *It is Etienne rolling in his grave,* unable to rest until his killer was dead.

And yet, there was another darkness that accompanied his dreams, something that crept into the corners of his eyes, flaking like dirt.

Sometimes, he heard laughter.

"Well, you appear unarmed," the lad finally said, breaking Volcrian from his thoughts. "If you'll follow me, I'll take you to the Temple. It's safer this way. We've been having...riots...."

Volcrian had hoped that the guard would leave him alone, but it appeared he had no choice but to follow him. Oh well, perhaps he would get free provisions and a place to stay the night. He was tired of sleeping on the cold, hard ground...and his horse wasn't much of a companion.

As they entered the town, Volcrian could see what the lad was referring to. People packed the streets, some of them setting up tents on the sidewalk, passing out food and rations amongst each other. They all appeared thin, sickly, some with skin that was covered with sores and blisters, or nails that had turned black. The sound of voices was even louder than the cacophony of bells outside.

He avoided their stares, focusing solely on the road in front, keeping his crippled limb close to his side. The people were superstitious in these parts; they wouldn't trust the disfigurement, and it seemed like a disease was already spreading. *Dirty humans,* he thought. *Disgusting. They live in their own filth.*

They reached the Temple after almost half an hour of navigating the busy streets. Volcrian took to covering his face with his cloak, trying not to breathe in the sour smell of the sick people. Their hot breath and heavy sweat was a thousand times worse to his sensitive nose. The Temple towered above the rest of the houses, a domed roof with ornate gold designs running along its border, and a golden emblem at its peak. Even more bells and whistles adorned its walls, howling and whirring at each stroke of wind. Volcrian ground his teeth together. He couldn't stand the noise—how could anyone sleep with that racket? His fist clenched so tightly that his muscles cramped. His nails dug into the palm of his hand, drawing blood.

They paused at the Temple's front gates, which were made of wide golden bars. Her smell was everywhere, and he had to stop himself from dropping to the ground, pressing his face against the walls and breathing in her essence. Yes, his prey had visited here...and as he took in the air, he could smell something else, a darker scent, crisp and spicy. The aura of the assassin. But were they still in the city? He sniffed again, pulled the air through his quivering nostrils. No, the smell was several days old...but he was catching up.....

The soldier pulled a tassel that hung next to the gates, and an especially large bell started to swing back and forth, chiming loudly. Volcrian winced. How could they discern one clang from the next?

But somehow, they did. After a few moments, the gate opened. A young woman, obviously a priestess, stood there. From her plain robes, he knew she was new to the Order, perhaps recently promoted from acolyte. He doubted she even knew the Song of the Four Winds yet. Volcrian was unimpressed.

"This traveler claims he is on a pilgrimage," the soldier said, cocking a thumb in Volcrian's direction.

Volcrian curled his lip. The irony was killing him; he supposed he was on a pilgrimage of sorts. A far more lethal kind, though. "Show some respect," he snorted. "I have traveled far to be here."

The young priestess looked him over. Her brown eyes were wide and sincere, but he saw something flicker across her expression, something he didn't like. "Who are you?" she asked.

"My name is Volcrian. I come from the north," he said. "Across the mountains. I have traveled far and I am in need of rest."

The woman continued to regard him with that strange expression. "You are no pilgrim," she murmured.

"I beg your pardon?"

"You bring no sage, no herbs as offerings for the Goddess," she said. "We don't cater to common thieves or riffraff. Find another bed for the night."

Volcrian was shocked. Then his eyes narrowed. "Turned away by the Goddess herself?" he said in disbelief. "Hypocrite. Her Winds guide all things."

"But not you."

He took a step forward, suddenly forceful, set on making his way through the door—but the priestess put out her arm, blocking his path. Something about her closeness made his skin crawl. He bared his fangs. "Get out of my way," he growled. "I have asked for shelter and I shall receive it! I have traveled far, looking for three companions of mine. Perhaps you have seen them? A girl...."

"There is a dark aura around you," she said, cutting him off, her voice hushed. Then she turned to the soldier with the dark hair. "Bring help. Evict him from the city."

The soldier stared at them both, wide-eyed. "Really?" he stuttered, as though she had said a foreign word.

She nodded sharply.

He continued to stare at them for a moment, then stumbled away. He turned and ran down the street in the direction of the guardhouse.

Volcrian watched him go, a sneer of contempt around his lips. He was a Wolfy mage—no jail could hold him. He turned back to the priestess. "You're afraid of me," he murmured, and took a step closer to her. He felt power surge through his blood, flood his veins. Her heartbeat called to him; he could see it in her throat, practically taste her blood. He wondered if her blood would be different from the others, sweeter, full of the potent blessing of the Goddess. Or perhaps, it would be bitter and cold.

"Stand back!" she said, putting her arm out again, blocking the door. He felt the power in her words; she spoke with the authority of the Temple, but it merely shivered across his skin. He hardly flinched. "Come no closer, demon!"

He laughed. Laughed! "Hah! Demon, am I? You are sadly mistaken, my dear. I am a Wolfy mage...and I have need of blood."

"I see what you are," the woman whispered. "And you are a demon. There is darkness around you. Your wrath surrounds you like a red cloak. You must turn away from this path. It is devouring your soul."

Volcrian laughed again. What fun! A priestess who thought she knew something about magic. Stupid human. They would never understand the Wolfy race; his power thrived on the very essence of life. It couldn't be cursed. He was above curses, above nature, above stupid superstition!

But, if they insisted on treating him this way, then he might just have to become a demon....

"There he is!" a voice cried from behind him. He turned around on the steps, looking down at a cluster of guards who had assembled, swords drawn and shields at the ready, and rolled his eyes. Simpletons. Did they truly think weapons could harm him?

With a sickly glint in his eye, he grinned at the guards. "So you think you have me outnumbered," he said. "Well...you are sadly mistaken." Then he reached behind him, grabbed the priestess, and bodily dragged her before him. He yanked her arms behind her and clutched her throat with his crippled hand, grasping her under the jaw, cinching her wind pipe. Pain shot down his limb, the muscles cramping and contorting, but strangely enough, it felt good; like an addiction, he needed more. For a moment, he imagined that the limb was even stronger than his regular hand. He could feel her quiver in his grasp, the warmth of her skin, the desperate shallowness of her breath. She was like a rat clutched in the talons of an eagle, fully aware of her fate.

"You called me a demon," he growled. Hatred surged in him. It had become a constant companion, this wrath. Always roiling beneath the surface of his skin, leading him, egging him on. He submitted to it now, bowing his head. He would not stand in his own way. "But I am nowhere near as evil as the demon I hunt."

Then he clenched his fist, crushing the woman's throat, feeling her bones snap in his hand. His long nails, like talons, buried themselves in her skin. Blood ran across his fingers, down his wrist, into the sleeve of his shirt. A shimmer of electricity shot through him, a bolt of lightning, every nerve coming alive.

He dropped the body to the ground, still twitching and convulsing. Unconsciously, he licked the blood from one of his fingers. When he looked back to the soldiers, he felt nothing but power. He could sense their hesitation, see the horror on their faces.

"Now," he said, "where are we going?"

* * *

Sora woke up with a stiff neck and even stiffer legs, but she felt wonderfully lazy and content. From the shadows in the room, she could tell that the sun was low in the sky. It had been only a few hours since she had fallen asleep, but she felt completely refreshed.

She stood up, looking around the empty room. She wondered where Crash had gone, and whether or not Burn and Laina were back. Then she let out a deep sigh. It was good to be alone. *Do I remember seeing a bath around here somewhere?*

She tapped on the door of her room, wondering if Laina was inside. When no one answered, she opened it and looked around. The beds were still untouched and the room was empty. Her eyes landed on the bathtub in the corner and she grinned wickedly. No one was around—the perfect time to take a bath! She dashed to the tub, suddenly paranoid that people would arrive at any second.

Upon inspection, Sora had to admit that it was the cleanest tub she had ever seen, barring her manor, of course. It stood on four porcelain feet upon a patch of white tile. Towels were hung over its side. But...how to fill it? Her eyes lingered on the brass pipes that arched over one side, where water was obviously meant to pour out. Now...how did she turn it on? She had never seen running water before.

She stood back and studied the odd metal mechanisms. Then she tapped one of the pipes and stuck her finger up the spout, wiggling it around a bit. Nothing happened.

Then she noticed the handles. With the utmost caution, she twisted one of the levers and leapt back in surprise. Water squirted out of the pipe, whining and hissing like a wounded animal. When she stuck her hand under the flow, she found it to be icy cold. Horrible! Quickly, she shut the water off, then fiddled with the opposite handle until it turned on. A steaming torrent spewed forth, so hot it could have boiled a lobster. She turned that one off too, then stood back to think. *How in the world do these things work?* The water was either too hot or too cold!

After several minutes of pondering in silence, Sora finally decided to turn both faucets on at once. This worked a bit better, and after a tweak or two, she found the perfect temperature. With a victorious smile, she left the bath to fill on its own.

As she waited, she undressed and wrapped a complimentary towel around her small form. Then she walked over and opened the windows, letting a brisk sea breeze blow against her face.

Sora took a deep breath and let it out slowly. Her mind wandered. She thought of the Priestess, of the Temple in Barcella and the journey ahead. She still felt a horrible sense of uncertainty when she considered the Lost Isles, and what she might have to do to kill Volcrian. *Will I have to remove the necklace?* The Cat's Eye weighed heavily on her neck, and for a moment, she imagined it was a collar tied to a strict leash. She touched the stone, wondering about its bond with her mind. Sometimes, it felt as though a ghost were living inside of her.

And to break that bond...to remove the necklace....A chill went down her spine. *Will my spirit be sucked inside of it? Half-alive, half-dead, trapped in a rock?* Or would she simply go into a coma, sink into darkness and disappear? Cease to be?

And what if, somehow, I survive? That, too, was terrifying. She could no longer remember what life had been like before the Cat's Eye; what her *mind* had been like.

How am I ever going to do this? How was she supposed to defeat Volcrian? She wore a Cat's Eye, sure, but she didn't know anything about magic or Wolfy mages. His spells were powerful; she would be dead by now if it weren't for the necklace. What would it be like to meet the mage face to face? She paused, trying to connect with the stone, hoping for some murmur of comfort, the familiar jangle of bells.

But it was silent.

Positive, Sora told herself. She had to think positively. She forced her thoughts to go in another direction—yes, her manor, before her father's death. She imagined her wide, green tiled bathroom; the endless corridors and richly decorated chambers. It felt like she had lived there so long ago. She wondered briefly about Lilly and the other maids. What had happened after her foster father's death? Who owned the manor now? What family member had come to claim it? She tried to remember names and faces, but it all seemed vague and washed-out, like a faded painting.

She returned to the giant tub and leaned over its edge, brushing her fingers through the water. It was almost halfway full. With this in mind, she undid her braid and combed out her hair with a boar bristle brush. It had grown since she had last braided it, and it flowed like a shower of gold over her shoulder. It felt good to release the tension from her scalp.

"Sora, we need to..."

With a yelp, she leapt to her feet, whirling around. "Don't you people ever make any noise?" she practically screamed.

She was met by Crash's stunned face. He stared at her, obviously stricken. She had never seen such a peculiar expression before. Then she realized she was in a towel...a very short, small towel, now that she thought about it...with more than a bit of skin showing.

His eyes flickered over her. They flashed a darker shade of green, almost predatory, and she took a startled step back. Then he blinked and the expression—or whatever it had been—was gone.

Sora gulped and pulled the towel closer around her, hoping to retain some dignity. Finally she found her voice, and raised her head a notch. "I was just about to take a bath, but I can wait as long as it's quick. Either get in or get out, just don't leave the door open."

The assassin stepped in quickly and shut the door, and thankfully, his eyes focused on the tub behind her. "I'll be going to look for a map of the Isles pretty soon. There is also a weapon maker in town known for his bladework." He paused. His gaze flickered over her once more before focusing on one of the beds. "I was wondering if you'd like to come. Laina and Burn are still out."

Sora blinked. "So, just what are they doing, exactly?"

"Touring," he shrugged.

Sora was quiet as she tried to make her brain work. "Touring at night?" she finally asked.

"I guess they're having a good time."

"At least somebody is," she muttered. "They better not be wasting money...."

"I'm sure they will." Crash's tone was wry.

Sora gave up with a sigh and looked back at her tub. "I'll be quick in the bath, though I was planning to have a soak." She ran her hand along the smooth marble. "I'd rather go with you than be stuck here alone."

"All right," Crash nodded.

She frowned. Was it just her, or did his voice seem rougher than usual? "Would you close the window?" she asked in concern. "It sounds like you're getting a cold. Do you have a sore throat?"

Crash's eyes darted to her face, and again they became that dark green color. The expression held longer this time, and Sora felt a peculiarly warm, squirmy feeling in her stomach. Abruptly, she wished there was more between them than just a towel and twenty feet of floor space.

He stared at her for a moment longer, then turned to the window. "No, I'm fine," he said quietly, though his pitch had dropped another notch. He shut the window anyway. Then he gave her one last look before stepping quickly out the door, closing it behind him.

Sora sagged visibly, relieved that she was alone again. She shut off the water before the tub overflowed and let the towel drop to the ground, then climbed into the warm water and felt her muscles relax immediately. With a long, luxurious sigh, she grabbed the bar of soap and started washing off a thick layer of road dust. Then she set about brushing and cleaning her hair, scraping the dirt from her nails and scrubbing her face. Finally she deemed herself clean and arose from the brownish water.

Sora toweled off and dressed quickly in fresh clothes. Then she threw on her cloak, allowing her damp hair to hang free. With a happy sigh, she stepped out into the main room where Crash was waiting.

Immediately he stood up from his chair. "Ready?"

"Ready as ever," she replied with a smile. "Where to first?"

She could have sworn Crash smiled in return, but he turned to the door so quickly, she couldn't be sure. "Let's get the weapons first, then we'll look for a map."

He opened the door and ushered her through, then shut the door behind them, locking it securely.

"You keep a lot of stuff under your cloak," she observed as he tucked the key into its black folds. She had seen him take a myriad of objects from beneath it: knives, lock picks, rope, sticks of dried meat.

"That I do." The assassin started off at a brisk pace down the hall, and Sora fell into step next to him. She cut off a sarcastic remark she was about to make.

Outside, night was falling, and she could already feel the chill from the ocean. Amazingly enough, she could see frost on her breath, despite the fact that winter was long gone.

Crash slowed down once they were on the streets. He seemed to be in no big hurry, and soon she realized why. All of the shops were still open! She looked around at the bright lanterns and twinkling lights. The sun was less than a gold tint on the horizon, and the streets were alight with paper lanterns. They reminded her of colored bubbles, strung from balconies and awnings, casting a rainbow of light across the flagstones.

In smaller towns, the stores began to close at sunset so that everyone could be home by nightfall.

"What time is it?" she finally asked, after they passed the third shop with lights on. Crash glanced at her, then up at the rising moon.

"I'd say around nine o'clock," he calculated.

"Then why aren't the stores closing?"

He gave her a strange look, then shook his head as he realized, "You've never been on the coast before, have you?"

Sora continued to stare up at him questioningly. He returned her look, then motioned to the buildings around them. "Here, the stores are open twenty-four hours a day. Well, most of them. You never know when a ship will pull into harbor. Sailors make good customers." He glanced back down at her. "Relax, we're in no hurry."

This was so unexpected that Sora almost choked. Crash—relax? As though he knew how! All of the times she'd seen him before, he had either been fighting or on the lookout for trouble. Except for once, almost a year ago, when they wrestled in the mud outside of her mother's house....

They walked down the streets and looked in shop windows. Most were pottery shops or carried similar merchandise, but Sora was still fascinated; she had never seen so many stores in a row; they seemed to go on forever. And she wanted to see everything: pottery, porcelain, glass blowers, fresh-cut flower stands and clockmakers. At first Crash was reluctant to go into the stores, but she dragged him along anyway, ignoring his stiff arm.

After almost an hour of wandering from shop to shop, they finally found the weapon maker. Crash led her to the front door and said dryly, "It seems we have come to a shop with some practical use. I'd invite you in, but regrettably, they don't sell jewelry."

Sora blinked, wondering if she should be insulted...but then she realized he was joking. Maybe. "We only went to three jewelry stalls," she muttered irritably.

They entered the shop. The building had a curious layout: a completely open floor with weapons strung along the walls, less of a selection than she had expected, brightly lit with oil lamps. The back of the building opened onto a wide dirt yard, where a massive cast-iron forge was sunk into the ground. Sora stared; she had never seen a forge before. It reminded her of a stone cave, perhaps twice her height. The flames were banked for the moment, but she could imagine how hot they could get.

Then a woman stepped inside, wiping her hands on her pants. She appeared to have been working near the forge, as her clothes were streaked in soot and ash. Sora was surprised. She had expected a giant, hulking man, but by the heavy apron that covered the woman, she guessed that this was the weapon maker. Her hair was short and silvery, her figure tall and willowy, and a pair of brilliant violet eyes stared through the shadows.

She had a cigar in her mouth. After a moment, she exhaled a puff of smoke, then put the cigar on a tray on the counter. When she spoke, her voice was unexpectedly deep. "May I help you?"

Sora turned around to find Crash glaring at the store clerk.

The woman offered a small smile, though it was decidedly cold. "Welcome to my shop," she said in that smooth, rich voice. "I take custom orders, or you can see what I have on the shelves."

"A poor selection," Crash muttered, and Sora looked at the assassin in surprise. He threw a pair of daggers on the wood counter; they were about nine inches in length and perfectly straight. The hilts were slightly more ornate than what he usually carried. She wondered where he had grabbed them—she hadn't seen him pull them from the wall. "This steel is low-quality. I won't pay more than two silvers."

The woman arched a pale eyebrow. "Then you have bad taste. I won't sell them for less than five."

"You couldn't pierce cowhide with these," Crash said; Sora raised an eyebrow. The assassin took one of the knives and tried to stick it into the wooden table. It fell over, blunt at the tip.

"Sharpening is extra," the woman glared.

"This steel won't hold an edge for long. Two silvers, and I'll sharpen them myself." He tossed the coins onto the table.

The two stared at each other for a long, acrimonious moment. Sora was mortified. Wasn't there such a thing as civility? Crash was acting like a complete barbarian!

Finally, the woman took the coins. "If only to get you out of my store," she said.

Crash grabbed Sora's upper arm hard; instinctively, she struggled. "That's it?" she growled, trying to tug free. She wanted to melt into the ground, she was so embarrassed. "I like it here! Let's look around a bit longer!"

Crash's grip tightened, almost bruising her. "Bad quality," he snapped. "Let's go."

The shopkeeper continued to stare at them with unblinking eyes. It was humiliating; Sora couldn't understand why the assassin was acting this way. Then her temper began to rise. First the man in front of the docks, and now this—why did Crash suddenly feel as though he had a right to bully her? Her noble upbringing came to the surface; *no one handles me like this!*

"Let go of me!" Sora said shrilly, and twisted in Crash's grip. She used one of her mother's techniques and slipped from his grasp. "This is a perfectly good store. You're being very rude!"

"If you don't mind me saying, miss," the shopkeeper said in a warm tone, "I wouldn't expect anything else from his kind. I'd suggest you find a new friend."

Sora was surprised by the woman's words. The assassin spat at the storekeeper, then turned and glared at her—a look that Sora had once found terrifying, but now only made her angrier. "Why are you arguing?" he snapped. "Come on."

She knew if she stayed, she would only provoke him further. With an embarrassed nod to the weapon maker, she allowed Crash to lead her forcefully out of the store. Once in the street, she whirled on him, livid with rage.

"What was that all about?" she hissed, her voice barely above a whisper. "You *wanted* to come here, remember? And why insult the shopkeeper? Why drag me from the store?" She glared extra hard at him. "You treated me like an animal! And that poor woman did nothing but help you!"

Crash's eyes hardened, and Sora instinctively stepped back. She lifted her head and resisted him.

"You wouldn't understand," he growled, "and I'm not going to explain it to you." She felt like he could burn her down with his eyes. "You're completely ignorant."

"At least I have dignity!" Sora's patience snapped like a string. "I've been raised since I was born to carry myself in a certain way. You can't just treat people like dirt! Learn some common decency!"

Crash made a dismissive motion with his hand. "Why cater to the feelings of others? You don't *actually* care about them, do you?"

"I do!" Sora exclaimed. "And that's beyond the point. It's just manners!"

"Manners?" he quipped. "Why, did I embarrass you?"

"Perhaps!" Sora admitted. "I don't like it when you're rude. It makes you incredibly difficult to be around."

"Then leave!" he said coldly. "Go back to the hotel. I don't care."

Sora paused. He didn't mean that, did he? *Of course he does,* she thought. Why fool herself into thinking otherwise?

The assassin took a step forward. Her skin crawled. She felt a sudden, unnerving aura of power around him. She swallowed her fear and braced herself.

"There is something you need to understand, little girl. I have *killed*," his voice was low and bitter. "I've spent a lifetime doing it. I am not a good man, so don't expect me to behave as one. Volcrian's hunt is justified. I am an assassin. *Manners* don't hide what I am."

Her breath caught. For a moment she was speechless—*what do you say to that?* Then she drew her anger around her. "You're right. You're just a criminal, a murderer!" she hissed. She thought he might have flinched. "I've tried to look past that, Crash. But you're right. You're a killer. You'll never change."

Abruptly he turned away, his face shadowed and his voice quiet. "Just because you have shared my food and slept by my fire, you assume to know me. You know *nothing*."

With that, he pushed past her roughly. She fell back against the wall of a building as he walked away. Sora stared at his back, stunned by his reaction, and placed one hand on the wall.

His words slowly took effect. She bit her lip, tears welling up inside of her. *Gods, I will not cry!*

His rage stung more than it should. No, it didn't sting, actually it ripped like a knife. With a force of will, she blinked back her tears. Sora didn't follow him or try to face him; instead, she made her way hastily out into the street.

She followed a cobblestone walkway that led her between two buildings; then onto another street that was identical to the first. She walked for several minutes, not paying attention where she was going, blinded by hurt and anger, not thinking coherently. Her fists were clenched tight and her head was full of harsh words and the look in his eyes.

The paper lanterns gave way to less decadent streets, farther from the docks. The houses became darker and lower, leaning close as though huddling together for warmth. Eventually, she found herself in a small courtyard; at its center was a weathered statue that might have been a likeness of Kaelyn the Wanderer. The pose was a familiar cast, the Wanderer standing with her hands poised near her face, a flute held to her lips. Except that the flute was gone from the eroded statue; the lady was playing on empty air.

The small square was vacant, but she was too upset to keep walking. She sat down at the side of the statue, hidden by shadows and curled up, her forehead pressed against her knees, alone in the night.

Crash's voice echoed around her head. *I have killed,* it said. *Manners don't hide what I am.*

And after all she had risked to come here....

She reached down, grabbing a pebble on the ground and hurling it against the wall in front of her. It bounced off harmlessly. *Bastard.* Hot, angry tears leaked from her eyes. Sora let them fall as she sat quietly amidst the dust and gloom. Why had she even tried to find him? Why had she left her mother? She should have let Volcrian take them all. Who cared about a plague, with so many evil people in the world? And why enlist the help of a dark, bitter man like Crash? She blinked through her tears and took a shaky breath.

Why did it hurt so much? She knew how he was, always moody and brash. Just look at how he treated Laina.

But this time, it was personal. She had thought she was different, immune to his anger. That perhaps he liked her, even just a little.

Sora let out a breath of frustration through her tears. She picked up another rock and hurled it. She was supposed to be stronger than this. Why couldn't she be like Kaelyn, fierce and proud, fighting for justice? Her eyes glanced up at the weathered statue, the empty indents for eyes, the partially crumbled nose. Even against the salty air and countless rainy nights, the rock refused to give way, standing strong against the elements.

But she wasn't a rock. Maybe she wasn't like her hero at all.

Sora sighed harshly. *I can't save the world.* She was going to die at the end of this journey. It was a nagging truth, one she tried to avoid thinking about. *There's no way out. I'm going to die—and for what?*

This was enough to renew the tears and soon she was having trouble keeping her sobs inside. She held her knees tighter and looked around at the dark, gloomy, abandoned streets. *How did I get here?* It suddenly seemed ludicrous, insane; how had she come to be in an alley, alone, somewhere on the coast, miles away from her birthplace?

This is a waste of time, Sora. Get yourself under control, her inner voice said. She had fought Catlins and risked life and limb before. Why was it so easy for a few harsh words to hurt her? *You have to carry on.*

The hard stone bit through the seat of her pants. It was growing colder, yet she could not make herself get up. *I can stay here all night,* she suddenly thought. She had slept on the ground plenty of times before. In the morning, she would go back for her horse and leave, return to her mother's house where she was loved and needed. Where she belonged.

A sudden shadow entered the courtyard. Sora tensed. She hadn't heard any footsteps, but as she watched, a figure emerged from the overhang of a building, as smooth and silent as a ghost. Just from the way he moved, she knew who it was.

He stopped in front of her, a mere foot away. She waited, unwilling to speak because she didn't want him to hear the weakness in her voice. She couldn't stand looking at him. Was he really here? Why? It was the last thing she had expected.

Sora pulled her legs up to her chest and pushed her forehead against them, closing her eyes, trying to disappear.

After a moment, a hand touched her hair. She flinched, uncertain. The hand continued to caress the same lock of hair over and over.

There was a stretch of silence; then the assassin said a little irritably, "Come now. Don't pout."

She could feel the tears start again at those words, and her resolve buckled. Against her will, a tiny sob escaped.

This time, Crash didn't just content himself with touching the lock of her hair, but took her hands and pulled her gently to her feet. She had little strength to protest. She kept her face turned away, clamping her eyes shut, trying to keep the tears from rolling down her cheeks.

In careful detail, she felt one of his hands brush the hair back off her face and tilt her chin upward. She blinked through the tears to find his green eyes staring into her, bright against the night, as though lit from inside. She wanted to hide, to bury her face against something, to pull away—but she could do nothing.

"I...I'm not strong," she finally confessed, trying to excuse her tears. "I'm too soft, Crash. Maybe I am too open and trusting. I try to see the best in people. I'm not the right person for this journey."

"*Shush*," he whispered, and pulled her to him. His arms went around her, and Sora found herself wrapped in his warmth. One arm went around her back while the other hand cradled her neck. Her head didn't even reach his shoulder, and she buried her face in his chest. He held her tightly.

"Why do you act so cold?" she said, muffled by his shirt.

"It's been...necessary...for me to survive," he murmured.

She understood that. A lifetime of killing couldn't be easy; she wondered what kind of demons he lived with, wondered if he had regrets, doubts. "I don't know why you're here," she said, struggling to speak despite the lump in her throat. "Why you decided to help me. It's a suicide mission. Honestly, I'm terrified, Crash. I try not to think of it, but...by the end of this, I might be dead." She looked up, though crushed against his chest. "I'm willing to die next to you— and I don't even know who you are. What is wrong with me?"

Crash gazed at her for a long moment, his eyes shadowed. She felt like she was staring up at a dark tower, a vague light at its peak. "I don't deserve it," he said quietly. "I can't lie to you about that. I don't deserve your friendship or your sacrifice."

"Why are you here, Crash?" she asked, just like she had asked him once before, back in the gardens of the Temple.

"To protect you."

She was silent.

"Sometimes..." Crash started, then stopped. "Sometimes the heart doesn't make any sense. Sometimes we don't even know our own intentions. You're trying to help the world, Sora. I don't think it's just your Cat's Eye. But you can't do it alone." He lowered his head slightly, and she felt his hand travel over her back. "You don't have to be strong all of the time. That's asking a bit much. You can be soft too, if that is who you are. I...I came to protect you."

Sora wasn't sure she had heard him right. She looked up at him, uncertain. *Protect?* How could a killer protect the living?

"It's weak to be soft," she said instead. "I should take care of myself." Weakness didn't belong in an adventure. How was she supposed to be like Kaelyn, like the Wanderer of old, if she was too fragile to handle a harsh word? "I don't want to be a burden...."

"All friends are burdens," Crash said quietly. "But we carry them anyway."

A typical statement, coming from him, and yet it was as though a great weight had been lifted from her; as though she finally had permission to be who she was. She couldn't take it. She buried her head against his chest again, trying to hide from his intensity. His hand continued to stroke her hair methodically, calming her, allowing her time to compose herself.

Finally, her throat loosened. She felt as if she could breathe, perhaps even better than before. She stayed in his warm embrace for a moment longer. Then, with a sigh, she looked back up at him.

"I think I'm okay now," she murmured hoarsely.

"Are you sure?"

"Yeah."

He let his arms drop and she stepped away, suddenly self-conscious. They had been so close...she could still feel his body imprinted on hers, his warmth thrumming in her blood. She wanted him to hold her again; she yearned for that close contact.

She smiled, trying to look cheerful. It was a sorry attempt. "Let's go." She tugged his arm.

Crash gave her a small grin in return. There was an openness in his expression that she hadn't seen before, something vaguely welcoming. For once, he moved slowly enough so she could walk next to him, at her own pace. They headed back down the cobblestone pathway, leaving the old statue behind, past the silent houses with their black windows, then traveled through a pocket of back alleys, gray and deserted.

After a few minutes, the pair found their way back to the main road. A gust of chill wind from the ocean reached them. Sora shuddered at how cold it was, and pulled her cloak closer. Obviously the moisture from the water was making the temperature drop. The streets widened and light from the windows began to illuminate their path. The bobbing paper lanterns returned. A group of people passed by them, laughing and stumbling into one another. Soon the streets were full of pockets of people, hanging around outside brightly lit taverns or houses. Everything looked more familiar.

Sora looked at Crash. They had been wandering somewhat aimlessly for a while. "So, where are we going?" she asked.

Crash glanced down at her from the corner of his eye, then back to the street. "The map maker," he finally answered, as though his thoughts had been somewhere else. "Hopefully he'll have something on the Isles."

The street took a downward path, and she altered her gait accordingly. Crash stopped sooner than she expected in front of a small, cramped shop with boards over the windows, through which a dim light slanted. Sora could see that the windows had been broken at one time. Across the street, a group of red-haired men sat, sharing a bottle of wine and laughing loudly. She tried not to stare at them as Crash led her into the shop. *Why are there so many redheads in this city?*

The inside of the store was warm and bright, and smelled like old pipe tobacco and dusty paper. There were rows of tables, and shelves covered in rolled-up parchment. The shopkeeper was in clear view, standing with his back to them, hunched over a table.

Sora stared in surprise at the scruffy old man; he was hovering over a large book, but his figure seemed familiar. She leaned to one side slightly, trying to get a glimpse of his face. Over a year ago, she and Crash had gone to a similar store in the town of Mayville. It seemed impossible, but...if her eyes weren't deceiving her, this was the exact same mapmaker!

Everything from his stiff gray hair to his large nose was the same as before, yet it seemed as though he had lost his hat. She leaned over so far to see him, she bumped into a table, causing it to inch noisily across the floor. The mapmaker stood up and turned toward them. Yes, even his piercing blue eyes were the same.

"Ach, customers, and at this time of night!" he said sourly. "How'd you get in?"

Sora was surprised. "Uh...the door was unlocked...?"

The old man snorted. "Nonsense, locked it meself 'bout an

hour ago. Oh, well! I'd be grateful for your coin, if you're willing to part with it. What are you looking for?" He stared at them, his eyes narrowing. Sora wondered if he recognized them, too. *He's a senile old man,* she reminded herself. *Can't even remember if he locked his door or not.*

"You," he said suddenly, unexpectedly, pointing a gnarled finger at Crash. "We have done business before."

Crash nodded. Sora wondered why the man remembered the assassin but not her. "We are looking for a map to the Lost Isles," he said.

The old man chuckled from somewhere deep in his throat and began shifting through piles of parchment on one of the tables. "An adventurer like myself, I see...why go there? The Lost Isles—better they didn't even exist. What about your lady friend? Certainly, she would like to go somewhere more...cheerful." The old man winked at her, a gap-toothed grin splitting his face. "Why not the King's City of Crowns? It is beautiful this time of year, and you can get there quickly by sailing north to the mountains, then down the Little Rain River. They'll be holding the winter carnival soon. It should be a mighty big one, celebrating 300 years of peace."

Sora shook her head, and the man waggled his eyebrows. "Oh? Then can I interest you in the Glass Coast?" He held up another map. "Half-price. I've got about a hundred extra copies. Beautiful beaches, caves where the stones sparkle like stars, and the sunsets turn green against the waves! The sand there has turned to glass over hundreds of years of lightning storms...it's quite the sight to see...."

Sora was shaking her head. The old man's speech stumbled to a halt, and he sighed. "Why the Lost Isles?" he repeated. "You know they are cursed."

Crash coughed. "Far from it, my friend. And I know that for a fact. We are going there for personal business, and you are safer not knowing about it. Do you carry a map?"

The old man nodded slowly. "I didn't make it myself, but yes, I do have a map of the Lost Isles. Bought it from a traveler a long time ago. I won't part with it cheaply."

Sora wanted to sigh. Was anything cheap anymore? "How much?" she asked.

"Let's have a look first," Crash said.

The old man traveled to the other side of the room, using a withered cane for support. He opened up a large chest near the far wall and rummaged through it a bit, then brought out a small square of paper. Sora was surprised. She had expected something larger and far grander. Instead, the map looked like it had been drawn on a scrap of leather, perhaps someone's handkerchief or bandana.

"It is a bit old, but I doubt much has changed out that way over the past decades. You are aware of the storms?" The mapmaker said, giving Crash a dark look.

The assassin nodded. They followed the man to a large table and he spread out the piece of leather, holding a light close to it. Sora stared at the scratchy ink and burn marks. She could make out a thick line where the coast was, and an indication of Port Delbar, but the rest was unreadable. Crash, however, was slowly nodding.

"We will need a compass as well," he said.

"Altogether, I'll give you the map for twenty silvers...and I'll throw in the compass for free."

Twenty silvers? That was enough to buy a new horse! Sora

opened her mouth to speak, then Crash said, "I'll pay no more than four."

"You cut a hard bargain. Let's say fifteen."

"Six, then."

Sora rolled her eyes, uninterested in haggling. She was simply no good at it; in all honesty, she found the process stressful. She had grown up in a safe, sheltered manor where she had never had to shop for herself. After moving in with her mother, haggling and bargaining had remained one of the great mysteries. She had no knack for it, and she hated the feeling of being cheated out of her money.

As the two men talked business, she wandered around the store looking at the items on the dusty shelves. Most of the parchments were untitled, but every shelf was either numbered or lettered. Some of the shelves were categorized by region, "Southland" or "Northland," all in regard to the King's city. And then there were more curious labels. *The Bracken, Valco, Ester*....She ran her fingers along the bookcases. Just how large was the world if it could contain so many maps?

"Ester," she suddenly heard from behind her. She turned to find the mapmaker looking over her shoulder. "A land far to the East, past the Bracken. Used to be a lush kingdom, but after the War of the Races, it's now a desert. They say you can still find the floating ships of the Harpies buried in the sand. There are entire ship graveyards."

Sora's eyes widened. She hadn't learned much geography in her manor; most of her studies had focused on propriety and arithmetic. She was always interested in the War. "Ester?" she murmured.

"Yes. We get treasure hunters coming through here, looking for maps. They seem to think there is a great treasure buried out there, something that the Harpies left behind."

She could see Crash behind the mapmaker, tucking his coin purse into his cloak. He grimaced at the mention of Harpies. Sora frowned. Come to think of it, she had seen him act that way before on several occasions. Maybe it was more than coincidence?

"And the Bracken?" she asked, pointing to another section of the store.

"A dark forest, not for young ladies like yourself," the mapmaker grinned. He seemed to be enjoying this. "I see you have a witch wood staff. That obviously came from the Bracken. It's the only place where the black trees grow. Nigh indestructible, that staff, and priceless. Try not to lose it."

Sora nodded slowly. She could remember the weapons dealer they had bought it from. He had mentioned something similar, though it was so long ago that she couldn't remember all of the details. "I've heard that the wood is magic," she said, her interest piqued.

"It certainly is," the mapmaker agreed. "It will react to certain areas, especially those that are sacred. But I don't know much about that. Not many sacred areas left. Magic is fading from the world."

Sora wanted to ask what he meant by sacred, but the mapmaker moved away abruptly, and Crash took his place. They seemed to be at odds with each other now, and she assumed Crash had talked him down to a good price.

The assassin looked her over quickly. "We're done here," he said.

She nodded. Honestly, she wanted to stay longer in the store, but she got the sudden feeling that they weren't all that welcome. The mapmaker was bustling around, apparently eager for them to leave. She reminded herself that the front door was supposed to be locked.

With a nod to the old man and a small smile, she turned and headed for the exit. There were many lands beyond their Kingdom, she knew that much, but she didn't think she would ever get the chance to see them. Their world was shielded by wilderness on every side, and they hadn't come in contact with any new peoples or civilizations for hundreds of years. Even the kingdoms they traded with were overseas, offering no threat of war. She wondered if it would remain that way.

As the two left the shop, Sora noticed that the band of rowdy redheads had disappeared, probably off causing some kind of mischief. She wondered if the man she had met near the docks was related to them. Perhaps they were a large family?

With Crash at her side, they headed off into the night.

CHAPTER 12

"Looks like we're at the docks," Sora said. The two had been walking quietly, each lost in their own thoughts, but she was tired of the silence. Now she looked around. The cobblestones spanned out in different directions, and there was an endless row of bobbing ships before them, their sails drawn in for the night. She was mesmerized by the sight of the black, inky water, the streetlights dancing across its surface. So beautiful...*how could I have lived my life without knowing of something like this?* The lights from the stores lit up the water, as though gold treasures lay hidden beneath the surface. After a moment, Crash nudged her shoulder.

"So...where do you want to go?" he asked, his eyes roaming up and down the docks. "Anything you want to see?"

It was unexpected. Crash—sightseeing? Was he serious? She looked at him, wondering if it was a joke. He was staring up the thoroughfare, at who-knew-what. She followed his gaze but found nothing of real interest. Many couples were out watching the sea, peasants and lords alike. There was a row of benches a little way down the boardwalk. Sora prodded his shoulder.

"That looks nice," she said, and pointed to the area. "I think I see an empty bench."

He nodded, and they started forward at a leisurely pace. It was as though they had all the time in the world. She watched as a young girl grabbed the arm of her lover and pointed toward one of the shops. They laughed, then headed in that direction. Sora got the sudden urge to hold Crash's arm in the same way. She glanced at him, wondering if he would mind. Dare she?

They reached the bench before she could make up her mind, and sat down on the cold wood. The boats drifted and bobbed in front of them, and she caught snatches of the far-away horizon. Her eyes traveled up to the stars, which were half-obscured by cloud cover.

"So what is this obsession of yours with the sea?" the assassin asked, after a few moments of watching the waves.

"What?" Sora blinked out of her trance. "I've just never seen it before. It's quite breathtaking."

"I know," he replied. "It is beautiful, though I don't think of it much. I grew up by the sea."

Sora leapt at the invitation to learn about him. Finally, a bit about his past! Despite her curiosity, the words that tumbled out of her mouth were, "You don't seem very fond of it."

She felt Crash grow uncomfortable next to her, and immediately regretted it. *Great, Sora, estrange him again,* she scolded herself.

"Brings back memories," he responded after a moment. "No, I don't like it much." A silence grew between them, this one more awkward.

"The only thing I don't like from the sea is squid," Sora said conversationally. She remembered, quite vividly, a doctor shoving the slimy stuff down her throat while she was sick with swamp fever. He had been certain it would cure her, but it had only made her throw up. Just the look of squid made her sick. "I don't like shrimp either. Spongy and tasteless."

Crash glanced at her. "I'll keep that in mind."

Sora settled back and continued vigilantly watching the ocean. The wind picked up a little, and the air began to cool noticeably. A slight mist was gathering. Before long, she was shivering in her thin cloak, though Crash seemed unaffected by the chill, as usual. She looked up at him, and he turned to look back down at her, his eyes flickering that darker shade of green, his black hair tussled by the wind. His jaw was sharp, firm, without the slightest hint of stubble. Their faces were very close together, and she found her eyes lingering on his lips, suddenly noticing how full they were; they looked unexpectedly soft, despite his firm mouth.

In an attempt to hide her flustered state, Sora turned back to the ocean and crossed her arms. She tried to keep her teeth from chattering as the temperature dropped another degree. She thought she was doing a good job of concealing the fact that she was cold, but Crash's eyes saw everything.

"We should go inside," he commented.

She shrugged nonchalantly, though she knew he noticed her discomfort. Maybe he had noticed from the beginning. "If you want," she answered.

The two stood up and started back to their hotel. The wind began to gust with unaccustomed strength. Now Sora was visibly shivering. They walked down the docks toward their hotel, but her legs were almost numb from the cold bench.

"Here," Crash said after a moment, and she felt him putting his cloak around her shoulders. She stiffened against it, doubly shocked. The material enveloped her short stature, almost comically. Despite the fact that it was ridiculously oversized, the cloth was incredibly warm, either naturally or from Crash's body heat.

She pulled the material closer after a moment. It held Crash's scent all over it, a strong odor of grass, woodsmoke, saddle leather, a tinge of sweat and a slight spice that was unique to the assassin. It was a good smell, somehow familiar. She closed her eyes for a moment. She could envision all of those nights under the stars and the days of trail dust. Years and years of it, his entire life.

She opened her eyes again and found that they were in front of the hotel. It had been a short walk. Slightly disappointed, she allowed Crash to open the door and usher her inside. As she became enveloped by the indoors, she reveled in the warm, bright atmosphere.

The hotel was alive with sound. The adjoining restaurant was flooded with people, albeit a more expensively dressed crowd than the pubs she had seen outside. No less rowdy, though. Dishes clinked and wine bottles were passed around the tables.

She handed Crash his cloak with a grateful smile, then looked toward the restaurant. Her stomach rumbled just as her eyes fixed on someone at the side of the room, waving at them animatedly. She recognized Burn and saluted him, then walked quickly over to his table.

Burn motioned for her to sit down and said happily, "Sora! So good to see you awake!" He chuckled. "We saw you briefly in the room while you were asleep. By the gods, do you snore! I'm surprised there were no complaints!"

Sora rose to the bait gladly. "We'll see if there are any complaints tomorrow, after all the noise you make!"

"Me?" The Wolfy sputtered, a peculiar twinkle in his eyes. "I'm sorry, but you must be talking about Crash. I'm as silent as the night itself."

"I think you both snore terribly loud," Crash said wryly, and sat down across from Sora. "Why do you think I'm always the first one up? I never get to sleep in the first place."

"Truth is, you're just scared of the dark," Burn smirked.

"Or nocturnal," Sora muttered.

Burn laughed outright and Crash gave her a look. It was then that Sora noticed someone missing from their party. "By the way, where's Laina?"

"Laina? Who's Laina?" Burn said with mock seriousness.

"Burn...."

"She went up to change." He shrugged his massive shoulders. "It's not like she needs help. She should be down any moment now. I decided to wait for you guys downstairs so we could have dinner." The Wolfy wiggled his thick eyebrows at her. "I expected you'd be starving by now, but then of course, you're always hungry. I still can't imagine how a little shrimp like you can eat so much; it's phenomenal!"

"Easy for you to say!" Sora teased back. "You eat up all our rations with your huge bulk!"

The Wolfy laughed loudly again. Apparently he was in a good mood tonight. Sora was glad; she liked it when Burn was happy. Her friends deserved a break. She was about to mention it, but then her eyes landed on a figure standing near the stairs, and the words died in her throat.

There, looking slightly flustered and a little lost, was Laina. Except that Sora hadn't recognized her at first. Instead of a small, mousy girl, there stood a young woman, just beginning to blossom. Her usual gray rags were replaced by a smart green outfit that accented her soft violet eyes. The exotic mane of hair, now clean, was the color of whitewashed silver and glistened in the light like water. Sora was astounded. Obviously, the girl had convinced Burn to buy her some new clothes; she only hoped they weren't stolen. Laina looked fidgety and uncertain in the pretty fabric, as though she had been much more comfortable covered in dirt.

Then Laina moved, and the effect was ruined by her awkward, swaggering walk. *I could teach that girl a thing or two about walking like a lady...*Sora thought, then checked herself. Where had that come from? She herself had hated being proper!

Laina spotted them and started toward their table with a quick, eager stride.

"Sora, good to see you awake!" she said with a grin, and sat down next to her. "Those baths are a pain, aren't they?"

Sora nodded. "But they're so convenient! I'm going to see if my mother can have one installed when I get back home." *If I ever see home again*, she thought, but didn't say.

Laina's lips turned up slightly. "I guess you need your mother's permission, huh? That's nice, but I like making my own decisions." Then she shrugged. "One of these days, I'm going to have running water too!"

Sora was slightly stung by the orphan's comment. Laina must not realize just how rude she had been. Or...or did she?

Suddenly, a dazzling smile came over the young lady's face. "Oh, I didn't tell you, did I? I saw this lovely green shirt in a store window and I just had to buy it! What do you think?"

"It's very nice," Sora said uncertainly.

"And a waste of money," Crash stated, without a glance at the new outfit.

"Crash!" she chided.

The assassin wasn't looking at Laina, but rather was staring at Burn. "Do you have any idea how costly it will be to buy a ship, Wolfy? This isn't the time to purchase useless accessories."

Burn frowned. "A few coins isn't going to make that big a difference in the long run. We can't afford a ship as it is. And we got it at a good price....Come now, Laina, don't feel bad." He turned to the girl with a smile. "The shirt looks marvelous on you."

"It's the nicest thing I've ever owned," she sniffed, then shot a glare at Crash. Sora, who could see Laina's bottom lip quivering, quickly decided it was time to eat something.

"I don't know about all of you, but I'm starving," she changed the subject. She waved a waitress over and asked, "What's on the menu?"

The woman bowed slightly before answering. "Black pepper tuna steak, slightly charred, over a plate of fresh greens and long-stemmed wild rice. We recommend a bottle of our sparkling white wine, made locally. It is very light on the tongue."

"I'll have that," she said easily.

"Do you have a room number, miss?"

"Yes, fourteen," Sora answered.

"All right, just let me check here..." the woman flipped through a small book she pulled from her pocket, then nodded. "Ah, the King's messenger, busy job you've got. Yes, your room covers meals. I'll be right back with your food."

"Wait, I'll have some too," Laina cut in loudly, "but make it shrimp."

The woman nodded. "Very well, but a special order will take longer."

"I'll have tuna also," Burn interjected.

The woman ran a hand through her neat hair. Then she nodded respectfully, as she was paid to do, and turned to Crash with an expectant smile.

The assassin sighed. "Do you serve anything other than fish?"

"We have venison, sir."

"Good, I'll have that then, and a brown ale," he added.

"Yes, sir, very good," the woman nodded again, then glanced around the table. "Is that all?"

"Yes, I believe so," Sora returned the smile. The waitress bowed one more time before walking back to the kitchen.

Sora looked at Crash curiously after the waitress was out of sight. They were sitting next to each other, so she leaned in close to speak. "I take it you don't like seafood?" she asked quietly.

"What?"

She leaned a little more toward him. "I said, so you don't like fish?"

"Not especially," he replied in an equally soft voice. Then a wicked glint lit his eyes. "Unless it has long, slimy tentacles and suckers, with tiny black eyes that have been boiled in soup...."

"Oh, hush!" Sora laughed. "Are you describing yourself? I think I've seen a few tentacles under that cloak...."

The assassin grimaced. "You're very clever."

"I learned it from you," she grinned.

"We'll have to put a stop to that."

Sora's grin widened. "You could always throw me to the sea."

Crash laughed. "That wouldn't work. As I recall, you're a very good swimmer." The compliment was unexpected. He had adopted a deep tone that Sora had never heard before. It sent shivers across her skin and she shifted in her seat, strangely excited.

"I could teach you," she said.

"Why don't we have our first lesson in the bath?"

Suddenly Burn cleared his throat from across the table. Crash quickly backed away from her, saying shortly, "Another time, then."

Sora nodded and sat back in her chair, looking around the room, avoiding her companions' eyes. What had just come over her? Teasing the assassin...!

Their order was brought soon after this exchange. The four ate in silence, too busy scarfing down the delicious meal to say anything. Sora felt that she could have eaten two plates of food, or perhaps three. She even drank her glass of wine, which left her warm and slightly light-headed.

Once she was through, she sat back with a sigh. Her friends were already finished and wiping their mouths with their napkins. Briefly, her eyes glanced over the populace of the hotel; all were high-class and richly dressed. Sora couldn't help but feel slightly out of place in her worn garments, but so far, no one had cast them a negative glance. That was the reality of being a peasant, she reminded herself. She was also invisible.

"So what do we do now?" Laina asked.

"Find a ship, of course," Burn answered. "What else? We'll just have to look around until we find one that's going to the Isles. If we can't do that, we'll see if we can buy one."

"Oh, that should be easy!" Laina agreed. She looked around at them expectantly.

"Not so easy. We need to make more money somehow," Crash said. "We'll start tomorrow, sell the rest of our equipment and see if we can find any work for hire."

Sora sighed, wishing things could be easier. She'd never had a real job before. She tried to think of what she was skilled at, besides riding horses and fighting. Not much. Perhaps she could find a few sick people to treat...but she wasn't half as skilled as a true Healer, and she didn't have the supplies that her mother always used. Her Cat's Eye didn't naturally cure the sick; it only worked on the plague, and so far, that didn't appear to have spread to the coast.

"How are we supposed to make that much money in just a few days?" Sora asked.

"I grew up by the sea," Crash commented. "There is plenty of coin in this city, if one knows where to look. Better to work honestly than to attract the attention of the guards. The King's army patrols these docks, and they are not fools." The assassin gave her a meaningful look.

She nodded, but her thoughts were of Volcrian. He was following them; she could feel it in her bones, like an oncoming storm. Her nightmares had been getting worse. She couldn't tell if they were connected to the Cat's Eye or not, but she could see his face in her dreams, as clear as a painting, even though she had never met the man in real life.

And she could also feel a boiling hatred grow within her every time she was reminded of him, the mage who had murdered Dorian. She had never hated anyone before; it was surprising that she could have so vicious an emotion toward a stranger.

Something caught her attention and Sora looked at the door. A red-haired man and woman had entered the room; they looked almost identical. She frowned.

"Why are there so many people with red hair?" she asked, wondering if her other companions had noticed.

Burn nodded thoughtfully. "Where have I seen red hair

before?"

"I know where I've seen it," Crash replied. "Sora was flirting with a young, red-haired street entertainer in Mayville."

Sora looked at Crash in confusion as she searched for the memory, and then the vision of aqua-colored eyes came to her mind. *"A pretty flower for a pretty lady."*

"That...that was more than a year ago, Crash!" she said, surprised. "And that's not fair. I wasn't flirting with him. He just gave me a flower."

"*He* was flirting with you, then. Not a big difference," the assassin said flatly. "What matters is that he looked incredibly similar to that man who was talking to you yesterday by the docks."

Sora immediately remembered the large crow. Her eyes widened. "Could it be the same man?" she asked. It seemed impossible, and yet....

"Most likely," Crash replied, raising his drink to his lips.

"But that doesn't explain all of the other people with red hair," Laina said.

Now Sora was confused again. What were her friends getting at? She looked dumbfounded until Burn chuckled.

"All the different races have similar features, Sora," Burn said. "Harpies all have pale blond hair, and Wolfy mercenaries all have my same height and build...."

She looked at him. "So you're saying the redheads are one of the Races?" she asked. "But which one?"

"Dracians," Crash nodded.

"Dracians?"

Burn leaned forward. "Yes, you can tell by the red hair and jewel-like eyes; also that awful sense of humor." The Wolfy grinned.

"Of course, that's just their outside appearance. They can change on a whim if they want."

Sora was interested. "Really? How?"

"Well, they sprout giant dragon wings, and grow scales." Burn took a sip of his drink. "It's supposed to make their magic stronger. They have elemental magic, you know. Each Dracian specializes in a different element: Wind, Fire, Earth or Water. Wolfies are so much more efficient, in my opinion."

She sat forward, suddenly excited. "So these redheads are Dracians?" She would have never suspected! "What should we do about them?"

"Nothing at all," Crash answered.

"They'll just get us in even more trouble than we're already in," Burn agreed. Then he gave Laina a stern look. The girl was staring at the red-haired couple. "They're bad news for all of us. Dracians have a knack for causing trouble. They enjoy mischief," Burn continued.

Laina remained silent. But Sora didn't like the look on the girl's face.

"Well, everyone, I'm heading off to sleep," Burn said abruptly, and gave a mighty yawn. "I'd suggest you all do the same if we want to be up bright and early tomorrow. Work doesn't wait around in a city like this."

At the mention of sleep, Sora let out a giant yawn and stretched. He had a point. "I guess I'm tired too," she agreed, and the wine was making her more sleepy. She stood up and turned to Laina. "Are you coming?"

"Yeah, I think I will." The thief followed, also standing up. "Tomorrow is going to be interesting."

I hope not. Sora looked at Crash, wondering if he was going to join them, but he shook his head. *Ah, well, it's not like he sleeps much anyway,* she thought. With that, the three went upstairs.

* * *

Crash watched them go.

Volcrian was getting closer, the assassin could feel it, and their money crisis was only slowing the four travelers down. He shook his head. He had been running from the mage for so long. Always running. Crash couldn't remember a time when he hadn't been looking over his shoulder. He couldn't even remember how long it had been since he had killed Etienne, the mage's brother. Years, for sure. If he had only known...if someone could have warned him, before he had taken the coin....*But then somebody else would have done it, and who knows, perhaps there would still be a plague.*

He took a sip from the strong ale in his mug; a dark, thick alcohol that tasted like it had been brewed in a tree trunk. It was good by other pub's standards, and complimented the steak. Too bad the meat's flavor had been overshadowed by the smell of fish from his companions' dinners. Crash had never liked seafood. He had eaten far too much of it as a child and outgrown the taste.

Slowly, his mind turned to the members of their party, and he grimaced as he remembered Laina's new clothes. The girl was nothing but trouble. She whined and complained, then sniveled at every harsh word. But he disliked her for other reasons—reasons that the girl herself probably didn't understand. Reasons he couldn't share with Sora without revealing too much of himself. The girl certainly had Burn under her thrall, but Crash wasn't fooled.

And what of this journey? he pondered, his thoughts turning to his moment in the courtyard with Sora, her admonition and their embrace. Silly of him, to have grown sentimental. It was not his usual state.

Why had he decided to help her? Was it truly to face his past—to stop running, after so many years? Was it really simply to protect her? Desire was a finicky thing, as was the heart, not something to risk one's life for; it could change on a whim. And why had she sought him out? Just for help? He wanted something more concrete, more stable...but he knew the world too well to expect that.

He had heard the legends of the Dark God, of the weapons, of the War. He knew a few things about the Cat's Eye too...but he did not how to survive a broken bond. Was Sora ready to die for this cause? No, of course not, he could already see that. Sora had no idea why she was here, why she had been called upon to stop the plague. She had chased after him on instinct, just as she had tried to run away from her manor. She didn't fully understand her own reasons...but perhaps the Cat's Eye did. Perhaps, the necklace could read its bearer better than he could, straight through the fine mist of circumstance, know her heart as surely as a seer knew the stars. It was the Cat's Eye who had brought her here, after all. The Cat's Eye—and all of the souls inside it.

He sighed, then drowned out the ambient noise with his ale. Whatever Sora's intentions, he was thankful for her help. He had to admit that to himself. He had lied back at the weapons shop, in the heat of their argument. He *did* need her. He couldn't defeat Volcrian alone; neither of them could. The mage's wrath had grown into something far greater than himself that couldn't be killed with a sword.

These thoughts were making him sick, or perhaps it was the strong drink. Crash set down his mug and stood up. Although he seldom slept, he was weary of sitting in the main room. He had spent all evening on the lookout, his eyes combing every corner, but no one appeared to be following him. He still felt the terrible sense of being watched, though.

Maybe upstairs, alone, he'd find some peace of mind.

CHAPTER 13

Sora had her hair tied up at the back of her neck and a basket of laundry under one arm. It wasn't really a job, but the lady at the clothing shop had given her a few coins to run a basket of silk to the dyer. After a morning of going from stall to stall offering her services, it was the only paying task she had found.

She had awakened early to Crash and Burn conversing in the common room of their apartment. Burn had left shortly afterward to sell the horses. Sora had made sure that her mother's horse was not to be sold; instead, she told Burn to release the mare into the fields and let her find her way home. She was confident that the horse would return directly to her mother. She had even attached a lengthy note to the horse, describing their adventure so far, what the Priestess had told her and where they were heading. The men had given her strange looks, but no one protested. They understood that it was quite a special horse, and well-trained—by a Healer, at that.

Laina joined them later at breakfast and then left with Burn. She seemed very attached to the Wolfy; Sora figured it was due to his fatherly nature. Then Crash went to find work unloading cargo from the ships. She hadn't seen any sign of her companions since.

Sora looked up at the sky and squinted. It was early afternoon and the sun was at its highest peak, though cooled by a strong breeze from the ocean. She slipped between alleys and dodged through traffic, making her way as quickly as possible to the dyer's shop, occasionally asking for directions. The accents on the dock were thick and foreign, difficult to discern at times. She had gotten turned around more than once. Crowds passed her on every side, jostling and yelling; everyone seemed to be in a rush, haggling over fish or running back and forth with packages.

She finally found her way to the docks and spotted the dyer's shop almost immediately. It was on a busy street corner surrounded by large crates; there appeared to be a shipment in progress. She could smell the dye from where she stood, and the surrounding cobblestones were stained different colors from years of spillage.

She blew a strand of hair out of her eyes and watched the sailors lingering around the door; they were big, bulky men wearing bandanas and vests. One of them, particularly large and gruesome, leered back at her. Sora stiffened and averted her eyes. She didn't need any trouble, for sure.

After only a slight hesitation, she walked boldly into the mass of men, trying to appear confident and aloof. Several voices called out to her, but she pushed her way through until they finally stepped aside.

Now she was faced with a new problem. Her hands were full, as she was carrying the basket of silk, but she had to open the door. She balanced the basket against her hip and tried to work the heavy handle. It seemed to be stuck.

A tanned arm, tight with muscle, reached past her shoulder and took the handle. Sora watched muscles bunch beneath his skin as a man's hand turned the knob. He pushed the door open for her.

"Thanks," she said, and half-turned to smile at whoever had helped her. There was too little room to turn fully, but she caught a glimpse of a tattoo on his forearm, a dagger with a snake wrapped around it. Her smile froze on her face, and she quickly stepped inside the steamy room to set down her bundle of cloth.

When she exited the building, her eyes landed on Crash, who was waiting outside for her, half- hidden by the shade of the building. She had suspected it was him, though she had only seen the tattoo once before—on their last adventure. She looked him over quickly as she approached him. He stood casually, his sleeves were rolled up. It had been a long time since she had seen his arms, and she couldn't help but stare at the well-shaped biceps. Why had she never noticed them before? She studied his tattoo again, partway up his forearm. The ink looked faded and old.

He was leaning up against the wall of the building. She stood next to him, also relaxing against the cool stone.

"So what have you been doing?" she asked, and reached up to undo her hair.

"Leave it up," Crash requested. She noticed that his own hair was wet and slick with sweat. It clung to his forehead in a black wave. She kind of liked it that way.

They stared at each other a moment; then he cleared his throat and continued, "I was chaining up cargo on one of the ships and asking around for passage to the Isles. It turns out there are no ships heading that way; the last one sailed almost five years ago and never returned. They say the waters are cursed with storms."

Sora looked up at him in worry. "So what do we do? We have no way of getting a ship!" she said.

"Not necessarily," he shrugged. "We just have to wait for an opportunity. We can find a captain that's willing to go. We'll just need a little extra money to put him on the job."

Translation: a bribe. Sora grinned wryly. "Oh, I see," she said, and looked the assassin up and down. "So how much have you made so far?"

Crash sighed and rubbed the back of his tanned neck. "Not a lot," he admitted. "And I doubt Laina and Burn are having that much luck."

"I'll be making five silvers at the end of today," she said, then flagged under Crash's gaze. It truly wasn't a lot of money. There were ten coppers to a silver, and fifty silvers to a gold. A ship would cost several gold.

"At least you're doing something useful. I doubt Laina will have anything by the end of the day." Crash's voice trailed off darkly.

Sora sighed, wishing he wouldn't be so gloomy. Laina was only thirteen, maybe fourteen at best. What did he expect? "Come now, she's not so bad, the girl has to be good at something," she joked.

He snorted. "Picking pockets, maybe."

"And you haven't done worse?" she retorted.

"Hey! You! Stop right there!" The voice was so loud, it made Sora jump. She and Crash turned as one. The shouting continued up the street. "Halt! Surrender, in the name of the King!"

Two figures sped past who looked an awful lot like Laina and Burn. They were followed by a group of red-haired young men and women, all shouting and laughing, the city guards hot on their heels.

Sora watched them dash by in surprise. Then she realized her hand was in Crash's and he was pulling her after them. The two raced after the fugitives, their feet slamming on the cobblestones, and almost too soon they caught up with them. Sora broke away from Crash and slipped her way through the pack of redheads, until she was sprinting along next to Burn.

"And just what do you think you're doing?" she panted.

The Wolfy looked down at her in pleasant surprise. "Why, Sora! So good to see you!" he grinned.

She narrowed her eyes. "That doesn't explain much," she replied.

Burn laughed between breaths. "Well, these fellows were interested in buying our supplies," he started off, and Sora looked around at the redheaded troupe. Their whoops and yells were almost deafening. "Turns out their money had a previous owner...bunch of thieves, the lot of them! And now we're all on the run!"

"Great fun, aye?" called a particularly short, redheaded man. He was scrambling to keep up, though he appeared to be thoroughly enjoying himself. She frowned, then turned back to Burn.

"Where did they come from?" she asked.

"I haven't the slightest idea. It started with just one of them, and then more kept joining the group as we ran...."

"Ahoy up there!" a voice shouted from behind. "Turn into the next alley!"

Burn abruptly threw himself into a small passageway, taking Sora off-guard. She scrambled to change direction, but was assisted by Crash's hand on her arm. He came up behind her and shoved her into the shadows. "Get behind those crates!" he ordered.

Sora tumbled down to the dirty ground, then scrambled behind a pile of large boxes. Laina was already there, her pale cheeks touched with pink. "This is bloody fun!" she panted.

Sora put her head in her hands and groaned. *Can't I stay out of trouble for one day?*

She looked up and across the small alley. Burn was crouched behind a pile of discarded posts. "What now?" she mouthed, not wanting to make noise in case she attracted the wrong people. He shrugged at her, then grinned. Someone shifted, and Sora glanced over to see Crash crouched nearby. His green eyes glinted with amusement. Was he having...fun?

Then she realized she felt giddy and light. For some reason, she wasn't truly worried at all. It was like they were playing a children's game: guards and robbers, or hide and seek.

A figure abruptly dropped down next to her, and Sora almost screamed. A hand went over her mouth, and then a gentle, rolling voice said, "There now, lady. Easy does it."

A giant crow fluttered down, hovering on one of the boxes, shuffling its wings. Sora's eyes focused on the new redhead. She recognized him immediately, noting that he still wore that brown hat. He smiled easily, then slowly drew his hand away. A merry blue-green eye winked at her. "Enjoying the city, I hope?"

Sora was speechless for a moment, then couldn't help smiling. "Very much, thank you."

"Very good!" he said, then tipped his head in a mock bow. "My name is Jacques, and I will be your tour guide this afternoon." He turned to her companions. "Now, you lot, listen up. This mess is our fault, so we're gonna help. We need t'move to the rooftops before those idiots stumble 'cross our hiding spot." He motioned to the roofs above them. "We're all ready for you."

Sora looked up and saw two faces peering down at her. She recognized one as the short man who had run next to her.

"André!" her escort called. The smaller man atop the roof nodded. "Here comes the first one!"

Abruptly, Sora was grabbed and hefted aloft, then pulled up by another pair of hands from above. She squeaked in surprise as she was dragged over the gutter and onto the slippery roof tiles. Her view changed from the enclosed alley to the open air and sky. When she stood up, she could see an endless series of rooftops stretching out around her, of all different colors and makes.

André reached for the next person.

Someone cleared their throat behind her. Sora turned to find a woman next to her.

"Don't make too much noise," she said in a low, husky voice. Sora took in the woman's long, brick- red locks. She had a strange, angular face with jutting cheekbones and slanted, almond eyes; beautiful, but sharp.

There was a thump, and Laina appeared on the other side of her. "My, I don't think I've ever had so much fun in one day!" the young thief giggled.

The woman turned to smile at her. "For us, every day is like this," she chuckled softly.

Laina beamed at the woman.

The sound of Burn's voice drew Sora's attention. She turned to find the giant Wolfy now on the roof, sitting opposite to her, chatting away with André. *What are these people again? Dracians? They seem so human!* She stared at André for a moment, trying to get some hint of his true race, but besides the brilliant red hair and jewel-like eyes, he looked normal.

Suddenly, there was a pattering of feet on the main street below; a group of soldiers went past. "Do you see them?" one yelled.

"Nowhere," another responded. "Let's check up that way."

Sora's heart pounded. Would the guards discover their hiding place? The energy of the Dracians was contagious; she felt drugged, dizzy and elated.

"They were right around here," the first soldier said. "I could have sworn I saw them."

"Yeah, I did too. Let's have a closer look around."

André stuffed a fist in his mouth, on the verge of laughter. Sora glanced over and saw Laina doing much the same. Crash crouched on the other side of them, moving silently across the roof. She didn't remember seeing him climb up.

Jacques approached her, and she recognized the large crow again. "'Tisn't quite what you expected, is it?" the man said, hunching next to her. He spoke softly, below the wind. "We've lived in this city our entire lives, and the guards know us well. This is routine for them. I don't believe I caught your name....?"

"Ah...Sora," she muttered.

Jacques smiled cheerily and shook her hand. "Quite brilliant to meet you, Sora, and don't mind me asking, but...are you traveling with a Wolfy?" he breathed.

Sora glanced at Burn and nodded.

A second later, Jacques was at Burn's side, shaking the mercenary's hand as if he were the King himself. "Nice, Wolfy, well met!" he gushed. "Why, if I had known I'd be meeting your kind today, I'd have done something with my hair! Jacques is the name, jesting's the game!"

Burn stared at the Dracian with a bemused expression. "Burn is the name," he replied. "Leaving with my hand intact is also very important to me."

The Dracian abruptly dropped Burn's hand with a small laugh. Sora watched the two in amusement, but was shaken from her thoughts as a voice called out from below.

"I know you're up there, Jacques! I can smell your wretched blood!"

The crow let out an affronted squawk. Jacques turned away from Burn, cocked his head and put a hand behind his ear. "And what is that I hear?" he said, intentionally loud. "Why, is that the native cry of the Captain of the Guard?" He leapt up to the very peak of the roof, then looked down and yelled, "Hey! Stewie! Up here!"

"That's Captain Stewart to you, you filthy dog!" the voice yelled back angrily.

"Did you forget to shave this morning?" Jacques called back. "Isn't that against regulations?"

"Archers! Take your mark!" the man roared in outrage.

"Uh-oh." Jacques fell flat on the roof just as two arrows shot by his head. He rolled over to look at the Dracians. "That's our cue to leave. Joan? Get everyone out of here. Take them to the hideout. Come on, let's go!"

Sora found herself being pulled to her feet by Burn. The Wolfy smiled down at her. "Dracians—they're a good sort," he confided.

Jacques' voice carried above the rising wind and the shouts from the soldiers. "André? Where are you? Ah, there we are, give me that smoke bomb you've been saving."

Jacques took a small black ball from the shorter Dracian and turned to the rest of them. "They've made the most wonderful invention in the kingdom across the sea. It's called gunpowder, and it makes quite satisfactory explosions. Watch this!" The Dracian scuttled down to the edge of the roof. He was quite dexterous on the slick tiles. "Hey! Stewie!" he yelled, and leapt to his feet. "Catch!"

Sora watched in fascination as he hurled the ball to the ground. There was a moment's silence, then the street below erupted into a clatter of shouts and curses. Someone grabbed her arm, and before she knew what was happening, she found herself leaping across the rooftops. Then a small explosion rumbled through her chest—*fuuuummmph!* Tiles trembled beneath her, windows rattling in their frames. Thick smoke billowed up into the sky, but she kept moving.

Sora had never run on rooftops before; it reminded her of the pole exercises her mother had made her practice. She used her staff to help her vault across alleys, but most of the buildings were so close together that she had little trouble. It helped that the houses were all of similar height and make. Her biggest challenge was keeping her footing on the roof tiles, which were slick and slippery from the constant moisture.

Jacques caught up with them quickly and ran next to her, his crow gliding above their heads. She looked over at him. "Don't you ever worry you'll hurt someone?" she panted.

He looked at her, then over his shoulder, where the smoke was quickly dispersing in the breeze.

"Naw," he finally said, and gave her a roguish smile. "The soldiers can take care of themselves. It's all in good fun!"

But an explosion like that could have cost someone a leg, she thought. Sora got the sudden feeling that she was surrounded by a pack of rowdy teenagers. Although the Dracians appeared to be well into their twenties and thirties, their eyes held a childish, carefree twinkle. She wasn't sure if she liked that.

After several more minutes, the group started to slow down. They paused on a pyramid-shaped wooden roof, layered with wooden shingles. A large window in the ceiling served as a skylight. As they arrived, it opened inward and three of the Dracians, André and two other males, slipped through. Next in was Laina, who looked exhilarated, then Burn. As the Wolfy passed her, he whispered, "Reminds me of my younger days."

Sora glanced around the rooftops one last time. She had no idea where they were; the city sprawled out on each side, a jungle of smoking chimneys, metal ladders and jutting towers. With a slight shrug, she dropped down through the skylight.

It was a short distance to the floor below. Sora landed softly and gave herself a minute to adjust to the shadows and dust. The space was clearly an attic, packed with old boxes and scuffed trinkets. If she listened, she could hear the sound of distant foot traffic from the floor below, voices and an occasional thump. They were most likely above a store.

The attic had been transformed into a cozy room with a tattered carpet and scratched paintings. The atmosphere was friendly and welcoming, which put her at ease. Her gaze shifted to Burn, who had been tackled by four of the Dracians. They were laughing in delight as he lifted all four into the air, two in each arm.

"I guess they've never seen a Wolfy before," came Crash's voice next to her. It undermined the laughter in the room. A wry expression marked his face, and Sora felt a momentary stab of pain, remembering Dorian. He would have enjoyed the Dracians immensely.

Sora frowned, trying to clear her thoughts. "I guess we won't be getting that money today," she murmured to Crash.

"Ah, well, we'll just have to try again tomorrow," the assassin replied. She hadn't been expecting his easiness on the matter, but his words were not comforting. Perhaps they weren't supposed to be.

"Jacques! I'm back!"

A trapdoor opened in the floor, only a few feet away from Sora's boots. A young man bounced through, probably a year older than herself and, from his coloring, obviously a Dracian.

"Tristan!" Jacques ran over to the young man's side and gave him a rough knock on the shoulder. "Courting a young love this afternoon, weren't you? How is the girl?"

Tristan put one hand on his forehead and groaned dramatically. "Woe, horrible! She is so demanding! You're a terrible man, Jacques, to pick her out of the crowd!" He scrunched up his face; he had strong, handsome features, dark auburn hair and bright blue eyes. "She must be the most selfabsorbed person I've ever met!"

"Aye...I thought you might make a good match!"

Tristan narrowed his eyes. "Very funny...."

Jacques laughed and put his arm around the younger man, tussling his short red hair. "Eh, there will be others, I'm sure. Anyway, I'd like you to meet a few new faces." He turned and motioned to their group. "This is Laina, she's from out of town. Quite the li'l charmer, aye?"

Laina's cheeks turned pink. The young man made a short bow.

"This is Burn, a mercenary Wolfy from...well, I don't know where exactly," Jacques continued.

The young man's mouth fell open as Burn turned around. It was a ridiculous sight. The mercenary had four grown men hanging from his arms, and was almost twice as tall as the Dracian.

Tristan was struggling to regain control of his voice. "Really?" he finally gasped. "A Wolfy? I thought your kind had perished long ago! No offense...." he paused nervously.

"None taken," Burn said, and managed to grip Tristan's hand, despite the extra baggage.

Jacques continued around the room, hesitating when he looked at Crash, then continued past him. "And this beauty over here is Sora," he finished.

Tristan's eyes fell on her and she noted his expression. It was the same look that the farmboys had given her back at her mother's town. She swallowed and tried to ignore it. "Nice to meet you."

"Tristan," he stuttered, coming up to her. "My name's Tristan. Nice to meet you, too. If—uh, if you don't mind me saying so, miss, you are..." he grabbed her hand and held it a little too tight for comfort. "Perfect."

Whatever that means, she thought. She looked around the room quickly, hoping that someone would rescue her from the embarrassing situation, but she saw only Burn's amused smile and Laina's angry glance. She blinked in surprise. Jealousy?

"So...you're a Dracian too?" she asked hesitantly. Tristan still hadn't dropped her hand.

"Half, actually, on my father's side," he said, a little too fast. Then he smiled. Two handsome dimples stood out on his cheeks. Sora sucked in a quick breath. *Oh, my.* Then he winked. "That's why I'm so much better-looking than the rest of 'em! How about you? Are you half Harpy?"

"What?" Sora asked, taken aback. She didn't know what Harpies looked like, so she didn't know how to answer that. "N-no, I'm not," she stuttered. "Or at least, I don't believe so."

"Are you sure?" he asked. "Because that would explain everything: your grace, your stature, your beauty...." He kissed her hand, lingering. She felt an urgent need to tug away. "You have a certain glow about you, almost like magic. Have you cast me under a spell? I feel absolutely bewitched...."

He straightened up suddenly, dropping her hand, and Sora was shaken out of her trance. An arm slid around her shoulders.

"Hello," Crash said bluntly. The assassin stared at the young man with a dead, cold eye.

She could feel his warmth, and for some reason, it was even more distracting than the handsome redhead in front of her. *What's wrong with me?* she suddenly thought, shaking her head. She looked at the two men, but was unable to understand the tension between them.

Crash, who was the older of the two and a lot more skilled at silent confrontations, stared Tristan down until the young Dracian was forced to look away.

"Come on, Sora, Jacques...." Crash straightened up and withdrew his arm. "I need to speak with you." The assassin turned toward the open window without another glance at Tristan.

Sora and Jacques shared a glance before following him. He led the three outside onto the roof, where they sat down to watch the sunset, leaving the rest of the party inside. Sora shifted around several times, trying to get comfortable on the tiles. She wrapped her arms around her legs and looked out over the city. The sea breeze was still brisk and fresh, and the distant rumble of the street was like calming music to her ears. She felt somehow above the world, untouchable.

Crash and Jacques both settled nearby.

"Dracian?" the assassin began.

"Jacques is my name, and you may call me by it." He sounded almost hostile. "Also, I would prefer it if you don't go spouting out the word Dracian and getting us into trouble."

Sora was surprised by the sudden shift in his tone.

Crash sneered slightly. "More trouble than you're in now? I hardly believe that's possible." He turned to face Jacques more fully. "Listen, *Dracian,* I'm not breathing a word about your kind, though your presence is obvious to anyone who knows what to look for. And I hope you won't breathe a word about us as well."

Jacques nodded after a long pause. "I don't intend to say anything of you, Dark One." He fixed Crash with a cold stare.

Sora listened to the discussion curiously, but held her questions in check.

"I know that you don't want me here," Crash said calmly. "But our quest cannot be further delayed. Sora, show him the rapier hilt."

Sora was surprised. She reached for her bag, wondering where Crash was going with this. After a bit of rummaging, she pulled it out and unwrapped it.

The Dracian looked at the hilt for a long moment, then back to Crash. "What is this?"

"Look at the symbols on the hilt. Here, hold it in your hand for a moment."

Jacques went to lift the device from Sora's hand, but as he did, he dropped the rapier, as though touched by fire. With a slight hiss, he shook his fingers. "It's colder than ice!"

"Exactly."

Now Sora was confused. "Wait, what do you mean?" she asked.

Crash nodded slowly. "The hilt doesn't affect you, Sora, because you wield a Cat's Eye. You can't feel the rapier's magic. I'm not surprised that you haven't noticed this before." Then he looked back to Jacques. "We are being hunted by a very angry, blood-driven Wolfy mage. He is consumed by a thirst for revenge. He has summoned three wraiths to hunt us from the underworld."

"Three wraiths?" Jacques asked, his eyes widening. They returned to the rapier hilt. "Three dead spirits?"

Crash nodded again.

"I am not a specialist in these things," Jacques said slowly. "But our kind, too, has legends. From what I recall, this magic is forbidden."

"And for good reason," Crash replied. "These are not just normal weapons. They are sacred weapons of the Dark God. The longer they remain in this world...."

"The more His power manifests." Jacques stared at both of them for a long moment. "And with his return will come plagues, war, chaos."

Sora was stunned that he knew so much. She looked at Crash, who had a satisfied glint in his eye. "Yes," the assassin finally said. "I'm glad I don't have to convince you of that. Sora has a Cat's-Eye necklace. We are traveling to destroy the mage...and hopefully set things right."

Jacques turned to look at her, sharing her stunned expression. "Well," he finally said. "You are a curious lot, indeed. Let me see this Cat's Eye."

Sora hesitated before pulling the necklace from her shirt. The Dracian's eyes lingered on the stone. He looked as though the breath had been knocked out of him. "'Tis a bit much," he murmured.

Sora nodded in agreement—'tis still a bit much for me, too! "We've come from Barcella," she said quietly. "We've already spoken to the High Priestess. A plague has started spreading across the mainland. It hasn't reached the coast yet, but it's on its way. Countless livestock have died. Crops have turned rotten. Now farmers and their children are getting sick."

Jacques nodded slowly. "I have heard rumors of this in past months. I thought 'twas just hysteria over a bad crop."

"No, it's not. It's real," Sora said, her voice turning serious. "The legends are true, and this is just the beginning. We need to destroy the weapons...and destroy the mage who summoned them. That's the only way to stop the plague."

Jacques' eyes darted back and forth between them. "Bringin' spirits back from the dead is tricky business," he finally said. "If the mage is unskilled, then the spirits can enter the world with all sorts of strange energy. Looks like you drew the short straw. It would be pretty hard to swallow if this hilt weren't right in front of me. What happened to the blade?"

"Long story," Crash said bluntly. "More importantly, we need to kill Volcrian to stop the plague."

"And how d'you plan to do that?" Jacques asked.

"The Lost Isles," Crash stated.

The Dracian looked at Sora, then at the Cat's Eye that she still held in her hand. He wasn't smiling anymore; his face was solemn. "All that, just to kill a Wolfy? Though, I suppose he is more than just a Wolfy now. Don'cha realize what awaits you on the Isles...?"

"I..." Sora's voice faded. She didn't know what to say.

"The Lost Isles are one of the few remaining sacred grounds," he said. "They contain a circle of stones that was once used for living sacrifices. Prisoners were placed within the circle, and a Cat's-Eye stone would suck the very souls out of them. The magical energy is still dense in the land, in the clouds and sea. There are strange storms out that way." Jacques frowned. "I take it you plan to do the same to Volcrian?"

"Something like that," Crash said.

Jacques nodded again. He stared at Sora for a long, hard minute. His silence was excruciating. It seemed to drown out the wind, the distant shouts from the streets below, even her own thoughts. "It could destroy the necklace, y'know," he said. "The stone itself. It might crack and break. Y'know what that means...?"

Sora hadn't heard of this before. She grew pale, cold. Yes, she knew what that meant—she would have to relinquish the necklace. A broken bond. And, most likely, her own death.

She could only nod silently.

"Then we will assist you, Sora," he said, his tone soft, almost gentle. He completely disregarded Crash. "If you are willing to sacrifice your life for this, then we will stand at your side."

Sora was struck by his sincerity. She opened her mouth, but still couldn't find any words. What could she say? She couldn't explain herself, and "thank you" seemed thoughtless and empty.

"We are in need of a ship," Crash said sharply, breaking the moment.

Jacques turned back to him. "There are storms out that way, y'know. Things of nature that the Cat's Eye won't stand against.

And the Harpies do not like visitors on their island."

"We have to go there."

"I know. And I said I would help you," he grunted. "Don't push me, Dark One. I owe you nothing."

Why do they keep calling him that? Sora wondered, giving Crash a searching glance that he didn't return.

"I'll see to it tomorrow," Jacques said abruptly. "The soldiers are still too active on the docks. I believe your party will have to stay here for the night." He grinned, the shadow passing from his face. "The soldiers will be swarmin' over your hotel by now, but don't worry. It's run by a good friend of mine and she would never let them touch anything. We'll be eating in a little while. Please, make yourself at home. I'll send out Tristan to fetch your bags later tonight."

Sora nodded and smiled a little uncertainly. Crash stood up and she followed suit. It was getting cold outside, and she wanted to keep her health. Somehow, despite the vivid sunset, it had grown dark and gloomy.

With a yawn and a shiver, she headed back through the skylight.

Crash and Jacques stayed out on the roof for a moment more, sharing a look that was almost tangible. Then they followed her into the building.

CHAPTER 14

The next morning was gray and stormy. Dark, angry clouds covered the sun in a thick mass. Looking outside, Sora felt reluctant to get her chores done, but she had to buy supplies with the money the Dracians had given them for their equipment. Of course, she knew the money was stolen, but at that moment it just didn't seem to matter...and definitely didn't matter to Crash.

The assassin had woken her up only fifteen minutes earlier and explained his plan to buy supplies for the ship. He would go to buy the fresh water they needed for the voyage. Sora would buy the food. He had given her a rough list of how many pounds they would need of dried meat, grains, rice, and vegetables; that almost made her eyes pop out of her head. He also gave her an address where she should have the crates shipped to the docks. After getting the supplies, they would meet and eat lunch at the hotel.

Laina and Burn had to stay inside, since the soldiers were doubtlessly looking for them. Sora had readily agreed to this. At least if they were indoors, they would stay out of trouble.

And so, Sora found herself hopping down from a low building into a narrow alley. She landed gently amidst a pile of trash, then wrinkled her nose at the smell. City life was definitely not as glamorous as it was made out to be. As she got up, she was startled by a sudden growl, and turned to find a dirty mutt standing in the alley, baring its teeth protectively over the trash pile. She was only worried for a moment. Crash landed silently next to her. The dog slunk away.

"Take this," he murmured, and drew something out of his cloak.

Sora gasped. "My staff!" she exclaimed, then looked at him suspiciously. "Where did you get it? I thought Tristan said he couldn't find it last night."

"A Dracian was sleeping with it. Don't take it personally. They'll steal anything and everything, even from their own mothers. Keep a close eye on your bags."

Sora frowned, suddenly uncomfortable. "Do you think the rest of our things are safe?" she asked quietly.

He shrugged. "It doesn't matter. We're out of supplies as it is, and we don't have much money. Let's get moving." After a pause, he added, "Be careful. I don't know if the guards got a look at us."

Sora blinked, and he was gone. She watched the tail end of his cloak disappear around the corner, then she slung her staff over her shoulder and headed in the opposite direction, to the food district.

The crowds were thinner than usual on this cloudy morning. The air was thick with drizzle. Most people moved swiftly, hunched against the weather. They were dressed in heavy cloaks and boots, prepared for a storm. The wind was notably stronger than yesterday, gusting through the streets in sudden force, blowing down flower stands and sweeping away paper bags. Soon she was shivering, despite her cloak.

Her boots clicked smartly on the cobblestones as she reached the front of the docks. The ocean was stone-gray, reflecting the dark clouds, and tossing with short, choppy waves. There were street vendors on every side of her, calling out their wares despite the threatening rain. Sora walked among the sparse crowd, mostly sailors and fishermen, with the occasional bustling housewife. Wiry old sea dogs sat under foyers and overhangs, rolling dice across upturned barrels and smoking pipes. Some leered as she passed, but she had learned to ignore them.

The shopping list included a series of stores; she found two of them almost immediately. They were giant warehouses, each taking up an entire city block. The lines were short due to the weather, and she didn't have to wait long before ordering. At the first store, she requested several hundred pounds of salted meats and even bought a few chickens, figuring they could eat eggs for breakfast. At the next warehouse, she ordered seaworthy vegetables, such as carrots, yams, beans, and a variety of pickled stuff that she didn't look at too closely. She gave each shop owner the delivery address; none seemed surprised by her request and treated her orders as status quo. Sora finally finished her shopping with only two silvers left and very, very sore feet. She looked at her coin purse in wonder. Sailing was far more expensive than she had anticipated. They were going to need more money.

As she exited the final shop, the first few drops of rain hit her nose. The sky had increasingly darkened until it felt like evening; the clouds were heavy and low. The wind swept by even more briskly than before, blowing fragile droplets of rain into her face. Sora blinked her eyes clear and looked around, trying to reorient herself. Now which way back to the hotel? She and Crash would check their rooms one last time before turning in their key and leaving for good.

The population of the docks was sparser than before; most of the vendors had given up and gone home. She leaned back against the cold stone wall of a building and took a moment to look at the ocean. Two ships were racing toward the docks, their sails billowing and flapping in the unstable wind, attempting to beat the weather. The waves jumped and leapt in the face of the oncoming storm front. Out at the breakwater, huge sprays leapt over the rocks, perhaps twenty feet, higher than the houses on shore.

Sora stared, awestruck. What power! She was suddenly fearful. *Will we be caught in a storm like this?* From what she had overheard at the market, this was mild compared to most weather. She suddenly didn't know what she feared more; being caught by Volcrian, or sailing into a storm of fifty-foot swells.

She was momentarily lost in the image of Volcrian catching them at sea, killing her friends and throwing them off the ship in the middle of a storm. *That's highly unlikely,* her inner voice chided, and she forced her attention back to the docks. She needed to ask someone for directions, but the few people on the street walked quickly past, heads down, hoods over their faces. A few sailors shouted to each other, but she couldn't hear them over the wind, which blasted by, howling, shockingly powerful. A spatter of rain arrived. She shook her head, her ears ringing, a headache beginning around her temples. The noise of the wind was loud, but the ringing in her ears seemed to drown it out.

Then there was a sudden lull in the uproar around her. She blinked. Her ears weren't ringing at all. In fact, the sound was...were....

Bells.

Oh, no! She put her hand on her Cat's Eye in sudden fear. It was unmistakable, far louder than a distant wind chime. What could be causing the necklace to react? She whirled around and scanned the empty docks, ready for anything, but several minutes went by and still nothing happened. Maybe she had made a mistake; maybe someone close by was selling bells, or carrying them around. She shook her head. *No.* She knew where the sound came from. Someone was using magic...and her Cat's Eye was warning her.

Suddenly, there was a strong tug on her neck, as though an invisible leash had been pulled. Her foot stepped to the right on its own accord. *Whoa.* That necklace meant business! She started walking in the direction it encouraged her to go, and the more she walked, the more urgent the feeling became.

And then, she had the feeling that something terrible was about to happen. But where? How?

Sora ran away from the docks, and soon found herself drawn to the inner streets, mostly side alleys. She didn't know where she was going, but the Cat's-Eye's compulsion was overpowering. She had to move fast—there wasn't much time.

* * *

Crash arrived at the bell tower. He doubted it was the only one in the city, but it was certainly the largest, stretching far above any other building on the docks by almost three stories. It was old and decrepit, the plaster stained and chipped. From the street below, the bell looked like it hadn't been rung in a decade or more.

He paused before entering the building and pulled his veils up over his face; he didn't want to be easily recognizable. He had the hilt tucked safely away in his cloak. Leaving it with the Dracians would have been a mistake; he didn't trust any of them. He doubted they knew about the Shade...but they were still thieves, and they wouldn't hesitate to sell it off for a bit of coin. And that would inevitably place the hilt in the Shade's hands.

The sky was dense and gray, the clouds low to the ground. After surveying the docks for a moment, ensuring he hadn't been followed, he slipped smoothly into the building, prying open the rotten door.

Inside, the bell tower was dark and musty, completely abandoned. The stone tiles were cracked and salt-worn. Mold infested the walls. Wooden scaffolds crisscrossed the interior, climbing all the way up the belfry, strung with old, gray rope. At one time, it looked like there had been plans to renovate the building, but those plans had been long discarded.

He stood there in the damp darkness, waiting.

About a minute passed, then something shifted deeper in the building. He watched. There was a long, slow silence. And then....

Wham! The noise was intentional. A flock of sleepy pigeons launched off of the higher rafters, cooing in alarm, fluttering out the broken windows.

Crash looked up. A figure crouched above him in the gloom, balancing expertly on a thin wooden beam. After a moment, he picked out two more figures, hanging back in the shadows. They were cloaked and veiled, their faces hidden, similar to himself. The veils gave them away immediately, more so than their faces would have.

"Where is the package?" the first asked coldly. Surprisingly, it was a woman's voice.

Crash was prepared for this. He reached into his cloak and withdrew the hilt. He held it in his hand, feeling its weight, allowing the three to see it.

"Where's my reward?" he asked.

The woman dropped to the ground. She landed smoothly, uncoiling like a cat. The other two swung to the lower beams, but stayed above the ground. "Hand it to me," she said.

He put the hilt back under his cloak. "My reward first."

"We need to verify its authenticity."

"I need to verify *your* authenticity," he countered.

The woman's eyes narrowed. She stared at him through the shadows. He could detect a feminine figure beneath her heavy cloak and black clothes, but besides that, she was unidentifiable.

"You are of the Hive," she said abruptly. "One of our own....?"

Crash didn't respond.

"Just kill him and take it," one of the men called down. "We don't owe him anything."

"Quiet!" she barked over her shoulder. Then she turned back to him. "Are you of the Hive or not?"

Crash stared. Her question was strange, unexpected. He let it churn in his mind. Was he? Once, perhaps. He raised his head slightly. "I am not."

The woman glared suspiciously. "Your manner of dress says differently. Why do you challenge us?"

"Enough of this," the man said again. "If you won't give us the hilt, then we shall take it!"

Crash took a slight step back, looking upward, his hands hovering close to his daggers. Beneath his veil, he managed a thin smile. "Try," he said.

The woman flung out her arm, signaling for her companion to stop, but the man ignored her. He leapt from the beam and landed smoothly on the ground, a cloud of dust rising in his wake. A sword appeared in his hand, a thin blade similar to Crash's own, and he lunged forward.

Crash stepped to one side, smoothly dodging the attack. He grabbed the man by the scruff of his neck, drew his dagger, and jammed it into the man's stomach.

Oof. A soft breath of air came out of his mouth, a low moan. With a shocked gurgle, the man dropped to the ground.

"Jackal!" the woman said sharply. It was not a sympathetic tone. She sounded furious. "I told you—*stay put!*"

Jackal didn't respond, but curled into a fetal position, wheezing.

The second man hovered in the beams above, silent, observing.

Crash knew this dance. He had grown up with it. Constant tension, always on edge, never knowing when a slim blade might pierce the darkness. He stared at the woman, impassive. She stared back. Then, slowly, she drew a heavy coin purse from her waist.

"One hundred gold," she said. "As promised." She flung the purse at his feet. "Now give us the hilt."

Crash didn't move to take the coin. Instead, he kicked the bag away, deep into the shadows, somewhere past the man on the floor. A pool of blood was spreading across the dusty tiles. It touched his boots.

"I didn't come here for coin," Crash said. "I came here for answers."

The woman arched an eyebrow, the only part of her face that was visible. Her eyes were vividly green. "What?" she snapped.

"I want to know who you are, and what you plan to do with the weapons."

"That is none of your concern," she said icily.

"Actually, it is." Crash patted his knife belt under his cloak. "Last I checked, I'm the one with the hilt."

"We don't know if it's real."

"Oh, it is. I can assure you." He glanced up at the second man. Somehow, during the conversation, the man had switched beams. He was lower now, closer. Crash hadn't detected any movement. He wondered what kind of weapon he specialized in; what his attack would be. Just a matter of time now....

The woman laughed suddenly; a dry, quick sound. "And last I checked, we have you outnumbered, *savant*," she said. "You are a savant, aren't you? Yes, I remember now. A worthless bandit leader out in the lowlands. Nameless. An exile of the Hive. That's who you are. Pathetic."

Crash hadn't heard that word in a while: *savant*. A name for the Nameless. Growing up the Hive, all assassins were called savants until they competed and won a Name. Some never did.

"I prefer the odds," he murmured. "Neither of you will leave until I have my answers."

The woman laughed again, her voice shrill. "And what makes you think we'll answer you?"

The man on the floor coughed suddenly, spewing up blood, then went limp, his final breath oozing out of him.

They all glanced at the body, then at each other, green eyes darting around the room. The woman stood up a little straighter.

"Widow," she said. "Kill him."

Crash looked up, expecting an attack, but the man had disappeared from the scaffolds. The Widow. He tried to remember which weapon that Name belonged to....

Shhhing!

A long chain whirled out of nowhere. Crash ducked to one side, barely dodging the hooked scythe at its end. It spun past him, humming through the air like a deranged wasp. *Chuunk!* It struck the side of the wall, embedded deep in the plaster.

Crash danced backward, watching the weapon with interest. With a firm tug, the Widow pulled on the chain, dislodging the blade. With another flick of his wrist, the scythe spun obediently back to its master. The Widow stood amidst the shadows of dusty boxes, sunk deep in the room. His hands spun the chain in a tight circle, the blade thrumming at its end.

Crash drew his sword. This was a fight for a longer weapon.

The man cast out his scythe again. Crash dodged a second time, and the blade smashed past him, obliterating a soggy wooden crate at his back. Splinters and wood chips exploded through the air.

He has good aim, Crash thought. He couldn't risk getting hit; one strike would break his bones, turn his gut to chowder. The chain was deadly at a distance, but useless in close combat. Throwing caution to the wind, he charged his opponent, his sword braced before him.

The Widow stumbled back, surprised, then tugged on his chain. The blade spun through the air like a trained hawk, directly at Crash's back.

At the last second, Crash dropped to the ground. The scythe went whizzing over his head, back to its master—and struck the Widow square in the chest.

"Agh!" the man gasped, staggering. Blood gushed from the wound, spilling down his shirt. The scythe was lodged firmly in his chest plate.

Crash sprung easily back to his feet. Then, with a two-handed swing, he sliced clean through the man's neck.

Shunk.

The Widow's head bounced across the floor.

Sudden silence clogged the room, stifling the air—but Crash didn't hesitate. He whirled on the woman, bearing down on her, his sword at the ready. She saw him coming and leapt onto the scaffolds, trying to escape, jumping from beam to beam. She held a whip in her hand, and used it to help her climb, lashing out at lightning speed and swinging from one perch to the next.

Crash didn't need a whip. Using only his hands and legs, he jumped expertly after her, catching the old ropes and shimmying upward. He was perfectly balanced, his muscles coiling with ease.

About halfway up the belfry, the woman stopped. She hung from the rafters on her whip, like a spider from its web. Her hood had fallen back, and her thick black hair fell around her face, long and glistening.

Her voice didn't betray her...but she was breathing hard; he could tell by the rise and fall of her chest. "You can't win, savant!" she said. Then, with a flick of her wrist, she sent a handful of needles flying through the air. They were long and sharp, perhaps six inches or more.

Crash had no time to dodge. He held up his forearm and caught three of them, blocking his face. The fourth pierced his shoulder. He didn't flinch, but tightened his grip on the wooden beams, staring up at her.

"Who are you?" Crash asked again. "Who do you work for?"

Her eyes narrowed. "I am no one," she said.

A predictable response, coming from one of the Hive. "I highly doubt that," he said. "Answer me."

"Never!"

Crash slipped a knife into his hand and flung it upward, deft and concise. The blade zipped through the air—*sssnt!* It didn't hit the whip. No—it pierced her hand.

"*Aaaah!*" With a clipped scream, the woman lost her grip and plummeted downward, the whip unfurling and falling after. Crash watched her plunge almost three stories to the floor below. *Wham!* she crashed into a pile of boxes, an explosion of dust billowing upward, covering the base of the tower like dense fog.

Crash leapt, diving into open space, graceful and measured, perfectly controlled. He fell several dozen yards, then grabbed hold of a rope and slid downward, entering the cloud of dust.

It was difficult to see on the ground, but he couldn't let the woman escape. Once he was on his feet, he ripped the sleeve off of his arm, dislodging the needles with it. He flung the bloody sleeve to one side, ignoring the pain.

He followed the sound of her heaving breath, dashing through a maze of broken boxes. Then he saw her shadow against the dust and took off at full force. He tackled her to the ground—*whumph!*— and rolled with her several feet, until he rammed her up against the wall. He pulled his dagger from its sheath and dug the blade into her throat.

She was coughing and sputtering from the dust. He pinned her like that for a long minute until the air cleared, swept clean by the fierce wind outside.

"Novice," he said, inches from her face.

She spat at him, hissing like a snake. Her veils had come undone, her face contorted with rage and pain. She was surprisingly young, perhaps a few years younger than himself, with a blunt nose and full lips.

"It would be easier for me to kill you," he said, speaking low and fast. "Answer my questions, and maybe I won't."

She glared, her eyes crackling like fire. Then her gaze dropped to his arm—or, more specifically, his tattoo. Her eyes widened.

He lifted the blade slightly, allowing her to speak.

"Y-you're...the Viper!" she gasped, choking on dust.

He waited.

"The youngest to win a Name...and you abandoned your Hive. Y-you're...."

"Alive?" he suggested, and grinned beneath his veils. "What do they call you?"

"Krait," she gasped.

Yes, that would explain the whip. Each Name came with a specialized weapon. His dagger was just as identifiable as his tattoo, if one knew what to look for. "You are a member of the Shade," he murmured. It wasn't a question.

She glared harder, but he sensed a quickening of her pulse under the blade. It was answer enough. "And your leader?"

"I-I...I don't know."

"Lies." He pressed the blade again, allowing her to feel its bite. She reached up and grabbed his wrist, trying to force him away, but her wounded hand was slick with blood, her grip slippery and useless.

"A Name," he repeated. "Who is your leader? Your Master?"

"I obey only the will of the Dark God...."

"A Name, you worthless, unskilled maggot. Talk or I will make you."

"I can't!"

He lifted the knife slightly and ran its tip along the bottom of her jaw, not deep enough to kill her...but certainly deep enough to leave a scar. A small stream of blood ran down her neck. "You have three seconds...three...two...one...."

"Cerastes!" she gasped.

He paused. "What?"

"Cerastes is my Master!"

Crash stared at her. The Name echoed inside him like a tolling bell. He searched her face....

Like a true assassin, she took advantage of his pause. Slick as water, she slipped out from under him and scrambled backward up the wall, using it to propel herself up and over him, flipping neatly through the air. Crash sat up, turning, but he was still stunned by her words. He watched as she dashed across the floor, grabbed her whip, and swung out the nearest window. In five seconds, she was gone.

He could have given chase—should have, probably—but he had his answers. Only, they weren't at all what he had expected.

Cerastes.

How long had it been....?

Abruptly a powerful gust of wind whipped through the building, howling through the cracked windows. The bell swung far above him, clanging with surprising force. It resounded in his ears, making him cringe.

Crash stood up, shaken from his reverie. Whether Cerastes was the leader of the Shade or not—it didn't matter now. Sora was waiting for him, and at least he knew that the order was real...and that they were after the weapons. He walked around the blood-stained room, picking up the forgotten bag of coins, tucking it into his cloak next to the sacred hilt. On sudden inspiration, he picked up the chained scythe as well, and swung it easily into his grip. He looked upward...took aim....

He threw the chain powerfully. It arched up through the air and hooked onto one of the highest beams, at the very top of the scaffold.

He tugged it, making sure it sunk deep into the wood. Then, with a firm yank, he brought the rotten beams smashing downward.

He left the tower...and a minute later, the walls caved in.

* * *

Sora felt as though the Cat's Eye had taken over her body, leading her up and down pathways, over fences, under a bridge. Soon she found herself in a scarcely populated part of town where the streets were dirty and uneven, lined by trash cans.

She glanced up at the sky to judge the time, but found it impossible, since the clouds were so thick. It was getting darker by the second, and the wind was now blowing her hair wildly.

She stopped suddenly as a sound drifted to her on the wind. Was that the tolling of the city bell? Noon already?

She paused, biting her lip, torn about what to do. The urgency of her Cat's Eye, or her meeting with Crash? If she went to Crash, they could both stand against the threat, but could she afford the delay? What if lives were in danger? The hotel and docks were far behind her, back the way she had come. *What if it's Burn or Laina?* What if Volcrian had found them? The city guard? Finally, her Cat's

Eye forced her into motion, and she turned back to the alleys. Crash would just have to wait.

Sora ran up the street, sensing she was getting close. The Cat's Eye's call was becoming stronger, the ringing more persistent in her ears. Chills ran across her skin, wracking her body, her muscles on the verge of cramping.

The buildings were starting to look familiar. Panting, she felt the pit of her stomach fill with dread. Her eyes shot up to a nearby roof, and recognition struck her. It was the same roof that she and Crash had jumped from that morning.

Panic. Hardly able to breathe, Sora leapt up onto a pile of crates, latched onto the roof's gutter, and pulled herself frantically on top of the roof. The tiles were slick, but she found her balance quickly. Once she was standing, she turned and looked around in all directions. The jingling in her ears had reached a fever pitch. She wanted to scream at the necklace to be quiet—she kept listening for the sound of voices, perhaps screams, but the Cat's Eye drowned out everything.

Finally, she spotted a dark shape moving quickly across the rooftops. It didn't appear to be jumping or running....It moved at impossible speeds toward a tall building. She recognized the Dracians' hideout. Her heart lurched, and she realized that the shape wasn't human, nor one of the races, nor even a living creature. *Dear gods,* she thought desperately. *It can't be. Another one, already?*

A wave of fear and memories rushed through her; suddenly she stood in the fields again, staring up at that dark shadow, its sword poised to strike. The wraith had skewered her through the ribs. She almost died.

Another one, she thought. *It's here. Now.* It had taken an entire year...but finally, the second wraith had found them. The thought of facing her own mortality again was terrifying.

She could still see the wraith. It was still a speck across the rooftops. It had paused outside of the Dracians' hideout and hadn't noticed her yet. It hovered close to the tall building, flickering about the air like a massive fly, bobbing and shifting. Every brush of wind seemed to flow through the apparition, blowing it around like smoke.

When they fought the last wraith, it had been like fighting mist; their weapons had whisked right through it, striking nothing. That was a chilling thought. Her companions would be helpless against it.

The creature was hesitating. It was trying to find Burn and Laina. She assumed it could sense that they were close...but it still couldn't see them. What had the High Priestess said? *They're not that smart.* Still several streets away from the creature, Sora started to run with new determination, ignoring her fear, focusing on the memory of Dorian's dead body. She couldn't allow any more of her friends to die. She leapt from roof to roof, past spiraling chimneys and skylights, barely glancing at the tile below her.

As she ran, the wind seemed to pick up, as if urging her to move faster. The clouds swirled angrily. They were still dark and heavy with rain, but now they were shifting, moving at a speed faster than natural. The wind tossed her hair into her face, stinging her eyes. Black clouds crowded the sky above the Dracians' hideout, growing darker and darker, even as she looked. They twisted faster and faster, as though stirred by some giant invisible hand.

Then a twinge shot through her, an electric shock, spurred by her Cat's Eye. Sora stopped in her tracks. Stunned, she stared upward at the sky.

The clouds were beginning to form into a shape. A tornado? No, larger than that...*impossible*....She gasped.

It was a head. Some sort of beast...a horse...? No, a *dragon's* head.

Magic.

Sora had never seen or heard anything like it. The massive jaws of the dragon reached down from the clouds, made solely of mist and vapor, so lifelike that she imagined scales. Her mouth hung open.

The giant stretched its jaws wide and roared. *Rrrruuuuuummmm!* It sounded like a hurricane, like the wind howling across a barren field. There was a crash of thunder; lightning crackled around its jaws. Then the monstrous cloud dragon dove at the roof, straight at the wraith, a thousand times larger than its black-robed prey.

Then she saw him. In the middle of the windstorm stood Jacques, arms raised, a tight expression on his face, on a roof opposite the dark specter. The wraith held a long, black spear in its gloved hand; a dark aura seemed to cover the weapon, fading unnaturally into the air. She remembered her conversation with the Priestess. Could it be the second weapon of the Dark God?

If so, then she needed to get her hands on it...somehow....

Jacques' voice reached her faintly above the thrashing storm. "Wind Dragon! Hear me!" he called. His arms started to glow with silver light. The wind whipped into a cyclone around him.

With a roar of climactic fury, the dragon dove upon the wraith, spewing forth crackling webs of lightning. The wraith held its ground, moving the spear in front of itself. The impact of the two magicks sent a shockwave across the surrounding houses; Sora's legs gave out. She fell down so hard on the roof, she could feel it from her fingertips to her toes. Even her Cat's Eye seemed stunned.

The wraith suddenly flickered out of existence and reappeared on another rooftop, out of reach of the dragon. Then it raised its spear at the giant head, and a stream of black fire poured from the point. It hit the beast's muzzle. The blackness spiraled around the dragon's head like a ribbon of night, bending the glorious horns downward, continuing its way up the neck and into the sky.

The giant beast let out a roar that shook the house beneath her. She could hear the sound of glass shattering, of tiles shaking and sliding to the ground. People stopped on the streets and stared, pointing, screaming, running into their houses or toward the docks.

The dragon tried to break free from the black fire, but it was overwhelmed. The black fire engulfed it, like a python squeezing the life from its prey. Lightning overflowed from the dragon's mouth like blood, creating a sight so spectacular that Sora had to close her eyes—she thought she would go blind.

The wraith let out an ear-splitting shriek. Then the dragon's mouth shut with a snap.

It vanished in a puff of vapor.

Sora stared up at the sky, stunned. Then her eyes fell on Jacques in disbelief. The Dracian swayed for a moment on his distant rooftop, then abruptly fell backwards, apparently in a faint. Or was he dead? He must have expended a lot of energy to create such a spectacle. She didn't know what kind of toll that would take on him.

Sora was filled with cold certainty. *They're going to die if I don't do something,* she realized. The wraith was too powerful, the Wolfy magic aided by the touch of the Dark God. It was too intricate for the Dracians' spells....

Another figure appeared on a roof nearby, and Sora recognized Tristan. He was only a few leaps away, and she headed in his direction, forcing her legs to work. She reached his side within a minute, but he was turned away from her, focused on the wraith, a bow and arrow in his hand. She could see that his arms were trembling. He was shaking too hard to aim.

"D-did you s-see that?" he stuttered in disbelief. "It j-just d-destroyed the d-dragon." He swallowed and cursed again, trying to sight down his trembling bow.

Sora moved on impulse. She had no words for him, but she could feel the Cat's Eye gathering itself, prepared for the challenge. She reached over and grabbed the bow, pulling the weapon easily from his grasp.

"Stand aside," she said through gritted teeth, her eyes burning. "I can do this."

Sora had only held a bow once in her life. She had never actually shot one, but at the moment she was filled with grim confidence. Her Cat's Eye would guide her; her father's spirit and the souls of countless warriors would steady her hand. With a cold glint in her eye, she drew back the bow and sighted her target.

The wraith flickered in the air, dodging left and right, but she watched it with a steady eye. It paused momentarily, and that was all she needed. She let loose the arrow, uttering a silent prayer to the Goddess.

Her aim was true. She shot the apparition straight through the back.

Tristan let out a cry of amazement, but Sora didn't stop to congratulate herself. The arrow sailed through the creature, as though it were nothing but air, and buried itself in the slanting roof, wedged between two tiles. She had known this would happen; she had only wanted to get the creature's attention, to distract it from Jacques.

It whirled around, facing her, nothing but darkness under its hood.

Sora dropped the bow and retrieved her staff. Then she threw herself to the next roof, and the next, until she was near the Dracians' hideout with the wraith. She landed in front of the apparition. It hissed viciously.

"Sora! No!" she heard on the wind. She glanced up to see Burn and Laina watching from a window, shock on their faces.

Laina screamed, "Run! Get away from it!"

Ignoring their warnings, she gripped her Cat's Eye and closed her eyes for the briefest of seconds. *Protect me,* she thought, and a feeling of power surged through her. She grabbed a dagger from her belt and dropped into a fighting stance, facing the wraith. It jabbed at her menacingly with its spear.

"Sora! What are you doing?" Jacques yelled. She didn't turn to look at him. At least he was still alive.

"Don't worry!" She yelled, more to convince herself than anyone else. "I've got it all under control!" *Hopefully.*

The wraith attacked without warning, throwing itself at her with such force that she flew off her feet. She crashed backward, landing hard on the roof. It took her a moment to realize that she hadn't actually been hit; at the last moment, her Cat's Eye had drawn up a shield to protect her. The stone flickered quietly, a rim of green light.

As a result of the shield, the specter was hit with a backlash of its own power, and an inhuman scream pierced the air. Sora leapt to her feet. The wraith recovered in seconds and was ready for her. This time, it was on guard.

It stabbed at her, tendrils of dark energy rising from the spear. Sora dodged each swipe of the weapon, her body moving with unaccustomed grace. She flowed around each jab, easily anticipating the creature's attacks. Then the wraith faked a left and stabbed to the right, so quickly that even the spirits in her Cat's Eye couldn't keep up. The spear struck Sora's shield, but this time, a little magical shock ran through her. When she hit the ground, she was paralyzed for a few seconds.

The necklace was fast losing strength. She could sense that the next hit would be the last one her Cat's Eye would be able to take. Whatever kept the stone from absorbing the wraith's magic was also working its way through her shield. *Dead spirits,* she thought. The creature wasn't entirely magic....

Sora rolled to her feet and dodged another attack, whirling to one side. The spear came again out of nowhere, but she deflected it with her staff, sending a shower of sparks in all directions. They continued moving across the roof and back again. She tried to think of a strategy. She needed to make her necklace stronger, feed it more magic so it could overcome the wraith's defenses...but how? She racked her brain, trying to think of what little she knew about the stone.

They're all relying on me, she thought, the faces of her friends swimming in her vision. *What if I fail? What will happen to them?*

And what about Crash? she thought suddenly. Was he still

waiting for her at the hotel, expecting her to arrive, wondering why she was late...?

The thought of him was like a touchstone—it gave her courage. And quietly, a plan formed in her mind. Desperate, perhaps, but it was all she could think of.

"Jacques! Tristan!" she called out. "When I give the word, attack me with all of your magic!"

"What?" Jacques asked incredulously, yelling above the wind. The black crow fluttered around his head, squawking in alarm. Although the dragon was gone, the storm still circled above them, threatening to pour down at any second. "Attack you? I think not!"

"Trust me, just do it!" Sora leapt as the spear whizzed past her, then dove as it came back around again. Then the wraith flickered, disappearing from in front of her, vanishing like smoke. *Damn.* It had shifted again. She turned, frantic, her heart racing. Where had it gone?

Her senses strained. She listened desperately, trying to see in all directions at once.

Then the spear came swinging out of nowhere, and she dodged. Barely.

The wraith was behind her now. She turned to face it, stumbling across the roof. She felt tired, weaker, the creature more fierce in its attacks.

This is pointless. I can't win like this. Her Cat's Eye needed more power, and she was going to supply it.

Panting and sweating, Sora ducked another swing and leapt back a yard; the spear barely missed her magical shield, which now flashed and danced like a flickering candle. She was off-balance, distracted, suddenly overwhelmed by the wraith's attacks. The next blow hit the forcefield with a resounding *crack!*

The Cat's Eye's defenses shattered, disintegrating into the air.

"Now!" she screamed. "Hit me now!"

Wham! Sora didn't know where it came from, or from whom, but a force of magic suddenly struck her from behind. *Fire,* she thought. *It must be Tristan.* Red flames engulfed her, covering her body, racing over her skin—but none of it touched her. Instead, the necklace gave out a fierce, melodic chime, and sucked up the magic like water. It drank and drank....She felt life surge into the stone....

Whooosh! She was hit from the other side, a blast of wind more than natural. Jacques was adding his own magic to the mix. Sora fell to her knees, stunned, her body overcome by the intense energy. The Cat's Eye buzzed at her neck, trembling as it absorbed the new magic, eagerly recharging.

Nothing left for it, she thought, forcing herself to climb back to her feet. The wraith hovered a few feet away, observing her, put off by the sudden surge of energy.

Sora took a deep breath. "Come on, is that all you've got?" she taunted loudly. Her hair kept blowing into her face, obscuring her vision. "You're pathetic! I suppose Volcrian just made you out of weak blood, huh?" She tried to think of another insult for the wraith, but couldn't.

Amazingly enough, it worked—much better than she thought it would. The wraith threw back its head and screamed an ear-shattering note to the sky, then lowered its spear. The tip was inches from her chest.

A ray of black fire shot out of the spear's tip and hit Sora's outer shield. The force of the blow shattered the barrier like glass. Despite the cries of horror from the spectators, Sora had been prepared for this, and reached out, grabbing onto the end of the spear. She focused on channeling all of the magic into her Cat's Eye.

It was not clean magic. The power from the Dracians felt cool and clear, like spring water. The wraith's magic was like vinegar. Her muscles burned and a sour taste filled her mouth.

With a gasp, she whispered, *"Now!"*

The Cat's Eye let out a burst of power, sending a bolt of energy up Sora's arms, through the spear and into the wraith.

She could feel the four magicks twisting, flowing through her, mixing like a torrential river. She was being sucked down by an undertow. The roof melted beneath her, the sky bled into the ground; all she could see was the spear and the wraith and endless streams upon streams of color....She wanted to scream, but her voice would not work and her body...her body was...gone....

Then—a roar. Monstrously loud. Out of the corner of her eye, Sora saw something shooting toward her. It was a wave of absolute darkness, a pitch-black tunnel. It approached her like a charging horse, and she thought she saw the vague outline of some unknown creature...something with giant wings...and horns....

The tunnel engulfed her.

Spinning....

A loud screech, like the cry of a dying animal.

The ground rolled.

* * *

A raindrop hit her face.

More raindrops. Her eyes were wide open.

She blinked.

Had it been a second? An hour?

What was she staring at? The sky?

Voices were yelling, strangely dim, and then there were live bodies all around her.

Laina, crying and hugging her. Burn holding both her and Laina, and Tristan and Jacques down on their knees, patting her arms....

"We got the spear!" Laina was saying excitedly, a long piece of black wood in her hands. Sora vaguely recognized the creature's weapon; the shaft was gone, just like on the rapier, leaving only the spearhead behind. She wanted to feel relieved at this—two weapons collected, one to go—but really, she was just tired. She almost rolled over and fell asleep. Then another raindrop hit and she jolted back to herself, as though pulled down from a cloud. "W-what...what was it?"

"A wraith, you silly girl! Another wraith! What would we do without you, Sora!" Burn shouted.

"No, Burn, the magic." She tried to grab his arm, but she felt heavy and awkward. "Didn't you see the blackness? What was it?"

"Ach, my girl, you're talking nonsense," said Jacques in confusion.

"No, there was something else...."

"Sora!" someone yelled.

The two Dracians were shoved out of the way. Crash took their place and grabbed her by the shoulders, running his hands down her arms. She felt warmth seep through her at the contact. "Are you wounded?"

"No," she said, shocked at that truth. She was untouched,

except for her exhaustion.

Crash leaned over her, looking more worried then she had ever seen him. Then Sora refocused her eyes. There was a...shadow around him, dark against the air....

Reaching up, she tried to touch the darkness, but her hand went right through it. Then the aura dissipated, as though it had never been there.

"Sora? Are you all right?" Laina asked, staring at her raised hand.

"Maybe not...." Sora frowned. "Sorry, my vision is still blurry." Crash was sweating. She had never seen him sweat before. And no, it wasn't drops of rain. "You're drenched," she said, trying to sit up, only to have both Burn and Crash push her back down.

"And you, Sora, are trembling like a man lost in the mountains in his undershorts...." Burn began.

"Why are you sweating, Crash?" she asked softly.

He looked at her strangely. "I had to hurry, Sora. I saw the wraith, and I knew...."

"Knew what?"

"That...that I might be too late," he said, his voice quiet.

He let go of her arms, beginning to close off. The other men in the group shifted uncomfortably. Had she embarrassed him?

She grinned. "I thought you'd have more faith in me by now."

Crash nodded, though her vision was getting worse and she could feel her body starting to drift away, pulled towards sleep. She let a weary sigh escape her lips. "So why weren't you here sooner?"

"I...."

"Are you two quite done?" Jacques cut in loudly. "This young lady needs rest!"

Crash leaned down, and Sora felt herself already losing consciousness. "I came as fast as I could," he whispered into her ear.

Then she dropped into a deep sleep.

CHAPTER 15

Lorianne raised her eyes to the top windows of the brothel. It was well past midnight, but of course the windows were still lit. *What am I doing here?* she asked herself for the third time.

Ferran stood next to her, his thumbs hooked in his belt. He swaggered up to the front door with a stride that she remembered.

"Really?" she called after him. "This is where you sold the book?"

He shrugged. "Had to pay the woman somehow."

"You're a complete mess."

No response. She wondered if he had heard her.

They had spent the last day in the small fishing village of Pismo. She explained her situation to him—the plague, the Cat's Eye, the sacred weapons, her daughter....

"So you have need of my...services?" he had said in a low voice, leaning across the table toward her, sobering up over a mug of tea.

She raised an eyebrow. *"You're still a treasure hunter, aren't you?"*

"All my life," he had replied.

He knew about the sacred weapons. More than once, he had entertained the thought of searching for them. He had owned a book a few years ago, salvaged from a burned library, that outlined how to find and destroy the sacred weapons....It had included a map, too. Priceless—if accurate.

But nothing had come of it. He had finally given up that life—*lost faith, you see, grew tired of it all*—and had sold the book to a good friend.

Yeah, a good friend, Lori thought, staring up at the brothel. She eyed the back of his head distastefully. The past day, they had sailed up the coast in his small boat to the slightly larger town of Cape Shorn. The brothel was a large red building, right on the docks. She really shouldn't have been surprised. They were quite common in port cities; sailors were eager customers. *I wonder what other kind of friends he keeps....*

"Not many," he said over his shoulder, and put his hand on the door of the brothel.

Lori's mouth opened in surprise. "What?"

"Friends," he replied. "I don't have many." Then he opened the front door.

Lori shook her head. She must have spoken her thoughts aloud. Right? He couldn't *read* her thoughts, that was impossible.

He glanced back at her, saw her expression, and grinned. "Come now, Lori. Your silence is an open book. You haven't changed that much."

Her cheeks flushed and she glared. "Sure," she said. That's what he thought.

They entered the brothel. It smelled strongly of incense. The inside was richly decorated in deep purple carpet with elaborate wall hangings, everything from floral paintings to tapestries of men and women, tastefully—or distastefully—posed next to each other.

With all the brash colors, Lori didn't expect the soft, low music that permeated the air. It was almost pleasant. Then her eyes landed on the harp in the corner, and she changed her mind. A naked woman sat behind it, softly plucking the strings, dressed only in a large gold necklace that dangled provocatively between her breasts. Lori stared, slightly jarred by the sight. *Oh, come now, I'm over thirty, this shouldn't be shocking,* she scolded herself. But she hadn't spent much of her life in these places. No, she had stuck to the country, to small towns and quiet ways.

Ferran walked past the harp and the harpist without glancing at them. He approached the front desk, which was made of beautiful dark rosewood. The woman who stood behind the desk was probably the only clothed employee in the entire building. "Is Beatrice in?" Ferran asked.

The woman glanced up. She had piles of black hair clipped messily atop her head. A large, dark mole kissed her upper lip. Her makeup was so thick, Lori thought it might be outright paint.

"Hey, Ferran," she said casually. "Haven't seen you around in a while."

Lori frowned. *How long is "a while?"*

Ferran shrugged. Shrugging seemed to be his favorite response to any sort of question. "Is Beatrice in?" he asked again.

The woman looked at him for a moment, then glanced at Lori, arching a black eyebrow. A mischievous smile twisted her lips. She pointed her long, feathered quill at a staircase to their left. "The pearl room," she said. "Upstairs. Door 24...but I'm sure you remember."

Lori wondered what that look was for.

Ferran nodded briefly, then turned, following her directions. Lori fell into step behind him. They started up the narrow staircase, the air around them heavy with perfume.

"A year," he said.

"What?"

"A year since I've been here." He glanced over his shoulder, surprisingly close to Lori in the cramped space. His eyes glinted wickedly. "You were wondering, weren't you?"

Lori sighed. "Stop this, Ferran. I get it, you fell in love with a whore."

"Who said anything about love?"

"Please don't make me think any worse of you," she said in exasperation.

Then he threw back his head and laughed. "And you haven't had a lover since Dane passed?"

The question shocked her—it was unexpected. She hadn't heard Dane's name from anyone in almost ten years.

"I've...I've met some people," she said evasively. Honestly, Lori didn't want to think about it. She had given up Sora when she was twenty. For a few years, she had tried to rebuild, meet someone new, but....

They reached the second floor and headed down a narrow hallway. Doors were evenly spaced on either side. *21...22...23....*Room 24 was a small, ovular white door with gold letters painted on the front. Despite the thick walls, Lori could hear soft laughter and deep groans coming from the other side.

Ferran didn't knock; he simply grabbed the handle and opened the door. Lori stared, shocked again. *You'd think it would be locked!*

"Hey, Beatrice!" he called, entering the room. "Remember that book I gave you?"

Lori hesitated slightly, then followed. She expected to be screamed at—she certainly would scream in such a situation—but there was no such rebuke. Instead, she shut the door softly behind her and looked around the room.

The pearl room was decorated in soft whites and silvers. The bed looked like a giant clam shell. A man was tucked under the covers, staring at them speechlessly, his mouth agape. He was an older gentleman, portly, perhaps a sea merchant.

Beatrice was a tall, voluptuous redhead with more than ample curves. She was dressed in a corset, tall leather boots and fishnet stockings. She carried a switch in one hand.

Ferran raised his hand, waving slightly to the client. "Pardon me," he said. Then he turned back to Beatrice. "About that book...."

The woman glanced over them with bored, hooded eyes, as though interruptions were common. "Really, Ferran?" she finally asked. "That was a year ago...."

"Turns out I need it."

"Hmph. Well, as I recall, I sold it. And it didn't even pay for half of your charges."

There was an awkward silence. Lori smirked at him, but Ferran didn't return her look. "Ah, well, money's a bit tight as it is," he muttered. "Sorry about that. Do you recall who you sold it to?"

"Yeah, a pirate, just like you," she retorted.

"Treasure hunter. I've never captained a ship," Ferran corrected.

"Like I care. He came by about a month ago and paid good silver for it."

"Did he say where he was going?"

"Aye," she said, and nodded to her left, indicating some distant, unseen location. "He's anchored up the coast a bit, towards Sylla Cove." Then she slapped the switch against her thigh—*snap!*

Everyone in the room jumped. "Is that all? I'm busy."

Ferran nodded and gave them both a short bow. Then he turned, grabbed Lori's hand, and pulled her from the room.

"What...?" she started.

"Well, we know where the book is," he said. "Time to head to the Cove."

"And do *what,* exactly?" she asked as they headed down the hall, back the way they came.

"I'm thinking we're going to have to steal it back."

Lori rolled her eyes. "Ferran, there's better ways of doing this, we aren't kids anymore....We should try to barter."

"Oh, and with what money?" He looked her up and down briefly. "Last I checked, your coin purse was quite light."

Lori grinned mischievously at that. "You checked my coin purse? When?" she asked, eyes glinting. "I stashed the rest where you wouldn't find it. I'm a Healer, you know. I make a good living...."

"Is that so?" Ferran asked slowly.

Lori returned his look. "Yes, it is. Anyway, we don't have the time to dally around."

"And we won't. We'll leave tonight to get the book."

They started down the staircase. Lori was eager to exit the building. The combination of perfume and incense were giving her a headache...and it was stiflingly hot.

"Think you could buy me a drink, then?" Ferran asked, as they approached the front door.

"No," she said.

"Oh, come on, Lori, what happened to you?"

"*Life* happened to me," she barked, and jumped out the front door into the wide, cool night. She started walking down the docks at a fast pace, forcing him to keep up with her, toward where he had moored his boat. A dozen or so ships sat on the cape, at varying distances from the shore. None of them were larger than a fishing vessel; there were no cargo ships or large merchant vessels. It was past midnight and the town was finally winding down; the only people on the street were sailors and questionable women.

"And what's that supposed to mean?" Ferran asked, coming up behind her. "Like life doesn't happen to all of us...."

"I'm a Healer," she explained sharply. She wasn't sure why she felt so defensive; somehow, she had hoped that Ferran had found a new life for himself, a successful trade or at least a supportive wife and children. Instead, she was faced with a late-thirty-something bachelor who still got into bar fights. "I don't drink. And you're not drinking anymore either, not as long as you travel with me. I'm going to need your head on straight. This plague is spreading. You might not have seen it yet, but...it's terrible." Her voice ended close to a whisper, her mind distracted by the patients she had treated. Her remedies had been useless against the sickness. That left a cold pit of dread in her stomach.

The treasure hunter groaned behind her. "Fine," he muttered. "I get it. You're stingy. I don't like it...and I *will* hold it against you."

She smacked his arm in annoyance. He grunted in response.

When she glanced sideways at him, he was staring straight ahead...and grinning.

* * *

Volcrian was enjoying his time, strangely enough.

He was camped close to the ocean, enough to taste its saltiness with each breath. The smell reminded him of clean, fresh blood. That alone would have made for a good night...but to top it off, he was spending it with a beautiful woman.

A beautiful dead woman.

He grinned across the fire at her, a small hen roasting over the open flame. The once-priestess of the Wind Goddess was clothed in her ceremonial robes, just as he had found her, though he had cut the neckline daringly low, displaying her mangled neck. Her eyes stared vacantly at the flames. He had never cared for a woman's chatter, but her youth and beauty were preserved on her pale face, like a porcelain doll.

"Eat, love," he said, offering her a piece of meat. Then he smiled. "Not hungry?"

"Release me," she replied. Her voice was dry, crinkled, like an autumn leaf.

"In time," he replied.

He had killed a dozen men first, then had dragged her through the city and out into the fields, where he had bled her dry. She had struggled, of course. A feisty one, this priestess. Even after death, she still had the gall to speak to him.

The rest of Barcella had watched helplessly. None had raised a weapon in her defense. He had seen fear shining in their eyes. Not even the remaining handful of soldiers had tried to stop him. He hadn't even been followed. Cowards. Of course the humans would abandon each other. There were so many; what mattered if one more died?

The memory of killing her brought a rush of excitement to him. There was something powerful about death, about mastering it. He felt invincible, more alive than ever before. He was getting better at using the blood magic, more controlled, his spells stronger than ever.

"So tell me about yourself," he said to the dead woman. "Tell me about your Goddess."

"She will come for you. She will save me."

"Ha!" he barked, and took a bite of meat. It wasn't quite done yet, but he liked the taste of uncooked flesh. "Then tell me, why didn't your Goddess stop your death? Why didn't she strike me down?"

The priestess turned her blank, glassy eyes upon him. Her movements were slow and stiff, suitable to a corpse. She did not answer. Volcrian threw back his head and laughed, a sharp sound. "I can answer that for you," he said, still chuckling. "Because my powers are not bound by a Goddess. No, sweet priestess, I am beyond Her reach...and soon, just maybe, I shall become a God myself...."

Volcrian paused. Become a God? Where had that come from? He hadn't considered it before, had never desired it. But certainly, all things were possible with blood magic. The idea was suddenly very attractive. He could begin a following, spread his influence, gather servants....Why not?

He felt an odd tremor inside of him. His head swam, looking for a reason. No...no, this wasn't about power, he reminded himself. It was about Etienne. He shuddered. For a moment, he had almost forgotten his brother's memory, his murdered body on the steps of the flower shop.

Forgive me, brother, he thought, and shook his head. He was giddy, high from the blood of the priestess, distracted. Of course he wouldn't forget his hunt. It had consumed his life for years. He *couldn't* forget.

He felt slightly sobered by the memory of his brother. A bitter taste entered his mouth. He turned back to the priestess and raised a thin, silver eyebrow.

"I'm bored," he said, grimacing. "This spell isn't meant for conversation. Dance for me." And he sat back against the grass, watching the young priestess with narrowed eyes.

"I cannot," the priestess replied.

It surprised him, and he glared, his temper rising. "You are my servant and my creation, little pet."

"The dead do not dance."

"By my command, *they do.*"

Then, as though pulled by invisible strings, the corpse rose to its feet. It staggered for a moment in place. Volcrian watched, waiting.

Slowly, she began to slide from foot to foot, her body swaying and spinning to the crackle of flames. He liked the way she bent against the fire, the way her shadow flickered on the ground, how the light licked across her white skin.

He even liked the streaks of blood that leaked from her eyes— perhaps tears, perhaps the natural decay of the body. He didn't care which.

CHAPTER 16

Sora slept through the second half of the day, but was rudely awakened close to midnight. According to the Dracians, the ship they were planning on "commandeering" had just docked, and it was time to get a move on. They quickly packed. Both sacred weapons were carefully wrapped up and stored. She felt exhausted and shaky upon waking, but the thought of boarding a ship seemed simple enough. *You just pack your luggage, walk up a plank and set sail....*

But of course, they weren't just boarding a ship.

Sora tried not to seem too obvious as she mingled around the perimeter of the docks, watching as cargo was unloaded from an incredibly large, seagoing vessel. *Not a boat,* she thought. *A ship. A true ship.* It was the size of several houses, two stories up to the deck, and a third level above it. She stood in her mother's cloak with her staff held tight to her chest, leaning back against the shadowy overhang of a building, hoping she didn't come off as nervous, which she certainly was.

It was dark, about an hour past midnight, and the docks were all but deserted. The storm had relented for a moment, but it was still freezing cold. The only light came from the ship, where dull lanterns swung slightly side to side. The buildings behind her were mostly large warehouses, used for storing cargo.

At this very moment, her friends were positioning themselves for a total takeover of the ship. All of their supplies had been packed onto rowboats, and the Dracians were sneaking them around the rear of the vessel, where they would be lifted aboard by ropes. It didn't seem very safe, but with most of the crew distracted at the front of the ship, the Dracians had assured them it would go smoothly.

"Don't worry, we've done this before," Tristan had winked. Sora wasn't completely convinced. From what she could tell, they were fond of taking risks.

Goddess take me...how did I get myself wrapped up in this mess? she thought. She was still tired from the wraith's attack, and now she was about to enter a new battle. Hopefully this one wouldn't be as draining. From what she could see, the sailors were of all matter of heights, makes and creeds—and they all had one thing in common: bulging muscles.

Glancing from left to right, she barely spotted Laina slinking about in the shadows of a doorway. The frost on her breath was more visible than the girl herself. Her eyes picked up another brief movement on top of one of the roofs. *That would have to be one of the Dracians.* Tristan, maybe, or André.

Sora felt the first drops of rain hit her face. The storm was preparing for another go, and she braced herself for a miserable night. Already she could feel the temperature dropping. The sailors sensed it too, for they doubled in speed, swinging pulleys back and forth, and the occasional net of fish.

Another shadow on the rooftop flitted by her eyes. Joan, perhaps.

The sailors appeared to be growing uneasy. They were looking over their shoulders, gazing into alleyways and dark windows. Sora knew she was fairly visible, and she had already attracted a few looks. There was nothing she could do about that. *What's taking them so long?* she wondered, and shifted nervously.

She was to lead the frontal assault, aided by Laina, Burn, and a handful of Dracians. The rest of their crew—about two-dozen in total—were already aboard the ship, quietly dispatching the few sentinels on duty. The sign for attack should come any second now.

Suddenly, one of the torches on board went out.

The sign.

It's time. Two more torches went out on the ship, and she brought her fingers up to her lips, summoning an earsplitting whistle. All of the sailors turned to look at her, their faces slack with confusion.

Then the docks erupted in a flurry of whoops and yells. The Dracians leapt from behind boxes and out of shadowed doorways. Arrows shot down from the rooftops; Laina and Tristan's work, for certain. From on deck, a scream split the night. Several bodies fell into the ocean.

The sailors began running about, drawing swords and knives, shouting to one another. It would only be a matter of minutes before they organized. Sora, staff in hand, plunged into the crowd of sailors, laying several out with sharp whacks to the head. *This isn't so hard,* she thought, pleasantly surprised. And to think she had actually been worried....

They were larger than she, though, and strong from pulling ropes and climbing rigging. A few started to catch on to what was happening, and after that, her task became a lot harder. As Jacques had predicted, most of the sailors rushed back to the ship to help the captain. Quickly, she signaled to a few Dracians and maneuvered herself between the ship and the rest of the sailors.

Gods, they're huge! she thought as they advanced. A half dozen broke through their line and made it aboard the ship. With a grunt of determination, Sora leapt in front of the rest of them. She rammed her staff into the thick chin of a charging sailor, then jabbed another hard in the ribs. Bones crunched. The man doubled over with a gasp, and she kicked him in the face.

With a whirl, she tripped another to the ground, then brought up her staff to deflect a sword blow. The blade went flying sideways, skittering across the cobblestones, glinting in the hazy rain. She smacked the sailor hard on the hand, breaking a few fingers. The man screamed in pain.

Then arms grabbed her from behind, and someone heaved her upward. Her staff was wrenched from her grip and sent flying into the darkness; then the world went briefly upside down as she was tossed over someone's shoulder. *Fight, Sora!* her inner voice screamed.

She shoved her elbow into the man's throat, jamming his windpipe. Immediately, she was released. She dropped to the ground, landing clumsily, off-balance. More sailors jumped her, and with a burst of energy, she started punching left and right, aiming at their enraged faces. She broke one nose, jabbed another sailor in the eyes. She tried to grab her daggers, but there was no time.

Heavy hands tried to pull her to the ground. It was difficult to see; she rolled to one side, barely evading a dagger thrust aimed at her chest. The sailors pressed in around her, a forest of broad arms and waists.

Then a knee drove into her back.

She gasped, momentarily paralyzed. She fell to the ground, a painful kick striking her ribs and a boot crushing her shoulder. She wanted to scream for help, but couldn't seem to recover her lungs.

"Keeeee-ya!"

The shout was sudden, ferocious. A body went sailing over her, and then four more bodies. The mob of sailors quickly scattered. Sora looked up in a daze, her head spinning, her body covered with a myriad of cuts and bruises.

Before her stood Joan, outlined by the light from the ship, her deep auburn hair like a glowing flame.

"You okay, sister?" the Dracian asked. "There were a lot of 'em! You're lucky I spotted you!" She extended a hand and pulled Sora to her feet.

There was a crash of thunder. The skies opened, as though waiting for the ideal moment, and rain poured to the ground, spilling down in torrents. Within seconds, they were both drenched. Sora slipped a little on the cobblestones, already slick from the pouring rain.

"Thanks, Joan, good thing it's over now," she said.

"Over?" Joan asked, raising an eyebrow. "Not yet!"

As though echoing her sentiment, there was a chorus of yells from the ship.

"Watch out!" someone cried.

"Goddess, grab the ropes!"

"Too late! *Aggh!*"

She turned, just in time to see a massive crate swing through the air. No one had control of the pulley. The crate hung from several flimsy ropes, which were quickly unraveling.

No, not a crate...a cage, with metal bars along its sides. Sora frowned—*but why?* The ropes finally snapped, and the giant cage came crashing to the ground.

Cru-crunchhh!

The wood exploded in a thousand shards. The metal bars were shaken loose, and several went bouncing across the docks—*tong, tong*—skidding wildly. One flew up into the face of a sailor, cracking him across the cheek. The man fell to the ground with a scream.

It took a moment for Sora to hear what the sailors were saying.

"Kraken!" one yelled, dashing past her. "Watch out! It's loose!"

"Aye, get to cover! 'Tis a Kraken!"

Sora stared after the running sailors, confused. *Kraken...?*

A long, thin yelp pierced the night, close to the cry of a wildcat. Sora flinched and looked around. She squinted. Somewhere between the sheets of rain, she could see a large, black shape rising from the wreckage of the crates.

Then Joan grabbed her arm. "By the Goddess!" she gasped. "'Tis a Kraken! Quickly, Sora!"

But the creature had already turned toward them. A sailor, the same one who had been struck by the metal bar, tried to run away but didn't move fast enough. The long, wiry shape leapt after him, flying through the air, landing on the sailor's back. The man let out a bloodcurdling scream, then tumbled to the ground. Only the sound of ripping flesh was heard.

When the creature raised its head, an arm was hanging from its mouth. It looked straight at them with glowing yellow eyes.

The Kraken was small, the size of a mountain lion, perhaps still a baby. She could dimly remember the name now; she had read about the sea monster in books, but she hadn't truly thought they were real. The beast had a horse's neck, a mane of black hair sprouting from its nape. The rest of its body was low to the ground, squat and reptilian. It was too dark to make out its coloring, but its face reminded her of an eel, with a hooked jaw and rows upon rows of razor-sharp teeth. The mouth was wide enough to swallow a man's head.

As she watched, the Kraken crunched through the body of the screaming sailor, limb by flimsy limb.

"Run!" Joan screamed, turning to flee. Sora turned as well, but the Kraken was attracted to their movement. It abandoned the body of the sailor and lunged across the docks, slithering and loping like a giant weasel, heading straight for them.

There was no safe place to run, and Sora wasn't fast enough to outpace the beast. Instead, she dove for her staff, which was tangled up in a pile of rope next to the ship. She didn't want to get close enough to the beast to use her daggers.

She skidded to a stop on the rainy cobblestones, reaching down to grab her staff. When she turned around, the beast was right behind her, and she raised her weapons just in time to catch its snapping jaws. Its teeth crunched down on the wood, mid-bite; she could imagine those jaws snapping a sword, but her staff held firm, without even a scratch. She let out a breath of relief. Witch wood.

Then the beast thrashed its head, and she almost lost her grip. With a mighty heave, Sora threw the beast off her, twisting her staff out of its mouth. The Kraken curled its massive head upward, flexing its thickly corded neck. Then it opened its mouth and hissed at her.

Sora was prepared for the next attack, but then Joan flew onto the scene, sword in hand. *"Keeey-a!"* She slashed and swiped at the rear of the beast, clipping off a chunk of its long, fin-like tail.

The Kraken shrieked, a sound like shattering plates, then turned around, tail lashing, jaws snapping angrily at the air. It lunged at Joan, spitting and hissing, leaving gobs of black phlegm on the docks.

"Hey!" Sora yelled, trying to attract the beast away from Joan. She brought her staff down on its hind quarter, hoping to break its leg, or at least distract it.

The Kraken shrugged off the blow. It turned to snarl at her, then went back to Joan, lunging forward, trying to bite around the sword.

"Run, Sora!" Joan yelled. "Get on the ship!"

"No way!" Sora yelled back. "I won't leave you!"

Then the monster lunged past Joan's defenses and bit down on her leg. The Dracian screamed, an ear-piercing shriek full of pain that made Sora want to cover her ears, her stomach curling in horror. She brought her staff down again, over and over, trying to beat the creature off the woman, but the Kraken was impervious to her blows. They bounced off its thick scales.

Joan kept screaming, and total panic enveloped Sora. Her friend would be eaten right in front of her, and there was nothing she could do! Her Cat's Eye was useless against such a creature. Her staff wasn't sharp enough to split the scales. She would have to fling herself on its back to use her daggers—and that was sheer suicide. She beat away at the Kraken furiously, but to no effect.

Sora opened her mouth and screamed.

CHAPTER 17

Crash's knife sung with the night, whirling through darkness, invisible death. In this moment, he felt more like steel than a man; sharper than the blade he fought with. He stabbed a sailor in the gut, then whirled around, swiping his knife across the throats of two more. He moved so fast that his enemies didn't even realize they were wounded. He watched their expressions—the slow blossom of understanding, the sudden flicker of horror. Their hands flew up to their throats, blood running between their fingers. With a mighty kick, he sent them staggering into each other, then stumbling overboard into the ocean.

There were no more sailors onboard. The ship was secured. Sheathing his daggers, he turned to join the rest of the Dracians, who were preparing to cast off. It had taken longer than he had anticipated, and he didn't like the delay. He had to leave the city before Volcrian reached them—or before the Shade made another appearance.

Abruptly the wind shifted, and his head snapped up. A scream pierced the air. It skittered across his skin and reverberated through his bones. He shivered. Suddenly, he felt as though a large hand was squeezing his stomach, tighter and tighter, making it impossible to breathe. Danger. Uncertainty. Fear...?

Sora!

That scream, that pitch, the direction it came from....Crash found himself running across the ship, bounding toward the docks.

Sweet Goddess—no!

* * *

The rain battered Sora's face, but did nothing to calm her fear; she was too scared to move. Her hands shook where they gripped her staff, wet and slick.

The Kraken had released Joan's leg at last, and the Dracian had stumbled away, unable to walk. It would have chased her down, but Sora had lunged between them. A foolhardy move, to be sure—but she would not let her friend die.

The Kraken snapped at her, lashing its tail, so close she could smell the stench of its breath. It was not as timid as it had been before. Its eyes flickered over her, and with a snarling yowl, it lunged, its body flying through the air. Sora raised her staff, her only defense, just as the beast made impact.

Wham!

She crashed to the ground, the Kraken's body on top of her, its powerful claws tearing up the cobblestones, snagging and ripping up wood and rock. It pierced her shirt and shredded the cloth down the front, grazing her skin.

She screamed again.

Then, from nowhere, a black shape sped past her, as brief and furious as lightning. The beast let out another roar—this time, one of pain. Abruptly the Kraken sprang off her, whirling to face the new threat.

Sora took a moment to regain herself, her head spinning with panic, adrenaline pounding. There were sounds of distress and grunts from behind her, and when she finally turned around, she could only stare in confusion. The Kraken was slowly backing across the docks toward the water's edge. A black shadow darted around it like a vicious wasp. Slowly, step by step, the monster was driven back, but it was fiercely enraged, snapping at its attacker, long claws slashing through the air.

Then Joan was next to her, limping heavily, using one of the metal poles to help support herself. Sora could see blood trickling down her shredded pant leg.

Joan grabbed her by the arm. "Let's go," she said.

The two began stumbling toward the ship. Sora's eyes remained on the wicked fight, the spitting Kraken and the deadly shadow, barely visible through the torrential rain.

"Who...who is that?" she finally asked, squinting through the darkness. "*What* is that?"

"I believe it's your assassin friend," Joan said through gritted teeth. She leaned heavily against Sora, staggering toward the ship.

Sora's jaw went slack. From this angle, she couldn't make him out clearly, only that he was somehow dodging the Kraken's spear-like claws. She felt cold. Shocked. The beast was twice his size and just as fast, and the cobblestones were as slick as ice.

No...I have to...I have to help him somehow, that monster is far too large...but what can I do? A slow, sinking fear crept over her. Nothing. She could do nothing. She would only get in the way.

Joan tugged at her and Sora realized she had stopped walking. With one last, desperate glance, she turned and ran the rest of the way to the plank, practically carrying the Dracian, her staff gripped hard in her hand.

Once on-board, a sailor lunged at her, one of the last of the crew trying to get off the ship. A Dracian, unrecognizable in the flickering firelight, kicked him down into the water.

Sora was too shaken to respond, even to the surprise attack. She stared at her rescuer for a long, stunned moment before she recognized Jacques. As though on cue, a large, dark crow fluttered down from the sky, landing awkwardly on his shoulder. A strip of flesh hung from its beak.

Tristan appeared too, standing slightly behind him. There were a few bruises on the younger Dracian's jaw, but other than that, he seemed to be in good shape. He was even grinning.

Sora let out a shuddering breath and shoved Joan into Tristan's arms. "Get her to the infirmary," she said. "She was bitten by a Kraken."

"Crikey!" Tristan exclaimed. "Crippled by a Kraken?" He grabbed Joan just as she began to collapse on the deck, and swung her up into his arms.

Jacques shook his head. "She'll be all right, Sora. Dracians are immune to the beast's poison."

"Poison...?" Sora asked, surprised. Then she quickly scanned herself for wounds. Shockingly, there were none, except the slight graze to her chest, which wasn't even enough to draw blood. She checked her arms and legs twice. Her adrenaline was still surging and she doubted she would feel a small cut.

There was a high-pitched yowl from below, and she looked at the docks again, feeling another burst of concern. What if Crash was bitten?

No one asked what the noise had been. Tristan turned to walk away, carrying Joan in his arms, and Jacques waved to the Dracians who manned the rigging. "Unfurl the sails!" he called. "Prepare to cast off! We have a good wind behind us and a long voyage ahead."

"Wait!" Sora cried, stopping Jacques from pulling up the boarding plank. "Crash is still down there!"

He frowned. "Are ye certain?" he asked, turning to look at her.

"Yes! Don't draw anchor yet!"

Jacques nodded to her, a grave expression in his eyes. Then he held up his hand. All of the Dracians stopped in their tracks. "Hold up!" he yelled. "One crew member is still on the docks!"

The crow squawked, as though echoing his command. Then it took off into the air, flying over the side of the boat into the darkness.

Sora nodded. She watched their small crew scramble to obey. Then she frowned. She wanted to ask where Jacques had been just a few minutes ago, and why she and Joan had been left alone on the docks with a Kraken in their midst. And why had no one helped them earlier, and why was no one going down to the docks to fight alongside Crash...?

But Jacques turned away from her, preoccupied. He cursed at one of the Dracians who was tangling up the ropes.

A sudden, shuddering roar rumbled across the docks, followed by the sound of a heavy body splashing into the water. Her insides quivered sickeningly, a horrible jolt rocking her chest, and she found herself peering desperately over the railing, trying to see through the darkness. Silence descended. Her heart lodged in her throat.

Come on, Crash....come on.....

The rain lashed down. It thrummed against the wooden deck like a thousand jabbing fingers. It was impossible to hear anything else. Sora was drenched, shivering with cold. Her stomach felt like it would slide right out of her mouth.

She knew Crash was a skilled fighter...but the Kraken was a vicious, powerful beast that had torn the sailors to pieces. No man could have won that battle. The vision of Crash's body, floating still and cold in the murky water below, or perhaps dragged under the waves to some far-off den, stayed firm in her mind.

Sora wished something would move, even if it was the monster. She just wanted to know what was happening, to break the horrible tension. The rain continued to pound. She listened with all of her might; she felt as though her ears were slowly separating from her head, she was straining so hard.

Then, dimly, barely above the rain, she heard the sound of boots treading on hollow wood. *Thunk...thunk...thunk....*

A figure formed out of the storm. A crow hovered above him, drifting in the rain like a strange banner. Swaying from side to side, bent almost double, Sora still thought he was the most beautiful sight in the world.

Crash stepped slowly and softly off the plank, into the light of the ship's lanterns. At first she thought he would walk right past her, without even sparing her a glance. But then he paused at her side. His eyes were trained on the wood beneath them, the expression on his face unreadable.

"It's dead," he said. His voice was cold, without inflection. It made the tiny hairs on her arms rise.

She gazed at him in silence, unsure of what to say. "Thank you" seemed close to ludicrous.

Crash let his head drop another notch and a shudder ran through his body. Then he closed the small gap between them. She stiffened, surprised. Slowly, unexpectedly, he laid his forehead against her shoulder. His breath was hot through the damp cloth of her shirt.

Neither moved for a long moment—a moment in which Sora thought she would completely crumble. She had never felt such worry, such panic, over another human being.

Then Crash said quietly, "You're shaking."

Of course I'm shaking! she wanted to scream, but she didn't want to tell him why. *Dammit, Sora, be strong!*

He stood up a little straighter, then slowly pulled her into his shirt and released a long, silent breath into her damp hair. Enveloped by his warmth, she couldn't think, stunned by the show of emotion. *Perhaps...perhaps I am finally seeing beneath the mask.*

"Are you going to cry again?" he asked, and she could hear humor in his voice. Of all things!

"Warriors don't cry," she whispered brokenly. And if she did let a few tears slip out, it was purely from exhaustion, and well-hidden by the wind, rain, and Crash's thick shirt.

He held her like that, motionless, for what Sora felt was a long time, though it was probably more like five minutes. She didn't want to move away; she liked the strength of his arms, his height, his scent. He burned like a slow fire, hot-blooded.

"Well, we should tell Jacques to set sail," she finally whispered. It was a nice position to be in, but it couldn't last forever, and there were still many things to do. She started to pull away, then paused when he didn't move.

"Crash?" she said. His arms stayed tight around her, almost too tight. After listening to his shallow breathing, she knew something was wrong. *"Crash?"* she repeated, alarmed, and pulled her head out of his shirt. His eyes were half-closed and his breathing was far too shallow. "Hello?" Still no response.

She jerked backward in sudden fear. His grip loosened and his body slumped to one side, almost toppling them both. She gasped as she caught his weight. "Crash!"

Sora laid him down on the deck and stepped back. Disbelief crept over her face. *No, no, this isn't happening!* she thought desperately. *Crash can't be hurt, it's not possible!* The only other time she had seen him like this was ages ago, while they were crossing the swamp and he had almost drowned.

The wind picked up. Sora felt something warm and sticky on her shirt. Looking down, she stared in horror.

Blood.

The whole front of her shirt was soaked in blood, deep crimson, almost black in the firelight, and still warm. She didn't know what to do at first; her mind couldn't quite grasp what she was seeing. Then she opened her mouth in horror.

"Jacques!" she yelled. "Tristan, Joan, Laina!" Then, filling her lungs with an impossibly deep breath, she screamed, *"Burn!"*

Now is no time to panic! her inner voice screamed. She dropped to her knees and looked at the assassin's face. His eyes were closed, his skin pale. She ran her hands over his body and found the wound in his side, a shallow gash where the Kraken's teeth had snagged him. Without hesitation, she ripped his shirt open and gazed at the bloody skin. The area around the wound was red and puffy, tinged with black. Poison.

She heard the thrum of feet against wood. "Burn!" she called, recognizing his footsteps. "He's hurt!"

The giant Wolfy dropped down next to her. He took only a

moment to gauge the situation. Then he grabbed the assassin and lifted him up, as easily as one would lift a child.

"We need to get him inside," the Wolfy said firmly. "This cold weather won't do him any good."

"What about the poison? What if it spreads?"

"There has to be an antidote on board," he replied. Sora couldn't tell how certain he was; his face was like stone. "If they went to the trouble of catching that creature, they must have come prepared...."

"What is *that?*" Jacques' voice rang out from somewhere above her, high on the rigging.

"It's Crash, he's hurt!" Sora choked, but the Dracian cut her off.

"No, those lights!" he pointed.

Sora glanced distractedly over the side of the ship, then stared. Several dozen golden lights had appeared silently on the docks below, bobbing up and down as if suspended in thin air.

Then Tristan appeared. He ran over to the plank, heaving the long slab of wood up onto the ship as though it were made of paper. Sora was stunned by his strength.

Suddenly, there was a massive burst of light from below. Sparks flew high into the sky as a large pyre was lit, illuminating the entire dock. What she saw in the new light was not reassuring.

The entire city guard force stood below, their flickering eyes trained on her and her friends. The Captain was in front. Sora breathed slowly in amazement. They must have arrived while the Kraken was loose and then hung back in the shadows, waiting for the chance to strike. *Cowards!*

Somewhere behind her, she heard Jacques' exasperated voice.

"Damn it all, do they ever sleep? Tristan, close the rail and get away from there, we're leaving! Hear that, boys? Raise anchor!"

"Jacques, I know you're up there," drifted the silky, arrogant voice of the Captain of the Guard. Sora recognized it from the previous day. "Why don't you surrender now and make it easy on yourself? I might even cut your sentence."

Jacques moved to the railing and yelled heartily, "Not a chance in hell, you pompous bastard!"

Then he threw a hard oval object at the docks below. Sora watched as it struck the dock, then exploded in a blast of mist and smoke. Jacques let out a loud whoop of triumph just as the ship groaned and rocked, floating away from the docks.

Then Tristan was standing at the rail. "Better luck next time, Cap'n!" he yelled. "We'll miss you!"

"We'll try to write!"

"Don't forget us!"

All of the Dracians began calling out, hanging from the deck and rigging alike, whistling and laughing. Smoke still covered the docks, and Sora doubted any of the soldiers could see them. She wanted to be amused, she truly did...but she bit her lip instead, irritated by all the noise.

Crash was injured. She turned away and looked around for Burn, but he had disappeared, taking the assassin with him. Fear raised its ugly head, and she began to look for them, trotting off into the darkness of the vessel.

The ship was massive. Sora scrambled down a staircase, below deck, out of the rain. It was lit by a few dim lanterns. The cabins stretched on and on, but it only took a minute before she bumped into the mercenary. He was exiting a room a few doors down the starboard side.

"How is he?" she said as she rushed up to him.

Burn looked at her for a long moment, then sighed. "I wouldn't worry your head about it. Crash is...very resilient." He gave her a gentle pat on the shoulder. "Why don't you get some rest? I'm going to search through the supplies to see if there is an antidote."

Sora opened her mouth in protest. *Rest? How can I rest with Crash wounded?* It seemed careless, selfish, absolutely irresponsible...."No," she started, "I need to help!"

"You won't be any help if you can't even keep your eyes open," Burn said. "You've had a long day...or have you forgotten the wraith?"

It seemed Burn knew her body better than she did. As if summoned by his words, a wave of exhaustion hit her, as forceful as the rolling ship. She staggered, the adrenaline draining out of her, and Burn caught her easily.

"Maybe...maybe you're right," she said, her muscles suddenly weak and sore. He nodded, his eyes gentle and quietly sympathetic. Then she staggered towards the long row of cabins with his strong arms assisting her, barely able to move her own feet.

CHAPTER 18

Sora woke up in an incredibly small room; a patchwork quilt had been thrown over her. The room swayed back and forth in a disquieting manner, but that wasn't what had awakened her. There was a rather loud argument going on; it seemed to be coming from the deck above her room.

Although she couldn't quite make out what was being said, she could hear Burn's deep baritone rumbling like thunder and Jacques' tenor trumpeting back at him. Two of the voices were female; so she assumed that Joan and Laina were there too, along with Tristan and a few others.

Yawning, Sora climbed peevishly to her feet and made her way into the hall without bothering to put on her boots. Hearing the rain pounding against the deck, she followed the sound to the staircase, and climbed straight out into the bad weather.

Immediately she was hit with a blast of cold wind. *Whoa!* Tiny bits of ice were mixed in with the rain, clattering against the deck before melting into the wood. She momentarily considered crawling back to her cabin, but curiosity pushed her further out into the pounding hail. She shivered as her feet touched the slick, icy deck.

The room above hers seemed much further away than it should be; between the ship tossing back and forth and the cascading rain, Sora found herself bouncing between wall and rail, trying to maintain her balance. She could see light spilling from a porthole ahead of her. The rolling motion of the ship almost knocked her over, until finally she was able to reach the cabin's door and turn the handle. She dragged open the heavy old door, then stepped into the room.

There was an immediate silence.

Sora stared at the bright lanterns that were swinging crazily overhead. It appeared to be the Captain's cabin, with desks and chairs scattered about, nailed to the floor to counter the movement of the ship. The walls were plain wood, except the one on her left, where several maps had been nailed up.

The cabin's population turned to stare back at her.

Burn's mouth hung open in mid-sentence. Jacques looked flushed and tense. There was Laina, the girl's eyes as wide as saucers, and Joan, who smirked in amusement, her leg wrapped in a tight bandage from heel to thigh. Tristan, André and several other Dracians stood at the back of the room, observing the argument. The group watched silently as she shut the door. The only sound was the hail hitting the window.

Sora had the distinct impression that she wasn't supposed to be there. "What's wrong?" she asked quietly.

"Nothing's wrong," Jacques said quickly. "We were just deciding the best course to take."

"Oh," she said, oddly numb. She frowned. "And what course is that?"

"Well, with the storm this bad...."

"How could you not tell her?" Laina suddenly broke in.

Tristan nudged the girl hard with his shoulder, a strained smile on his face. Then he turned to look at Burn. The giant Wolfy stared at Tristan, then at Sora, but he didn't say anything.

"Where is Crash?" she asked abruptly.

"Resting, I should think...." started Jacques.

"Don't trouble yourself, dear," Joan said.

"I shouldn't think he's that bad, eh, Burn?" Tristan added to the confusion.

"North by northeast," Jacques continued, pointing to the wall behind him, where the largest map was pinned. "Away from the eye of the storm."

"Yes, but can we outrun the weather?" Joan called.

"*Where is Crash?*" Sora asked again, slower and a bit more loudly. The turmoil of voices came to a halt. The Dracians looked at each other in embarrassment; finally Burn stood up. He motioned to the chair he had been occupying.

"Would you like to sit down?" he offered.

Sora didn't remember agreeing, but suddenly she found herself seated, maneuvered to the chair by the firm roll of the ship. She glared up at Burn, wondering what he was keeping from her.

"Tell me," she growled.

"Sora...." He scratched his ear in an agitated manner.

"Just say it."

His eyes turned away. He let out a long, slow sigh. "We couldn't find an antidote."

Sora waited. It took a long moment for his words to sink in. "Then...?"

"He's alive...but the wound is worsening," Burn ended reluctantly. Sora realized he was trying to protect her from the truth about Crash, but it was still annoying. How was she supposed to help if she didn't know the problem? She pulled in a tight breath, her mind racing for a solution. *Worsening by the minute...and* there were few of the right supplies on board for her to use.

"Aye," Joan added. "He isn't a Dracian like me. The poison is deadly to humans. We need to draw it out...but none of us are Healers."

"His cut is deep and needs to be stitched," Burn added quietly. He watched Sora, waiting for a response.

The room was enveloped in an awkward, suffocating silence. Sora put her head in her hand, trying to think clearly. *I should have brought some Healing remedies....*Her mother had taught her a few small things, but without the right supplies, her knowledge was useless. She should have prepared for this. The sailors had unloaded most of their cargo from the ship, and probably the antidote with it, if there had ever been one. *Maybe there are still a few things left on board.* Mint was easy enough to find, and sweetgrass and redroot. She could at least treat the infection....

This is all because I'm weak, she thought suddenly, guilt roiling in her stomach. If she had handled the Kraken like she was supposed to...not given in to her fear....

Finally, she blinked her eyes and took a deep breath. "I know a few things about Healing," she said.

There was a brief pause. "What?" Burn asked.

"Well, I'm not a sworn Healer per se, but my mother taught me some things. Let me see him. I've drawn poison out before...." But never a Kraken's poison. She had only worked on a few snake bites and a scorpion sting, once. "And I can stitch him up."

Burn stared at her for a long minute. Then a slow smile spread across his face. "My," he said quietly. "And to think, a year ago you couldn't shine a shoe. Learning a Healer's trade....Dorian would be proud."

Sora blushed, then grinned slightly. "You know what he would say?"

Burn's eyes glinted. "What?"

"She shows potential!"

The Wolfy laughed, placing a hand on her shoulder, his ears twitching. It was a good moment. Sora could remember those words on Dorian's lips; he had said them often, when she had first learned to use her staff. She laughed as much as she could at the memory, then shook her head and glanced around the room. By the looks she and Burn were getting, the Dracians thought they were crazy.

"There's no time to waste," she said quickly. "Take me to him!"

"Right," Burn said. He held out his hand and helped her to her feet, balancing her against the rocking motion of the ship. "Jacques, carry on, find that course for us and don't forget the map Crash gave you. We'll be back...."

Jacques nodded solemnly. As Sora got up, she looked around. Her eyes landed on Laina. "We'll need your help," she said. "Can you fetch me several bowls, hot water, a needle and thread?"

The young girl nodded. Joan stood up as well, balancing on a wooden crutch. "I'll go with you," she said, nodding to Laina. "No use getting lost on this big ship."

Sora smiled gratefully, then addressed Tristan. "I don't know if there is an infirmary on board, but I'm assuming so. Bring me every herb, weed or pill you can find. And I'll need towels."

Tristan nodded as well. He, Laina and Joan headed out the door, stumbling as the ship rocked from side to side.

Sora and Burn followed the three others out into the night. Burn waved to her over his shoulder. "His cabin is this way!" he called above the crashing ocean. The hail had stopped, but now fog was gathering beyond the railing, and the rain had turned to a stubborn drizzle. Swaying with each wave, Sora followed Burn closely, using his bulk as a shelter against the storm. She couldn't see anything in the pitch blackness, but obviously Burn could since he led her confidently around the side of the ship and down yet another set of stairs.

He stopped about four cabins down the hallway, swung open the door and hustled her inside. The swaying ship slammed the door shut behind them. Sora blinked. A dim lamp barely illuminated the room. The space, small and cramped like a walk-in closet, was mostly taken up by a wide, fluffy bed. The ceiling was so low, Burn had to bend almost double to walk around the room. Even Sora was close to hitting her head on the ceiling.

A figure rested quietly in the large bed.

Feeling suddenly nauseous, Sora moved over to the bedside and looked down. Tentatively, she pulled back the covers to look at Crash's face. Although she couldn't see clearly in the dim light, he appeared pale and drawn.

"Burn, get the lights on," she hissed quietly, and paused as he lit two or three more lanterns, hanging them from the ceiling. She looked at Crash's face again, and her former observations were confirmed. His skin was unnaturally white, beaded with pearls of sweat, and his eyes were clamped shut. Gently, she placed her hand on his clammy forehead; heat radiated from his skin.

The moment Sora's palm touched his forehead, the assassin seemed to relax. The stiff lines on his face eased. His mouth moved as if he was saying something, and she leaned forward, wondering if he was conscious after all....

The door opened and closed. Laina rushed in, a wide reel of pink thread in her hand, along with a small box that looked like a sewing kit. Tristan was right on their heels with a large basket of herbs and dried plants. Sora spotted several dark bottles mixed in with the herbs, and a pile of towels stuffed under his shirt, apparently to keep them dry. Joan couldn't fit in the room, so she waved briefly through the doorway, placing a jug of water just inside the door. Then she hobbled out of sight down the long, dark walkway.

Laina and Tristan stood there, panting and wet, and stared at her. Nobody moved.

Finally Sora motioned to a small, empty table in the corner of the room. "Set your things there, then you all need to leave...even you, Burn." She met the Wolfy's eyes apologetically. "I need as much space as possible, and this is a small room." She motioned again to the desk, then shook her head when Laina tried to speak. "Put your things down and get out. All of you."

There was a scrambling of feet as the items were set down; then the group filtered awkwardly out, casting glances in Crash's direction. Sora was surprised that they all seemed worried; she hadn't thought Laina or Tristan were overly fond of the assassin. Finally, Burn nodded to her and shut the door.

Sora took a moment to regain her nerve, then pulled back the blankets to inspect her patient. She found, with a start of surprise, that her assassin friend was already shirtless. She watched as his chest rose and fell in small, abnormal bursts. She could hear his wheezing breath, hinting at an infection. The poison was acting quickly. Sora tried to think back on the books she had read at her mother's house, the things she had learned about treating poison.

She would have to draw as much poison out as possible. With a bit of help from the herbs Tristan had brought, hopefully Crash's immune system would take care of the rest.

Her eyes landed on the deep gash near his diaphragm. It looked like the beast had snagged him with its teeth. She winced. The slash was covered in dried blood, but she could still see the dark purple flesh beneath it. A sure sign of poison. The wound had been washed, she could tell, but it needed to be sewed shut, as it was still oozing fresh blood.

She quickly inspected the rest of Crash's body, looking for any other damage. His legs and head were fine, and she rolled him slightly to one side, quickly glancing over his back, trying to ignore his tight, powerful muscles. All seemed in order, though she noted a myriad of scars covering his body, nicks and dents, white streaks and rough patches. Some older scars were overlaid with newer ones, a chaotic history of his life. She would have to ask him about some of them when he woke up....She ran her finger over the longest one, which started at his jaw and went all the way down his chest, past the cut muscles of his abdomen. This one, Volcrian had caused.

Then she inspected his arms, over the faded tattoo of a green snake. Her eyes landed on his right side, and widened with surprise. There were several bloody holes up the side of his forearm, as though he had been pierced by a very thin knife, or a thick needle. Strange. The wounds were also tinged with black. *Poison?* She felt the skin: hot, swollen and red. It looked like a fairly fresh wound, barely scabbed over. *But how...where....?*

There was no time to linger on it. Who knew where the assassin got all of his cuts and bruises? Perhaps he had stepped on a garden rake and gashed his arm. A poisoned garden rake? She grinned at the thought.

Sora grabbed a towel, wet it with hot water, then turned back to clean the wound. She started at his torso. At first the blood was stubborn and hard, but after a minute or so, it softened and came off easily, exposing the deep gash beneath. She continued to clean it, wiping away pus and dead skin. She pinched and prodded the wound a bit, waiting to see if Crash would react, but he stayed unconscious throughout the entire process. *Good, because this is about to get nasty.* Sora finally pulled out a knife from her belt and wiped it clean. She stared at the gash, noting all of the blackened flesh. It would be difficult to suck the poison out...but she had to cut away all of the infected area. Otherwise, the poison would continue to spread.

She started small, cutting off tiny chunks of infected flesh. The new blood that filled the wound was a healthy red color, which was a relief. She had to stop every minute or so and dab up the excess blood.

As she moved deeper into the cut, the blood turned a darker, blacker color. Sora knew she would have to suck it out somehow—and only one way presented itself. The gash was only about an inch deep, but the thought of putting her lips against it made her want to retch. *I can't stall on this....If I wait too long, the infected skin will return.*

She forced herself to lean close to the wound and place her lips against it. She had done this before, but not on such a grand scale. She did her best to suck out the infected blood, spitting it into a bowl on the bedside table. It was sour, putrid, and stank of infection. It made her want to gag.

When she was done dealing with the poison, she wiped her mouth and rummaged through the bottles that Tristan had brought in. She finally found a familiar one—*sprig juice*, it read—and she opened it up. It was a natural disinfectant. She gargled the solution, then poured more of it onto the wound. She repeated the process on Crash's arm, sucking out the poison and cleaning the small cuts. It went a lot quicker the second time.

Finished with the poison, she stood up, opened the door, and tossed the infected waste into the sea.

Shockingly, Crash didn't make any noise through the painful process. He was completely unconscious. She kept thinking he was dead, but his steady breathing reassured her.

Certain that the wounds were clean, Sora turned and rummaged around in the pile of herbs. *Yes!* She found a bundle of white willow bark, a strong painkiller. She dropped the bark and a few other leaves into hot water to make a tea. Then she grabbed another cloth. She dabbed it in the jug of water next to the door, then placed it on Crash's sweating brow.

The tea was finished after a few minutes. Sora propped up her patient's head and carefully poured the concoction down his throat. At first he coughed, but after a bit of coaxing, the liquid flowed smoothly. Soon Crash moved into a deeper, more natural sleep; only then did Sora start threading her needle. She looked at the thread in amusement. *Pink*....She wondered if her assassin friend would mind.

The texture of skin was tougher than cloth. Sora had never gotten used to this part, though she had practiced countless times with her mother, stitching everything from flayed pig's hide to real, human patients. She still shuddered as the needle punctured his flesh. She tried to imagine that she was in sewing class, way back in her manor, creating a grand tapestry. Stiff with concentration, she made surprisingly neat, small stitches.

Sora's scalp prickled suddenly. She was almost finished, but she glanced up—then dropped her needle in surprise.

Crash's eyes were wide open. He watched her with the calculating look of a caged predator. She froze at the expression, unsure if he was angry...then slowly, she frowned. Her breathing eased. There was a peculiar glassy look to his eyes, despite their shrewdness. She had seen this in a few of her mother's patients, especially those with high fevers. He wasn't truly awake...but wake-dreaming. His eyes were open, but his mind wasn't in the room.

"You should lie back down and rest," Sora murmured softly. She picked up the needle and pulled it through the wound, continuing the last few stitches.

Crash didn't even flinch. His eyes followed her hand, and his gaze changed at the sound of her voice. Then, he slowly sat back. "I was dreaming."

"Really?" Sora asked. She quickly finished the stitches before he could start moving around. She tied off the end neatly and snapped the string with her teeth. Then she said, "Dreaming about what?"

Crash shook his head, closing his eyes. Sora could see him shaking slightly. Shivering? Unnerved, she reached out a hand to touch his forehead, to check his fever...but his hand caught hers in mid-air.

"I thought someone else was here, not you," he said quietly. "In the dream, I was young."

"Your mother, maybe?"

A dark cloud passed over his face. His eyes were still closed. "I have none."

Sora gently pulled her hand back. She watched him warily. She had seen patients throw fits before, become violent in their delirium. If Crash became upset, who knew what he would do?

She looked for something that would make a good bandage. She spotted an old sheet in one corner, and moved carefully over to it, ripping off strips of fabric. Then she returned to the bed. With a bit of prodding, she got Crash to sit up straighter, and was able to wrap the bandages around his torso. She couldn't help but watch him in concern.

"Are you a dream, Sora?" the assassin asked suddenly.

Sora blinked in surprise. "Of course not," she answered. "Why?"

"Because...perhaps this is the dream. I am asleep now...and before, I was awake, and you were gone. In fact, you never were." Crash's green eyes snapped open, looking directly into hers. A strange, dark smile touched his lips. "I've imagined it all...I've imagined everything, since the Hive...." He caught her hand again and pulled it against his chest. "What do you have to say for yourself...? What do ghosts say in dreams?"

Sora swallowed in surprise. His words were confusing, but she thought she knew what he meant. She still had dreams of Dorian, of hearing his voice, as clear as a real conversation. Dreams of returning to her manor, of seeing her stepfather, the house as vivid as her waking life. She knew that bewilderment, unable to tell which was more real, her mother's house or her stepfather's, the scent of expensive perfumes, the heaviness of her blankets....

"Is this a dream, Sora?" he asked, his voice suddenly frantic.

"Is this whole damn thing my imagination?"

"No, you're not dreaming. I'm here."

"But you can't be."

"What are you talking about, Crash?"

"I'm talking about...about...." There was an abrupt, wild expression in his eyes. They darted around the room, narrow, cunning, as though he anticipated an attack.

Sora pulled away, alarmed, but she couldn't break his grip on her wrist. *Goddess, is he hallucinating?* Perhaps the poison's residue was affecting his mind. *I know what he needs...more tea!* She grabbed the teacup with her free hand and forced it to Crash's lips. "Drink!" she ordered. "Your fever is coming back. You need to rest."

The assassin seemed grateful, and drank with long, hard gulps. Sora practically drowned him with it. The tea was a painkiller and would put him straight to sleep. After a minute, his eyelids drooped.

"Rest," she murmured, and lightly brushed the hair from his forehead.

A faint smile formed on his lips, though Sora knew he was unconscious. She could tell by his breathing that he had fallen back to sleep. She allowed herself to smile as well. *Disaster averted.*

With a sigh, she turned to stand up. She was halfway to her feet when she realized that she couldn't go any further. Crash still had a death grip on her hand.

"Crash?" she whispered, turning pink. "This isn't funny. Let go!"

He was dead asleep.

Sora stood there for a moment, writhing in silent frustration.

Outside, a brief fork of lightning flashed, followed by a roll of thunder. She glared down at the sleeping figure on the bed, then around the room, as though the lanterns were somehow to blame. Finally, she let out a resigned sigh. She climbed into bed next to him. If she was stuck here for the night, she could at least get some rest. The bed was certainly big enough for both of them.

She curled up next to Crash's side, digging herself under the covers, enjoying his warmth. *I'm not going to snuggle with an unconscious man,* she told herself. Still, the thought was tempting...and he probably wouldn't remember....

As the night wore on, the lanterns died out, leaving the two in stormy darkness.

Crash's hand was her anchor through the night.

* * *

Sora awoke to the sound of someone pounding on the door. She felt heavy and exhausted, but her nerves were so tightly strung, she would have awakened to a pin dropping.

"Sora?" came a voice she didn't recognize. She wondered who it could be, and straightened up from her cramped position. She stretched. Then she gave a start, remembering the previous night. She looked down in horror, her mouth slightly open....

Crash was sprawled next to her, still firmly asleep. Even better, her hand was free.

There came another knock at the door, this one even louder, and Sora stood up. She rushed to the door and poked her head out, taking a deep breath of the chill morning air.

"Yes?" she asked.

A Dracian stood before her, one she didn't recognize by name, but whom she had seen around. He bowed his tousled red head and offered up a metal tray, which Sora looked at suspiciously.

"I have breakfast for you, sent from Jacques, along with some soup for the patient."

Sora stared at the food, surprised. Then the ship rolled beneath her. Her stomach flopped; for a moment, it was as though she had swallowed her tongue. *Ugh. I don't know if I can eat...but Crash needs his strength.* She took the tray carefully and nodded to the tall Dracian.

"Thank you," she murmured. From the dampness in the air and the turbulence of the ocean, she figured the storm was not finished yet. *I doubt this is going to be a very easy ride*—no, far from it. The ship hadn't stopped rolling since she had set foot on it.

She touched her Cat's Eye briefly, trying to see if the storm was magical or not, but there was no response from the necklace. She frowned. Could it be natural? She had never seen such horrible weather. The wind gusted in sudden, violent bursts, whistling down the hallway, and Sora's teeth chattered.

"I'm letting all the warm air out," she said, giving the Dracian a small smile. "Thanks for the tray." Then she started to shut the door.

"How is he?" the Dracian burst out, as though his mouth had been corked up to that moment.

She blinked. "Tell Jacques he's doing all right," she answered. "I think he'll recover soon. And tell Burn not to worry." Then she shut the door.

Sora walked across to Crash's bed and set the tray down on the side table. She carefully placed her hand on his forehead and winced. Still burning hot. She silently berated herself for not checking him during the night. His fever had obviously returned.

She began to mix a new batch of tea. The tray included a kettle of hot water, which was a very good thing. Then she peeled back Crash's bandage carefully. She really should clean the wound once more and check her stitches. It had been late at night when she had treated him. She hoped she hadn't missed anything....

Sora was surprised. The wound, although still angry-looking, was a good deal smaller than it had been the night before.

"Unreal," she murmured, or was she just imagining the change? Her hand trailed over the wound. She could see where the skin had already healed over her stitches. It should have taken days, at least....

She looked at her friend's face. She had seen her mother treat countless humans, and none of them—not even the most physically fit—could heal so fast. *What is it that I don't know about you?* she wondered. *That poison would have killed an average man.* Her eyes traveled to the scar that ran up his chest and neck. She set her finger on it gently and traced its length, then swallowed. That wound should have killed the assassin, too. *But you're never injured for long....*

She remembered that name everyone called him, *Dark One.* Was it some sort of code? A term amongst thieves? Or...something else?

Sora's finger traced the scar lower, across his chiseled abdomen, closer to the waistband of his pants.

Abruptly, his stomach muscles twitched.

She let a slow, sneaky smile spread across her face. "Crash?"

"Mmm?"

Only his sleepy murmur answered her, but Sora wasn't fooled. She continued inspecting his wound, despite his stirring. "How long have you been awake?" She jabbed her finger against the cut, perhaps a little harder than she needed to, testing the stitches.

Crash groaned and sat up. "What time is it?"

She placed a hand on his chest and pushed him back down. "Oh no! You're staying in bed until I say you're ready to get up."

Crash's green eyes narrowed to slits, and then gave a small, amused grin. "Yes, mother," he joked, then his tone turned biting. "Are you going to spoonfeed me, too?"

Sora was surprised by his mood, then grew annoyed. She stopped checking his wound and looked him in the eye—glared—then reached for the bowl of soup.

"You were going to die," she said, and picked up the bowl with careful hands. She wasn't sure why she said that; maybe she was hoping it would change his attitude.

"I'm aware of that."

"Yeah, well, I saved your life again. That's twice now...."

"Right, and I've returned the favor...how many times?" He raised an eyebrow. "Let's not forget who saved whom last night."

She rolled her eyes. He was being difficult, not the best thing after a restless night. Sora held the bowl steady as she looked around for a spoon. His eyes widened again at the smell of food, and he looked at the bowl dubiously.

"That's right," Sora muttered. "And you'd better behave, or else you're not getting fed at all!"

"That's fine, I'm not hungry," he sniffed.

"Nonsense, you've been a full day without food. You'll eat if I say so."

"No."

Sora sighed at the finality in his voice. How could anyone be this stubborn? He reminded her of a grumpy old man, the kind her mother used to treat in the village, who would complain about the weather, about the farmers coming and going, about tired, sore bones—but would refuse to take any medicine.

She closed her eyes and begged for patience, then looked back at Crash. He regarded her with a flat look; he plainly wasn't about to give in.

"Why?" Sora finally asked. "Why are you being like this?"

He let out a slow breath. It seemed that her calm words had done the trick. He raised a hand to his face and rubbed it viciously. "Seasick."

"Seasick?" she asked incredulously.

"Surely you can feel it, too?" He nodded. "Like your stomach has turned inside out?"

On second thought, Sora did feel a bit woozy, and the thought of food didn't agree with her at all. Her eyes dropped to the bowl in her hand, and she felt her hopes plummet. If Crash wouldn't eat anything, how would he ever recover?

"Crash, you need to eat," she muttered.

"Why? I'm fine," he retorted. "And if you knew how I felt, you'd never want to eat again."

"You're not fine! You almost died last night."

"It's not the first time."

She set the broth down and sat back, wracking her brain for a solution. *Tea. Maybe a sip of tea will bring him out of it.* She stood and moved to the other side of the room, a short distance away, where a hot kettle sat on the bedside table. The tea had been dropped off along with the soup.

"How do you feel?" she asked, gingerly picking up the kettle of water.

"I'll live," he answered simply. "That concoction you're cooking up isn't the same from yesterday, I hope. It tasted as foul as it smelled."

Sora couldn't keep the thin expression from her face. She turned her back and concentrated on the tea. *Why is he being so nasty?* Couldn't he show a bit of gratitude?

"Pink thread?" his voice murmured behind her.

"Yup," Sora bit out.

"Is that all you could find—pink thread to sew with?"

"Well, would you rather be dead?" she finally yelled, and whirled around to glare at him. "If you don't like pink, it's not my problem! Gods, Crash, sometimes I wonder what I see in you! I'm tired, I'm dirty, and I'm trying to be nice, okay?" Her voice grew choked. "I've just had the worst ordeal of my life. I'm seasick, I'm hot, it's stuffy in here, it's about to rain, and all I want to do is go back home, crawl safely into my bed, and go to sleep! So if you don't want my help, that's fine. I'm leaving anyway!" She threw up her hands and spun away from him, abandoning the tea.

"Wait, Sora!"

She was already out the door and walking away, seething with anger, hot tears stinging her eyes. *How could he be so ungrateful, after all I went through?* She kicked at a pile of ropes in her path, wishing she could break something. One of the ropes snagged her boot and almost tripped her. Stumbling in anger, she slammed her fist against the wall and a hot, seething breath escaped. She should have never helped him in the first place!

After a minute of angry wandering, Sora found her cabin by sheer luck. She recognized the filigree carved into the wood. She went in, slammed the door, and threw herself onto the bed with a grunt.

She rolled over and tried to fall asleep, hoping to make up for the restless night, trying to put all thought of the assassin out of her mind. *We made it,* she reminded herself, trying to think positively. *We have a boat and we're headed to the Isles.* And they had found the second sacred weapon. No one had died. There was no more need to panic. Volcrian would follow them, certainly, but she doubted he would catch up.

And far across the wide plains, her mare would arrive at her mother's house, her letter attached. Lorianne would be reassured that her daughter was safe.

See? I've covered everything, Sora thought confidently. All she had to do was enjoy herself, her first time at sea. She forced her breathing to slow, her heart to calm. She shut her eyes tight and tried to imagine that it was a pleasure cruise; that they were heading to some strange and exotic land, full of wildflowers and giant fruit. Sleep drifted over her....

Her rest was foiled, however, by a tide of unhappy dreams. She was at her mother's house, miles and miles away, watching Crash and Burn leave. Their backs were to her, and she watched them ride down the front walk, sinking into the distance...over and over again....

* * *

Miles and miles away, a dappled mare trotted up a long

pathway, through the forest, and up to the log cabin where it had been born.

Cameron was mucking out the stalls when the horse appeared. He stared in surprise, recognizing the steed, though it took a long moment for his thoughts to catch up.

Sora's horse!

The steed was covered in dirt and mud, its legs scratched, its hooves full of pebbles. It was in terrible condition, malnourished, bones sticking out on its haunches and shoulders. He approached the horse carefully, running his hands over the ruffled fur of its neck. *Poor thing.* Cameron could remember training the horse, when it was just a young foal, circles and circles on a rope in the pasture. The horse neighed softly and pressed its nose against him.

He was about to take the mare to the stables when he noticed a slip of paper tied to its mane. He took it, unfolding it in his small, blunt hands.

The writing was tight and neat, with fancy loops and flourishes. He frowned, his head starting to hurt. He rubbed the large knob on the back of his skull that was left over from the accident, the one that had robbed him of his thoughts. He couldn't read anymore, but he recognized the handwriting. He had sat next to Sora on countless occasions over the past year, watching her write recipes and notes. She thought he had been trying to learn how to read again, and she tried to teach him, though he hadn't paid attention. Really, he had only wanted to watch her tiny, curling letters flow across the page.

He stood for a moment in the shade of a tree, shifting nervously from foot to foot, trying to decide what to do. He wished he could read the letter. He didn't know much about the situation, only that his mistress was worried for her daughter, and an unharnessed horse was a bad omen.

His thoughts turned to Lorianne. She had left almost a fortnight ago, but had given him detailed drawings of how to find her. His mistress was always prepared for an emergency; it was the duty of a Healer.

What if Sora was in danger? What if Lorianne came home, and it was too late to do anything, and she blamed him? Kicked him out?

The thought made his hands shake so hard, he almost dropped the note. He had lived with Lorianne ever since the accident, almost ten years now, and he could imagine no other life.

He folded up the scrap of parchment, tucked it securely in his vest, and went to gather his things. He had to deliver the message. It was his only choice.

And now, a special preview of...

VOLCRIAN'S HUNT

THE CAT'S EYE CHRONICLES

BOOK 3

T. L. SHREFFLER

Available
September 30th, 2013
on Amazon, BN.com and
other ebook retailers.

Prologue

Born into the colony, they lived without names, without parents. They became in all ways invisible. Brothers and Sisters. Servants of the Shadow. The Hive.

And the highest members of the Hive, those who fought and lived by the teachings of the Dark God—only they were given Names. Titles earned through combat at fragile ages, when children were the most eager to spill blood.

There was no word for *child* in their tongue. Only the word for the unnamed—*savant*. The same word for silence and sand and stagnant pools of water.

By the age of fourteen, he had waited long enough. He was ready to take a Name.

It was early, early morning. The shrine stood in a clearing of tall grass, covered in dew. It was the day before the Naming ceremony. The grass had a grayish hue, as did the dawn. Clouds covered the sky, drifting inland from the nearby ocean, which he could hear if he listened carefully. The air was heavy and brisk with moisture. Trees surrounded him; long, narrow things with smooth trunks, branching into wide canopies above. He had grown up with the smell of salt water; the rush and hiss of the waves.

His teacher, Cerastes—one of the Grandmasters, who had held the dagger of the Viper long ago—always trained him next to the sea.

"*Look at it,*" Cerastes had said the night before, speaking in his low, rough voice, like the curl of waves against rock. "*At how it moves, coming and going. At all of the life that spills out of it. The ocean regurgitates life like a drunken sailor.*"

The nameless savant had studied the ocean with his teacher.

"*If it weren't for us,*" Cerastes had said, "*for our kind, life would overtake the world. It would cram itself into every corner. Multiply out of control. Do you understand the danger in that? Just like the ocean waves, all things have a balance. The wave rushes in, then rushes out. It cannot just come in and in and in— then the whole world would be an ocean.*"

The savant had nodded, watching the sea, alert.

"*It is not beautiful or glorious, what we do,*" the Grandmaster had continued, "*but it is necessary. We are the outgoing wave. The harvesters. Hands of the Dark God. Soon you will enter into our tradition. Are you ready to take a Name?*"

Savant had nodded slowly. In that moment, it felt as though he had waited a lifetime, counting each passing minute. *A Name,* he had thought. *A presence. A history.* He would become more than just a shadow—more than an unknown child of the Hive.

Then they had meditated, looking out across the iron-gray sea. He didn't let himself consider failure. Those who failed at the Naming were scorned and shunned, often forced to leave the Hive. He didn't have to compete. He could refuse. At least then, he wouldn't risk losing his home. *But that's the way of a coward, not an assassin.*

And now it was morning and he was ready.

He walked across the meadow to where the ground caved downward abruptly. Grass turned to gray, rough stone. The shrine of the Dark God was underground, hidden inside a massive cavern, formed by a centuries-old stream of perfectly green water. The dancing water could be heard throughout the cavern, resonating off the granite rock.

He stood at the edge of the pit for a long moment, looking through the ancient crags. Between the rocks, only darkness gazed back.

After a final glance around the clearing, he started down the rocky crevice. He gripped the loose shale with his feet. His fingers found crooks and handholds in the rough stone. He was quick and nimble, and slid easily downward.

Shadows enclosed him. It was a familiar darkness, soft and cool. A brief walk through the cavern brought him to the stream of green water, vaguely illuminated by shafts of sunlight, which shifted through the layered shelves of the ceiling. He leapt the stream easily.

On the opposite side stood a brass door embedded in the wall, wedged into a natural fissure in the rock. It, too, was centuries old, dating back to the founding of the Hive. The door had no key, and it took only the slightest shove of his shoulder to crack it open.

He entered the shrine of the Dark God, a long, stone cavern perhaps a quarter-mile long,. The walls were almost five times his height. Dim lanterns hung from the rocky ceiling, rusted by age and moisture. The stone was colored green by its high copper content and crumbled under his fingers, but the room itself was well-swept and maintained. The ceremonial offering of a dead shark had been laid on an altar the night before, toward the opposite end of the hall. This morning, the corpse had no stench. A sign that the Dark God had accepted.

Along the greenish stone wall hung an expansive collection of ancient weapons: dirks, maces, claymores, battle axes, pikes, staves, crossbows, chakrams and whips. Almost every kind of weapon that the world had to offer. The Grandmasters maintained them regularly.

But these weapons were not of average make. Forged from superior metals, blessed by the Dark God's fire, they were each imbued with a Name. When a warrior displayed the right skills, he earned the weapon and its title—and status within the Hive.

There, hanging from the ancient wall, he saw the one he wanted. The weapon he would use in the fight.

It was a recurved dagger with a trailing point, serrated towards the hilt, about twenty inches long. It hung from the end of the bottom row, where all the unclaimed blades were stored. He couldn't touch it, not yet. But it was the same one his Master had used, the one he had been trained for. The Viper. *He who hides in the grass.*

"Aye!" a voice suddenly reached him. It echoed around the stone walls with startling volume. "I know you're in there!"

The voice was immediately familiar. He glanced out of the shrine, into the shadows of the underground cavern.

She stood ankle-deep in the dewy green water, a piece of oatbread in one hand, her shoes in the other. His eyes flickered over the girl's plain black uniform. Although most in the colony were without names, he always thought of this girl as "Bug," both because she was small for her age, and because she often trapped moths, putting them in small boxes or jars around her hut.

"Preparing for the Naming?" she asked, a slow smile spreading across her face. A dimple stood out on one cheek. He was surprised by it. The Hive did not encourage smiling—or any show of emotion, for that matter. He felt something swell within him: a certain strength.

"I am already prepared," he said. "Will you be watching me?"

"I will be competing too."

"What?" He stared. She was only twelve, far too young to fight for a Name. Most of the boys competing would be older than even he was, sixteen or seventeen.

She nodded. "My Master says I must. She says that she has no other students to compete in her Name."

He watched her with careful eyes. There was uncertainty on her face. Adults knew how to mask their emotions, but she was still young.

To fail at the Naming was to be shunned from the Hive. Everyone knew that. He wondered why Grandmaster Nitrix would force her to fight....Maybe she wanted to get rid of her. It was not unheard of, and Bug had always had it rough. She was small for her age and showed too much kindness toward animals. He couldn't count how many times he had caught her leaving food out for wood-cats and squirrels.

"Come on," he said, and held out his hand. "Let's look at the weapons. Show me which one your Master used."

She nodded. As they entered the long, cool stretch of limestone, she turned to glance at him, her green eyes still uncertain. All members of the Hive had the same make and coloring: black hair and green eyes. It was a trait of their people.

"I knew I would find you here early," she said, perhaps shyly; he couldn't tell. "I watch you practice sometimes. You are very good. They say Cerastes sired you himself; that is why he wanted you as his student."

Savant only shook his head. "That's rude," he said. "We're all brothers and sisters in the Hive."

She shrugged, still grinning. "Perhaps. But not by blood. The humans say that you can only be related by blood."

"We are different."

"You think so?"

Savant didn't answer. The only ones who knew the true bloodlines of the Hive were the women, and they kept that knowledge well guarded. Biological siblings were usually traded with other Hives, to keep them from intermixing blood. Every now and then, a mother would be reprimanded for favoring her own child over others. All children of the Hive were supposed to be raised communally, and all elders were to be treated with equal respect; except for the Grandmasters, who were revered.

"Which weapon?" he asked, turning to the wall, hoping to change the subject.

She pointed at a short, curved sword. "The Adder," she said. Then she wrinkled her nose. "To be honest, I don't want that one. I want the Krait or the Asp. I'm much better at them."

He glanced over her in thought. She referred to the whip or the shortbow. To be honest, he couldn't imagine her with either one. She was too small. Too skinny. He felt his heart sink at the thought, though he quickly quelled the feeling. It was not the assassin's way to show pity.

And yet, here they were. "Do you want to practice?" he asked slowly.

She blinked. "Practice? With the Named weapons?"

He nodded.

"But...it is forbidden!"

He shook his head. "Only if they catch us. I've been training for the Viper for seven years. Let's try them out."

She watched him warily for a moment, her assassin's mask slipping back in place, then she grinned again. "Alright," she said. "But only for a half hour, and in the forest where they won't find us!"

He nodded, looking up at the dagger of the Viper. *What's come over me?* he wondered, suddenly uncertain. He wasn't one to break rules. It was especially forbidden to touch the weapons in the shrine...but something about Bug made things different. Something about her large, wide, slanting eyes. Their particular shade of green, like moss grown over a lake.

And the fact that he truly felt sorry for her. He doubted that she would win a Name. She might even be killed.

He grabbed the dagger before he could change his mind.

At first she went to take the short sword, but then she hesitated. She took the whip instead.

They dashed into the forest, the dawn light ever brightening, leaving the gray meadow behind.

* * *

Toward the back of the cavern, the rocks narrowed into a series of tunnels, leading to a secret exit, shrouded in ferns and bushes. The green water of the stream led to a dense woodland. They walked into the forest and found a place about a half-mile away from the sacred ground. Large, mossy elm trees swayed on each side. Ivy coiled across the ground.

They waited to regain their breath, then Bug loosened the whip from its coil, dangling it in front of her. "Prepare yourself," she said, eyes glinting.

He leveled the Viper before him. It was a long, thick dagger, the blade jagged and sharp enough to pierce metal. He gripped it backwards from the handle and went into a crouch.

It was difficult to tell who lunged first, but suddenly they were fighting. Her whip lashed out, faster than the eye could see. But he heard it snapping through the air. He leapt to one side, the whip striking the tree behind him, tearing off a strip of bark and moss.

Then he lunged at her. She tried to engage him in combat, but he quickly slipped under her defense and grabbed her by the arms. Within seconds, he had her pinned against a tree, the knife against her throat. He was skilled enough not to cut her.

Her eyes widened. Then she glared. "Again!"

She ducked under his arms as soon as he released her, then spun, kicking him behind the knee. She was fast—faster than he. She caught his foot and he fell to the ground, but was up again within seconds. They circled slowly, each studying the other opponent, looking for a weakness.

Then she flicked the whip, catching him on the cheek. A

shallow cut. He could tell that she had avoided his eyes on purpose.

He touched the thin streak of blood.

She lunged at him while he was distracted, drawing a knife from her belt. He hadn't seen the short blade, wasn't prepared for it. He turned slightly out of reflex, and the knife barely missed his neck. Then he ducked under her short arms and grabbed her by the shoulders. Rammed her up against the tree again. Pushed the Viper to her throat.

She dropped the small blade. "I give!"

He released her, barely even panting. It was somewhat disappointing. He had hoped she would be better than this.

"You'll never win a Name with these skills," he said.

She avoided his eyes. She knew the truth. "I know," she said quietly. "What should I do?"

Savant couldn't answer. He could only look at her, that peculiar feeling swelling in his chest again—pity.

There was a sudden crackling in the underbrush.

They both snapped to attention, then Savant grabbed Bug and shoved her back behind the tree. They crouched low among the roots, breathing lightly, painfully alert. They shared a wide-eyed glance. If someone caught them with the sacred weapons....

The crackling in the underbrush continued. Savant turned slightly, angling his head to see between the leaves. At first he couldn't make out much...but then he caught a shuffle of movement. A peculiar glow seeped through the ferns, like a highly concentrated patch of sunlight. It shifted across the forest floor.

The light moved closer.

Savant felt his mouth turn dry. He had heard tales of such a light, but he could scarcely believe his eyes. He could *feel* the light, too. It vibrated against his skin in an annoying, buzzing way. The hair on his arms stood on end.

Only one of the races glowed in such a way....

There was the low mumble of speech. He turned his head again, straining his ears.

"We only need one," he overheard. "Don't put yourself at risk." The voice was small and distant, as though held in a cup.

He shared another glance with Bug. She had overheard it, too.

"I know. I'm waiting for a young one. An adult will cause too much trouble." This voice was far stronger than the last, only a few yards away.

Savant gripped the handle of the dagger. The Viper was still new in his hands, yet it felt comfortable, familiar. It gave him courage. With a slight nod to Bug, he crept around the tree and darted forward, staying low to the ground, using the underbrush as cover. His footsteps were absolutely silent; not even a crunched leaf. Stealth was the first lesson of an assassin.

Bug scampered after him, mimicking his every move.

The light was fully visible through the trees. It hurt to look at it. Savant found himself averting his eyes, even as he crept closer. He wanted to hear more of the conversation....

He paused again behind a thick copse of trees. The light was brightest on its opposite side, perhaps only a few feet away. In this position, he could hear the conversation clearly.

"Make sure you're not followed," the thin, hollow voice said.

"Don't worry," the person replied, soft and melodious, his words dripping with nectar.

Suddenly, the light vanished.

Bug let out a small breath, barely audible. Her hand clutched at Savant's sleeve.

Then a shadow fell over them.

Both savants turned, their expressions guarded. The man who stood behind them was strange indeed, not of the Hive. His coloring was far too exotic. Pale, pale hair, like the white sands of the beach. A white tunic and fawn-colored breeches. His skin held a strange glow, barely visible. In his hand was a small white stone.

"Who are you?" Savant asked. He raised the Viper before him, brandishing it viciously.

"Just passing through," the man replied. He stood only three paces away. A strange smile was on his face: cruel and sharp. Then he turned to Bug. "Here, little one. Catch this." He tossed the stone.

Savant's hand shot into the air, trying to intercept the throw, but Bug was too fast. She easily snatched the stone, perhaps out of reflex.

"No!" Savant yelled.

Bug screamed.

White light flashed, exploding outward like the a miniature star. The force of it actually pushed Savant back, almost toppling him to the ground. The whiteness pierced his eyes and he clamped them shut, ears ringing, pain splitting his head like an ax.

"Don't look at it!" Savant yelled. His eyes were tightly shut, his head buzzing from the intensity. "It's a sunstone! It will blind you!"

"How considerate," that melodious voice spoke again.

Savant didn't hesitate. He lunged toward the voice, the Viper singing in his hand. He plunged the blade into thin air, missing his target, but he didn't stop—no, he kept lunging, kept listening. The handle felt hot, as though warmed over a fire.

Savant now recalled lessons about the sunstones, about bright lights and white-haired strangers. He had heard all of it while studying the War of the Races. He should have thought of it sooner, but he had never heard of a Harpy traveling so close to the Hive. This stranger was a child of Wind and Light, one of the First Race— and a sworn enemy of the Dark God.

And a sunstone was not just a pretty pebble. It was a dangerous magical weapon used for hunting and killing the Dark God's children.

"Where are you?" Savant roared, anger rushing through him like hot fire. He could hear scuffling in the underbrush and a dull moan. Bug's voice. He followed it. His vision was beginning to clear and he blinked his eyes repeatedly. He could now make out vague shadows and outlines, imprints of leaves and branches.

There, to his left. The Harpy!

He lunged again, knife plunging, and this time hit flesh. He sank the dagger deep into the leg of the Harpy. The man let out a cry of pain and outrage, then whirled, backhanding Savant across the face. The blow was fierce and Savant stumbled backwards again, still sensitive to the light, hardly able to focus his eyes.

The sunstone flashed again. It felt like having his face thrust in a fire. He cried out, throwing up an arm to shield himself, dropping his dagger. The ground tipped—his head swam.

He tried desperately to recover, to open and focus his eyes. He could see Bug—or at least, he thought it was Bug—scrambling through the bushes, biting and scratching at her captor. She was screaming in pain, smoke rising from her hand. The sunstone was burning through her skin and into her flesh, where Savant knew it would fester. The light would bind her limbs and steal her senses. Eventually, it would burn out her eyes.

He was overwhelmed. His blood felt like it was boiling in his veins; his head pounded. He pulled himself to his feet and tried to follow them through the forest, tried to listen, but his ears were consumed by an intense ringing. The ground kept tilting beneath him.

He fell to his knees, curling up in pain.

The light grew and grew...and then faded....

* * *

An hour later, he came to. He hadn't expected to still be alive.

The forest was empty. After a brief, desperate search, he uncovered the Named weapons, the whip and the dagger. That eased some of his tension, but he was still worried about Bug. *Assassins do not worry.* But he could not quell the sense of guilt and panic.

A few scuffs marred the dirt, but besides that, there was no sign of Bug or the white-haired stranger. He searched for a trail and found a few white feathers littered in the underbrush, but they led to nowhere. No path, no evidence. Upon examining the feathers, Savant wasn't surprised. Harpies could fly. How did one follow the air?

There was nothing more he could do. He took the Named weapons back to the shrine, mounting them carefully on the wall.

His ears were still ringing, his eyes sensitive. In the dark, cool recesses of the cavern, he knelt by the green water and plunged his head into its cold depths, allowing the current to run through his hair. The peaceful shadows slowly permeated his mind, calming his heart, soothing his skin.

Finally he sat back, taking deep, moist breaths. He felt numb and uncertain. Should he address the counsel of the Grandmasters? If he told the them about the Harpy in the woods, they might gather a team of huntsmen and track down Bug, rescue her....

Or perhaps not. The Grandmasters were not warm or understanding. They would ask what he had been doing in the forest. Ask about the Named weapons. About the nature of his friendship with Bug.

And he would be severely punished for using the weapons. They might disqualify him from the Naming—perhaps permanently.

It chilled him. The thought of waiting another year for the Viper left him sick and uneasy, if they even allowed him to compete. Perhaps his actions would render him unworthy of the title. Another Savant could take his place. Cerastes had other students to compete for his Name.

Cerastes. He let out a slow breath. He couldn't go to all of the Grandmasters about this, but perhaps he could speak to his own. The bond between student and teacher was built on loyalty and unquestionable trust. Cerastes would know what to do.

It took a half-hour to return to the beach, a stretch of sand on the outskirts of the colony. He found his Grandmaster easily. Cerastes sat above an alcove of rock that sank down into the ocean, like the mouth of a gaping giant. Ten foot swells crashed against the rocks—the giant's breath. His teacher was deep in meditation, perfectly still, almost invisible against the dark rock.

Cerastes opened his eyes, aware of his student's presence. "You are late," he said. "In four years, you have never been late for our training. What happened?"

Savant fell upon his knees before the Grandmaster, propping his hands against his legs, bowing his head. "Master," he began. He had rehearsed the words, but they failed him now. His mouth grew dry. "There has been...an accident...."

"Assassins do not have accidents," his Master replied automatically. Then his brow furrowed. Cerastes was far older than his student, well past his prime, and yet his forehead was still smooth, his black hair long and sleek down to his waist. "What happened?"

Savant hesitated only for a moment, then he rushed through the story, explaining the morning's events. He kept his voice soft, his tone quiet. Those of the Hive had ears everywhere.

When he finished, Cerastes lowered his head in thought. He remained silent for a long stretch of time. Savant almost relaxed, lulled by the rush of the ocean and the caw of gulls.

"I know the female you speak of," he finally said. "She was Grandmaster Nitrix' student. She was weak."

"We must save her."

"*She was weak.*"

Savant looked up sharply, unable to hide the surprise on his face. He stared at the Grandmaster for a long moment, countless words on his lips, tangling his thoughts. He shook his head to clear it. "But, she is of the Hive."

"You are not listening, Savant." Cerastes spoke slowly and clearly. "You are my best student. The best I have seen in twenty years. Your logic is as keen as your blade."

Savant waited, forcing himself to listen, barely contained.

The Grandmaster carried on at a leisurely pace. "Harpies are not weak. Their very nature, in fact, is designed to destroy us. Their Light burns our eyes, their Voice binds our limbs. Does it make sense for the Hive to send full-fledged assassins—some of whom will be killed, I assure you—to rescue a weak child?"

Savant felt anger spark to life. It rushed up from his stomach, burning his throat like molten rock. "But...."

"You were friends with this girl?" Cerastes' stare pierced him. Savant lowered his eyes. Friends were not encouraged in the Hive. They were tolerated, perhaps, but only as a thing of childhood. He was too old for such sentiment, now—a friend was a weakness, a crack in one's armor. "No, Grandmaster."

"Then give me one reason why we should save her." Cerastes' words were unexpectedly direct.

Savant looked up and opened his mouth. Paused. He had no reason.

The Grandmaster nodded. A slow, knowing smile spread across his lips. His green eyes glinted coldly in the afternoon light. "This is the way of the Hive, savant," he murmured. "Now let me ask you a far more important question. Are you sure that you are ready to take a Name?"

Savant gazed at his Master, still reeling from the day's events. "Yes," he finally said.

"Because your weakness is most apparent right now."

The words shut him down. Savant realized what he was risking; what his Grandmaster was threatening. He locked his jaw, wiped his expression and cleared his thoughts. He let out a short, tense breath. "It was an unexpected morning," he said abruptly.

The Grandmaster nodded again. "Understandably. Take a run on the beach. Clear your mind for the Naming."

Savant bowed, his head touching the rock, then stood up. He reminded himself that he was lucky. Cerastes was far more understanding than some, and he was true to the ways of the Hive.

He climbed to his feet and turned, leaping nimbly across the slippery rocks.

Cerastes called from the peak of the giant's mouth. "You did not fail her, savant," he said, and his student turned briefly, catching his eye. "Remember. *She was weak.*"

Want more of the world?
Visit *The Cat's Eye Chronicles* website!

WWW.CATSEYECHRONICLES.COM

LEARN ABOUT
THE RACES
THE WORLD
THE CHARACTERS
THE AUTHOR

VIEW
FAN ART
BOOK TRAILERS
TRIVIA GAMES
WRITING PROGRESS
PERSONALITY QUIZZES

AND BUY GIFTS FOR FRIENDS!

About the Author

T. L. Shreffler is a noblewoman living in the sunny acres of San Fernando Valley, California, a mere block from Warner Bros. Studios. She enjoys frolicking through meadows, sipping iced tea, exploring the unknown reaches of her homeland and unearthing rare artifacts in thrift stores. She holds a Bachelors in Eloquence (English) and writes Epic Fantasy, Paranormal Romance and poetry. She has previously been published in *Eclipse: A Literary Anthology* and *The Northridge Review.*

Feel free to connect online! She loves hearing from readers, reviewers, orcs, elves, assassins, villains, figments of her imagination and extraterrestrials looking to make contact. Her online accounts are as follows:

Email: therunawaypen@gmail.com
Author Website: www.tlshreffler.com
Facebook: www.facebook.com/tlshreffler
Twitter: @poetsforpeanuts

Made in the USA
Lexington, KY
05 May 2014